# The Earth Cries
## Book One

# CRIES:
# The Captive Mind

by

**Christopher J Reeve**

The Earth Cries Trilogy:

Book one – CRIES: The Captive Mind

Book two – CRIES: The Souls of Derra

Book three – CRIES: The Book of Daniel

*This book is a work of fiction. References to past figures and occurrences are for fictional effect only and hold no historical value. Similarity to other persons, living or dead, is purely coincidental.*

No part of this work may be reproduced or transmitted in any form or by any means, electronic or mechanical without written permission from the author.

Copyright © 2017 Christopher J Reeve
All rights reserved.

ISBN-13: 978-1544606057
ISBN-10: 1544606052

Cover Design by Christopher J Reeve

**For my treasured family.**

## CRIES: The Captive Mind

### Prologue

*'Awake Child of God, it's time to return.'*
'I don't know if I can... I'm so confused!'
*'Yes, yes you can, focus...'*

I'd just seen God die, there before me, slain. It was as if I'd taken a mortal blow myself.

*'Yes! Yes! He is vanquished!* I am *THE one!* I am *THE Lord! All bow and worship me! ME! All powerful, all beautiful...'*

'All beautiful?' I shot.

The Creature turned its narrowed eyes onto me, in a look that I felt should have slain me. Where had we gone wrong? In that moment all my mistakes, all my inadequacy, seemed ready to condemn me. *Focus...*

...blackest darkness, a rushing of the wind...

'The last time I saw you, you were holding me. It was early in the morning. The birds were singing the dawn chorus. You were asleep. There was still a little colour in your hair.'

Fire!    Blood!    No!    *Focus, focus, it's nearly over...*

It was high Summer, the gentle kiss of a fragrant breeze heralded the arrival of our family. It was an annual event; my children, grandchildren, and even great grandchildren, here, because I could not manage journeys.

For many years my personal response had been one of absence. Physically I was there, but mentally... well, I struggled to hold a thought, let alone value the respect my story generated.

It had become a family tradition you see, to help the grandchildren understand; then because they asked again and again, and then because of their children.

Each year my wife's narrative chipped away at the disorganisation within me, until I recognised my life again.

My family was oblivious to my awakening. To them I remained

unresponsive, a blank, a frail old body in a chair. How I longed to thank them for their continued visits. How I longed to throw my arms about them.

My oblivion was respite, convalescence you might say. Only recently had that reached completion, only these last few years had I been able to use my wife's words to return.

There was a tangible anticipation when she was ready to begin. A hush. 'Are we all here?' She'd ask. 'All ready?'
I would be held by an expectant pause, a silence of gibbering recollections, a cessation of the back and forth that I had otherwise stumbled about in. I was eager for what was coming, even though there would be pain within it. Why? Because the stability and control I once enjoyed would be there. Each word about to touch my ear would restore, for that moment, life as it was lived. I would become saturated by the memories and recall... no, live again, more than the teller could tell. She began with my own words, the story as I'd told her...

## Chapter one
## Hitting the Ground

'Something's missing,' I thought, as I stood on my patio at the edge of a pristine lawn. The thought had long been on my mind. Nothing happened here, good or bad. Not that I wanted anything bad to happen... I sighed, I knew I should be grateful for what I had - great job, nice home - I just felt that I lacked something... Someone, yes, someone was missing, and the strength of that feeling was unlike anything I'd felt before; it engulfed me...

I remember seeing the prettiest, most perfect face I had ever seen; my body convulsed and everything became dark.

I could hear breathing; heavy, laboured breathing... my own! I was on my face, my limbs somehow paralysed. A heavy, pounding rain beat against my back. I lifted my head, coughed, and sprayed the grass beneath me with a mix of blood and saliva. What happened? My mind reeled. I knew here, but now there were other memories - certainties, experiences.

The strongest memory was Hope. I wondered if she would come, then remembered how distant she'd become. I shook my head as I realised a deeper truth, she wouldn't come because the Great Suffering our world had endured - without the intervention of the Val'ee - would mean she could never have been born.

The rain stopped abruptly. The sun shone. A still emptiness compounded the numbness of my senses. I tried to cry out but my voice was stifled to a whimper. I felt broken, my heart stuttered erratically. I knew what I'd done! I'd changed the outcome! Changed history! The battle I'd fought was won. Earth was safe, the Val'ee destroyed, history belonged to us.

Mrs Gray's cat from four doors up hopped down from the fence and, watching me closely, crouched down to relieve itself in the flower border. I could do nothing, I was instantly infuriated, then I started to laugh inwardly to myself. How ridiculous all this seemed against what I'd faced. A resigned sigh escaped me and my head lolled down onto the bloodied turf.

Suddenly a razor-like agony shred through every sinew of my being. I found my voice in an ear-splitting scream and felt the muscles of my limbs burn and spasm into life. Strength pulsed through me and I flung myself onto my back, sending the cat darting down the garden path.

Filling my lungs with air I attempted to drag myself up and failed, achieving a slumped, awkward position. Pins and needles cried out in my hands and feet. I tipped my head back, eyes rolling. I felt alone, crushed, exhausted. Blood dripped off my chin from my injured tongue. The garden began to spin. I paused, waited, breathed. I could feel the heat of the sun on my head, the brightness through my closed eyes. Could I stand now? I pulled myself up on a patio chair.

In the background I could hear my mobile ringing on its charger in the hall. I couldn't get to it to answer, and it went to voice mail.

I could see my reflection in a window and edged my way towards it. On getting close I stuck out my tongue, the gash was nasty, I'd need medical attention. A puddle of water was forming around my feet, I looked at the sky – a sheet of cloudless blue – my hands and neck seemed sunburnt, the patio was only wet where I'd collapsed.

'Hmmm, liquid time must have followed me out of the conduits,' I thought. It was a thought alien to here, but not alien to memory. I clambered into the house to seek dry clothes.

I'd been a bit of a loner in this life. Perhaps that's why no one had responded to my cries. I needed solace. I heaved myself into the lounge to the media screen for some music, "David Ertis - Acoustic Glastonbury" would help. To my surprise the screen was on. Had I been using it before I went into the garden? I thought not. I couldn't find the album I seemed to crave either. I abandoned the search; cleaning myself up was the priority - I'd look again later.

It was strange to have access to the memories of another life. Hope's mother had made it possible. I longed to see Hope again. To me she was as beautiful as any woman could be. Her loss hurt me deeply.

I made my way upstairs, wiped the unclotted blood from my face with my wet shirt, and consigned it straight to the bin. I pulled on a new one from a wardrobe full of similar, plain white shirts. An uneventful life seemed bliss to me against the horrors that I could now recall. I could picture Hope's face and was momentarily lost in her eyes as I stepped back out onto the landing. Fresh blood dripped down onto my shirt. I sighed and turned abruptly into the bathroom for a flannel to hold to my mouth. There was a sudden crash downstairs. 'Hello?' I called, there was no answer. I looked down the stairs, 'Hello.' Slowly I descended. I could see a pot plant on the hallway floor, the pot was cracked and a little compost was on the laminate. I made my way to it, the back door was still open. I must have knocked the plant when I came in, a breeze must have caught the foliage. I picked it up and carried it to the patio, I'd repot it when I felt up to it. I needed to see a doctor. In the distance I could hear a great number of sirens. I stepped once more onto the patio, and from there I could see several columns of smoke rising into the sky. My stomach turned, I stepped back into the house and shut the door. Stepping into the lounge I sought a live news feed on the media screen. Obviously halfway through his report the man on the scene was gesturing towards a motorway pile-up.

'….in conjunction with what some have already labelled as a mass swoon, with scenes like this across the country and, indeed, the world.'

I was becoming aware of what I'd done and why it hadn't occurred like this before. Almost everyone had died by this point; only those in the fleet had survived, devastated by Earth's destruction. My heart was heavy with

*Cries: The Captive Mind*

guilt, but I knew the alternative. I felt sure I was justified.

My eye fell on my mobile phone; it would have a message for me on voicemail from after the swoon. I picked it up and tapped the icon for voice mail.

'You have one message...'

'Hello, er Dace I guess you're out, so um, it's me anyway, Fredrick, your Dad's colleague, but then you know that. Anyway, your Dad collapsed, he's OK now...'

The rest of the message was lost to me, my new memories had told me that I'd lost Dad again and again; in the levelling of Sylvestris, in the catastrophic annihilation of Earth, at the hands of my adversary, and yet here he was alive. I laughed, I had been with him just last weekend, chatting over lunch - as we did every alternate weekend.

The anger present in my new memories seemed to lift off me, the absence of its weight discernible. I fumbled with my phone, seeking to replay the message.

'...your Dad collapsed, he's OK now but I'm taking him up Central anyway for a, er, check-up, yes. He keeps saying stuff about... oh I can't trouble you with that, it will probably make more sense to you coming from him. Well er, perhaps you could meet us at the hospital, or, er yes, looking at this traffic you'll get there first, but you're not in so um, hope you're OK. My MADS estimates about an hour until arrival, it's four fifteen, good grief - it'd be quicker to walk...'

The voice mail, set for short messages, cut Fredrick clean off in mid-flow, but my attention was back with the television. The situation was unfolding, and I could feel a frown burrowing into my brow. One shot showed a fire appliance that would ordinarily be manned by a team of seven, but only two fire-fighters were present to tackle a raging conflagration. Things were worse than I'd imagined and any sense of being justified faltered. I had not considered how a change, from almost total extinction to a position of complete unpreparedness, would affect a population that had lived ignorant of any threat. To be unaware of any impending change had left them vulnerable to that point of retort as time cracked into its new place.

Dad had passed out because his experience of life had *never* reached this far. It must have been like running into a brick wall.

I punched off the television. What choice had I had? Could I have prepared humanity somehow? Could they have been persuaded to pause their lives at a specific moment, without any understanding of their circumvented obliteration, of war or an enemy bent on their enslavement?

No, I *was* right, the people of the earth would recover from this, as it had recovered from "The Great Suffering". This would spell the end of our woes, the last spasm of a war that disrupted the very flow of time.

## Chapter two
## Precursors and Suffering

I contemplated what had happened since I'd made the change, since I'd destroyed the Val'ee. I smiled, what I'd achieved had a positive spin. We'd done everything without the "aid" of the creatures that had destroyed the Earth. In going alone, the world now stood unified. All children were taught about "The Great Suffering", and the good that came to us through it.

Once we were divided and blind. We lived in a world where many were consumed with real and ingrained hatred for each other, where sides were drawn, and where innocents were caught up in hostility. Now mankind was only divided by two simple "Pre-GS" ideologies, that of the Concordant Nations, and that of the Eastern Coalition; their coexistence peaceful.

Before this unification, fear of a terrorist attack on a nuclear facility held the Concordant Nations in high anxiety. The fear proved justified when plans were exposed during a Police operation. Unable to fully contain the terror cell the Government was forced into drastic and compulsory action. All nuclear facilities were locked down, each under military control. Nearby towns were evacuated and levelled as a "reasonable precaution".

The threat continued growing, so the Government channelled resources into removing the risk altogether, providing dedicated funding towards research into a viable alternative energy source. It was against this backdrop that a physicist, Dr. Ottily Hayvan, appeared. The discovery she made was extraordinary.

Assisting in a failing collision experiment - designed to observe the energy output of elements impacted from opposed trajectories - Ottily had the strangest of thoughts. The project leader, however, was unapproachable. He had seen the elements repeatedly miss and had shut down his equipment due to overheating. He had raged, cursed all his staff, and insisted that the project be scrapped.

Made responsible for the deletion of any "embarrassing" data, Ottily found herself making an illegal copy of the file before wiping it from the laboratory records. She travelled home that evening with all the details of the experiment covertly stowed in her handbag. She felt sure that something more than an impact had been missed that afternoon, and it didn't take her long to find it.

An energy peak, tiny and easily overlooked, had upset the paths of the elements. The energy had remained present, unobserved - due to the head technicians focus on achieving a collision - and was merely added to every time the test elements missed. It wasn't long before the growing charge started interfering with the apparatus, ultimately causing the failure of the hardware. Strangely though, it wasn't the damaged equipment that had allowed the final readings to be saved but the power generated by the collision elements as they passed repeatedly in their opposing paths.

Dr. Hayvan's failure to return to the facility led to her dismissal, but she was too absorbed with her own experiments to really care.

Three months later, her eyes wide with anticipation, Ottily flicked a switch. Within seconds the starter cell was burnt out by the increasing electrical charge created by the elements as they looped through the device Hayvan had created. She was unsurprised, that was the point of the cell, it had performed its role, the reaction had begun and was self-perpetuating. What now raised her pulse was the unrelenting rise in output. Ottily stood up and backed towards the door, heart pounding; then it happened. A rolling aura of light appeared, emanating horizontally from the collector plate between the opposing loops of the generator. It was beautiful like a great, curving wave tube that some surfer might exploit. But, more importantly, the appearance of this phenomenon had heralded a plateau in the reaction. The power had reached a point of balance.

Further experiments confirmed that the reaction was reliable and that the attachment of electrical equipment even resulted in a measurable rise in output. Ottily had created a new form of power generation and she had only to contact a single dedicated number to register her discovery.

Government officials found the generator irresistible, safe, pollution free, easy and cheap to construct, and the prototype she had bought to the test facility - barely the size of a brief case - could produce enough energy for a small town!

Observing the aura around the device one official wrote "Hayvan's Wave" on his documents, and the name stuck.

Hayvan's Wave rolled out across the Concordant Nations and those states not restricted by poverty. Its incredible effectiveness was soon understood by the ambassadors and representatives of the Eastern Coalition, and the device spread into every affluent society on the globe. Dr. Hayvan was honoured, and her subsequent response to power poverty - a violent reply from exploited poorer nations - was rewarded with the Nobel Peace Prize. Hayvan insisted the atrocities that resulted from the power poverty uprising be set aside, and that the Wave be gifted to these communities as an act of peace. Peace ensued, but it was uneasy, the deeds perpetrated during the uprising had led to some of the worst bloodshed outside of military action ever recorded. The conduct - left unpunished - harboured a smouldering, hidden animosity. It was that hatred that was blamed for Dr. Hayvan's disappearance. She was never seen alive again.

All this occurred five years before I was born. The fact I was born at all was truly amazing and would galvanise efforts to solve the catastrophe that had overtaken mankind, "The Great Suffering".

It had started some three years before my birth. In that year no infant was delivered in the Concordant Nations that did not die within moments of its first cry. Only those peoples associated with the power poverty uprising continued to bear viable young. It was this fact that caused a backlash of accusations: Had these violent people instigated this terrifying condition? Was this some plot to reduce their enemy's ability to engage in conflict at some future point, due to a diminished and aging fighting force?

The finger pointing stopped almost as soon as it had begun, as a great cry ascended from the accused and they joined in the alarming lament of Earth's people.

The condition effected humanity alone. The natural world and its cycles of life continued.

*Cries: The Captive Mind*

The world, in its fragmented, suspicious, conflicted state was in no position to face this enemy. Representatives of nations criss-crossed the globe demanding information on the angles other communities were taking regarding research into a cure, even threatening consequences for withholding information.

That's how it had continued until I was born. Until that point no progress was made.

Her name was Vanessa North. She was my mother and she was very poorly indeed. Despite the possibility of treatment for her condition, Mum chose to risk the extra time that was needed to give her unborn child the greatest chance of survival. The doctors fought her on her decision, telling her that her baby would die just like the others were dying.

'Save your own life,' they urged. 'The Great Suffering may end one day and you will live to try again.' Mum refused to listen. She sacrificed herself to bring me into the world. She died two days after the Caesarean section that her consultant had forced her to undergo so that treatment could start.

I arrived eight weeks early, lifted from my Mother's womb and set aside like something awaiting disposal.

A screen had blocked Mum's view of the procedure, but the sensations of being moved about, ripped, tugged at and pressed upon were already forgotten. Her senses were consumed by the strength and lasting nature of my plaintive cries. All other sounds stopped as the delivery room accepted the truth. The theatre staff seemed lost as to what procedure should follow. No infant had survived this long for years. Then a nurse swept me up off the cold metal trolley. Her eyes wet with welling tears she lifted me so that my Mother could see.

'Your little boy Mrs North,' she said, almost choked with emotion.

Dad would often talk about the two days I shared with Mum, days I could never remember, days she never left me, how happy she was that I was a healthy babe, despite my early arrival.

'She would gaze at you,' he would say, when I was old enough to understand. 'As if you were the very answer to the troubles of the world.'

Sometimes we would talk and cry all night so vivid was the picture my father could create. But I'm getting ahead of myself.

At two days old my Father's words would protect me, soon after they would begin something no one had thought possible.

News spread quickly of the birth of Dace North. The world knew me long before I'd processed the existence of existence around me. Officials, journalists, well-wishers, even holy men pressed the hospital for all manner of information: interviews, photographs, access, a sight of the miracle child.
The hospital, to my father's horror, was all too willing to introduce me. Such publicity about its role in the arrival of a living baby could serve it well in the acquisition of funds and acclaim for its research projects.
Dad held the line. He insisted that I be safely out of the Special Care Baby Unit before I was assaulted with flashbulbs and random pathogens.
I was strong, surpassing my father's expectations I quickly progressed. Dad pulled some strings at the Government facility he worked at and had me secretly airlifted to a secure location. Over the following weeks he met with those who had managed to hand him contact details, introducing me to them in his strong, protective arms.
Some thought I was the first of a flood of new life. But I wasn't.

Within a few weeks questions began to be asked. What was the secret of the North child? Why should he live when all others continued to die? Attention turned to my mother, what drugs had been administered during the pregnancy? But there had been none. What about the method of delivery? Some copied this, but many of the dead had been premature, and the outcome was no different. Even the fact that I had been placed onto a cold, metal trolley was seized upon, but nothing made any difference. The Great Suffering continued.

I was seven before I saw the newspaper cuttings my grandparents had kept. Gramps and Nana Edding were my mother's parents, Dad had moved them in so that he could continue his work - my safe keeping, in a secure Government house, still necessary.
The three of them were as close as any family could be and it was a wonderful environment in which to spend my formative years. One particularly wet afternoon - when I'd been feeling particularly bored - Nana had brought me the scrapbook.
It had seemed extremely novel to me. I was used to information being presented in digital form, but Nana had kept all the details - neatly and

*Cries: The Captive Mind*

tidily presented - in a hardback book with a carefully embroidered cover she'd made herself.

That was the first time I saw the articles, with grand titles like "Great North Star" and "North Gathers South, East and West". They recorded eyewitness accounts of a stirring speech my father had given when a multitude of people descended on our home, overwhelming the security.

My father sent Gramps, Nana and me to a panic room for my protection; one group sought access to tissue samples, blood and more, until my survival was understood.

The crowd was agitated, but these times were offering no solace. There was no direction of action; no progress. Dad recognised reporters, he recognised people from his recent circles of activity and, most importantly he noted that his visitors included many of different nationalities.

My father called for their attention. 'You have come here tonight because humanity is lost into darkness. Though we strain to see a pin prick of light that might suggest an end to the tunnel of our despair, we see nothing. I believe we can lift that blindness, and that we can start to lift it tonight. You are here because a miracle of life has left you desperate for more. I thank God for this light at my time of sorrow and loss, but the child cannot help you - no.'

The crowd fell silent, every eye fixed on Dad.

'Tonight is about what *we* can do, what we *must* do. Our Governments bicker and fight over direction, each pursuing its own work. Studies are being replicated, error repeated, dead ends revisited, time wasted. Our minds were created to fathom the mysteries of our world, this "Great Suffering" is one such mystery; perhaps the greatest of mysteries. But we remain divided in knowledge, skills, technologies, resources, manpower - all the things that will be needed to beat this foe.'

Heads were nodding now; Dad was voicing what was starting to be circulated amongst the populations, amongst the people that had created the governments that could not work together. Shouts of support for Dad's opinion began to grow…

'This very second is another second lost in gaining victory against the very extinction of humanity. A world-wide problem demands a world-wide solution, unity of effort, collaboration. People, go home. The answer is here only because it is in your own hands. Go home and rest. Tomorrow I will join you, and we will not leave any course unexplored until we pass from this blackness into the brilliance of day! Tomorrow sees the beginning of an end to our pain.'

Within a half hour Dad collected us from the panic room, the crowds had gone, and I remained oblivious to it all.

The unfolding tomorrows saw a unity that had seemed impossible; a world pouring itself into action, nothing held back, material or intellectual. Amidst it all was Dad, heading a multinational taskforce to see the job through. A diverse group of the world's finest scientists, thinkers and experts. Some may not have spoken to each other just weeks before, but now they were working together.

## Chapter three
### Vanessa

Dad's work took him away sometimes but that was OK. Nana and Gramps were always there making life good. He was never away long and never missed my birthday or Christmas.

He had quickly become *the* Government overseer, liaising with representatives at all levels of the fight against The Great Suffering. He and his team co-ordinated the methodical research that enabled a systematic ruling out of all potential pathogenic, organic and allergenic causes, without any wasteful repetition of study.

Dad's ability as an encourager was invaluable, people had quickly become disheartened when the obvious "disease" cause had drawn a blank.

'Nothing is working to find a cause, let alone a solution.' came the cry.

Dad would just smile at his colleague, the Government official, the civilian or the lens of the camera held by a reporter and say, 'We're doing well. As each cause is excluded the list of possible causes is reduced. We *are* getting closer to our goal.' Somehow - when there seemed little hope - that was enough. His drive, conviction and positive tone took the work onward.

With no schools open that catered for my age group I was tutored at home by a small team that included my father when he wasn't busy. I absorbed what I was taught quickly, causing some excitement that managed to leak into the tabloids. "Miracle Child a Genius" blurted the headlines. It was tabloid media, and after some enquiries Dad replaced my tutors with a Government colleague, who quickly and adequately filled the role with complete dedication and absolute discretion. It was she who recognised my fascination with how things worked, and who cleverly used this interest to help my understanding of the workings of areas of study I had more difficulty grasping. Dad was very pleased.

I believe now that Dad had intended me to join him in the battle against The Great Suffering, but by my tenth birthday events took over. Dad discovered something.

We were playing cricket with my tutor Miss Knight, and a few young men from the village nearby. I had bowled a superb ball and was expecting the wicket to shatter, but Aid - the son of a farmer who owned the adjacent land - struck it hard, and it disappeared under the hedge at the top of the field for a six.

'That's mine.' Dad called, trotting after it. He pushed himself through a sparser section of the hedge and began searching for the ball. It lay alongside the rolling waveform of a D-Series wave generator that the hedge had been planted to screen.

Dad noticed something as he bent down to pick up the ball, a tiny, resonant vibration in the blades of grass where the waveform travelled through the ground. The vibration had a sort of pulse to it that moved laterally away from the generator. Dad's eye followed it to the hedge, squinting, leaning towards the coniferous fronds, seeking, seeing the pulse travel through it.

'OH MY!' Came a shout, quickly followed by Dad as he burst through the hedge.

'What's up?' asked Miss Knight, as he ran by us like a man pursued.

'We've been blind Kerry, blind, but please carry on with your game. I must go, so sorry.'

Pausing his haste briefly, he firmly pressed the ball into my hands. 'Best bowling I've seen in ages son.' He flashed a smile then hurried quickly away.

Dad's suspicions prompted a massive investigation into Hayvan's Wave generators. The puzzle was how something heralded as so safe could now be the cause of such woe. After all, it had been supplying power for a number of years before The Great Suffering ever occurred. Dad felt sure his team would expose the truth.

I clearly remember the night he came home and gathered the family..
'The generators are perfectly safe.' He announced in a flat, saddened voice. He shrugged and gave a heavy sigh. Still, something about his eyes convinced me that we weren't gathered for news of failure. 'It's the waveform itself.' He continued. 'But only in generators that allow the waveforms to cycle through earth, a factor we've called "Going Terrestrial". The D-Series generators need to be raised so that the wave doesn't do this. There are low-slung vehicles, and military applications that will have to be dealt with too. The problem is created when the wave reacts with other elements, just like one chemical reacts with another. We didn't think waveforms had physical attributes, but they do. These properties have formed something quite unique, we lack the language in science to describe it, so we've called it "Product A". The closest thing is a signal, like that of a mobile phone or Data Pack, just different. It can have an effect on human tissue, it's here in this room now, passing through all of us...'
We shifted awkwardly.
'...Oh, it can't harm us, we are beyond any harm, but the lab projections confirm that the new-born heart *is* effected by "Product A". Computer simulations show that the womb and amniotic fluid protects the child until delivery, and then, well...' He paused, obviously trying to find some analogy that best suited what they had observed. '...well, "Product A" just seems to say "stop". There's this little part in our hearts you see, no bigger than a grain of rice, that is responsible for its beat and, well, this "signal" shuts it off.'
'So we can cure it.' Gramps stated.
'We're going to have all D-Series generators off by morning, with B-Series replacements. I've got Fredrick on the press release for recalled vehicles and exchange pool; that bombshell comes tomorrow.'

Looking back on these new events - knowing what had happened in my regained memories - I began to appreciate the fools that the Val'ee had turned us into. They told us that our own unsustainable activities had led us to our own bitter downfall. We had poisoned ourselves, robbed ourselves of a future. Their methods seemed obvious to me now, demoralisation followed by altruistic, benevolent assistance.

I had ended this, it had never happened, we'd found the cause of The Great Suffering without false aid, we'd solved.

I thought back again to that ground breaking night. Dad cupped my cheek. 'We've done it my little miracle.' but the following weeks were about to reveal the full horror of the nightmare.

At first Dad became withdrawn, spending less time at home and more in the Lab. Within three weeks D-Series generators were shutdown, all vehicles had been recalled and were in the process of being scrapped, including the F660 high speed train, Flack Air Carrier and Dormst YY80 tank.

The problem was that couples had protected themselves from the horrors of pregnancy. Few dared to conceive. Who would want to endure such pain? To feel life within but lose it so abruptly?

The Government had provided incentives to try, and there were always occasional "accidents", but even with abortion banned in all but the most severe of contraindications to mental health, only a diminished flow of life came. There was simply a long wait to test the theory.

When it did come it was tragic. Excited by the news that a cause had been found the expectant parents had chosen their child's name, a practice that had all but stopped. Evie died.

Dad was beside himself. It was as if Evie had been his own, and, when the date for the next delivery was identified, the six-day gap seemed too short. Dad was in a pretty dark place, but he refused to be beaten, especially now that the enemy was known.

The horrible truth came two days later. The fact that no new "Product A" was being produced mattered very little, old "Product A" was still with us, bouncing around the atmosphere like some possessed rubber ball. Not dissipating, it mimicked the reaction that had generated the waveform, that self-perpetuating reaction meant that the "signal" persisted in the environment. The cause could be switched off, the effect couldn't, but then, Dad refused to believe that.

If he'd had more time the answer was simple, create something that would cancel the "signal". Dad and his colleagues spent two more days on computer simulations that Dr. Lyn had already been working on. The device was workable, it used a pulse that would strip parts of the "signal" as it passed, causing it to break down over time. Unfortunately, a network of apparatus would be needed, and there would be no way of fabricating it in time, let alone running it long enough to make any difference to the Allen child. Dad called off that line of investigation freeing the entire team to independent thought.

That evening I'd found him in his study staring at a photograph on his computer. Seeing my reflection in the monitor, framed by the light from the hall, he turned and beckoned me to come closer. I walked up to him and pulled myself onto his lap, 'Who are they Daddy?' I asked.

'Magda and Daniel Allen, participants in the Government "Hope for Life" program…'

'Why are you just staring at them?'

Dad chuckled, 'I want to help them son. I can focus on a problem better when I can see who the solution helps. I like to pray too.'

Dad used to pray with me and read Bible stories at bedtime when I was younger, but this had diminished over the last couple of years.'

'You see, Dace, Magda here is due to give birth on Monday but the babe will die like all the others if we can't figure out how to protect it from "Product A".' Dad sighed and returned to staring at his screen.

'Is there any "Product A" in space?' I asked.

Dad chuckled again, 'Ha, Ha, if I could get Magda up into space without damaging her or the baby, and if I could get a maternity team up with her to deliver the child I would; there's no "Product A" there, it bounces back to the earth off the atmosphere, the babe would survive.' Dad gave a little frown, then began uploading his Lab Site. 'Time little geniuses were in bed… please.' He kissed my head and I trotted off.

The next day Dad had already left for the Lab, we didn't see him until Thursday; he needed a good shave and shower, and carried a little pink bundle which he passed to Nana.

'Her name is Vanessa. I named her after your daughter, my wife, because she's precious and beautiful. She is our secret for now. Look, I've got to get cleaned up. I'll fill you in shortly.'

I remember gazing down on my little adopted sister. She was so delicate, so pretty, so tiny. 'Was I that small Nana?' I asked.

She smiled, 'Oh you were smaller, seven weeks premature, though a healthy size just the same. No, she's a bonny thing.'

*Cries: The Captive Mind*

She gave a little wiggle scrunching up her plump, dimpled face. I was lost in her, her tiny nose, tiny fingers, tiny nails, everything so small, so vulnerable, yet, here under Dad's care, so safe.

Gramps came into the room carrying a case he'd retrieved from Dad's car, he looked at the child. 'I wonder why Douglas had to bring her home?' He sniffed.

'Oh Lionel, you know Douglas, there's been some sort of complication...' Nana paused for a moment as if she'd thought of something terrible, 'Oh no, that's not it, it'll be because the mother's resting. We'll have her a night or two and then...'

'No, something's up.' Gramps interrupted. 'He's named her himself. Vanessa. How personal can you get? No, she's here for the long term.'

Nana fretted around for a few moments then started unpacking the case. Nappies, bottles, formula, sterilising kit, some changes of clothes...

'The long term.' Gramps repeated.

Dad returned twenty minutes later - looking much fresher - to find all of us gathered around Vanessa, silent and expectant.

'Gorgeous isn't she?' He declared.

'Quite.' Nana replied. 'But why is she *here* dear?'

## Chapter four
### The Nature of Leeches

Dad beckoned us over to the big sofa that curved around the coffee table. 'If you want the whole story we best get comfortable. Oh, and keep the interruptions down or I'll have to stop for baby's feed.'

Dad had a gift at retelling events, and this one seemed to excite him a great deal - it was, after all, the story of how he and his colleagues had beaten The Great Suffering.

He looked directly at me, 'Do you remember what you asked me about space last Thursday night son?' he began.

I nodded, 'Was there any...'

'That's right! Was there any "Product A" in space, and I laughed, er, sorry about that. Well, it got me thinking - why *wasn't* there any in space?

Ha! A no brainer really. Some quality of the atmosphere just bounces it back; it never reaches space. Anyway, I got to wondering what it was that caused the 'bounce' and whether it could be removed or recreated on the ground to provide a safe zone for birthing mothers. I emailed Dr. Stanway for his feedback and retired to bed, but I couldn't sleep. If anything could shield an infant in those first critical moments of life, well, we had to get moving on finding it. My mind was full of ideas that only the Lab could help me explore. By two forty-five I'd contacted the others and we were all heading to the facility.'

Dad picked out an apple from the fruit bowl on the coffee table and took a large bite. Before the mouthful was quite gone he continued.

'After a little while none of my ideas had survived the appraisal of my learned workmates. Their superior knowledge on practicalities left me flat, and I'd considered them such plausible directions. A fear pressed in on me that we would never find a method of blocking "Product A".

'Stanway's notes on the atmosphere gave some thoughtful and beautiful illustrations of atmospheric structure around the point at which the thermosphere gave way to space, but none of it suggested a barrier impassable to "Product A". Not the vacuum of space, not the solar wind, not even the rotation of the earth could provide an answer; it was all covered.

'By Sunday evening I was hopelessly running simulations on my computer, trawling a second time through Stanway's notes just in case I'd missed something, and, to my shame, I began to accept the Allen baby as yet another statistic…'

Nana tutted, 'Douglas, that's a horrible way of putting it…'

'Now, now Maria,' Dad cautioned, 'Don't spoil the build-up. I'd told the others they could head off, only a couple actually did; the rest felt obliged to keep trying to the bitter end. Then - just half an hour later - Stanway exploded into animated life. The shockwave of his discovery leapt from scientist to scientist, my own understanding of it hindered by the burly man bounding towards me waving a much scribed upon piece of paper that ended its journey too close to my face. Stanway's eyes, bloodshot from much research and total absence of sleep, stared right into my soul.

'Half out of breath from his short sprint he blurted "Troposphere, stratosphere, mesosphere, thermosphere…" the words blurred together almost lost to his broad Texan accent. He pointed brutishly at the crumpled paper, which was almost illegible. The heavy number crunching challenged my eye regarding where the beginning of the discovery was. I was also semi-aware that some colleagues had begun applauding!

'Suddenly Stanway's revelation and exertion seemed ready to cause him to black-out, he hovered faintly beside me, but my ignorance wanted answers. "Don't you dare let me down now Vince!" I exclaimed applying a hefty slap to his cheek. "Pull yourself together!"

'The glazing of his eyes lifted instantly, he frowned, "Hey!" He exclaimed, flushed red with fury, then mellowed, "I guess I needed that; anyhow looky here." He pointed at the paper more specifically, saying. "We nearly messed up Douglas."

'Now *I* frowned, drawing the page closer, attempting to keep it still as Stanway's finger tapped at it. All suddenly became clear. "Ha!" I exclaimed, jubilant and yet ashamed for having not realised it myself.

'I glanced at my watch, if the Allen child was to survive, the usual protocols would have to stand aside. This was going to be close. I grabbed my jacket. "Fredrick, call Commander Reece at Jaro, we need a Flack Air Carrier, before they scrap them all. Heather, call the midwife and her team, get them to the Allen address to coincide with my arrival. Track me on my usual frequency."'

When Dad used phrases that moved my childlike mind into the realms of his world - the people he could mobilise, the hardware he could request - I was always enthralled. I would often gather my models and re-enact his stories after he had told them. He continued…

'It was night, the lights of the facility disappeared behind me and I knew I had many hours ahead, but this was the moment we'd been working towards, and I felt sure Stanway had cracked it. I just hoped that our response would be enough, and that it would bear up to the weight of service we would require in the months and years to come.'

Dad looked at us all, 'That's why she's our secret, there's no way this method's going to cope with the flood of life that *will* come if our success goes public…'

'What about her own parents!' Gramps protested. 'Can't they accept the need for silence?'

'I'm getting to that Lionel. It's more complicated I'm afraid.' He turned to me. '*You* want to know what Stanway found don't you?'

I nodded, wide eyed.

'For pities sake Douglas!' Gramps moaned

'Lionel dear, there's going to be a good reason.' Nana calmed. 'There *is* a good reason isn't there Douglas?'

Dad bent closer to me, 'Stanway had realised that we'd been looking at the atmosphere as a single expanse believing that "Product A" bounced around within its entirety, but the atmosphere is layered. Stanway's calculations demonstrated that the activity of "Product A" persisted only within the lowest of these layers, the troposphere.'

I looked at Vanessa, then back at Dad. 'You took Magda and Daniel up and she had the baby safely!'

'Good deduction son, but not quite right I'm afraid.' His face became stern and his voice low, he seemed irritated, flashing Gramps a look that said "Now you'll know".

Gramps responded with a grunt and a shrug of his shoulders.

'I'd driven six hours, not really knowing if I'd reach the Allen residence on time or if our efforts would already be too late. I'd been fuelled by adrenaline but this had faded, and the sleepless days began to play on me. Fortunately, during the most mundane moments of the journey, I'd been able to talk to my colleagues, gain encouragement, share my objectives and instigate my plan.

'As I pulled up towards the entrance of the Allen's Government accommodation, the sun finally peeped up over the horizon. A security guard took a retinal scan, and the heavy gates swung slowly open.

'Fredrick was waiting on an open line for my instructions. "All OK Fredrick. Site is suitable. Come in on my coordinates. Over."

"Right you are Douglas. ETA two minutes. Out."

'My car rolled up the gently curving driveway that skirted a great circular lawn, more than ample for a Flack AC to land. As I pulled up I could see the front door opening. We had called ahead, so this was no surprise - I dismissed it as the mother-to-be preparing to leave the house. I made a call to my PA, Heather; my gaze held down as the phone rang.

"Yes, Dr. North." Heather responded.

"I need an ETA on the maternity team please, Heather."

"Their tracking icon is right on top of yours, Dr. North, so they're as good as with you."

'I looked over my shoulder at the gate. Sure enough a car bearing medical insignia was awaiting entry.

"Confirmed Heather thank…" I turned looking in horror as a baseball bat hit the windscreen, totally crazing it.

'Heather was left hanging on the line as I flung the door open and leapt out. To my astonishment my attacker was Daniel Allen. "Hey! Wait! We're here to make sure your child is delivered safely!"

'Anxieties towards the due date were normal but this was aggressive and extreme, and I questioned how this man had passed the psychological assessment necessary to be part of the program.

"Jus' go away Doc!" He was pointing the bat directly at me.

"We're going to help, Daniel!" I could see Magda staring wide-eyed from the door of their exquisite home. Glancing quickly over my shoulder I could see both the medicar and security staff heading towards us. Above them, distant but visible over a nearby woodland, was the Flack AC on approach. Daniel's agitation grew.

"Look Daniel," I insisted. "We've got the answer. We can bring your child safely into the world."

'He glanced up at his wife, eyes filled with despair. Then, swinging wildly at me with the bat, he nearly decked me with his words.

"We don't want it Doc, go home."

'I was stunned as the truth struck home to me. Daniel and Magda were Leeches! Many couples on the Government program were genuine. They desperately wanted a child. They knew that one day a cure might be found, that their risk might help restore the future of humanity. But a minority played the flip side. Government provision for couples on the program was luxurious, compensation for loss ran into seven figures, it was lucrative.

'Leeches had given up on a solution, they believed that The Great Suffering would never end. They would exploit the system, and, when the lump was gone, they would walk away, handsomely rewarded for their attempt. It was this which betrayed the first Leeches. Genuine couples needed counselling.

'A rage blew up in me, stepping forward I swept the bat away with my left hand, striking Daniel hard across the chin with my fist. He faltered backwards over the car bonnet and onto the driveway, out cold. I stepped quickly over to Magda, she attempted to close the door but a through draught had blown the door curtains over the latch. I thrust the door open and grabbed Magda's arm just as the Flack AC touched down on the lawn.

'I strode towards the aircraft, wincing at how the waveforms from its engines cut through the turf, leaving no sign of damage but, without doubt, releasing more "Product A" into the environment. This said, it still remained our only hope for reaching a High Altitude Platform in time, and I felt sure that time was running out.

'Suddenly one of the security guards levelled a gun at me and demanded that I "Let the woman go!"

'For a moment I wondered if I were the only sane person in the garden, then the second guard sent the first flying with a rugby tackle, clearly more aware of my purpose, and the nature of Leeches.

'Within moments we were on board. The pilot gave a thumbs up and we were away.

'The Flack AC is a medium commercial freight carrier, capable of vertical take-off and landing, but more importantly it can hold a geostationary position and is capable of stratospheric flight. Passenger space is minimal, but enough for a three strong maternity team, the prospective parents and myself.

'With Daniel on his way to a detention centre, I invited Fredrick to join us. He'd arrived with the AC, intending to return the staff car to the facility. The broken windscreen had meant calling for recovery instead and I told Fredrick that he would be useful to me. The truth was he'd been working longer hours than me, and my old college friend looked in need of a diversion.

'Magda sat between me and the aircrafts hull. Her eyes seemed to scratch at my face.

"I don't want it!" She shrieked, fumbling crazily with the belt release.

"There is no reason why you should worry. This is just an experiment; chances are you will lose it just like all the others did..."

"But you told Daniel..."

"That was before he helped me understand your real motives. No, it's just an experiment. No need to try and comfort *you*. Things have to be ruled out you know. Just relax. It'll soon be over and your reward will be safely in the bank." The Flack AC's heaters kicked in.

"Experiment?" Magda hissed almost inaudibly against the powerful hum of the engines.

'I glanced calmly at my watch then back, gazing straight into her eyes. "Yes. Good observational science. We have a theory. We're going to test it. A theory that cannot be tested is just a story, however agreeable that story is to your paradigm in life, it still remains weak science." I leaned closer, "You're a test. None of this is going public, even if it miraculously works. We wouldn't have the hardware in place to cope with the increasing birth rate. We'd be compounding grief. I don't hold too much optimism…"

'I had hoped that the cold despondency of my tone would stir some maternal instinct in her but I was wrong, she smiled, then frowned.

"What's the catch?" She queried, then - snorting in disgust - snapped, "I'm going to prison, right? I'll fight you know, very convincing I'd be as a woman who's lost a little one. I would sue you…"

"If the child dies you'll walk away; if it lives you'll walk away. Your cooperation sets you free. I don't think your husband's violence was quite the home life the program envisaged for a child anyway."

'Magda shifted in her seat to attain what little comfort she could. "That's fine then…" She agreed, waving her hand dismissively and closing her eyes.

'Of course she was going to prison, but an agitated, resistive mother was no good for the baby, and we wanted to give this little one every chance.

"Stratosphere in ten seconds, 9, 8, 7…" The pilot announced. Our momentum slowed as the vessel's long, tapering wings and fins extended from the machines body, the aft engine rallied and we shot forward, stratospheric.

"ETA seven minutes. All OK back there?" The pilot enquired. I gave him the thumbs up and he began to converse with approach control.

"Actually I feel a bit sick." Fredrick piped up. "It's the absence of a window. It was bad enough coming all the way from Jaro airfield."

'The Midwife pointed to a pouch on the wall next to him. Inside was a sick bag. The whole cabin fell silent…'

'To say I was excited would have been short of the truth, I was buzzing! There was no "Product A" where we were. The baby could arrive safely right there; not practical, sure, but possible. Only one concern remained, would it thrive once returned to a "signal" rich environment? It would be awful if the baby died on re-entry into the troposphere. We were sure that the vulnerable moment was the point of birth. After that moment the properties of the infant heart changed, accepting its function independent of the mother's circulation; it had every chance.

'The aft engine eased, the AC began to slow down and arc to the left. I stretched to get a view through the cockpit; ahead was the Britcom High Altitude Platform, "B-HAP-4". A science facility fused with a massive solar powered airship, created to provide a geostationary telecommunications hub. It was the small number of these facilities that posed the greatest problem. The positive news of a successful birth would have to be delayed as long as possible, in order for the production of new facilities to be set in motion.'

Dad sighed 'There will be couples that miss out on being parents for the sake of these few months we are seeking, but so many children will be lost if there's a rush for that limited space.'

'What happened next Dad?' I urged.

'We docked with the B-HAP. A maintenance "Hopper" flew clear to provide us with a docking hatch. Hoppers are the only other craft that can reach a HAP, but they are compact and single seated. The Flack had done us proud.

"Docking sequence complete." announced the pilot.

"Thank God!" Fredrick announced. He was no longer a healthy colour.

"B-HAP-4, we are docked. Over." relayed the pilot.

"Docking stability confirmed. Crew and cargo are welcome to disembark for a twenty-five-kilometre-high cup of tea. Not the best in the world but hot and wet and moderately refreshing. Er, Over."

'Fredrick made a strange noise.

'A screen door slid up and over the bay revealing the facilities entrance hatch. A gaunt, wizened face appeared at the window. With a clunk and a hiss, the door swung open revealing our short, white coated host, waving a pot of tea. It was quite surreal and we all laughed, relieved to have arrived, all accept Magda - who just rolled her eyes - oh, and Fredrick, who was looking for somewhere to put a small bag he'd filled.'

Dad seemed too amused by Fredrick's misfortune. Nana tutted.

'The tea was actually quite nice, the view stunning, but, after all the haste and anxiety about getting there, we now had to wait.

'The Maternity team set up quickly. Fredrick and I headed for our bunks for the first sleep in too long. Magda paced the viewing deck for six hours refusing food, drink or conversation. Monday ran its course.

'We thought Tuesday was going to pass too, at six thirty that evening I was on the viewing deck with the Flack pilot.

"They really create some sort of signal?" he said nodding towards the idling waveforms emanating from the fore-engine as it ticked-over, maintaining the magnetic coupling.

"We wish it were that simple. Signals can be scrambled these days, effectively cancelling them. No, this is what we've called a "Complex Resonant", that's the best descriptive name we can come up with…"

"My best descriptive name." Fredrick interjected as he joined us from the kitchen with a steaming hot-chocolate. "And it's only an issue when…"

'Suddenly our host burst in, "Please hurry," he demanded. "Your patient has collapsed!"

'We rushed to the scene. This wasn't how we wanted our journey to end. The medics were already there. The midwife filled me in.

"Seems she's had a serious stroke. We're prioritising the baby. Magda's chances are practically non-existent." She fixed me with a cool stare. "We weren't prepared for this drama; we can operate but we'll need an extra pair of hands. Someone with a strong stomach."

'Fredrick squinted. "Any other time, but I'm not settled from yesterday yet."

'I looked at the pilot. He just smiled and shrugged, raising his eyebrows unevenly.

"OK, lead the way." I said and followed close behind.

'As we walked the Midwife shared that her colleague had spotted behaviour consistent with substance abuse, but they had no idea how long she'd been unconscious.

'We soon arrived in the makeshift theatre. I was impressed. It was as good as any I'd seen in a real hospital; the team was clearly very professional. Memories of *my* Vanessa bubbled to the surface. How frail she'd become, how hard that team had worked to give us two precious days.'

Dad allowed his tears as he told us the struggle the medic undertook on Magda's behalf and how hard he himself tried to fulfil every request made of him. They'd nothing but praise for him that evening.

Evidence came to light afterwards, explaining Magda's collapse and death. A drug user throughout the pregnancy, Government money had funded her cravings for Pink Sugar, a stash of which she had stowed on her person prior to Dad's arrival. In the haste, however, she hadn't pocketed a measuring device known as a thimble. That afternoon she had accidentally overdosed. Feeling pain in her head, it seems she'd sought help but had fallen just metres from the medics' billet. Dad told us that he will always presume that Magda had tried, and succeeded, to save her child. The baby was quiet for a new-born but alive.

Before spending his last night on the B-HAP Dad had gazed down from the viewing deck at the cities illuminated by Hayvan's generator, musing as to whether all this pain could have been avoided. 'If only the need for ground clearance had been known.' he mourned.

'No-one knew.' Nana offered.

'She's here now anyway.' Gramps added softly.

'We stayed up there for twelve hours, just to satisfy our own minds that she might have a chance when we returned to the troposphere. She needs tests to see if her mother's habit has harmed her. The midwife says she's unnaturally quiet, but time will tell.' Dad stepped into the kitchen to prepare a bottle, Vanessa's crying face was accompanied with silence.

Tests confirmed that Magda's habit had robbed Vanessa of a voice. As she grew her fair skin responded little to the effects of the sun, the red colour of her hair amplified by the contrast. Her green eyes were a constant fascination to me and I adored her.

A new generation started to appear. Dr. Lyn's "Product A" absorber began the long process of eradicating our enemy.

A central school was created as child numbers rose into the hundreds, and - after seven years - conception figures were equal to records taken before The Great Suffering.

Flack Air Carriers lifted prospective parents to new High Altitude Platforms, designed for maternity care. Each airlift safely performed from docking towers fifteen metres clear of the ground.

We were victorious.

Nessa was seven and I was eighteen when I joined my father working for Morrello, the privately owned Government department for science.

That was years ago now, so much has happened since, happy times more than sad. Gramps died six years ago and Nana shortly after, but we were all free, free to exist without the Val'ee. That's all that mattered.

## Chapter five
## The Opening

I gasped, I had neglected Nessa. She'd never existed in any of my previous experiences, but here I loved her deeply. I retrieved my mobile. My fingers typed the familiar number. I waited for the soft sound of her voice - made possible by a prosthetic larynx.

She had never articulated words with her lips, tongue and teeth. She'd remained Dad's secret, a classified Government secret. Many applauded the Government funding to help older couples conceive, but if they'd known of Nessa's arrival some may not have needed it, and there was still a litigation culture in our society.

Dad developed the device that gave Nessa her voice, it was clear and feminine, and to hear it generated no great attention. To see her speak was something else, her lips did not move; it was as if you heard her in your mind.

Nessa's answer phone clicked in, my heart sank.

'Vanessa North is currently unavailable---' There was a click and a pause which made me pay attention.

'There is a Voice Memo for your number, please confirm Dee as recipient after tone---Beeeep---'

Dee was her pet name for me. 'Confirm Dee.' I responded, waiting for the machine to compare my voice with its library, hoping my hurt tongue had not slurred my speech too much.

'Caller confirmed, press one for message, two to leave a message without hearing memo three…'

I pressed one, Nessa's face appeared, lovely but concerned.

'Hey Dee! I tried to call but you were engaged, I'm cleared to come home from school. Something weird happened. I didn't notice anything, but most of my class fainted. I'm freaked so I'm heading home. Really need my Dee. See you there. Bye! Kiss, Kiss!'

Home was Dad's place. I guessed she hadn't heard from Fredrick about the hospital. I sighed, a journey from the school would take two hours ordinarily, I couldn't imagine how long it would take today. Nessa wasn't prone to a great deal of anxiety, but she'd be seeing a lot of turmoil on that journey. Again I felt a pang of guilt.

Ironically she had been enrolled at the school as being a year younger to avoid the obvious questions. She hadn't minded that; she'd excelled.

Had she kept her age, she would have finished school last year!

Leaving a message for her was futile, she'd already be travelling. I'd see her at Dad's. She must have called when Fredrick was leaving his message. Oh well, she was safe. I would head for Central Hospital, find treatment for my tongue, seek Dad, and join her later.

I retrieved my card key and headed for the garage via the kitchen. The MADS, retrofitted on my classic Nissan, sensed my approach and unlocked the car.

'Good afternoon Dace, please state driving preferences.'

The voice was calm, and was the only personality setting I had selected.

'Hi MADS, full auto please.'

MADS stood for Morrello Automated Drive System. In Full Auto the system took total control of the vehicle, but various levels of control could be requested. Auto would control the gears, Drive was like cruise control linked to road speed limits and Manual reduced MADS to satellite navigation.

I would normally select Manual but I was excited about seeing Dad again, it just made sense to let the system drive, especially as I had so much on my mind. I stepped into the car.

'Please state destination.'

**'Central Hospital please.'**

'Destination Central Hospital, loading.... Distance Two point two one kilometres, ETA, six seventeen P M.'

The duration puzzled me. That was one and a half hours. Fredrick was right, the distance could be walked quicker.

'MADS, justify duration.'

'Processing command... Duration subject to - RTA, multiple, - Safety Cordons, six, - Diversions, seventeen, - CDS, multiple.'

CDS were the predecessors to MADS. The "Complete Drive System" was soon referred to comically as a sofa on wheels, as it possessed no driving interface. Everyone was a passenger. Although disliked in retrospect, the system had been widely adopted. I expected that it had saved lives that day, as the on-board computer would have made it impossible to crash. The creator of the MADS had simply programmed the CDS as another obstacle; a joke that didn't feel that funny anymore.

'MADS, cancel destination and power down.'

'Destination cancelled, powering down, have a great day!'

*Cries: The Captive Mind*

The car door opened. I sighed, it *wasn't* a great day. I stepped out of the car and walked to the garage door which had opened as the MADS initiated.

The day was gloriously bright, although the smell of burning plastic tainted the air, and everywhere I looked there was smoke trailing into the sky.

I could see a queue of vehicles at the end of the street waiting to join the gridlocked main road. I stepped forward to let the garage door close. I would have started walking if it wasn't for the scratching noise coming from my front door. Mrs Gray's cat was trapped inside! 'Oh,' I thought to myself. 'It wasn't the breeze that knocked over my spider-plant.' I opened the door, expecting the cat to bolt home, but it stood with its back to me, hissing at the hallway, backing up slowly, heckles up with a tail like a fox. Suddenly it broke from its defiance and darted away, disappearing over the low wall next door.

I stood motionless, then, just as I shrugged, convinced it had merely become trapped inside when I shut the back door, I heard music coming from my lounge; the missing David Ertis! I felt my heart pounding. Something really wasn't right.

Anger took hold of me. I'd had enough. I wanted control back. 'Had I ever had it?' I heard myself think. All I knew was that things had been manipulated before I'd entered the house.

I stepped into the hallway, approaching the lounge quickly and quietly. It all seemed like some sort of prank. Who would break in and play music?

Entering the lounge, I became aware of something dreadfully familiar under the volume of the sound system, a multi-rhythmical slaving tone that was starting to grip on my senses. The room seemed instantly fuzzy and I began to lose awareness. NO! this I could beat; I'd learnt how on Derra. I concentrated on the memory of Hope's face, her beautiful face, her soft lips, dark hair, her freeing smile.

Focusing, I pinpointed the source of the tone; a small silver box placed hurriedly under my chair. I bent down to retrieve it, just as the understair cupboard in the hallway burst open. I spun around, box firmly in hand, as a slim, short figure landed more heavily than its stature could explain, on my back. My head was wrenched sideways by a thin, warm arm that wrapped itself around my neck. The heel of one foot pressed uncomfortably into my groin, the other leg pressed firmly into my ribs, winding me. I flailed wildly with the box, hoping to strike my assailant with its sharp corners but it dropped to the floor, succeeding only in ending the tone it emitted.

I reached up with both hands and took a firm hold on my attacker's head. I tried to pull my enemy from my back but its strength left me in no doubt as to its identity.

'You're all gone!' I shouted.

The reply was gentle and calm, more like a lover speaking from the warmth of an embrace than from a figure contorted in a violent and physically awkward hold. *'Really? It would seem not wouldn't it?'*

I attempted to ram my back against the wall half knowing that this might be my last chance to subdue my foe.

A slight gasp betrayed the fact that I'd hurt it, but I knew *that* wasn't enough. I caught a glimpse of our reflection in the mirror on the mantlepiece. Its free hand, raised high above my head, appeared to be holding some intricate contrivance which it now plunged down towards my head.

'Get Off!' I barked.

*'Not until I know why!'* It retorted, in a tone that sounded like a rock guitar power chord.

There was now something on my head. Desperately I tried to swipe it away, but a jolt of devastating pain sliced first down one side of me, then across; I crumpled and fell.

The arm jerked cautiously away from my windpipe and my conqueror pulled a trapped leg from beneath me. *'Just one day and you have become so resilient, so strong of mind. I've never seen anyone shrug off the tone before. How did you do that?'* The words were like a harmony, wonderful and restful, calm and assuring. I wanted to answer truthfully, but that struck fear into my heart.

*'Do you even know what you've done? I think you must, you declared us gone. You must realise how weak this generation's technologies are. The future your kind could have had is lost, our records show it. You must know it too. What we found was not of this generation. Tell me, when did you first see us?'*

I felt the melody of those words loosening my inhibitions. I felt a desire to help; it was horribly recognizable. I could feel the question in my mind, scratching around for a way in. I attempted to talk.

'Leave our world alone.' I rasped.

*'No.'* The word resonated like a little bell. *'It's our only hope. All I need is your open mind, think to me.'*

*Cries: The Captive Mind*

I felt a hand glide up my back, so soft, so tender, it glanced across my neck with its fingertips and came to rest on the device that had left me captive. The pain pulsed more strongly.

*'Dace, the pain is there to occupy all your violence towards me, to lock it away. I had assumed your heat from your deeds so long ago. Now, let what remains be opened to me, to my words. Let your mind respond. Give me your thoughts, yes, that's it, I see them. How intriguing. Do you recall all of this or just your time here and now?'*

'All of it.' I heard myself reply.

*'Oh, I doubt that. I can help you, let me in. When did you first see us? When did you first sigh at such glorious beauty?'*

Yes, they were beautiful. I felt my mind opening. It shouldn't be opening, I thought myself immune, but then there was the device... I tried again to fight it, but without any hope of rescue it seemed pointless, other than the inconvenience it obviously caused.

*'No! No!'* Chimed the bell, and I felt my body being lifted. I was over six feet tall and of comparable proportions for my height, but this creature swept me up and placed me on my back. I forced open my eyes.

*'How are you doing that?'*

There before me was Chorda, a Val'ee Overseer, a vision to behold, perfection. Desire filled my soul, but my fierce hatred prevented a complete surrender.

Chorda sat on my chest. I knew what these creatures could have inflicted on the world by now, but humanity - in my experience here - knew nothing of them. I felt drawn to give Chorda what she wanted. Her cerise gaze filled me with yearning, despite the sensation of being pulled apart.

Chorda stroked my face, moving again to adjust the device. *'So strong.'* She asserted, and her words became the only tangible thing, nothing else held substance, even the pain seemed to vanish... *'I like your resolve very much, but it must end.'*

'Why now?' I heard myself think. 'Why wait?' She seemed taken aback, and in the link of our minds I perceived a long held desire that this meeting would one day take place. Within that desire I saw flames, and twisted metal evaporating in fervent heat. There was a need for an answer, but it was jubilant at my capture, what was one more answer before she sought her own?

*'My timing is perfect. Yesterday you would not have known me, today you*

*would gladly have shot me - whatever that would have achieved - Now you remember all, before... you knew nothing.*

*'It took me a while to figure out when you would know, but the clues were there. Then it was just a wait; a wait for the Rip to become apparent, and oh! HOW apparent. Do you know how many died because of what you did? Your means of attacking my kind is hidden in you. You hold a secret I can only unlock now, that is why we waited.'*

Chorda adjusted something on the device. I glared defiantly at her eyes, they settled in my gaze, radiant, deeply segmented. She leaned closer. I could feel her breath on my lips. My mind screamed out, not in pain but in the torment of the inevitable. I knew I would buckle. Chorda alone I could have resisted but her device was cutting through my resolve, forcing the opening, and my heart longed to allow it.

*'Tell me when you saw us first,'* Chorda chanted, sensing my faltering will. *'Tell me, show me.'*

My will began to seek. I felt the lives I'd lived dropping away one after another, the Rip was gone, Nessa was gone, this life was gone, replaced by the events that led to it, those in turn replaced; such different circumstances. I could sense Chorda's excited fascination, but she remained focused on her goal. She wanted the beginning.

Here with Chorda, ceased to exist, my consciousness returned to youth, but it was too tangible to be a memory, I was really there. This was where I saw them first.

I no longer perceived Chorda's probing questions or the sensation of her legs straddling my chest.

All mankind fell to them then, in their hearts, and I was a mere child.

## Chapter six
## The Calls of Youth

How different it had all been that time around...

I was only two when the Val'ee came to the earth. The Great Suffering had been endured for five years. My father had unified the world, but this was a period that was devoid of any progress and all were at their lowest ebb.

My birth had been a mystery which no test could explain, resulting in constant intrusion by the media. Circumstances would move us to a less secure home and Dad's involvements left me vulnerable and bitter.

My young age gave no recollection of the Val'ee arrival. Nana had told me of the silence that fell on the earth and the concern it caused; three hours without sound, no birdsong, no voices, no whirr of a wave generator, just deathly silence. She told of the descent of the Val'ee transport ships; neat Y shaped craft dropping slowly from the sky. Thousands of vessels landing all over the world, humanity watching transfixed and fearful, ready to run.

The first sound to break the silence was theirs. Their voices, cut into the void and dispelled our fears, the familiar sounds that had been absent followed quickly after.

To the relief of many, they claimed peace and benevolence. By the time I became truly aware of them it was as if they'd always been here, working with us, guiding, mentoring.

They had visited me soon after their arrival. They'd learnt of the "illness" that had befallen us and of the miracle child who shouldn't have survived. They'd gained Dad's permission to scan me and seemed to find the answer with little effort.

They warned us that the cause of our suffering had been our ignorance, that we needed to develop our understanding if our species was to avoid extinction. They promised to help us; so began the salvation of the Val'ee.

They invited Dad to play a key role in the project. He had, after all, been instrumental in bringing a violent and indolent people together, into - what they called - a state close to civilisation!

Dad told me of the praise they rained down on him for his work and efforts for his people, his powers as a peace maker and mediator; the ideal choice for running the project that would end The Great Suffering. Dad felt privileged to be considered useful by such an advanced race.

Work began immediately on the "Sylvestris" project, an amalgamation of earth's forests and alien technologies. Huge curved apparatus rose up above the canopy of the trees. Each shell-like structure was festooned with gill-like ribs that sucked in the air, passing it over elements that cleansed it of the pollutants the Val'ee insisted caused our suffering.

It was at one such array that Dad started work. It encompassed the Thetford forest in Suffolk, close to where my mother's parents had lived, and it made sense for us to leave the secure Government accommodation and move into their old house. It seemed the Val'ee had found a cause through scanning me, and there was no longer a need to protect me from those that had wanted to study me more invasively.

As Dad worked he became disillusioned. He'd looked into atmospheric pollutants long before the Val'ee came and had drawn a complete blank. He came home loaded with statistical data. He just had so little free time. When he *was* with us he poured out his dissatisfaction with the Val'ee provision, marvelling that children were indeed being born on the Val'ee mothership.

Dad became withdrawn. His pride was broken. His motivation, gone. He'd missed the cause. Aliens had come and exposed his oversight; put the world right in days. How many more years would have gone by before he'd realised his mistake? He didn't deserve praise at all, it all belonged to the Val'ee. They, and they alone, had saved us; but I knew Dad didn't believe it.

The Val'ee enjoyed their accolades from us. They seemed to need nothing else, except a few resources to fabricate strange, metre square tiles. Apart from this our company seemed enough, and they would seek it regularly. Their concern for our wellbeing led to their offer of a device that would help them respond to accidents and illness quickly. A little chip that sat under the skin, monitoring vital statistics. The "MIT", or Indicator Tag, flagged up early signs of illness, and many benefited from early intervention and rescue from potentially fatal injuries. The device was universally accepted.

When my father felt I was old enough he decided that it was time for me to formulate my own opinion, rather than be poisoned by his. It was a noble gesture on his part, for all, but a grumbling minority - led by some

*Cries: The Captive Mind*

man called Jayes - held the Val'ee in high regard. There was a joy returning to the earth that Dad wanted me to be a part of, so he invited our "rescuers" to revisit the anomaly of The Great Suffering.

This was the first time I remembered meeting them - I was four - but the impression they left on me remained strong, it was so great in fact that a little of my subdued perception grasped that this memory I was living was an illusion, that I was not a little child enraptured by his visitors, but a grown man entrapped by one. They weren't solving our problems; they were pretending to. In reality they were holding us back, grooming us...

I forced my realisation into silence, anxious that Chorda would notice my awareness and shut it down again. I feared that nothing was hidden from her sight. Nothing happened. I allowed the memories of the Val'ee visitation to flow, feeling I could use this knowledge to break free at an unexpected moment and subdue my captor. I wrestled with my excitement letting it spill into the memory of the child's experience to disguise it.

We were deeply under their spell when I was a child; subtle creatures that seemed to float effortlessly, their elegant raiment fluttering constantly as if in some unfelt breeze. They presented all the demeanour and appearance of femininity; gentleness, grace, radiance, poise, they even accepted the use of such gender related words in their dealings with us, even though there seemed to be no sexual divisions within their kind.

To gaze into their eyes was to experience beauty beyond comprehension, turquoise, gold or cerise irises bounded by jet black segmentation, seemingly denoting rank or caste. The perfection of their faces was to be found in a symmetry that humans lack, the left and right sides of our faces differ slightly, theirs do not, they are flawless.

Their voices play on the human mind. Oh those voices, that, even in the most mundane of conversations, dance like a song on our ears. All of us were drawn to them, men, women - it mattered little - what mattered was that we pleased them, served them to our highest ability - that the blessing of their approval might come to us.

Twenty Val'ee came to my home that day. At first I'd hidden behind my Dad's leg, shy but curious. Soon their playfulness enchanted me. They were not the professional, serious creatures I'd expected. They seemed like children themselves, innocent, happy. Dad, for all his intellect, seemed cold, impatient and miserable by comparison...

It was now or never, the recalled doubt regarding my father's love for me and his pain urged it. The delighted play of a child, with new found friends, must be enough to mask my intent. I would have the advantage for sure. I shot my hand up towards Chorda's throat, opening my eyes as I did so. With her soft flesh in my hand I felt a sudden elation pulse through my being, but her eyes gazed back at me with a bemused disparagement. My grip would have done considerable damage to a human neck, engorged as it was with adrenalin and desperation, but she smiled. This was no grip at all, it would have had the assurance of what was soft beneath it giving way. No, it was me who was held.

Chorda eased herself off of my outstretched hand, leaving it suspended in the air like the last call for help of a man drowning in quicksand. A moment captured like some macabre tableaux.

*'The device has safeguards...'* She sat momentarily, just staring at me from the rug in front of the wood burner. She shook her head in disbelief. *'You knew the great benefits our kind gifted to your people. I see that you recall them. You would have had so much more by now. I must know your reasons. Show me through your eyes, that I might understand you.'* The words spilt over me like a lament, her pain discernible in my consciousness.

*'Where were we, Dace?'* The words affected me like a heavy sedative. I watched my outstretched hand blur into fog. I felt her settle down next to me, holding on around me, her head resting on my chest. Did she need the closeness to make her connection work?

Darkness consumed me, I felt genuinely lost this time. Part of me was happy to let go, touched by Chorda's melancholic tones. Part of me was grateful to give in. The very essence of what made me didn't see this as a struggle against death, therefore the outcome needn't worry me. 'Let it, let it,' it seemed to urge. My physical senses fell away; my desire lay in a pool of light, that emanated joy.

Sounds of laughter thrilled my heart and an awareness of time passing at the pace of a child's experience pulled me closer. Ah, there was innocence here, and my tired will longed, even yearned for it.

I was again with my Val'ee audience, playing and dancing. I was happy, euphoric. I felt special, they said I was.

I cried when they said they had to leave. I'd never been surrounded by so much intense love, such focused praising attention. I hadn't felt *that*

*Cries: The Captive Mind*

from Dad in months. I hadn't wanted it to stop. Then one bent down and told me they would return frequently, that I was of particular interest and would grow to accept them as family.

I stood waving until their ships disappeared beyond the limits of sight above me. Then I stood, just gazing up, dizzied by the scudding clouds.

When I eventually looked down Dad was stood on the patio by the door, tears running down his cheeks, and I knew his regrets. I ran to him and flung my arms around him.

'I want to be here son.' He cried, 'I want to play and laugh. I don't want to miss you growing, you're so big already, I'm going to have to get you some new trousers, just look.' He took in a deep breath, 'Your mother would be mad at me right now, for putting *them* ahead of you, but I'm not, not really. I hope you'll understand one day.' His hug was a hungry hug, a hug starved hug, as was mine.

'Speak to them Daddy.' I replied, 'I think they will be nice and let you come home more.'

'You are right. You are so clever. Mummy always said you would be. I will ask. I promise.'

Nana appeared next to us, her apron flapping in the breeze. 'Best come inside, looks like a storm blowing in.'

We looked at the sky. Heavy clouds were gathering over the nearby forest, a dull rumble echoed distantly, and the trees stirred and heaved under a steady wind that blew through them. We gathered the toys from the garden and headed inside.

Dad spoke to his Val'ee Overseer and was amazed at her understanding. He was simply to choose a colleague to play his role and he could have as long as he felt he needed.

Things became better; he eased out of the depression he had fallen into. His attitude began to change from one of self-persecution for his failure to help humanity, to one of gratitude that most children now survived thanks to the off world facilities of the Val'ee. The few that could not be reached in time for their baby to be delivered on the Val'ee mothership still lost their child, but surely the alien filters would end that soon. As long as mankind now survived who cared who had achieved it? Deep down he was still tormented by one question, how did atmospheric pollutants, absent from a delivery room, cause cardiac arrest at the point of birth?

*Christopher J Reeve*

I spent many happy times with my Dad during those few years, one time in particular would never leave my memory. I was eight, and was suffering at school. It wasn't due to being enrolled with children three years older than me, no, I was a natural academic and had been doing well. I was also well liked, the weird kid who had survived, and weird was cool. I should have been up to my usual standard, but I'd let my Val'ee companions distract me. My mind would be far away during classes, and my performance suffered.

Dad saw an opportunity to jump start me. A new motivation to learn was the answer and he requested the necessary help.

One night I overheard him at the front door discussing the opportunity to ride in one of the Val'ee transports. I froze, waiting for the reply...

*'We have grown fond of your family, Douglas.'* Came the melody of words, *'We would like to offer you more. A journey to the ship that brought us to your world...'*

I dropped the model I was playing with and made my way to the top of the stairs for a better view.

'Well, er... if you're sure that's not an imposition...'

*'We offer our gift gladly. We could not have helped a world that was primitive and violent. Your actions were timely and provident. Your company, and that of your boy, will be a blessing to us.'*

'Thank you, hey Dace, did you hear...'

I jumped up and down, clapping my hands.

*'Tomorrow then.'* Sang the Val'ee official and she moved away like a gentle breeze.

I didn't sleep that night. Soon I would see their home, not their world of course, but what had carried them from it. A structure formed by non-human hands with knowledge and technologies we could not yet conceive. It would be astounding; I just knew it.

*Cries: The Captive Mind*

<u>Chapter seven</u>
Time and Mortality

Dad found that morning playing with my models. My bed was the mothership. We had landed on it and were doing a spacewalk.

'Come and have your breakfast Dace, we're being picked up in an hour and it would be rude not to be ready.'

I was through the door and halfway down the stairs by the time Dad had said "ready" and I'd poured my cereal before he'd caught up with me.

'Now that's what I call motivation.' He laughed. 'I'm the same though. I've given these creatures too little respect. They really do seem to care about the people of the earth. There are conditions we could not cure before they came, and now we can. We'll be living longer with greater health.' He winked at Nana who gave a tut and a little smile. 'I'll not fathom the pollution thing.' He continued. 'I guess it's just beyond me. Thank God they came when they did, that's all I can say.'

I was pulling my trainers on when I heard a noise outside. I peered out to see a Val'ee Loader, a chunky, solid looking craft with a large domed flight deck. 'They're here!' I screamed, eagerly.

Dad smiled sweeping my coat around me. 'OK, Let's go.' His hand trembled in mine. He was as excited as me.

It wasn't as pretty as the transports our usual visitors used but it was a fascinating design. Some portions of the floor were transparent affording a phenomenal field of visibility. A large black plate was slung beneath, and two little arms were held in a passive folded position.

Our companion's eyes were the chilly turquoise we'd come to associate with the Val'ee worker class. Dad preferred the colour to any other, it being closest to a human blue. They welcomed us warmly. There wasn't a breath of a breeze in that cabin, but their delicate clothing still danced to their every turn and gesture. They helped us to our seats.

'*We have been selected today for the joy of showing you our home from home, the magnificent ERUWAI.*' Said one.

'*You will be amazed at her beauty; she will affect you on a deeply spiritual level.*' A second insisted.

The pilot turned in her seat '*We will not be docking, there is work to be done. We will be collecting materials from the release bay and transporting them to the forward sector, then we will return you here. It is our great pleasure to have your company.'*

'Thank you so much.' Replied Dad holding me close and tightly.

The pilot turned back to the controls, slid her fingers up a metallic panel and we rose smoothly, effortlessly, up and up, above the house, through some broken cloud, up with immense velocity but no sensation of movement.

A little tone was explained as an indicator that notified of the ships passing into the stratosphere, another confirmed the correct functioning of cabin parameters.

Above us I could begin to see an outline. I tugged on my Dad's sleeve and pointed.

*'Yes, that is the ERUWAI. Feel free to question us.'*

Dad needed no other invitation. 'Why don't we see this massive vessel at night? Surely it would reflect the sun as the moon does.'

*'ERUWAI likes the sun, it follows it, it is never in your night sky.'*

'How big is it? I ventured, astonished that we had travelled through our atmosphere now and out into true space and yet the transports that were regularly passing us were disappearing into the distance long before reaching the great vessel.

*'Nose to tail ERUWAI would still overlap the motorway that encircles your country's capital - the one you call the M25 - by a great margin.'*

I wasn't particularly happy with this answer. I'd never been on the M25. I knew it went around London but had no comprehension of its size.

The ERUWAI was very much longer than its width, comparable, I thought, to a felt tip pen, but perhaps with a stretched, curving, roughly rectangular cross-section. As we drew closer we were able to see that it was constructed of two great surfaces, an upper and a lower. Both these surfaces were covered in crazed tiles that had a surface patina, rainbow-hued like a polished, brass fire surround. The surfaces were separated by a wide black valley, the contents of which were hidden in shadow. The top edge was illuminated rhythmically by white and green static lights, accompanied in sequence by a red light that pulsed along the edge of the lower plate.

'Why aren't we weightless?' Dad piped up.

*'Our loader plate generates a gravity field; would you like to be weightless?'*

'Yes please!' I exclaimed

*Cries: The Captive Mind*

Our companions seemed pleased. The pilot strapped in and slowed to a halt, brilliant green lights flashed a warning to other approaching vessels and we separated from the black plate beneath us.

The two Val'ee not involved in piloting the vessel now took our hands and eased us into the space afforded by the flight deck. *'We do not get to do such things much; life is very busy.'*

'I understand,' Dad nodded. 'I've been foolish and judgemental, the pressures that face your kind - with such hardware as this ERUWAI to maintain - well, it makes what I grumble about look pathetic.'

*'Do not condemn yourself, you have much potential.'*

Both our companions glowed radiantly as they held us.

'How many of you are there?' I asked mesmerised by the speeding Y ships and sundry other craft as they flurried by.

*'Many thousands of us have not needed to leave our duties on the ERUWAI. look at the ships you see, they are but a fragment of those serving your world below.'*

Again, I didn't feel that my question had been answered. But it didn't matter, I was floating in space, spinning somersaults in a bubble of glass!

My eyes then fell upon the earth below. How fine it looked. It had a more profound impact than that promised for the Val'ee mothership. I was not ungrateful - it would have been impossible to be that - but the stronger draw for me was my world. I felt an urgent desire to protect it although I didn't know what from...

*'We must now collect our cargo.'* The pilot instructed. The others lowered us and held us, so that we wouldn't be roughly pulled down by the plate.

Dad's companion stroked his hair into place and helped him to his seat. I pressed my face to the glass as the vessel again sped forward along the side of the EURWAI.

The pilot slowed down as she approached the docking bay. Beside us, at a safe distance, the dark shadow between the great upper and lower surfaces gave way to an illuminated docking portal. Numerous personal transports darted like little yellow wasps at the entrance of a nest. Occasionally one seemed to stop dancing and hold a stationary position. The manoeuvre heralded the arrival of an icy blue beam that drew it towards the gaping dock accompanied by a green tinged laser that cleaned the surface of each craft with an efficient flourish.

The pilot smoothly accelerated towards a row of blocks that floated into space from a release bay. We were close enough to this opening to perceive some of the structures in the gap. Sweeping gill like structures, similar to those used in the Sylvestris project - only much larger - spanned the void from top to bottom creating regular divisions. Between each of these divisions twelve interlocking domes of immense size extended out from the body like wide cones with their points buried deep within the ship, the position of each cone suggested that their points met. 'What are the domes for?' Dad asked.

*'They are part of the ERUWAI's propulsion, I can say no more.'*

'Then that's enough for me.' Dad acknowledged, and I noticed his face adopting a familiar, thoughtful expression.

*'We have clearance to collect and proceed.'* The pilot informed, taking position above the nearest crate. The crate held a number of the tiles that had been fabricated on earth.

Without noise or jolt it became part of the loader and we accelerated to a phenomenal rate along the flank of the mothership.

'Woooo Hoooo!' I screamed with delight, causing all to laugh happily.

It took us ten minutes to reach the forward end of the ship. It was just as busy there as it had been at the docking bay. Large triangular craft sat above the activity, as if overseeing the work. More than fifty loaders, like ours, were releasing their cargoes onto the hull. Countless, suited workers collected the tiles and fitted them to scampering, crab-like machines that deposited them into place where other machines had cleared away the old. These came away in brittle fragments that floated into space in all directions. Each of the new ones, their fabric a sort of ceramic, slotted into a ridge on each side, sliding perfectly underneath the rear edge of the tile in front of it.

Then we saw the front of the ERUWAI. Two great structures, like the jaws of a stag beetle, curved out then in and forwards to a fine, needle-like point a further mile ahead of us. The whole array, apart from the needle, was covered with the tiles, all pristine and renewed.

'You are renewing all these tiles...' Dad ventured as more of a statement than a question.

*'Yes, it will take a few more years to complete.'*

'And after that?' Dad pursued.

All three Val'ee appeared saddened. *'Then it will be time to leave.'* The pilot sighed.

'NO!' I cried, 'You must stay!'

One smiled, stepped forward and held me in her arms. *'We have not got the time, but we will return I am sure. The Overseers are drawing up plans to involve your people and extend their range; you will see.'* She squeezed me tightly and gave off a radiant aura of light. I felt tired. *'Perhaps your advancement will be so great that you will come and find us, will you do that Dace?'*

I nodded, 'Yes.'

She eased out of the embrace, *'You will have to study hard; challenge the ideas that hold your kind back. You know that don't you?'*

I nodded again, and she flashed a smile at Dad.

Dad admitted later that his objective had been reached, that my motivation to renew my studies had been met in that very moment.

With hindsight we'd always known our visitors wouldn't stay forever, but the news coming from one of them left Dad and me a little flat and rather quiet for the remainder of the trip. The Loader delivered its cargo then, taking a route around the frontal array, we sped along the underside of the ERUWAI and headed towards home.

How jade and sapphire hued the earth looked as it grew beneath us, veiled in part by wispy nets of cloud. How good it felt to be returning, and how amazing to have travelled away. Dad must have felt the same, he stood watching the ERUWAI until daylight robbed him of its form. He was deep in thought, perhaps committing to memory that sight which he might never see again. We'd been away for only a couple of hours but both of us were drained and tired.

As we landed Dad thanked our pilot and guides for their time, and he wanted them to know that his gratitude was so much more than he had words to express, and that if there were any way to repay the kindness...

They responded by assuring us that it had been even more of a pleasure for them, so any return of kindness could be considered fully paid by the shared experience and closeness they had enjoyed.

I had always been quite transfixed by the Val'ee before. I could never leave them, it was always them that left, so I'm not sure why I did what I did next. Could it be that I was getting familiar with them? I couldn't tell; all I know is that I saw my school friend. He'd pulled his bike up on the pavement the other side of the road, to look at the Loader on my lawn. I could appreciate his interest. Usually a Y ship came when a Val'ee paid a call, Loaders were more unusual.

I waved, then, filled with a burst of adrenalin, felt the need to run to him and spill the whole story of my trip.

Dad was still expressing his gratitude when I reached the gate. I hadn't seen the van approaching - my short stature had left it obscured by a couple of cars parked on the road.

The pilot realised the danger first and warned Dad who, failing to stop me with a shout, made a vain attempt to catch up by sprinting across the lawn.

I had heard Dad, but my desire to share my story with Craig just seemed to override everything.

I was on the road when I saw her. She wasn't shouting or screaming like a number of other people now were, no, she was running, running straight at me. I was terrified. She had appeared from nowhere. My initial reaction was to try and dodge her but my eye fell beyond her at the horrified face of a van driver who was wrestling to stop his vehicle from hitting us, dust billowing up from his locked wheels.

The impact winded me. I found myself pinned beneath the woman as the sound of screeching tyres juddered to a halt. The fabric of her tracksuit was blue, soft and unfamiliar.

I heard the pounding of footsteps hurriedly approaching and a van door opening.

'Were they hit?' A voice shouted.

'No, but it was close.' Someone answered.

'OW!' I cried.

The weight of the woman suddenly lifted as she responded to my discomfort, 'Are you OK Dace?' She asked, her accent clearly American. The sun glared at my eyes but I felt sure I didn't know her. I didn't know how to react.

'H-How do you know my name?' I stammered.

'Your Dad was calling you, are you OK?' She replied.

Dad *had* been calling, but was it so obvious he was my Dad when others were shouting too? It seemed odd...

'He's bleeding!' Came a startled cry.

I was too. Seems I cut my head on the pavement as the woman swept me off the road, and a pool of blood became visible as I sat up.

Suddenly Dad was alongside us. 'Thank you! Thank you so much!' His voice was charged with emotion as he threw his arms around me. 'Dace,

*Cries: The Captive Mind*

what were you thinking?'

People were crowding around. 'You OK Dace?' Craig called.

'I've got a first aid kit in the van.' The driver offered.

'Let me see,' A woman insisted. 'I'm trained in first aid.'

My face came clear of Dad's embrace. I looked frantically about. I couldn't see my rescuer, just a flash of blue visible between the gathered bodies. She'd gone without trace, apart from the life she'd undoubtedly saved.

An absorbent dressing firmly in place Dad walked me back to the house, repeatedly thanking everyone for their help and concern. The Loader had left.

'She just left…'

'I guess they saw you were OK.' Dad suggested, 'They probably knew you weren't badly hurt by checking your MIT…' He rubbed my back.

'No, not the Val'ee…'

Dad looked blank then realised what I meant. 'Oh, yes…' He looked back over the street from the gate we'd reached. 'I really didn't see her properly. Well, it sometimes happens I suppose, a rescuer who doesn't want a lot of fuss…' Dad's voice betrayed his disappointment. He wanted to reward my fast acting rescuer. He sighed, and we headed up the drive to the house.

A later newspaper article and photographs would declare the near death experience in grossly exaggerated detail, but I was, in fact, fine. Gramps helped me to the sofa and Nana fussed around me all afternoon, but it really was just a scratch. All other outcomes I dared not entertain.

## Chapter eight
## Tears in the Night

Dad attempted to find my rescuer. He threatened to take a certain newspaper to court over the melodramatic way it had treated the accident. In doing so he gained repeated space in its columns to urge her to come forward. Every effort was made to find her, but two women who claimed to be her, were not her. She'd just vanished.

Soon, however, the search came to an abrupt end. The "involvement" that the Val'ee on the Loader had spoken of was upon us. Dad was drawn once more into the elite circle, with little time for anything else. I felt robbed of something important. I'd never said thank you.

The Val'ee plan soon captured the interest of everyone. They considered us to be a promising race of creatures who might join them beyond our own portion of space one day. They would equip us to begin that journey. They would not give away the answers, we'd have to feel our way and find solutions for ourselves. But whilst they were still with us they would give us a project to work on, giving us a foundation to progress from. This project was the construction of numerous Sky Cities, providing safe locations for the delivery of our young. They would also give us a tool that had helped them forge their own society; The Envisager.

It quickly became apparent that the Envisager was not a device that humanity would easily master. It actually created matter from focused thought, but few could maintain their attention long enough to make anything, and of those who could, only a handful had the innate prowess and understanding to fabricate anything that fulfilled its intended purpose. Eighteen months had to pass before there were enough skilled men and women to move the project forward.

The Val'ee had been as assistive as ever. In space they had constructed foundations for the first three cities, then waited for us to solve the problems of placement and support. They looked to the team that Dad had brought together to tackle The Great Suffering. Dad had known they were the best chance for humanity in those dark days, now, given "lesser" difficulties, they were unstoppable.

The first challenge they vanquished was that faced by the Envisager Operators, or EO's. They needed to be able to use the tool *and* understand the materials necessary for specific tasks, but these abilities were two very separate things. Dad had colleagues who were well versed in the structure of most materials, and who were able to explain them. He learnt from their conversations, picking up everything they described, and he was soon able to help in these instructive roles too, increasing productivity.

The project gained pace. The skeletal superstructures were lowered onto tropospheric stabilisers - Great platforms that exploited the recently discovered fact that two giant wave generators arranged in opposing positions created a potent hydrophobic reaction enabling them to "sit" on the atmospheric moisture found at the leading edge of the tropopause - Once initiated above this veil of water the stabilisers could not pass back through it.

Dad missed my tenth birthday due to his workload. I was devastated. He was the only person I longed to see. He explained that the Val'ee required him at all consultations, but in truth he was becoming fascinated by the Envisagers. When he eventually came home he would talk of his wonderings regarding the full technological capabilities of the Val'ee and seemed to have little interest in how I was.

One morning, just as he was about to return to work, I'd challenged his apparent disinterest. He wasn't amused by my outburst at all. He snapped something about targets and how important it was that we learnt as much as we could before the Val'ee left, then his transport arrived and he hurried off like some anxious servant responding to the instruction of his master. I felt hollow, and my schooling began to suffer again.

The following year saw an increase in EO's thanks to a system of selection that recognised the most promising candidates.

Dad had also been busy. He'd been helping many other members of his team to gain the skills to explain materials, even structures, systems and circuits, to EO's. Productivity accelerated but Dad was becoming a stranger. One leave day he appeared at the door with a beard having not shaved for three weeks. I hardly recognised him, and over the following few months he was noticeably losing weight.

Then came the moment that seemed to take him away completely. An EO took a break leaving his Envisager on charge near where Dad was working. Unable to resist, Dad took up the tool, pointed it, and created. When the EO returned, he discovered that Dad had outstripped the work target for that day. On seeing that his work was also so refined and pleasing to the eye, the EO sought an Overseer to share in his amazement.

The Overseer wasn't pleased, but he couldn't stop him from working because of the structural risks disturbance propagated. She would have to bide her time. Then Dad did something that would cement his status as a master EO. He would have had to stop when the Envisager's charge pack ran down but his feel for the device seemed to comprehend the impending decline in performance. Quickly he assessed the tools cells and connections, envisaged a miniature, clip-on wave generator, attached it and continued with the work. The Overseer left to inform more Val'ee officials. Nineteen hours later, they persuaded him to stop, and insisted he take two days leave to rest his mind; he had achieved all the targets for the next four weeks.

In a day Dad had become the most accomplished EO yet and as he arrived home, boiling over with adrenaline and excitement at his new powers, I felt he would never be the Dad I wanted, or needed him to be, again.

At the age of eleven I felt my grandparents had completely taken over Dad's role. With all the progress on the Val'ee project, and the ongoing speculation about the timing of the Val'ee departure, the media spotlight on my life had eased.

Some days, when I was free of the drudgery of school, I'd travel to the city on an overlooked card that had once belonged to Dad but which now lived firmly in the back pocket of my jeans. I would sit in the city centre watching the people pass by. Looking, waiting to see if she'd pass by, that stupid woman who had pushed me out of the path of that van. I wanted to tell her how she'd wasted her efforts, how miserable my life had become, how I'd have been better dead like my mother; but she never passed. I just sat rubbing the scar on the back of my head where the pavement had cut in. It was a reminder of the last day I'd ever felt the protection and love of my father. Now it was just Nana and Gramps day after day, a couple of "olds" with no grasp of what young people needed.

That said I was never late home, *I* actually cared. I didn't want Nana to fret any more than she already did about Dad. I'd hear them talking late at night. Nana would cry when weeks had gone by without word. News would reach us through a colleague of Dad, a man called Fredrick Evans. He'd visit occasionally - usually close to meal times when he'd always be offered a bite - He knew Nana and Gramps too, something about how Mum and Dad met.

Apparently Dad had started sharing the Envisager techniques he'd discovered with other EO's, and his methods were much better than those taught by the Val'ee. Many EO's drew close in skill to Dad, and trainees quickly signed on to his Data Pack address for tips.

One hundred and seventy EO's now worked on the Sky Cities and the first was nearly complete. Fredrick felt sure Dad would be home again soon, but then, he always said that, and he always said he'd have a word with him; a friendly push in the right direction. I remained despondent. Why would I want him here if he needed a push?

The first Sky City was completed soon after Fredrick's last visit and Dad actually did come home, albeit unannounced. He looked drawn and tired, and I discovered that I still loved him enough that his appearance worried me. Nana had started fretting, as was her normal reaction to health matters, but this time Dad didn't brush the concerns aside, he just sat down heavily and suggested that some of her delicious home cooking would help get him back to normal. 'Oh Maria, I have missed your food…'

'Did you miss me though!' I remarked as I stood just visible behind the door.

'Dace, my boy, where were you?' His tone was the same as it had always been, the happiness in his eyes hard to ignore.

*I* was in my room, of course, just a flight of stairs away, but the retort stayed firmly inside and I stomped off into the garden, fuming.

I headed straight for the old Eucalyptus tree. It had been there longer that Nana and Gramps had been alive. Its twisted limbs were easy to climb and Gramps had fixed some boards to the lower boughs to make a deck. The day was getting late, the sun was setting, the air cool. I felt alone and of little importance.

Dad's voice appeared from beneath me, 'Hey Dace, I'm sorry…'

'*You're* sorry?'

'Yes…'

I looked down on him over the edge of the deck, 'What for?'

'For not being here.'

I pushed myself back out of sight, a lump in my throat. 'It's not as if you missed anything…' I snapped.

'That's not true. I've missed the company of my brilliant son…'

I heard his foot stepping up onto the buttress of the tree below me. 'I didn't say you could come up here.' I said coldly, and the sound of movement stopped.

'I wanted to be here…'

'Then why weren't you?'

'They are going soon, a couple more months and their repairs are complete…'

'I don't care!' I retorted, 'Good riddance!'

'You don't mean that, Dace, you knew we had to get as much from them in their remaining time. I had to do all I could to…'

'Oh just leave me alone…' I heard a hand pulling up on the edge of the deck, 'I said leave me al…'

'You told your Dad that, not me!'

I turned my tear streaked face to meet the soft gaze of Gramps.

He smiled, 'He won't bother you again tonight, I've sent him in.' He sat next to me. 'Aren't you the littlest bit cold up here?'

'No.' I lied. My tears had damped the neck of my T-shirt and it was getting uncomfortable. Gramps knew, he threw his cardigan around my shoulders.

'Don't tell him I admitted it, but your Dad's achieved an awful lot of work…'

I shrugged and turned dismissively away, staring down towards the meadow. A subtle comfort struck me. This had always been my vantage point when Gramps had finished one of his remote control planes. He built them from scratch with various levels of success, but he was improving. He'd join me in the tree when he'd mastered flying one, revelling in the fact that he could observe the plane from above as it made a pass or landed on the neatly mown, level strip he'd created.

'…he's a workaholic Dace, but none of its been for himself, it's been for the future, no one else could have achieved what he's done.'

We sat in silence for a little while, the stillness broken only by my occasional sniffs and the evening song of a blackbird.

'Here…' Gramps dropped a wave lamp and a scrapbook into my lap, 'Consider what he's done in the light of this. His motives weren't selfish, they still aren't. He doesn't want fame or attention, he did it so…'

I still sat with my eyes fixed on the meadow, a haze of mist was forming above it.

*Cries: The Captive Mind*

'...Oh, Dace. Just look at the book.' With that Gramps lowered himself, with a grunt and a few puffs, down onto the grass below and wandered inside, rubbing his arms for warmth.

I pulled his thick cardigan around me, initiated the wave torch and opened the scrapbook with an indifferent flick. In front of me were articles relating to an event that had happened shortly after I was born, when we lived in the Government house. A great gathering of people, from all walks of life and many nations, had overwhelmed the security and sought to take me away for further "investigations". Dad had spoken to them and brought about the origins of the unity the world now enjoyed, a unity he intended would bring an eventual end to The Great Suffering.

'So what?' I thought, 'He never achieved it...' then my eye was caught by one sentence, it's text bold and important looking.

"I want a future for my son, one where he'll find love and have children of his own, and have purpose."

I suddenly understood his motives, they were still the same as then. If the Val'ee had gone before all was in place, the future would be lost...

I found Dad on the old easy-chair by the fire. I squeezed in beside him, hugged him and cried. We both did.

## Chapter nine
## Avoiding Speculation

Dad had pushed himself very hard indeed. He became very weak and needed a lot of rest. His sleep was broken by dreams of Envisagement, creations far beyond human capabilities. It was as if he was unable to switch off from the device. When he woke a depression would sweep over him as he realised that his works were not real.

'I dreamt I made a star ship, like the ERUWAI.' He told me. 'With a wave of my arm I made great swathes of its upper and lower plates. I am sure that was how the vessel was created, do you remember Son? How seamless the plates were?'

It was impossible to know, the surfaces were covered with tiles; I agreed with him, then left him to rest.

It was that day that the announcement was made; it was all over the news - the Val'ee would be leaving at the beginning of next month.

'We knew,' Dad sighed as he sat with us that evening. 'That's why we pushed so hard to complete S. C. Britannia. I wanted to ensure that the first Sky City was finished. That way we'd know we'd be able to finish the others when the Val'ee left. It was the only way to be sure that children could still be safely delivered when the Val'ee mothership departed. I've had some EO's working on transport solutions, and the Val'ee are willing to leave us a small fleet of older craft that are surplus to their needs and on a par with our technological level.' He burst into exhausted tears. 'We'd still be lost now, if it wasn't for them. The oversight regarding atmospheric pollutants was mine…'

'Rest now Douglas…' Nana urged as she helped him up and assisted him to his room.

It took Dad a further week before he actually showed signs of recovery, 'Want to see the Britannia Dace?' He asked.

I hated the thing, it had kept Dad away for so long but I knew it meant a lot to him; that it was part of a future he was ensuring for me.

'Today?' I replied.

'Yes, the Overseer visited last night; she was happy to see my return to strength and said that she would be sending a transport in the morning.'

I felt a little uneasiness. I blamed the Val'ee now for allowing Dad to

*Cries: The Captive Mind*

overtax himself, for being away from his family for so long and his poorly condition.

I had begun to consider that the Val'ee had darker motives, even if they appeared totally benevolent. What freaked me out most was that whatever they asked for, whatever they commanded, would be instantly provided, instantly obeyed, no questions asked.

'You OK Dace?' Dad queried as he witnessed my pained expression.

I was not prepared to share my thoughts, 'I'd like to see it, but I've got homework.' It was a good excuse, it was true and hid my actual lack of desire to go.

Dad just rested his hand on my shoulder. 'It's OK son. I know you've been struggling. It's my fault. Losing pace with a class that's older than you isn't anything to be ashamed of. I've made new arrangements. My colleague, Kerry Knight, will be joining you at school to adjust your workload. She will support you, assist if necessary, push where you excel and generally gear your experience of school to your level. So...' He clapped his hands making me jump. 'You can forget your homework; Kerry will look into its relevance.'

This was great news. My despondency had knocked my momentum and the assignment had been daunting.

Dad ruffled my hair, 'Go get ready.' he urged, 'Don't forget your camera; the views are amazing!'

The camera had been a present for my eleventh birthday. He'd come to deliver it but had gone again within an hour. I don't think I'd even opened the box. Still, better now than never and I ran upstairs trying to recall where I'd thrown it.

Our transport was a little less refined than we'd experienced before. A bulky wedge shaped craft with a small, single seated cockpit, a barrel shaped passenger compartment and a yawning hold that, being empty, echoed the hum of the engines. It had dropped purposely to a position approximately a metre off the ground before easing forward and down for a controlled landing.

'Look,' Dad observed. 'it's just like Hayvan's wave technology...' Two spiralling waveforms sliced through the lawn, not damaging it but sending quivering patterns through the grass.

An Overseer appeared, beckoning for us to join her inside. As Dad approached he pointed at the waveforms.

*'Yes Mr. North,'* She acknowledged. *'Our technology was once similar to your own. We call them spiral emanations, but since observing your oceans we like your name for them much better. Vehicles like this one are well within your reach now. Please strap yourselves in, the flight will not be as smooth as you have experienced before.'*

I was becoming more aware of the constant put-downs these creatures employed. If you listened carefully you'd spot them. They'd be veiled in praise but they'd be there. Yes, now we were advanced enough for unrefined, uncomfortable flight...

'OK Dace?' Dad asked, seeing the agitation on my face.

'Er, fine, I... feel a bit sick. I think it's excitement...'

Dad held my gaze for a moment. He'd noticed the disjointed tone of my answer and I feared he would challenge my response. Instead he cupped my cheek with his palm, winked and told me to take deep breaths.

By the time we arrived I really did feel sick and Dad asked the Overseer for a few minutes so that I could steady myself. I'd been OK until we entered the stratosphere. The Val'ee headed away to perform some sort of procedure and Dad started to grin over-widely.

'What?' I insisted.

'You liked that bit about their old vintage stuff being close to our own technology didn't you?'

'How do you do that?'

'What? See right through you?' He patted me on the head. 'Because you're just like me.' He sat me at a table looking out across a landscape of clouds. 'Great view, even on a cloudy day, and I doubt we'd be looking at it now without a regular helping of superior Val'ee criticisms. They see us like we perceive a toddler, unstable and with little understanding of the world. Wait until you see the transports I specified to the EO's though, that'll shake them up!'

The mischievous look in his eyes intrigued me.

'I instructed the EO's on a new engine specification based on my observation of the Val'ee ships. Should bring us right up to the level of troubled teenager screaming for attention!'

We both laughed out loud.

*'You feel better now?'* We turned around. The Overseer who had brought us was standing close, and neither of us had heard her coming. *'How does it make you feel...'* She said, addressing me directly. *'...to*

*Cries: The Captive Mind*

*understand that the bulk of this great City came from your father's mind?'*

'It's more the aesthetics really.' Dad corrected, 'The EO's before me performed the spatial elements and the Val'ee created the superstructure…'

I had drifted from the conversation. My eyes followed the great curve of the dome above us. They darted left and right and everything they fell upon amazed me; the great docking bay doors with their intricate opening mechanism, the graded tint of the glass that became almost opaque at the apex. Even the floor we stood on looked like a single slab of highly polished slate.

'It's so beautiful…'

*'The Envisager brings thought into physical existence. Your father and the other EO's possess a faultless understanding of materials, structures, mechanisms and systems and a stability of mind to produce what you see before you in a completed state.'* She smiled, *'Would you like to see?'*

I nodded.

*'Observe the chair you were sitting on. It would take hours to produce it conventionally. Douglas, if you would kindly demonstrate…'* She handed Dad an Envisager. Dad instantly obeyed, taking the tool in both hands and aiming it towards a space next to the existing seats. Before my eyes, like juice filling an invisible tumbler, a chair appeared that matched the existing seats. To me the process looked effortless.

He smiled and pointed 'Ha! I couldn't resist it…'

On the back of the chair Dad had created a little metal label, a symbol combining his initials.

The Overseer looked bothered by this and Dad later shared with me that the Val'ee considered any ability to envisage multiple materials simultaneously, impossible. The techniques that Dad had taught himself and shared, enabled many EO's to do the same. I had never seen a Val'ee look cross before, it troubled me, so I attempted to change the subject…

'What's that?' I exclaimed pointing towards a fanned structure stretching from beneath the floor upwards towards the very top of the dome, branching regularly to form a framework for the panes.

'Don't you think it's just a structure to support the dome and windows?' Dad chuckled.

'I suppose so, but does it do something else? It's tubular, thick at the bottom, narrowing with each division, and the top ends join that curved central column that sweeps down the far end of the dome back through the floor again. Ha! It's some sort of heating system!'

Dad tipped a glance at the Overseer who was nodding approvingly.

'You *are* the observant one son. You're exactly right. The stratospheric temperature is displayed over there. It's currently minus fifty.'

'Ow! That's cold!'

'Ha, ha, sometimes it's colder. The tropopause beneath us can be over ten degrees less. These thermal structures were the first thing created after the spatial decks. We were so glad to be warm and rid of our bulky environment suits when they came online.'

'But how come it's warm in here? We just came in. Surely that amount of cold would strip the heat right out when the docking bay doors opened?'

'Jets of hot air are expelled into the outside air to counter heat loss, but hey, you're impressing me with your understanding.' Dad ruffled my hair and I smiled broadly. 'I begin to think you're suffering more from not being pushed hard enough at school rather than through want of ability.'

My beaming grin slipped a little.

*'Please, my friends,'* The Overseer interjected, *'It is time we moved on.'* She gestured to a double arched panel that seemed to anticipate our intentions to pass through, opening in a blink of an eye. My awe regarding the abilities of EO's, especially Dad, had surpassed all my expectations.

We headed out of the docking bay into a refreshingly cool corridor, the floor moved like a conveyor belt in an airport, one side one way, one side the other, its momentum nearly floored me.

'Takes a little getting used to,' Dad apologised offering me a little support. 'It's not all perfect yet!'

Up ahead a broad archway yawned over the conveyor. We'd reached a road!

'A road!' I exclaimed.

'Five miles long,' Dad replied. 'With side roads coming off at intervals. Do you want to do the driving?' He pointed at a box-like structure, one of many that were lined up beside the conveyor.

I looked at the box then back at Dad with a puzzled shrug. He grinned and stroked the side of the nearest box. A previously seamless doorway slid upwards and he gestured for us to enter. Inside was big enough to stand in and the walls, opaque from the outside, now appeared clear. At one end - I assumed the front - stood a wide panel. Dad stood in front of it, rested his hands on the screen and the whole vehicle came to life, flying quickly forward.

For a moment I wanted to sit down or hold on but, like the Val'ee Loader that had taken us to the ERUWAI, I felt no movement.

Every now and then the road opened into a junction hall with side roads labelled retail, leisure, business, research and residential. I even saw the Medical facilities and the maternity units that would replace the ERUWAI.

I had never appreciated the size of this place from the ground. Now I began to appreciate it; this was not just a city in name, but in character and scale as well.

'Here's our turn.' Dad announced. Sliding his hand left across the screen, the vehicle took the turn, pulling up in front of a wall. Dad looked at me, his excitement too much to conceal. Scrolling the icons on his panel he brought up a keypad typed a ten-digit code and...

My eyes grew wide at the sight of the whole bulkhead dividing horizontally, revealing a secure chamber. Dad pulled up to a checkpoint and lowered the opacity of the vehicle's front surrounds. The guard recognised him, nodded and waved us through.

Rounding a corner, it became obvious to me that we'd entered some sort of fabrication area. There were more people here than I'd seen on the whole trip. Then I noticed that anyone doing anything was doing it with an Envisager. These people were EO's.

Dad drove from this area into a cavernous room with an articulated bay door at the far end. Along the side opposite us was a row of unusual vehicles, all the same, with a group of people gathered together in front of one that was clearly being prepared for some demonstration.

'It *is* Douglas.' I heard as Dad raised the doorway, and a champagne cork popped loudly. Hands were shaken enthusiastically, I was quickly introduced and beamed with pride as Dad was toasted. These people loved him.

It turned out that they were celebrating another completed project; the first human transports capable of travelling to a Sky City. It was a surprise to the Overseer, who had only known of the EO's desire to celebrate the completion of Britannia. Her interest at the speed of the vessels construction swept Dad away from me, and an inspection of the craft began.

Suddenly, I noticed something unusual. I was standing further back from the row of vehicles than the others and I could see movement behind the one on the end.

A small ball, about the size of an egg, rolled into view. I looked towards Dad and the Val'ee but they were consumed in their deliberations. Bemused, I wandered across. Behind the craft were a number of balls scattered about, and a small girl.

'Hey!' I said, intending it as a greeting but achieving a response of startled guilt.

'I'm not touching anything!' She lied, as she leaped to her feet and stowed something behind her.

'What's that behind you then?' I asked tipping my head to see.

'Oh! I thought you were a grownup.' She pulled me out of sight behind the ship and raised a finger to her lips, 'Shhh, I've got my Mum's Envisager. She held it up. 'I can make balls with it, look!' Giggling, she pointed at the floor. Four balls lay there already the same size and buff colour as the one that had first gained my attention. I bent down and collected it so that none of the adults would see, and slipped it into my pocket.

The girl was concentrating hard, and I watched as a little sphere appeared. She giggled again, 'Are you Dace?'

I sighed. I was bored that everyone knew me already. 'Yes I'm Dace…' then I realised something, 'How old are you?'

'Eight.' She replied.

I laughed, there was a gap of three months between the first two survivors. To be eight now meant only one thing. 'You're Hope Emmerson, the first child to be born on the ERUWAI.'

'You know me too!' She trilled, giving me a hug. We had met once before, soon after her arrival on earth from the Val'ee mothership. It was a big media event - the miracle boy and the Hope of humanity. I was three, and had only the vaguest of memories. Hope wouldn't recall it at all.

I stepped back a little to see how Dad was getting on. The Overseer was standing with him, and a number of others had gathered further back. Three more were busying themselves around the transport.

'Do you wanna try?' Hope asked, holding out the Envisager.
'Mum said you can make anything with it.'

I glanced at the tool then up at Dad again. He was absorbed in his work. Surely if I could make something it would please him. 'You just thought "ball" and made a ball.'

'Kinda.' Hope replied.

*Cries: The Captive Mind*

I hesitated briefly then took the device. I didn't want to make a ball - I wanted something complicated and exciting! I pointed the Envisager and thought really hard. Nothing happened.

'I think you need to think through it. I try and imagine the ball appearing, and it does.'

I tried again. Something began to form but it lacked the shape I'd intended. I started to lose my concentration. When I lowered the tool I was confronted by a large, formless, metallic blob.

'What is it?' Hope gasped.

I looked at it. I was too embarrassed to say that I was trying to make a model of a Val'ee Y-Ship, but what *did* the blob look like? 'It's a…'

Hope sat on it. It was soft, possessing little substance, quite the opposite of what I'd intended.

'It's a cushion!' Hope exclaimed.

'Er…yes. That's right…'

'Hope! What are you doing? Oh! Dace, I didn't see you there. I thought you'd be watching the test flight. What's this? Dace? Is that my Envisager?' Hope's mother Patricia had discovered us. I'd been hidden from her by the craft I'd been standing close to, but now I was in full view with her Envisager in my hands. Patricia was surveying the objects we'd made and was looking flustered. 'Dace? Did you make these things?'

I glanced at Hope. Her eyes expressed the shock of discovery, they cried out for rescue.

'Erm, I…did, but I didn't mean any harm.'

'What's the silver thing Hope's sitting on?'

'Er…first attempt.' This at least was not a lie. 'It was supposed to be a cushion.' I fibbed.

Her eyebrows lifted in recognition, 'Oh! OK, yes, first attempts are often quirky. But the balls, you made them too?'

Again I found myself in Hope's eyes. 'Please don't tell her it was me.' They seemed to beg.

'Just thought I'd try something simple…'

'Simple!' She stooped to pick one up, 'These are rubberised and perfectly spherical. You show great promise Master North, make one for me…'

My heart seemed to stop, my eyes felt wide enough to cover my face. The moment seemed to hang for far too long. 'Well,' I thought, 'It's got to be easier than a model Y-Ship.' I lifted the device and started to think

59

'Rubber Ball'.

'Patricia, we're ready…'

Hope's mum spun around, 'OK Michael, I'm on my way.'

Seeing her attention turned I grabbed the little ball I'd put in my pocket, dropped it to the ground and stopped it bouncing with my foot. Hope giggled again.

'It's not as good as the others but I felt a little pressured.'

Patricia turned back to me. She was initially speechless due to the sudden appearance of the ball, then said, 'Goodness Dace, you're certainly your father's son, he works quickly too. I would love to let you carry on, but it's illegal to allow untrained use of an Envisager. It's an important rule relating to structural integrity and post creative use. I hope you can appreciate that I let you try and that I will not be reporting this incident…'

'Patricia! We're go!' Came a shout.

'I won't use it anymore.' I promised.

She nodded, smiled and hurried away. I followed a little way, then stood watching the activity.

'Thanks Dace, you're my hero.' Hope announced, 'Mum can be real strict. I picked up the tool and just didn't wanna put it down. I'm soooo glad you came.' She was hanging off my arm uncomfortably, but I was transfixed by the human equivalent to a Val'ee transport that now hovered effortlessly and silently in the middle of the great room.

'Wow,' Hope sighed. 'I'd love to fly one of them.'

'Yeah.' I agreed.

The EO's, Dad and the Overseer moved around beneath the ship pointing. The Overseer seemed a little animated but Dad beamed happily, briefly making eye contact with me and winking. He lifted a hand-set to his mouth and gave some instructions. The pilot in the craft began a three sixty manoeuvre followed by a complete sideways roll.

The engines were still based on Hayvan's Wave but it did seem more refined than the power generators. Four slim waveforms, like elongated cones, extended from the 'shoulders' of the transport, transforming it into a shape reminiscent of a dragonfly. It was truly beautiful.

The rest of the visit continued in the same way, inspections, discussions, even external test flights viewed from an enclosed viewing deck. The transport's 'skin' was fitted with a lattice of heating elements preventing frosting and preserving the cabin temperature. It was just one fact in a

*Cries: The Captive Mind*

multitude that helped me understand how amazing my Dad's mind was, not just for creating such a vessel but because he also had the ability to explain his design so well that another EO could create the same. An astounding feat.

As a final perk to the trip Dad took me to the Britannia's main control deck. It was as busy as the fabrication facility but these people were not EO's. The data that constantly scrolled across their screens defied my understanding, the whole thought of the adult world worried me. If I wanted to thrive in this particular arena - and I really did want to be the pride of my father - then I'd have to get back into my studies. Thanks to the Val'ee the future was upon us.

As we returned home, Dad answered numerous questions on how the Sky City was achieved, then he said he had a question for me. He handed me a rubber ball.

'Busted.' I thought. I knew Dad would see right through any lies so I told him about Hope, and all that had happened. He wasn't mad at all, he just assured me that an amorphous blob with no substance was a common first error and that the cavity panels in the first room he made on the Britannia were full of the stuff. 'I called it insulation.' He smiled.

Dad went on to explain that ninety-nine percent of the population would never create an atom with an Envisager. They just lacked the ability to focus. I, on the other hand, had demonstrated a 'link'. 'What you made is the first thing I made. Now look at what you've seen today. That could be you too. Your blob is very promising, as are the balls that Hope is already capable of...' He paused. Taking back the little ball and rolling it around in his palm. 'I wonder how long she's been "playing" with her mother's Envisager...?'

'Please Dad, she didn't want her mum to know.'

'OK son. I expect her mother will discover Hope's talent, so I'll focus on yours. You said you'd wanted to create a model of a Y-Ship. That's ambitious. You need to decide on the substance of the model. A solid fabric that the shape is formed out of, say plastic or metal. What I expect happened to you was "speculation".'

'Speculation?'

'When you don't know the fabric or workings of something your mind speculates, guesses. In a trained EO a guess can be as good, even better, because he or she works from an understanding of materials. To the untrained mind the "speculation" is always fatal to the outcome.'

'But Dad, you never trained…'

Dad laughed, 'Then I'm a natural! Really though, is it any wonder? My whole career has centred around physical and material things, and prior to using the tool I'd spent months explaining things to EO's. I'll give you the key Dace, Focus. Focus and its maintenance is key to creation.'

## Chapter ten
## Departures

Those last few weeks went quickly, and although I had come to dislike the Val'ee, their departure did bring me some sorrow; I just couldn't recall a time without them.

Everything moved so fast. Earth had a fleet of old Val'ee transports, which Dad nicknamed 'Tinnys'. He felt they were bulky and unrefined but was thankful that we had them; they would ensure the safe transportation of pregnant women to S. C. Britannia for the arrival of their child. Even though Dad had personally seen the completion of a number of the transports I'd seen on the Sky City - now affectionately known as 'North Dragonflies' - they were still not numerous enough for the expected workload.

The maternity facilities on the incomplete Sky Cities were to be completed first, in readiness for the expected rise in need.

The Val'ee had placed restrictions on pregnancy, due to the relatively small facilities on the ERUWAI. For although the mothership was vast, it was not originally designed for the reproductive needs of an entire planet. These restrictions were scheduled to be lifted over each area served by each Sky City as its capabilities were due to come online.

The Val'ee gifted us a thousand Envisagers, including training equipment. They considered this plenty as only two hundred and twelve humans had acquired the skills to wield the tool in two years.

*'You must figure out how to form them yourselves.'* They insisted.

During the last few days Fredrick joined us at home. He seemed excited as he sat with us at dinner. With a nod from Dad, Fredrick filled us in.

'I was notified yesterday that a place has been reserved for me on ERUWAI...'

We all sat still, our eyes fixed on our friend.

'...I have accepted the offer and will be travelling with about two thousand other specially selected individuals, to the Val'ee home world...'

I was now looking at Dad. Had he been selected too? Was he about to break his news? Would we lose him again? And for how long? Forever? Fredrick allayed my fears.

'Douglas, or so the Val'ee seem to have suggested by their omission, is too important here...'

'I wouldn't have gone even if I'd been invited.' Dad stated.

'Really?' Fredrick replied his response loaded with disbelief.

'I've worked hard because the world needed it, not to gain a ride to another world that neither needs me nor sees me as an equal. I was here at the right time with the right skills. Dace's arrival was like God telling me to get involved, to help bring children back to the world before the last chance was lost and it became too late.'

Fredrick sat back in his chair, shaking his head. 'I can't remember the last time you spoke of God Douglas, but really! The Val'ee bought the children back, not some outmoded supernatural force. Yes, you worked hard, but in your own strength, not by a divine hand...'

Dad stopped him with a gesture, looked at me then back at Fredrick. He frowned. 'My parents used to tell me Bible stories Fred,' Dad began. 'I sat and listened, and believed. The stories were wonderful and exciting. More than that, they were an historical account of how God had brought His chosen people through adversity, and rebellion, and finally provided a substitute to bear their sins in the form of His own Son, not salvation by any human work but by faith in the Son alone. Now that, Fred, that appealed to my young mind.

'As I grew, school taught otherwise, TV documentaries taught otherwise, friends opinions taught otherwise. No creation, just slow, relentless pain and suffering; a striving towards a greater level of development.

'Looking back now I see the first challenges to that atheistic paradigm, the realisation that biological life exhibited a downward trend not a progressive one. That mutations, long the source of new and novel change, were proven only ever to corrupt and destroy genes. That DNA was one-hundred percent active, no junk DNA Fred, and it had different languages, a discovery that changed biological classification radically! At the time however, school impressed on me the doctrine that man alone determined his destiny, and I was the rebellious sort, you know that. Then Morrello appeared on the scene, you remember, the Morrello report? He demonstrated, flawlessly, how we'd adopted an unproven theory as unquestionable fact. He warned, that a great deal of what we thought we understood about ourselves and the world, had been created under the assumption that evolution had happened. You realised it then too Fred. For a while it rekindled my erstwhile faith, that's when we met Vanessa, the event we all attended…'

'And look where that led…' Fredrick burst in. He seemed to be getting overly warm now as he unbuttoned the top of his shirt revealing the interesting, bird-shaped birthmark on his neck. I found it strangely fascinating. You usually only saw it in the summer when he was wearing a T-shirt…

'The Morrello report created a vacuum, I admit it Fred. So many religious groups claimed ownership of the truth, but Morrello told it like my father had - it made sense of everything…'

'Even your parents' death?'

Nana shifted uneasily in her chair.

'The destruction of the Morrello Exhibition hit many people Fred. The loss of my parents left me questioning the love of God, and one last doubt embedded itself as an immovable barrier until the Val'ee brought us the Envisager. My problem was how nothing became everything. Not the Big Bang, *that* had always been nonsense "nothing exploded" and created every element known to science - total piffle. No, I was troubled by how *God* created everything. I had a cause but no means. My minister tried to persuade me that "God created because He could. Some things are just beyond human understanding." But I was reeling from my loss and to Vanessa's despair, I slid from my faith again. Then the Val'ee gave us the Envisager…'

Fredrick laughed, 'And did the Val'ee give God his Envisager too?'

'Fred, the Envisager is about focus. It's about will. The product is what the creator desires. I don't believe God needs anything the Val'ee possess. What the Envisager shows us - though its function still eludes us - is that creation *is* possible.'

'Hold on.' Fredrick interjected. 'Doesn't the presence of the Val'ee show that we abandoned Evolution too quickly, they are alien…'

'Fred, they don't believe in it either! They admire our research demonstrating genetic decline. How speciation is the result of environmental factors that reduce the gene pool in isolated populations, revealing genetic novelty. Not a path to higher development but a weakening, a thinning of the information already present in DNA. No Fred, I think the Val'ee will have a surprising origin. I guess you might find something out about that on your journey...'

'I really must question the soundness of God as a way of living. Why can you not take credit for your efforts? Why would you, a scientist of the highest calibre, not want to explore the technologies of an advanced race? Douglas, this is the future. Look at what they've achieved. Life has returned, the cry of babies is heard again. *They* have given us direction and purpose, not God.'

'I would be careful who you place on a pedestal Fred. If they have ended our suffering, why do we need the Sky Cities? Would you let your own daughter attempt a delivery on the earth? Caution, Fred my friend. The cause of The Great Suffering isn't pollution. The cause is still here, still causing death when it has the opportunity. Are the Val'ee so clever that even observable fact is wrong?'

'There!' Fredrick blustered, in a state of animation I'd never seen in him before. 'That's why you haven't been invited. You've never stopped questioning them. I'm amazed you were able to bring our mad world together in the first place.'

'Like I said,' Dad retorted, getting up from his chair. 'It was the right time... Enough!' He headed for the door of the dining room. '...I am happy you've been invited to go. *I* did not want to. *My* place is here. There is much to do.' He paused at the door and looked back at Fredrick. 'Be observant, my friend.' Dad turned and left the room.

For a moment Fredrick was quiet, then he scooped up a few more mouthfuls of Nana's roast quickly. Thinking, perhaps, that he might get a little more in before he was seen to the door. Then he smiled again. 'Maria, your cooking is the best. I wish you'd been invited to come with us...'

'You just be mindful of what Douglas said,' Nana scolded. 'There's a lot we don't know about them Freddy.'

Gramps offered his opinion too. 'Fred, have you ever seen a Val'ee use an Envisager?'

Fredrick frowned. 'Well, no, I guess they ran the risk of exposing advanced technologies...'

'Fred, they came to the earth and made ceramic tiles from London clay to cover their great ship... It took them ten years... Why didn't they 'Envisage' them?'

The conversation continued, similar themes were explored until Nana insisted that it was my bedtime. I lay in bed staring at the ceiling, concerned that Dad and his best friend had fallen out, just before one would be leaving for an unknown period of time. I considered evolution - it wasn't something I'd come across much, probably just in jokes - the idea of gradual change over time was intriguing. I marvelled at how an idea might create such an uproar between two intelligent people, and resolved to make time to study it a little closer.

As I lay there, I heard Fredrick saying his farewells to Nana and Gramps. I could hear him putting on his coat ready to head into the winter chill. Then the study door opened - it was definitely the study as the hinges clunked when the door swung - Dad's voice, calm and full of friendship, echoed up from the hallway.

'Come here...' There was the sound of two good friends giving hearty pats to each other's backs. The sound of Dad's hands gripping Fredrick's winter jacket sleeves as if holding him at arm's length to fix a memory of a moment in time.

'I've something for you Fred...'

'Really?'

'Yes, I got it after we spoke yesterday. Knowing of your journey, I thought you'd like some things.' The study door swung again, there was the rustle of a carrier bag then an exclamation of gratitude.

'It's the latest Data Pack,' Dad continued, 'I've put a load of photos on it, a few books I know you haven't read, and the software is set up for you to record your observations...'

'You shouldn't have Doug...'

'No, I'm going to miss you Fred. You just take care, OK?'

'Sure thing Douglas.' The voices sounded rather sad now but resigned. Nana and Gramps re-joined the conversation. A flurry of jumbled comments followed, then the front door was opened.

'Oh, a thin layer of snow!' Fredrick exclaimed. 'Don't let your heat out...'

Nana interrupted, 'I'll watch until your car disappears around the corner, if you don't mind.' There was a brief moment of shared laughter and a last exchange of farewells. I felt happy that things seemed better. I got up and pressed my face to the window.

As Fredrick pulled away he waved. Seeing me he lifted his hand higher and waved again. Moments later, all that was left of Fredrick's visit were tyre prints in the snow and the sound of the front door closing.

Dad stood at my bedroom door, 'You should be in bed.'
I ran to him and hugged him, 'You and Fredrick are friends again?' I asked.

'We'll never be anything but that Dace. True friends can be like that. A good debate keeps the brain working, corrects error, solves problems, tests, refines... It's not a bad thing. Not between real friends. Now, bed.'

I jumped back under the duvet. Dad kissed my head and moved to leave the room.

Dad?'
He turned, 'Yes son?'
'Am I the reason you wouldn't have gone?'
He smiled, 'You and a million other reasons, but chiefly you, yes. Sleep now eh?'

I pressed my face into the pillow and Dad drew my bedroom door closed. For a while I lay there mulling over all that Dad had said, then, slowly - with the muffled rhythm of adult voices softly spoken - I drifted off to sleep.

The day of departure came. A grey drizzle and icy wind prevailed, but the snow that had fallen the night Fredrick had visited, was gone. Many had turned out to see off the chosen representatives of earth. We had joined them, hoping for a last glimpse of Fredrick and some others that Dad knew. 'A few too many.' Dad grumbled on the drive down, but that didn't stop him from amazing the crowds at the pick-up point in Hyde Park.

All EO's now carried their personal Envisagers in a secure jacket holster. Dad took his and instantly erected huge windbreaks. Great transparent screens that caught the dampness and wind alike, killing the bite of cold and fostering a warm celebratory feeling that spread through the great gathering.

'There!' A voice called out, and a finger was joined by a forest of hands all pointing in the same direction. Voices called out, chanted and sang as the first Val'ee passenger vessel approached, on time and on target. It descended rapidly, stopping level with the platform of the departure pavilion, just feet from the ground. It was big enough to hold a hundred passengers comfortably, was dome shaped, elongated from front to back with lights that busily flashed, up and down, white and red. A second ship joined the first, and a third emerged from the cloud cover and hovered patiently.

We saw a group of passengers file onto the first ship, but we were too far away to see whether Fredrick was amongst them. We had a reserved place on the Terrace for V.I.P. guests. I looked at Dad. My own father an Important Person. Known, respected and esteemed. I felt so privileged to be his son. It was a feeling that had been so out of my reach just months before.

Dad's face told me everything. He was like a child excited by a firework display, then something changed. As the first transport eased slowly forwards, levelled, rotated to face away from us, and began to ascend, Dad's brow furrowed, then frowned. His smile seemed to drop away.

'You OK Dad?' I shouted above the throng of the masses. He glanced briefly down at me with an almost inaudible grunt of affirmation, but his arm encircled me in some sort of protective embrace.

The second ship now prepared to leave. The third moved forward, a fourth descended, a fifth and sixth held positions above. Dad lifted his Data Pack and started recording the underside of the departing vessel, shaking his head as if unable to comprehend something.

'What's wrong Dad?'

'Nothing, first time I've seen these ships, that's all.'

I shouted for him to speak up as the farewell cries peaked once more.

'It's the first time I've seen these ships,' He repeated, 'and yet they seem familiar…' He trailed off again, obviously subject to a deeper, louder cry of thoughts. I looked back at the pavilion, the loading was well organised and the third Val'ee transport now edged away. Their timing now perfected, the arriving craft formed an orderly chain of gradual descent.

Thirty times that morning groups of men and women boarded those ships; almost three thousand people representing humanity. Dad had also departed somewhat. We hadn't been able to see Fredrick or any of Dad's colleagues. I wondered if his deliberations regarding the ships had led him to any worries about his friends wellbeing. If so he wasn't telling, and on the trip home he made only light or evasive conversation.

At six that evening the ERUWAI was scheduled to leave, and we all knew what that meant. The silence that had puzzled the people of the earth the day the Val'ee arrived, would occur again.

I didn't recall the previous time. I'd been too young. When it happened it felt weird; perhaps less frightening than not knowing the cause, but weird nonetheless. Bed time came. We gestured our goodnights and I headed for my room. I lay there in the dark troubled by the roar of soundlessness around me and it was some time before my dreams replaced it.

## Chapter eleven
### Interlude

When morning came Dad had already left the house. Birds sang, the neighbour's dog barked, car tyres crackled on the grit surfaced road outside and Nana's kettle whistled.

'Dad out?'

'Yes dear,' Nana replied. 'He got an e-mail last night, said he would call us to let us know his plans.'

'Did he say anything about the departures yesterday?'

'Only how impressive and well organised it had been. One ship after another like that, takes good communication and no little skill.'

So he hadn't told Nana his thoughts either. The doorbell rang and Nana headed off to answer it. I sat down to eat my breakfast and tried to picture the event again in my mind, had I read too much into it?

'Good morning Dace.'

I spun around in my chair. Miss Knight stood in the kitchen doorway, warmly wrapped. 'I hope you're in a mind for some learning.'

'But it's not the right day.' I sputtered through a mouthful of cornflakes.

'Dace! Manners…' Nana protested.

'That's fine Mrs Edding, Dace is right, but Dr. North has made alternative arrangements. You're with me today and Thursday and I'll attend class with you on Fridays to assess your study levels.'

It was a good day. Miss Knight had accurately judged my academic level. I felt challenged and stretched, but happy. Any ideas that this mediator would take my studies and reduce their content to better suit my age were soon gone; instead I was encouraged to strive forward, thanks to a constant stream of encouragement from this remarkable woman. The encouragement was not hollow either, it wasn't to give some artificial boost to confidence, no, I really felt like I was learning.

'Your father is right about you! You're not just a miracle from those bleak years, you're special. You're smart. There's no reason why you shouldn't surpass your older classmates. She cupped my cheek with a warm hand. 'You're not going to do my reputation any harm whatsoever!'

She left in a fresh flurry of snow. Big, white blobs covered the windscreen of her car. Nana ushered me inside just as the phone rang. It was Dad. Speaking through Nana, he said he loved me, and hoped that I'd enjoyed my first proper day with Kerry. He was pleased with Nana's confirmation. The conversation turned to the reason for his absence. It would be for just a few weeks, but then, that was nothing new to us. He told Nana that the reason was classified, this meant he'd returned to his Government position now that the Val'ee had gone.

As it happened, it wasn't a bad thing that Dad wouldn't be travelling. We had the worst snow I'd ever seen, school was cancelled and I didn't see Miss Knight for three weeks.

With empty time on my hands I began to worry that Dad would be too busy now to make it to my twelfth birthday. It was important to me, he'd missed my tenth and stayed only long enough to finish half a cup of coffee on my eleventh. This was Dad's opportunity to show what mattered most to him.

The following weeks did nothing to ease my angst. Dad's work pattern was irregular, he became absorbed in his work as if he'd been starved of satisfying food and was now surrounded by the choicest delicacies. Sometimes he'd work through the night and seem surprised that it was morning. Then he'd be away, sometimes days, sometimes weeks. If Kerry hadn't been so perceptive my studies would have slipped again, but she knew my concerns. Her words were Dad's words and - for the first time - I realised that she and Dad must be very close indeed.

My birthday fell on a school day and, although Kerry was there in an observational capacity - even though it wasn't Friday - nothing else seemed out of the ordinary.

Dad was away. He had been for a week and a half and he hadn't telephoned either, so I wasn't being very sociable with my classmates. I'd even snapped at Craig, who really was my best friend. Stranger still, no-one had reprimanded me for it. By the end of the day - with Miss Knight hovering around beyond her usual time - I felt that something was up. I started noticing smiles from my fellow pupils, and Harry Pearly was spending more than his usual length of time gazing out of the window.

I looked straight at Miss Knight. I could see from her knowing smile that she knew I'd realised. She looked beyond me, smiled and waved. I spun around. A North Dragonfly hovered, silently, just feet from the glass. Harry stood there, wide-eyed. The rest of the class, who'd been in on this from the start, erupted into a chorus of "Happy Birthday", then I recognised the pilot.

'Dad?' I mouthed, voiceless.

Kerry approached me from behind. She signed something to Dad who replied in a series of similar hand movements. She rested her hand on my back and suggested - as the school bell was about to ring anyway - that I might, if I wanted to, catch a lift home with my Dad. I needed no further urging.

Miss Knight accompanied me along the hall, down the stairs to the school entrance and out onto the playing field. Dad had touched down and stood, back straight, chest out, saluting embarrassingly. A number of teachers stood at the staff room window waving, and looking up I could see that the windows of all the occupied classes were filled with smiles and waves. I felt the most special I'd ever felt amongst my older, fellow students.

Miss Knight ushered me forward and Dad lifted me on board. He turned and offered Kerry a hand. Her eyes betraying total surprise she declined, 'Oh! No, that's fine Douglas, you don't want a crowd!'

'Nonsense! I insist you join us. Dace wants you to.'

I nodded, so she edged nervously towards the Dragonfly allowing Dad to lift her slowly into the passenger compartment.

Leaping up, Dad flicked a switch that sealed the door behind him, striding swiftly he spun into the pilot seat.

'What's the fastest you've ever travelled son?'

I started to answer that it was on the Val'ee loader, but Dad's grin stopped me, 'Umm…' I said feigning thought. 'I think it was this afternoon in a North Dragonfly…'

'What?' Kerry fretted.

'That's right son!' Dad exclaimed, turning to his controls and sliding his hand up the screen.

'Now hold on!' Kerry protested, but we were already three kilometres above the school. 'Wow!' She gasped sitting back in her seat.

We climbed to the edge of space. Looking down we could see a number of Sky Cities like boats on a sea of clouds.

'The two near completion are S. C. Paris and S. C. Madrid. The others lack the Val'ee superstructure so they're not so advanced.'

They all looked finished to me. I turned from the window to find Dad and Kerry gazing at each other. Dad noticed me staring.

'We can get right around the Earth in twenty minutes. A Val'ee loader can only get two hundred and forty-six kilometres in that time.' Dad stated.

'But it can do that inside *and* outside an atmosphere.' Kerry pointed out. Dad's eyes travelled back to her.

'A temporary matter…' He dismissed. His eyes flicked back to me. 'Sorry it's not space, but how about circumnavigating the planet for your birthday?'

I nodded frantically.

'Are we allowed?' Kerry asked.

Dad shrugged, 'Are you going to tell on me?'

Kerry's eyes widened and she bit her lip. 'Might cost you!'

Dad turned back to the controls and I gazed at Kerry, well aware that the relationship between these two people had grown. The thought made me happy inside. I liked Kerry and wondered if she was similar to my mother. I turned back to my little window. The whole world seemed to roll beneath us, an illusion made all the more believable by the silence of the cabin.

The clouds made fascinating patterns beneath us, darkening into night as we left the influence of the sun.

'Look.' Said Dad, pointing left and tilting the Dragonfly. I leant over Kerry to see and the sky beneath us flickered violently. 'We're over Asia,' Dad informed. 'Seems they've got a rather stormy night!' Dad circled widely so that we could watch the storm for a while.

Kerry rubbed my back and smiled. 'Having fun?'

'This is the best birthday ever!' I confirmed.

Leaving Asia, we found the sun again over the Pacific Ocean and were soon over the coast of America. Dad altered course to take in the Grand Canyon but it seemed tiny so far beneath us. The Atlantic was soon ahead and as we began our run towards home Dad joined us in the Passenger compartment.

'Dace,' He began, then noticed my alarmed face... 'Oh! Don't worry; full auto pilot.' He crouched down in front of me, resting his hands on my knees. 'Dace, there's something I need to tell you...'

'He already knows.' Smiled Kerry, as she rested her left hand on Dad's, revealing a shiny new ring. There was a brief and, perhaps, slightly tense moment of silence.

'This *was* the best birthday...' I began, placing some negative emphasis on "was" to make it seem as if I wasn't happy. 'Now it's awesome!'

We fell into a group hug and I cried with joy. It took me the rest of the journey to regain my usual composure.

We landed in the meadow where Gramps flew his model planes. There waiting for us was a man who turned out to be the pilot, he'd delivered the Dragonfly to Dad about forty minutes earlier. Dad thanked him and we all sat by the Eucalyptus tree watching the pilot check over the craft prior to taking it away.

Kerry and I couldn't resist chuckling when he popped his head out of the side door and queried the readings for the distance of our flight.

'I think I must have set it up wrong, Simon.' Dad suggested.

The pilot smiled, 'What? Y*ou*, make a mistake?' He shook his head. 'Anyone else and I'd be cross.'

'Yes, and rightly so.'

Simon waved his hand dismissively. 'See you Monday!'

'Monday week,' Dad replied, smiling back at us. 'I'm having some family time.'

Simon nodded, and the passenger compartment hatch swung into flight position. We watched, huddled closely together as the sleek machine lifted effortlessly into the air. Its "waveform" wings passing gently through the branches of the big Eucalyptus tree.

## Chapter twelve
## E.O.A.

The news of Dad's engagement spread quickly and was met with much happiness. A stream of cards and letters from well-wishers all over the world reminded me of the high regard in which he was held. The media was also respectful, agreeing to only one interview. The wedding - which took place a week before my thirteenth birthday - was actually televised!

During the engagement and after the wedding, Kerry continued to be my tutor. My advancement became fuelled by contentment and the adoration I felt for this woman. She had brought joy back into our home, and her consistency of presence compensated for Dad's continued absences.

In May of my thirteenth year, Kerry insisted that I sit a number of exams with my older classmates. What I did not know was that Kerry's guidance had led me along a different route. I was aware that I'd covered a great deal more substance in many subjects, but felt that it was Kerry's way of feeding my desire to know more. I had found the extra work interesting and distracting, and reasoned that my school friends had only revised the information they required in order to meet exam criteria.

On the days the exams took place, I found I couldn't share in the post exam discussions. What the others talked about just didn't tally with what I'd done, and my comments were met with blank looks. It quickly became clear that my papers were different. When I quizzed Kerry she smiled and simply said that I'd been on a different course since she'd been involved, and that it had been Dad's express desire from the beginning.

I'd actually sat higher level papers. Despite this I'd passed with percentages in the high nineties.

Dad's superiors suddenly paid me more attention. It had been one thing for them to hear my father's accolades, but these grades, at this level, so soon - they were more objective, more interesting.

'Dace,' Dad began one morning. 'How would you like to attend the EOA?'

The Envisager Operators Academy was difficult to get a place in. The criteria for entry had become very tight, only certain individuals stood a real chance of ever using the tool at the standard the Government sought. Others were a waste of resources and time. Some unsuitable candidates had even succumbed to depression and it became important to safeguard against this.

The major factor in selection was intellect. It didn't rule out those without formal qualifications; you just needed a recommendation from an appropriate individual, and to pass the entry interview that assessed your suitability. Even then there was no promise that a qualifying person would make it through training, simply that the percentage who didn't make the grade would be minimised. With a restricted number of placements annually only the most likely candidates would be selected, maximising the number of EO's generated and leading to increased productivity and innovation.

My mind ran through the obvious objections, chief of which was my age. I considered myself to be much the same as other school children, I played, studied, went for walks and cycled, built models, enjoyed music… If I gained a place at the EOA I would be the youngest candidate ever.

I looked at Dad. He could see that I was really giving the offer careful consideration. He seemed taken aback, impressed that I had mulled over my response with such thoroughness. Eventually - and perhaps with some agitation - he urged for my answer.

I looked at him. It would be cool to get my hands on an Envisager again. It was as if something had been missing from my life since the encounter with Hope on Britannia. 'You really think I've got a chance?'

'No harm in taking the opportunity. You've already shown the ability to create matter through the device. I believe you've got a very good chance, yes…'

I shrugged my shoulders, 'OK then.'

Dad swept me up in his arms, 'That's great! I'll get the ball rolling tomorrow. Let's go and celebrate!'

We spent the afternoon on the beach at Southwold, skipping pebbles across the water and eating ice-cream. Any observer would have seen a child playing noisily with his father, not a potential EO.

To my astonishment my interviews led to the offer of a place. I filled the final position that year, which meant that the others had all been better candidates, and that I was deemed most likely to drop out at some point through the course. Dad put it to me that I was a kind of wild-card. I wasn't sure I liked that! I felt like some sort of guinea pig, but I had gained access to the EOA and that was very special indeed.

September saw the gathering of those selected. I was expecting some considerable bemusement from my fellow students that such a young person had joined their ranks. On arrival, however, I found myself faced with a group that possessed great diversity, age, stature, even dress sense. This was no stereotypical military unit by any stretch of the imagination, and despite my initial worries, I found the welcome to be wonderfully warm and genuine. I discovered quickly that they all knew me already, as was usual at social gatherings, but they all seemed keen to know me as a person rather than an article in a newspaper, and that made me feel quite accepted.

'You know Dace,' said a voice with a relaxed, American tone. 'I never met a Val'ee, not all the time they were here…'

The voice belonged to the oddest looking girl I'd ever met. Pierced nose, ears and eyebrows, a tattoo of some plant that trailed down her neck, disappearing under a delicate lace topped undergarment that protruded above a thin, low cut woollen cardigan. Her purple hair was held up and forward in a style I could only believe possible with the contents of an entire can of spray gel. I concentrated on the only normal thing I could see, her grey eyes.

'Rue.' she stated, offering a hand to shake from within an arms folded posture.

I shook her fingertips. 'You're American. Don't they have their own Envisager Academy?'

'AEON, yeah, why? You think I'm using "Brit Space"?' She replied.

I wasn't sure how to answer, it did seem unfair to British applicants, but she wouldn't have got a place if she wasn't a good aspirant herself.

Her frown evaporated. 'You're OK, kid. My family moved to the UK a few years ago.' She chuckled, but seemed to notice quickly that the term "kid" hadn't been received comfortably.

'I guess you're quite used to those guys.' She suggested, gesturing to a bank of photographers.

'Dad manages the media quite well. I've never really considered it strange to have a camera clicking nearby every once in a while…' I realised, painfully, that my comment might have come across as arrogance, 'I didn't mean that to sound arro…'

'You're nervous, that's fine, I'm nervous too…' Her observation was absolutely spot on.

'You don't look like the sort who'd be nervous…' I almost kicked

*Cries: The Captive Mind*

myself. What a thing to say, so judgemental, so rude.

'It's a front, under this beautiful cocoon I'm a freak Trix, you don't mind if I call you Trix do you?'

I minded a lot, but found my attention taken totally from Rue. Her voice blurred away, I could hear my heart pounding in my ears. *She* was here, looking straight at me, approaching me…

'Welcome to the EOA Dace, I've been looking forward to meeting you. Your father has spoken about you so much over the years…' She was old, but held herself in a more youthful way, even her high collar and accent reminded me of that day.

'I remember you.' I blurted out.

'I don't believe we've met before, Dace…' She began, almost laughing.

'You were there…' I felt absolutely sure, and yet her expression cultivated an uncomfortable doubt. A flash of panic burst through me. I had never forgotten that face, and here it was.

She looked over her shoulder, 'Dougie!' She called and turned back to me. The memories were so vivid I felt myself reaching for the old scar. Dad appeared from behind the lady.

'Something up Elizabeth?' He asked. I'd never heard anyone call Dad Dougie before. Dougie was so informal, rather intimate. Dad looked at me in a concerned sort of way.

'Oh, no Dougie.' She replied, giving me a sideways glance as she turned to address him. 'Have Dace and I ever actually met?'

Dad seemed puzzled by the question, 'No. I don't…'

'I didn't think so. Perhaps we can get to know each other better in some of your free time Dace. I fear you've mistaken me for someone else.' She turned to Dad and said something I didn't catch, then she strode off towards the entrance foyer.

'What was all that about?' Dad demanded - clearly unsettled.

'Don't you remember? The woman at the accident.'

Dad looked confused for a moment, then he shook his head, 'What?'

'She pushed me away from the van…'

Dad half smiled now, 'You think…'

'You saw her!'

'I shook the woman's hand but I didn't really make eye contact. I was more concerned about you… No, no Dace, you're wrong. It couldn't have been Elizabeth. I don't want to hear any more speculation. It's been, what, five years? Elizabeth Verne arrived in the UK three years ago…'

The statement floored my mind, I felt sick and foolish.

'She's been the one to convince about you attending the course Dace...' He sighed and his voice softened, 'You've just made a *really good* first impression. You're going to have to work to get Elizabeth's respect; she likes a steady mind son. He drew closer to me and pulled me into a hug. 'I don't know, perhaps she is similar, but there's no chance my boy so...' his voice betrayed that he was still agitated, 'So move on.'

Verne was clearly a superior member of Dad's circle. It was important to Dad that I impressed her. I hoped I could.

## Chapter thirteen
## Govern Your Mind

It was soon time to enter the academy. The eighteen strong group posed for a press photograph - an event I learnt was a tradition and not simply because I was there - and we headed through the facility doors, doors we wouldn't pass back through until the end of the pre-Envisager assessment period. It was important that we stayed on site. The school was located in the Morrello Complex, it's great Double Cherry logo held boldly for all to see, atop the tallest research building. It was the Government facility where Dad and Kerry were based - so there was every chance that during our studies we might come into contact with classified information; staying on site kept us safe.

'More like controlled.' Rue grumbled as she ate breakfast three weeks later.

The facilities that were provided specifically for the EOA were very small indeed; one lecture room with a curved wall that accounted for three sides of the space. There was a small store room, a kitchen/common room and eighteen private bunk rooms, all reached through doors in the curving wall. The bunk rooms were simply furnished with a bed, two seater couch, computer, clock, shower room and toilet. A window and door led out into an enclosed courtyard garden that would have been square had it not been for the curving wall of the bunk rooms protruding into it; the garden was green and airy, and I felt it would be quite a welcome retreat from lectures. The fourth side of the lecture room provided the main entry door and a multimedia screen. The floor was the most interesting thing in the room, in its centre was a large rectangular slab, like polished marble, metallic plates at each corner, all flush with the ground.

Our guide, a Matthew Quaid, then smiled and alleviated the rising sense of claustrophobia by outlining the number of shared Complex areas available to us. If we wanted to pursue leisure activities there was a gym, swimming pool, sports courts and a fully enclosed park planted in such a way as to give a feeling of the wilderness at its central pavilion. The Facilities refectory was shared with the EOA, but employed relatives had to eat at alternative times to students to prevent any resentment felt by pupils who wouldn't be seeing family for long periods of time. There were times when I'd not seen Dad for weeks on end, so this didn't bother me at all.

Library and research areas were quiet, just as they should be, but all other areas bustled with life and activity, so much so that none of us really missed "the outside".

We all began the process of settling in. We had two days before our studies and training actually began, so we spent much of it getting to know each other and find our bearings.

We were even more diverse than I'd thought. Most were science based as I had assumed but some had come from entirely different routes. Ed Lackey and Pearl Riss were both artists. Davey Collins had been a school caretaker who, over many years, had read his way through every course and book the school's library held. David Ertis was a young man who spent much of his time strumming a guitar and writing lyrics, and, of course, there was Rue.

Rue James was fascinating. She was twenty years old and had spent most of her life in the care system. Few families had coped with her as a foster child until the last one, which enabled her to throw off her addictions to alcohol and sundry narcotics long enough to enter into adulthood sober. It wasn't so much a family as a single woman, but Rue referred to her as the family she should have been born with. It was this woman who had discovered Rue's amazing ability to understand people's feelings. Her phenomenal observational skills and clarity of thought eclipsed us all. If she had utilised them in science class at school - instead of clouding them with drugs - she would most certainly have been the most accomplished individual in the group. She just shrugged saying, 'I had a really troubled mind when I was young.'

Soon we were plunged into our workload. Heavy and intricate, it was met with no little despair by a fair number of the class. I felt challenged and excited.

I didn't have to wait long before Elizabeth Verne noticed the real me; not just my academic skills and comprehension, but also the fact that I was a very popular and sought after member of the class. One month into the syllabus she called me to her office. As I entered she stood up and, in a disarmingly friendly way, moved quickly around her desk, approached me and shook my hand.

'Dear Dace, I've been overly judgemental towards you and I want you to know that I've changed my mind. You are even more remarkable than your father told me.'

I stood and blinked! The warmth and familiarity were the same as I'd witnessed when she addressed Dad as Dougie and I wondered how such a personality had landed such a role.

My problem came from seeing her at all; it always brought flashbacks of the incident I'd experienced, bringing instant recognition and a conflict that was led by my father's insistence that I "move on" from believing Miss Verne to be my rescuer.

'Tell me about your brush with death Dace.'

The request nearly knocked me off my feet but I responded immediately.

'It was all over so quickly, to be honest it's a bit disjointed now. I used to elaborate on it to make it sound more exciting to my classmates but my best friend, Craig, saw the whole thing and told me that I was wrong to tell tales…'

Miss Verne laughed, 'An insightful boy, maybe we should enrol him next year?'

I smiled. I was feeling more at ease, 'He'd like that!'

'Was *she* very much like me… the woman who rescued you?'

It was clear from her expression that she knew she hadn't pushed me from the road.

'It's like I've got a photo of her face pinned up in my brain. You could be her twin!'

*Cries: The Captive Mind*

The concept seemed to concern her briefly, then she just nodded, 'Fascinating.' She cupped my cheek with her hand, 'I've never had a twin.'

I felt foolish but her manner showed no disdain.

'I hope you find your rescuer one-day Dace, I'd love to meet her,' She glanced at her watch. 'I believe you have a lecture to get to. Oh,' She fixed me in her gaze and smiled broadly, 'Time you got your hands on an Envisager again!'

She was right of course. Up until now we had been immersed in the study of simple materials, but today we would each get an opportunity to try one of the training units. The outcome would not be assessed; the objective was simply to promote calm and focus, and attain what, for some, would be an initial "link" with the tool. 'Thank you for your time Miss Verne.' I said as I turned and opened the office door.

'My pleasure. Oh, and please, Dace, call me Elizabeth.'

'OK.' I agreed without turning. I'd seen her face quite enough that day, and in the back of my mind I just felt there was more to the whole story, something she wasn't telling me.

By the time I reached the lecture room I was laughing to myself. 'Elizabeth is top brass at a Government science facility, there's probably hundreds of things she knows that she wouldn't tell me!' Then I stopped dead in the doorway; I'd not asked after Dad whilst I was with Verne. I stared back up the corridor towards Elizabeth's office, feeling a little saddened, when a sharp, ear-splitting whistle brought my attention back to the lecture room.

Mr. Quaid turned to Rue, 'No need to whistle Miss James, Master North is on time. Calm and focused remember?'

'Wasn't hurrying him Sir, his mind wasn't with us, govern your mind Trix!'

The nickname grated but she was right, I couldn't afford to let my concentration slip now. I raised my hands in acknowledgement of Rue's insight. 'Guilty, Sherlock's right.'

Quaid flustered momentarily, 'Really!? Very, er, well... settle in Trix, er Dace.' and I stepped into the room.

81

## Chapter fourteen
## Focus is Key

I collected my chair and sat in my usual place beside Rue, as I sat my eye glanced down to my already seated friend. I guess it was normal for a thirteen-year-old boy to do it but the fact that I did actually took me by surprise; I looked down her top!

I slumped into my seat a little heavily, causing another student to Shh me. I was supposed to have a focused mind but Miss Verne's questions about the accident, my disappointment about not asking for news about my father, and now the image of two soft breasts, entwined in the vine tattoo that descended from Rue's neck, had me in complete disarray.

'The trainer Envisager,' Mr. Quaid began. 'Is not a complete device…'

I thought I'd seen a bit of nipple near the edge of her bra. I shook my head for some measure of clarity.

'…the parts that pool the user's thoughts into physical matter are absent, being replaced with…'

'Freckles.' I heard myself say.

'Pardon Dace?' Mr. Quaid asked, eyebrows raised.

Davey chuckled, he'd heard me. Rue looked at me, then looked down. From the corner of my eye I noticed Rue securing a button on her cardigan that had come adrift, 'Oh he just belched Mr. Quaid.' She said, matter-of-factly.

Davey sniggered.

'Cucumber sandwich at lunch Mr. Quaid.' I announced, 'Should have known better really. Sorry.'

A light flurry of laughter circled the room but Rue wasn't laughing.

'Really! Class compose yourselves.' Mr. Quaid insisted.

The group hushed. Quaid continued. 'The parts have been replaced with emitters that link to the plate you are sitting around; Val'ee technology, it is essentially a holographic plate. The effects of using a training Envisager are profoundly real; objects can be handled, moved, even disassembled where numerous interlocking or moving parts have been Envisaged. The object created will however, disappear when the platform is switched off or the object is moved outside of the properties of the plate. I will demonstrate…'

Quaid moved to the top end of the plate and initiated the Envisager; the metal plates that were inset around the slab now rose like pillars from the floor almost touching the ceiling. Quaid flourished a parachute shaped object into existence, it floated motionless in the air, lacking any apparent weight. Quaid lowered the tool and set the object spinning with a flick of his finger. The object earned him a ripple of applause and I found myself clapping too, although I wished I could grab the parachute and leap away from the wrath of Rue which I felt sure would come soon after the lecture.

'Dace!' I looked up, startled from my meditations to find Quaid standing in front of me offering the trainer. He seemed unperturbed by my look of minor shock, 'You have held an Envisager in the past. Perhaps you would like to lead by example. Show us your technique...'

'That's OK,' I blustered. 'I'm happy to wait my turn.'

Mr. Quaid turned the handle of the tool towards me and the parachute disappeared, 'Just a simple shape made out of any of the materials you have been studying.'

I took a deep breath and stood up. Taking the trainer from my tutor I offered it up like a handgun. There was some nervous tittering.

'Really!' Quaid snorted, 'Let's take this a little more seriously please.' He lifted my free hand. 'Both hands Master North!'

'Focus.' I thought to myself, 'That's what Dad told me.' Strangely I found a place of reasonable calm in my mind that seemed entirely separate from everything that had been happening, and I initiated the device.

I had spent all my spare time, since learning that we'd be using the Envisager that day, deciding what I'd make. I wanted something as complex as I knew I had understanding for, but could not forget how "complex" had become "embarrassing" on S. C. Britannia. I had resolved to keep it simple, a plastic cube perhaps or a pyramid. I had toyed with a sphere but it just reminded me of Hope's rubberised balls and I felt sure that it would strain my focus.

The rest of my mind seemed to be attempting to access my still zone. It didn't feel stable but I felt sure I could achieve what I'd planned; a simple wire structure, a cross, and as I neared completion of it I felt a wave of relief. What happened next happened quickly; my mind faltered. I could see the vine tattoo that traced down Rue's neck, weaving - as it descended - around her... I snapped myself from the image and looked to see what I'd done.

The cross was good, made as if from a single wire thread and standing on the point of its base in perfect balance. This was truly remarkable to me as the balance was achieved despite the entwining, wire vine that had sprung up from the point of near completion and trailed around the cross quite organically.

There was a stunned silence. Davey had talked earlier about being happy if he could create a standard house brick! The most elaborate planned object had been Ed's. He'd pointed at this being an opportunity for him to realise an expression of his innermost artistic flair - we were all looking forward to that - But this, this cross with its trained vine had surpassed all aspirations.

Only Rue seemed unmoved, her puzzlement was for the reaction of the class. She stood up and approached the object. With a gentle touch of her hand it began to rotate as Quaid's piece had. Then she noticed that each leaf seemed to have been made individually by hand in a medium such as clay, then cast in the finished metal. Some of the others joined her. She stared at me with an expression I didn't understand, then started clapping. 'What's wrong with you all? We thought Trix was special, now we know it.' Her leading generated further admiration from the group, even Mr. Quaid was applauding.

'Really Dace, quite outstanding.' He leant over me and in a quieter voice admitted, 'I had hoped that in your distracted state I would gain for the class a lesson in the importance of focus.'

'But focus, and its maintenance, is the key to creation.' I heard myself boast, and felt instantly ugly.

'With focus like that you could probably use an Envisager in a hail of mortar bombs.'

I moved to turn off the Envisager.

'Ah Pah, Pah!' Quaid blurted, staying my hand, 'This needs to be shared.' He took the trainer from me and sent Clare Tamiway - one of the six students with an engineering and material sciences background - off to find the rest of the EOA staff. 'They'll be in the staff room around now. Everyone else, we're having an early break. Please gather your thoughts, focus *is* key.'

I went to my room and sat on the bed. I felt like a fraud. I hadn't been fully in control and lacked any comprehension regarding how I could have produced such detail. I sighed, at least it was the tattoo that had come to the forefront of my mind and not Rue's skimpy bra!

Davey stepped into my room. How slow witted of me not to have closed it. He slumped onto the couch.

'That was amazin' kid.' He said shooting me a bizarre double point with both hands. He was the oldest on the course, aged fifty-one, and had been put forward by the principal of the school he had worked in.

He'd never excelled academically in his youth, but had taken immense pleasure from answering the questions of students when he was performing his daily tasks as caretaker. This delight spilled into intensive study regarding anything the children were due to look into. As a result, pupils always sought Davey if they were struggling.

'All that time in school tha facts never stuck,' He'd shared one evening. 'Once tha pressure were off, I retained an' understood everythin' I red. Principal sed that if I din' make EO someone might at least see 'ow well I could explain thin's, and tha's important too.'

Now Davey was sat in my room waving his hands as if he'd burnt them on something. 'Phew-ee, ya gonna surpass yer dad sonny boy!'

'No Davey, I'm a total fraud...'

'Sorry? I din' see anyone else wiv an Envisager out there, you were 'oldin', you were aimin', you were thinkin' Dace lad, yep that were wholly you out there.'

I couldn't deny that it was me, but he didn't realise what had happened. He'd been a true friend over these opening weeks however, and I felt the urge to share my problem.

'It was Rue's...'

'Tat'oo.' He interrupted and I realised that he was as aware as Rue regarding what had taken place. He winked, 'Truth is... I peeked over 'er shoulder meself before ya got back from Verne's office, 'ey, tha's one tease of a vine ain' it? Ever wondered where it stops?'

I realised that I'd never considered the end point of the tattoo, and the posing of the question sent my adolescent mind reeling.

'That's no one's business but mine old man.' Rue had appeared in my doorway. 'Out please, I want to talk to Trix.'

Davey stood up, and in a mock-comic way edged around the wall of the room towards the door crying, 'Be gentle wiv 'im Miss James, gentle now, ee meant no 'arm!'

'Out!' She snapped. Davey flashed me a grimace and was gone. Rue looked straight at me, head tipped and eyebrows raised as if expecting my defence. I stared back for a moment then wondered just where the vine tattoo did end. I glanced down at her ankle…

'Trix!' I looked back at her face. Always it was as if I'd spoken my thoughts. She looked over her shoulder at the empty doorway then turned back to me, whispering 'It ends in a loop around my waist.' She laughed and perched herself on the bed next to me. 'I was high when I had it done. It cost my foster parents so much they dumped me back at social services the next day. I got my drugs with their bank card that night too.' She lolled her head backwards, her hair, not constrained by any form of styling gel these last two weeks, cascaded down her back. 'I've let so many people down, Trix.'

'I-I'm sure you didn't mean to.' I piped up.

She swung her head back towards me, 'I did though Trix, I always meant it. I've always been a very deliberate kind of girl.'

She placed her hand on my knee. I felt my eyes widen. If she could read me, as well as I thought she could, she knew exactly how this was affecting me. I suppressed a cry of anguish as she leant towards me her lips parting slightly then suddenly, she lifted her hand and the heel of it struck me on the forehead sending me flat out on the bed.

'Ow!' I protested.

'Flattered,' Rue exclaimed. 'But if I catch you looking down my top again I'll gouge one of your eyes out!' She stood up and headed towards the door.

'OK.' I surrendered, remaining flat on the bed.

She stopped, turned, smiled and added, 'You really are cute Trix, just not ten years older. Even I've got my rules, babes. That's just a minimum to me yeah? You understand don't you?'

I nodded pathetically

'The pitfalls of real beauty.' Rue sighed as she continued towards the door, coming to a halt just outside. 'How much did you hear?' She asked.

'Oh I wouldn' wanna "Waist" yer time wiv that Rue, me Darlin'.' It was Davey, he'd been listening! Rue's hand flicked upwards, the action was followed by a sharp slapping noise and a brief whimper of pain before she finally disappeared from my view, in the direction of her room.

Davey stumbled back into my room, rubbing his cheek vigorously. 'Wow! That gal's got spirit, and di' ya hear?'

I shrugged my ignorance.

'I stand a chance wiv 'er, ten years older minimum!'

I remained quiet.

'You a'right kid?' His concern was genuine. I nodded. 'Tha's good cos Mr. Lock an' Mrs Faulkener jus' arrived…'

I pulled my pillow over my head.

'Ya can't be brilliant an' hide away lad…' I stayed motionless. 'Suit yerself, I'll 'av ter tell 'em yer 'eds grown too big ter fit through yer door…'

'OK! I'm coming.'

The tutors complimented me on my work, recording the object and insisting I give some comment about the achievement.

Mr. Lock assured me with his thick American accent that the production of remarkable first objects by trainees was not unheard of, they happened with most intakes of students in EO facilities worldwide, simply due to the reliability of the selection process.

'That said,' Lock chuckled. 'this one'll take the wind right outta the sails of my old buddies at the American EO Network.'

AEON had produced some of the most accomplished EO's in the world, but I comforted myself with the fact that this had only been the case since Dad's visit to them two years ago.

'We'll talk again soon Dace.' Lock informed me as he and Mrs Faulkener departed.

The day returned to schedule, my cross dispelled with the flick of a switch. Everyone produced what they'd intended, Davey was very pleased with his brick and Ed's free expression was somewhat darker than we'd expected, but he seemed very happy.

Rue created a simple but well-proportioned knife and asked if it were possible to stab someone with it inside the field of the plate; she was looking at Davey. Quaid insisted that the field could not pass through flesh, 'That would have the same effect as removing the object from the plates influence.'

Rue looked around the group, 'Just a question.' She insisted.

Since the EOA opened, no complete intake of trainees had been able to create something the first time; *We* all had. The selection process really was as good as Lock had suggested. We were all well on our way to becoming EO's.

## Chapter fifteen
## A Li'l Friendly Competition

I sat with the others that evening in the common room, chatting about what we'd achieved; Davey was the most excited. 'I jus' feel like, wow! I made somethin' wiv me mind, somethin' from nothing', jus' look at me 'ands.' Davey's hands were visibly shaking.

'Steady on old boy,' Rue commented, looking up from her Data Pack. 'Don't want you keeling over with a heart attack.'

'Luvley tha' ya care Rue, me darlin'.'

Rue rolled her eyes and returned to composing an e-mail.

'This'll steady you up bro.' Quin suggested, handing him a bottle of beer, icy from the fridge.

'Quin me latest bes' friend,' Davey exclaimed, clinking his bottle against Quin's. 'If it adn't been fer tha boy wonder...' He pointed at me with his beer bottle, spilling some, '...yours would 'av been tha bes' piece at there today.'

Rue coughed, 'We're giving out rewards now are we?'

Davey looked blankly at Rue. So blankly that even I could tell that she couldn't read him. She seemed visibly perturbed.

'Jus' sayin' it as I see it, me luv.'

Rue shook her head and glanced at me, 'You're quiet Trix, what do you think? Was Quin's the next best after *yours*?'

I didn't know what to say. I'd sound pretty conceited if I answered; it would hint that I really did think mine was the best. Fortunately, Davey spoke first.

'Ge' off tha boys back, Rue, yer know ee meant nothin' by it.'

'By what?' Quin queried, with the tone of one not yet in the loop but keen to give an opinion.

'I didn't like my cross half as much as I liked Clare's vase.' I interjected in an attempt to draw the attention away from what was getting close to being embarrassing.

Clare smiled.

Rue, taken aback by Davey's defence of me and perhaps realising the embarrassment was shared, backed down seemingly content that I'd avoided sounding smug.

'What did I miss?' Quin pressed.

Rue looked straight at him, head slightly tilted, eyes narrowing, 'What exactly *was* yours?'

Quin and Davey burst into fits of laughter. Rue raised an eyebrow.

'A track wheel!' Quin and Davey announced simultaneously as if it had been obvious.

Rue laughed. 'Quin invents the wheel and his friend Davey "The Brick" Collins thinks it's great! Hey, Davey, you probably remember the first wheel!'

'The first brick' I added.

'Hey yer yon brat! I've been defendin' you!'

'Actually we've moved on. Keep up old boy.' Rue teased.

'That track wheel is a component part of a Nexar robot's caterpillar tracking.' Quin stated, perhaps feeling it needed more clarification and shouldn't be confused with a "common" wheel. 'I've spent most of my working life with robotics, it's what I know best. I guess I kept safe with what I made, but I'm pleased with it.'

'I'll drink to that.' Davey toasted. 'Bes' track wheel I ever saw.'

None of the banter that night was harsh really, although an outsider may have considered some to be so. In reality the strength of the group, its cohesion, was coming to the fore; there were friendships forming here that would remain in place for a lifetime. Ed was a bit of a loner and the engineering lot - accept Clare - were quite tight, but the rest of us were bonding. I remembered my Dad telling me of the welcome he'd received into the ranks of the EO's after his remarkable first use of the Envisager. 'It's like marrying into a warm and supportive family.' He'd told me. I'd felt worried at the time, but now I understood. His love for his own family hadn't diminished; just as mine had not diminished for him, Nana, Gramps, or Kerry, but EO's seemed innately capable of a similar understanding, acceptance and openness. They were very practical attributes, perhaps even the very reason why such people were most compatible with the device.

As my chosen time to retire to bed loomed Davey gave me a little nudge. 'I were thinkin' Dace me boy, seein' 'ow easy I found usin' tha tool, I've decided I'm gonna up tha stakes a li'l, reckon I could 'av trumped yer showy piece 'ad I 'ad tha confidence I got tonight...'

I had watched him down a few beers that evening and wondered where his stated confidence had actually come from.

'Are you challenging Trix?' Rue laughed.

'No, no, no,' Davey shook his head and waved his hands in an exaggerated manner, upsetting an empty bottle on the arm of his chair. 'No, Rue, me dear, all I'm s'jestin' is a li'l friendly competition.'

'You made *a brick!*' Rue began, as if gearing up for a new tirade of teasing. Then she noticed the look of contemplation on my face. '*Trix?*' She stated, with a tone of disbelief, 'You're not going to accept Davey's challenge are you?'

'I've always liked a little competition.' I sighed. I looked at Davey. 'But don't you think I'm a little out of your league?' One or two uninvolved faces turned to face the conversation.

'Wha'z tha' s'posed to mean?!' Davey retorted.

'Well, I'll have to have some sort of handicap to make the contest fair…'

'Why, yer li'l…'

Rue saw the glint in my eye, 'Yes Trix, if we half your assessment scores and put them up against Davey's total that should be fairer wouldn't you say?'

'On the first assessment perhaps, then we might have to half mine again to really give him a chance…'

Davey realised we were joking and chuckled; he offered me his hand. 'I'm not messin',' he said. 'Truth is, if I don't 'av somethin' to buck me ideas up a bit, I reckon I'll struggle. This way I'll wanna keep stretchin' meself. What do ya say Dace? Jus' fer fun?'

I took hold of his hand, shaking it firmly, 'To the death my friend.' I yawned, then, making my excuses, retired to my bunk room.

My room was furthest from the common room but I could still hear the rhythm of happy voices. My mind dwelt on Rue. She'd been changing. Not only was her hair free to flow naturally over her slim shoulders but her make-up was less severe and her voice more relaxed, softer. Her earlier statement echoed once more through my mind as if she were here with me in the room. "You really are cute Trix, just not ten years older. Even I've got my rules babes. That's just a minimum…"

I sighed. I felt out of my depth in this adult world; respected for being selected, yet still a child. 'Maybe I could prove my maturity to Rue during my competition with Davey.' I wondered, then smiled, it wouldn't make me any older. I rolled over in my bed and pulled the duvet tightly around me. The unseasonable warmth we'd enjoyed through October was now giving way to a standard autumn. I closed my eyes, 'Best to enjoy the journey.' I thought. 'Just enjoy it.'

### Chapter sixteen
### Mixed Media

The next assignments would be assessed. Each assessment would lead to a grading which, when added to the scores achieved using fully functional Envisagers in the new year, would eventually lead to an EO rank. A high rank meant greater freedom of creativity, like Dad. Davey and I had agreed to complete our competition with the last Trainer assignment - the "Lock test" - as it was more important to remain focused with a full function Envisager; you couldn't do that whilst engaged in rivalry, however friendly it was.

I'd woken up on the morning after Davey's challenge believing he would have either forgotten his tipsy suggestion or, perhaps, be too embarrassed to ever mention it again. When I got to the materials lab - part of the shared facilities in the complex - I discovered that Davey had been there for two hours already!

'Mornin' Dace, ya might wanna get crackin'. I've already gen'd up on granite, flint, limestone, sandstone, slate an' basalt, it's like an 'ole chunk of me brain's been unlocked an' opened fer info.'

I feigned disinterest, 'No point in rushing Davey, but hey, if you need the extra time to absorb the basics, that's up to you. I'm a strong believer in quality over quantity...'

We both laughed and were told to be quiet by a researcher we'd never met before.

'Jus' ignor'im,' Davey whispered. 'I reckon a bit of camaraderie is wha' we need rand 'ere.' He returned to his observations.

It took me all morning to get close to what Davey had claimed he'd covered. I wondered if he'd been wholly truthful and feared he had, for a number of times I watched him flit tirelessly from work station to reference books to internet, checking and double checking his findings. He had a method that was proving very useful to him and the list of materials he'd prepared to tackle that day quickly diminished.

The following day I noticed his appetite for information again. The lecture had been about twenty-five percent Mr. Lock and seventy-five percent Mr. Lock answering Davey's questions; no one minded, we just made notes, it was good stuff.

Davey's look of satisfaction when the first assignment was handed out made me realise that I'd agreed to compete against a man of real character and resourcefulness. I knuckled down.

As we prepared to receive our assessor at the end of that week Davey moved his seat forward so he could whisper a final little piece of scheming into my ear.

'Nerv'us?' He enquired.

'Nope.'

'Tha's wonderful. Must 'elp not 'aving Rue's vine on yer mind eh?'

The memory came flooding back, but Rue had overheard him.

'I didn't have you down as a cheat.' She scolded

'No, no, Rue me darlin'. I was jus' pointin' out to Dace...' He turned close to my ear again, '...that ee 'asn't 'ad tha misfortune of glancin' dan yer cleavage and becomin' distracted an' outta fo...' His statement was cut short by a sharp blow that Rue dealt to his calf with her boot.

The damage had been done. My calm meditations before the assessment were a loss to me. Rue could tell, and stated in a justified tone as Davey franticly rubbed his leg, 'Guess that'll even up the odds a bit.' She'd taken on the role of unofficial referee in our competition and tried to suggest that we right off this assessment, as both of us would struggle now.

'You struggling Davey?' I asked.

Davey looked up at me, a tear rolling down his cheek, 'No, er no, I'm kinda good, ya kay yerself boy?'

'I've got you to thank for how lacking in struggle I am.'

'Yer wanna, ow, include this one then?'

'Bring it on.'

Mrs Faulkener arrived.

Three specific items were required to be Envisaged by each student: A vessel that could hold exactly one litre of water. A bar, one-centimetre-thick, that could support twenty kilos of suspended weight, and a cube, one metre square, through which light could pass.

I was happy I wasn't first but the obvious difficulties experienced by my classmates didn't fill me with confidence.

Ed struggled, claiming that the assessment was not as artistic as he would have liked. 'The parameters are pretty rigid.' He argued. Faulkener told him to complete the task as best as he could, the evaluation incorporated more than the obvious.

Ed's vessel leaked, his bar bowed and his cube, well, that was good, nothing had detailed the colour of the light as it emerged from the cube, only that it passed through.

My turn arrived and I stepped up quickly to afford myself the maximum pre-operative meditation time.

'Please begin.' Mrs Faulkener's calming voice urged.

The vessel turned out well, but if the requirement that it held one litre was both a minimum *and* a maximum, then I'd messed up; my bowl could easily have held a cup more. Undaunted I pressed on. I felt my bar was excellent - I'd Envisaged titanium, which easily fulfilled the requested function - Later I felt I'd been guilty of over-engineering.

My glass cube was my best piece. It was perfect, unflawed, and I awaited permission to retire from the plate.

Mrs Faulkener keyed in a few last observations. Downloaded data from the Trainer and gave me a reassuring smile, 'Thank you Mr. North. Mr. Collins next please.'

Davey rose and limped to the floor. Rue smiled. Davey scowled at her; she mouthed 'Sorry' with an expression of true repentance. Davey gave an audible sigh and raised the Trainer. His vessel - a very elaborate vase - seemed, at first, to be too small but held the litre volume to the last drop. I found myself clapping and was promptly hushed. Davey was allocated a few extra moments to focus.

'The next object in your own time Mr. Collins, then straight into the third.' Faulkener directed.

Davey wasted no time. It was obvious that he was clear regarding what he wanted to achieve. His steel bar was actually nine millimetres thick but held the weight, and his Perspex cube met specifications amply. He waited as I had done. Then, leaving the plate, offered me a high five, which I took.

Rue had waited until the end but seemed quite cool as she took her place. Like me her container could have held more but her attitude remained light and she even flashed me a smile, to acknowledge the shared error. Her bar was jet black and I didn't recognise what it was, but it held the weight and Faulkener was nodding, so it was a good choice. Then she did something none of us expected. Her cube was ice. Despite this being the last operation of the Trainer for that day, the rumble of appreciation that reverberated around the room was just as harshly hushed as my ill-timed claps earlier.

Mrs Faulkener finalised her records and looked up. 'Thank you, Miss James. Thank you everyone for your almost perfect cooperation.' She peered over her bifocals at me particularly. 'The rest of the day is your own. Please do not be worried regarding anything you may or may not feel you've achieved today. No one has failed this assessment, this I can already assure you, so well done.'

Announcement complete she tucked her Data Pack under her arm, powered down the holographic plate and - with no further formalities - left the room.

'Park?' Ventured Davey. A handful of us agreed and we filed out of the room pulling our coats around us.

The chill November air found us huddled together on the benches of the central pavilion by the pond. A vent structure - designed like a piece of modern art - threw excess warm air from the surrounding Complex in just the right spot to warm our feet.

'That was tense.' Quin opened.

'Harsh.' Clare agreed, 'I didn't pull off the cube right, but she said none of us had failed so...'

'Yeah, what's that about? None of us got it perfect...' Quin continued.

'Matt did.' David corrected. He usually played his guitar to unwind but had joined us for the fresh air.

Quin shrugged, 'That's what I mean. Shouldn't he have been the only one to have passed? Envisagement requires absolutes. That's what they taught us in the first week...'

'Psychology.' Rue interrupted.

'Huh?' Quin responded, voicing the sentiment of all of us. This idea was new.

'The Trainer does a lot more than holographic Envisionment. I watched Faulkener a lot. Her responses and things that interested her, they mostly came *after* we'd made something...'

We remained quiet. Rue continued, 'The Trainer records a great deal of data. It's taken into the device from your hands; pulse rate, perspiration, tightness of grip, shaking, loads of detail. It all relates to how appropriate we are, what our potential is. We all proved we had a link last time, this time we proved we were stable enough; flaws in our creations can be addressed over the coming months, psychological limitations will rule us out.'

'Go Davey!' David exclaimed. 'Dace's round of applause didn't even phase you.'

'Wha' can I say? I enjoyed meself!'

'It was two claps, hardly a round of applause. Anyway Davey's vase deserved it.' I began clapping again. Everyone joined in forcing Davey to acknowledge his success.

'It was how you constructed it man, in layers that increased in diameter and gave that twisted finish to the design. How did you figure the volume would work out?' asked Quin.

'It were a mafmaticle form. As long as tha base were righ' the rest were jus' a formality.'

We sat quietly for a moment.

'But how did you come up with the idea?' Clare puzzled.

'A book I read. Part of tha 'igher level mafs curriculum at tha school I werked at.'

'How many books *have* you read Davey?' Rue pressed.

'Dunno, p'aps ninety-eight p'cent of tha' library we 'ad.'

'Big library?' David added.

'Three floors.'

'Daveypaedia!' Clare giggled.

For some reason this was the funniest thing Rue had heard all day.

'So what didn't you read?' David asked.

'Home Economics...'

Rue was in fits. Davey continued, 'There were some books on dress makin', didn' read 'em, but tha models were cute.'

Rue eased up a bit, 'You're rank.' She chuckled.

We all chuckled.

'There were a section on bereavement.' He sighed. Sitting next to him I became aware that he wasn't quite with us any more, his eyes, a little watery, gazed out over the pond. 'Jus' guess I thought I knew enough 'bout that subject.' His voice was almost a whisper.

I quickly changed the topic of conversation, 'So Rue, what was the material your bar was made of? I didn't recognise it.'

Everyone turned to Rue, equally keen to find out.

Rue turned slowly towards me, fixing me with a stare that I'd come to know as her evasive answer look, 'You really want to know?' She asked with a quiet voice.

'Well if you don't want to tell us…' I began, in a mock can't-be-bothered tone.

'No, please tell us. I didn't get it either.' Clare pushed.

Rue's head swung slowly around to Clare, then her eyes looked around the rest of us.

'It was cold, stubborn, hatred.'

Silence, and a little frowning followed.

'I figured nothing was as rigid and unyielding as hatred.'

'Hold on…' Quin responded, squirming a bit in his seat next to Rue. 'You Envisaged an emotion as a material?'

'She's messing with us Quin.' Said Clare anxiously.

Rue shrugged, 'You asked.'

'You're a real freak Rue.' Clare protested.

'Guilty!' Rue celebrated, clearly flattered.

A nervous round of laughs circled the group but I noticed that Davey was still distant.

Passing Davey's room later I paused and listened. I could hear sobbing. I wondered what the earlier chit chat had unearthed. I knocked and entered without waiting for permission.

Davey was standing by his window, pale, red-eyed and rather cross looking…

'Thanks fer waitin'!' He snapped.

'You were upset earlier. I wanted to help.'

His head dropped and he ran his fingers through his thin hair. What anger there had been dropped away. 'It's been s'long.' He admitted, 'Then it all comes back like it were yesterday.' He moved to the chair by his desk and sat down heavily, resting his head in his hands. I sat on the desk and waited.

'I 'ad a fam'ly once Dace me boy.'

This came as a surprise, although I could not think why. To assume he didn't have a family was perhaps stranger.

He looked up at me, his eyes heavy with tears. 'Me wife Emma and I were goin' to take tha kids to tha Morrello Exhibition.'

I gasped, 'That's where my Dad's parents died…'

*Cries: The Captive Mind*

'I 'ad me a shed load a' problems back then,' He confessed. 'Short tempered, distracted. I 'ad to werk late at tha school. I 'adn't been there lon', an' I wan'ed to be indispensable. I fergot me promise to take 'em. Emma got cross I'd fergotten, I got defensive and said I shouldn' av to werk me fingers to the bone to feed a fam'ly of moaners…' He sobbed. I let him. 'So she took tha kids on 'er own, an' I wen' to werk fumin'.'

'You lost them all?'

He cried again. I rested my hand on his shoulder, 'Davey mate, I had no idea. I'm so sorry.'

'Emma, Tommy and Jenny. All I 'ad lef' were werk, an' me anger. Tha kids from me school were me salvation. First a li'l boy 'bout nine, came an' asked me a question. Well, I didn' know tha answer so I nearly snapped at 'im, then I looked up from tha drain I were werkin' on, an' I see 'is eyes fulla tears, I knew ee 'ad no one else ee felt ee could ask. So I told 'im I'd find out tha answer, and I did. After tha' others started coming an' I made a point of elpin' them too. After several years I'd learnt so much an' gained such a reputation tha principal 'ad me runnin' after-school clubs an' catch up classes.

'When tha Grea' Suff'rin 'appened; it made no odds at first, not 'til tha school years moved up a few times an' tha nursery emptied. Tha' were a dark time. I remember you bein' born, 'ow opeful folks became, but you turned out to be an anomaly. I think tha' were me lowest point, lad.'

I felt bad that I'd been the cause of dashed hopes; it had never occurred to me that I was anything but a positive factor, but I could see now how the lack of normality returning would cause compounded despair. Davey suddenly brightened.

'Then tha Val'ee arrived, came an' 'elped us. Life began again an' me school got selected as one of them Central Academies, so I kep' me job too.' Davey sighed, 'Thanks lad, ya really 'elpin' jus' bein 'ere. Lord I mus' look a silly ole fool…'

'Not half as silly as when you set up our competition.' I joked.

'Wadda ya mean?'

'You'd had seven bottles of beer!'

'Wait 'til we get our results t'morra'. I'll 'av tha smile off yer face!'

The evening saw Davey's steady recovery, although my ten percent higher score the next day did nothing to speed it up.

## Chapter seventeen
## Something Not for Me

Assignments were weekly and tiring. We Envisaged springs and pendulums, mechanisms of increasing complexity. Each time there seemed a little room for error, it had been acceptable. The next project, however, demanded absolute precision.

'We have been concentrating on characteristics, spatial factors and component relationships,' Mr. Lock pointed out after the morning lecture. 'As long as the outcome achieves the desired result, you've passed. There are many arenas for EO's of this calibre, but it will be down to you to find them; Morrello will only take up individuals who pass a Lock test. Yes…' He smiled. 'I did create them. So you know ya gonna be stretched. A number of you will fail, but it's not the end of ya training; ya'll form a sub-group - under Mr. Quaid - to have ya abilities honed at the level you've reached and at the end of the course ya'll be released with references. Only those who pass will be allocated a personal, full function, Envisager. Morrello will then contact you regarding ya own aspirations, and steps will be taken to match you and ya skills to fieldwork placements; these will form part of ya ongoing studies, you will have earned ya wings people.'

There was a murmur of excitement. This meant - for those who passed - that a real Envisager would be waiting for them when they returned after the Christmas break.

'Please,' Mr. Lock urged, 'Leave nothing to chance. Revise and cross reference ya studies. Review what you think you know; a number of you are making repeated errors, find them in ya evaluation notes and sort 'em out. I want as many of you back in the New Year as I can possibly have. At three this afternoon the "Lock 5" assignment will be uploaded to ya Data Packs; I consider this task to be the one most of you will be capable of achieving - *all of you* if you knuckle down. Practice time will begin on Tuesday from ten in the morning, ya allocated times displayed as usual; which just leaves me to wish ya'll good luck, I'll see you Friday week.'

And - without any call for questions - Mr. Lock gathered his Data Pack and left the room.

Glances were exchanged. A few remained confident but some - aware of their limitations and the thought of stumbling at this high hurdle - had doubts etched on their faces.

*Cries: The Captive Mind*

'So what did yer get fer the generator assignment Dace?'

I turned to the enquiring Davey, 'Dunno, haven't checked yet, hold on.' I reopened my Data Pack.

Quin chuckled, 'You must be the only one who didn't check their result…'

'But it was scheduled to upload during Mr. Locks lecture…' I noticed a few grins, 'What? You all checked during the session? I'm afraid I lack your confidence.' I opened the assignment file.

'I checked between Gases and Vapours.' Rue admitted.

Clare nodded.

'Vapours?' Quin exclaimed. 'Er, can I quickly check something on your notes Rue?'

Rue reopened her Data Pack and scrolled for vapours; I shrugged a "no surprises there then" sort of shrug and glanced down at my score, '94.'

'Oh blow!' Davey snapped, 'I got 92!'

'Well done Davey.' Rue complimented

'I fel' sure I'd trumped tha boy this time.'

'It's not going to happen is it?' I teased, 'What say I release you from our contest? We'll call it a draw.'

Davey looked shocked, 'I've ne'r backed outta anythin' in me life.' Then, seeing the cheeky look on my face, he acquired a devious expression himself. 'I got a betta idea, le's scrap tha scores. Highest score on tha Lock test wins?'

'That goes nicely in your favour, being fifteen points behind.' Rue stated coldly.

'That's alright Rue, I accept.' I said, shaking Davey's hand firmly; I wanted to be sure my friend would get through and felt this was his way of keeping the pressure on himself. At fifteen behind he might suddenly feel the gap was too great.

'Ha, ha!' Davey exclaimed, clearly amazed at my acceptance, 'I'm gonna whip yer…'

'Oh that's nice,' Rue mocked. 'No "Thanks Trix, moytie nice er yer mee boyee!"'

'Hey! I don' sand like tha'.' Davey shot with a distraught tone. 'I jus' wanna beat 'im once!' A familiar broad smile appeared.

'Best get to work on your flagged up errors Davey old boy, or the only one doin' any whippin' around here will be me.' I laughed.

'Now tha's fightin' talk.' Quin added.

'Boy's becomin' a man.' Clare giggled.

'Oi, lay off me accent!'

'I don't know why you're still standing there…' I continued as I headed towards my room and its computer. 'I'm off to address my failings before I live and breathe the assignment from three o'clock.'

Davey's face became serious again, and he very nearly sprinted to his room.

Soon after I closed my door, I heard other doors opening and closing as other students followed my example. I hoped that they would all be able to correct any issues that might prevent their progress. Perhaps my insistence and Davey's haste would be the witness that enabled more to succeed than would have.

'Now,' I thought, 'To my inconsistencies…' and I brought my personal evaluation file up on the computer.

The details showed nothing of consistent error regarding materials or understanding; in fact, a tightening of understanding had occurred over the last few weeks.

Concentration and focus had also remained stable - earlier fluctuations fully comprehended and addressed.

High scores seemed to settle it. There was little more I could do to improve my chances, and confidence was always promoted as a positive attribute.

Strangely I noticed a flagged link on my profile. Some feedback added by Mrs Faulkener.

I clicked on the link. It related to those fluctuations in concentration that occurred during my first two uses of the Trainer; I knew that they were due to Rue, and it seemed that Mrs Faulkener had drawn a similar conclusion.

"Daces excellence masks a potential failure of concentration that is unusual and dangerous. We forget his age when his work is presented, but we must remember that this is a boy going through changes. I believe the anomalous readings presented by the Trainer relate to adolescence. Although I cannot account for his ability to complete those tasks, I must warn that this period of life presents real risks; brain pathways are altering and distractions may lead to dire consequences. The greatest danger is to the integrity of made materials, and the risks associated with their value in any engineered structure.

*Cries: The Captive Mind*

"Dace will be a master EO like his father, of that I am sure, but I must insist that we delay him; adolescence passes, it would be negligent to qualify Dace into the field now. I therefore recommend failure of the pre-personal Envisager test..."

Suddenly I realised that this note was not intended for me at all, it was for the heads of Morrello. I felt sick. It seemed that however I performed I would be failed. I read on.

"...failure of the pre-personal Envisager test on grounds of concentration stability."

Below this was a response.

"Absolutely not..." I seemed to have an advocate. "...It is imperative that the subject links with a complete device as soon as possible; failure at this stage might result in his departure from Envisagement."

Faulkener had responded with a suggestion. "We can retain him. I suggest an apprenticeship with Morrello, to guide him in the direction of the corporation, providing a quality of living that will generate loyalty to the organisation. We can then, at an appropriate time, find cause to re-enrol him. I cannot stress more greatly the safety issues that will arise from his handling of a full specification Envisager. I can arrange an adequate distraction during the test to ensure failure. An offer of work - perhaps linked to his father - must then come from Morrello to prevent his move to Matthew Quaid's group."

The notes ended with a comment from my advocate. "We will observe his performance and make our judgement based on the data from the Trainer. Do what you feel is right for the assignment, if he succeeds he will stay. *We* will not fail competence." At that the notes ended.

I slumped back in my chair. What should I do with this information? Who was the other person in the debate? What was so important that they should be concerned about losing me?

I needed fresh air. I flung open the door that led into the courtyard. An icy chill struck me but I found myself stumbling into it towards a low concrete bench. I sat, rocking slightly, deeply troubled. It was almost too much of a revelation for me. I'd felt almost invincible in the last test. I'd proven my earlier doubters wrong, gained the respect of pupils and tutors... but wait! What if Mrs Faulkener was right? What if my adolescent mind was going to alter like she thought? It was a well-known fact that pathways in the brain changed during this event. Could I be sure

I'd create what I intended? Could my structures possess inherent flaws?

Maybe Faulkener's suggestions were wise. I'd be physically and mentally mature on my return, and would have gained other experiences working for Morrello.

Then a horror crept through me, the nameless response wanted me to continue regardless of the risk. It wasn't on my side at all! I was torn. I was just as excited as the others regarding the possession of a fully functional Envisager, but... My thoughts started reading more into the "facts"; could it be that my young *mind* was at risk? I started spiralling off into fears that I was actually more of a guinea pig than a potential EO. Had someone funded me as an experiment? I shook my head, 'Speculation,' I thought out loud. 'I know nothing, just Faulkener's concerns and recommendations.' If I passed the test her advice would rob me unjustly, but if I was going to be a hazard her suggestions were appropriate and made provision for my future return. But then why would I need sweeteners, "a quality of living that will generate loyalty?" What was that about? Wouldn't I want to stay with an organisation my Dad worked for anyway? The scheming didn't sit well with me. My mind circled over my findings without gaining any further grasp of their meaning.

Rue spotted me through her window as I came to a conclusion; now I knew "down time" employment would be an exercise in promoting loyalty it would have quite the opposite effect. I had no choice but to go all out to pass knowing that a difficult situation - intended to distract me - was going to happen. I'd just have to be mindful afterwards regarding the quality and integrity of my creations.

'Trix!' Rue exclaimed, from her door. 'What the hell are you doing out here in a T-shirt?' She swept towards me flinging a thick, woolly cardigan around my shoulders.

'Nothing...' I lied, knowing already that such a response was futile with Rue. She'd know already from my face that I was troubled; who in their right mind sits outside on a damp bench, in the middle of December, wearing nothing but a T-shirt and jeans?

'You've decided that acute pneumonia is a good step towards your "Lock Test"?' Her words were loaded with disdain and seemed to shout "idiot" into my face.

I felt her push me to my feet and march me into my room; she sat me on the couch and wrapped herself around me. I felt a little shocked...

*Cries: The Captive Mind*

'Trix, you're freezing! You silly boy!' She felt soft and warm; her breath hot on the back of my neck, but the acceptance of it was innocent; it was a comfort and I was in serious need of comforting.

I offered a little of what I'd discovered, 'My record flags my weakest area as age. It suggests that changes associated with adolescence may make my creations dangerous...' A tear rolled down my cheek but was quickly dashed away by Rues hand.

'You're as dangerous as...' She glanced around the room for inspiration. '...as that plastic dinosaur on your shelf.'

'Dad stood on it once and cut his foot. He said I should keep it off the floor out of harm's way, before it tripped Nana or Gramps and broke a hip.'

Rue stared at me.

'So what you're saying is, I'm as dangerous as a plastic dinosaur stored safely on a shelf?'

'Yep...unless it falls off on your head.' Rue chuckled, thumping my head softly.

I didn't feel ready to join in with her laughter - refreshing though it was - but at least her care was helping; care provided despite her own need to prepare for the test.

Rue stayed with me until a few minutes before the download. On seeing a chess set she had challenged me, regretting it ten minutes later as I produced a devastating checkmate, generating an onslaught of abusive terms such as 'nerd' and 'brainiac'.

Then she'd introduced me to a reaction game. I had to avoid a slap on the hand. It had overly complicated rules, and my hand was quite red before she insisted that we stop and practice another day. It was only after she'd left that I realised she'd fabricated the game in order to repeatedly inflict pain on me for beating her at chess.

## Chapter eighteen
## Lock 5

My Data Pack bleeped. I spent five minutes looking at the flashing light, my catatonia finally broken by the sound of other students heading undoubtedly to the research facilities. I flipped open the screen.

A confident female voice announced the task. 'Congratulations for progressing to level two entry assignment Lock Five. This download cannot be re-played, mimicking instruction in the field. It is recommended, therefore, that you make notes.' The voice paused to allow acquisition of suitable note taking materials. I switched on my camera and set it to record.

'The Morrello DXT44T robotic arm is used in transport assembly lines. Constructed from lightweight materials, strength is provided by the fine honeycombed latticework within, visible in this dissection.' The 3D representation on screen divided and zoomed in to reveal a network of hexagonal cells within.

'The DXT44T has seventeen components relating to its positional capabilities; these allow for rotation, abduction, adduction, flexion, extension and a number of pneumatic features relating to grip.

'You will be tested on your knowledge of the DXT44T, and - in simulation - diagnose and repair a fault relating to the aforementioned components. This will involve the removal of a component and its in-situ fabrication by Envisager.' The screen went blank and I moved to switch off my camera, but there was more. An image of the EOA floor plan appeared and rotated into a positional view of the room. The area where we usually stood to use the Trainer now gave up a secret; the plate began to rise revealing a cubicle beneath.

'The Simulator is Val'ee technology,' The voice resumed. 'and will provide a realistic environment for the duration of your test. Please be aware that this may hold challenges to focus; common distractions faced by EO's in the field. These will be randomly selected to play on the individual's psychological readings. Good luck!'

The screen went blank and a quick scroll through the download files confirmed that the information was unplayable. I watched it back on my camera and saved it to the movie file of my Data Pack.

The assignment was devious. There was much to learn that would never be needed for the exam, but would become good grounding for any standard piece of Morrello hardware. Knowing that the research lab would be busy now I headed to the kitchen for a glass of milk, then settled down in front of my computer for an online search.

The lead up to that Friday was perhaps the most frantic we'd experienced to date. Those of us who usually met in the common room each evening agreed that the exam came first. We would meet one night that week, then focus fully on the task.

We weren't the usual jovial group that evening; there had been concerns regarding missing data. The librarian apologised but there was nothing she could do if the Data Line was out. Clare had remained level headed, finding the information through contacts; sharing this had made her the most popular student in class, with cries of "Long live material engineers!"

We'd all taken a similar line of study. The specific materials, including a complex alloy, dissection and assembly of a DXT44T arm in the works labs, and some had looked into the history of the arm's development, its predecessors' failings, and the schematics for the DXT46T scheduled to replace it next year.

All in all, we felt we were on track although the newness of the Simulator had many of us perturbed, not least of all myself with the knowledge that a distraction would be used to ensure my failure.

'I'm just gonna ignore everything that ain't in front of me.' Quin stated.

'Hey, do you think they can make the arm grab at you?' Clare replied.

Quin hadn't thought of that one and became just as concerned as most of the rest of us.

Rue laughed, 'You heard the brief, distractions are based on psychological readings. The more focused you are on the task the less likely the distraction will even bother you.'

'That's one way to look at it.' I said.

'What do you mean?' Rue frowned.

'You've assumed the distraction lessens as focus increases. It didn't say that. It said distractions will play on the individual's psychological readings. It could be that the fewer the readings the greater the distraction.'

'Tha's not fair!' Davey protested.

'But it might relate to score,' I continued, 'even to EO designation. Only the best EO's worked on the Sky Cities before they were enclosed; lesser

EO's wouldn't have been able to maintain their focus in all the protective clothing needed to counter sub-zero conditions and cross winds.'

'Ya think they can sim'late temperatures?' Davey squinted.

I shrugged.

'Hey, guys, I wrote you all a song.' David announced, instantly gaining the full attention of the group. He'd often be strumming away in his room but this was the first time he'd offered to share anything with us. 'I just thought tonight was about escape, yeah?'

He'd made a good point. Our objective had been to relax but we were only making ourselves feel worse.

David pulled his guitar onto his lap, 'This is called "The Crew", er, that's you guys, yeah?' He began plucking out a precise rhythmic tune that ebbed and flowed, making Clare sway. Then he started singing.

His voice was a little throaty but clear and appealing. The song rolled and flurried expressing the delight of the singer regarding his friends and what they'd come to mean to him, the chorus made us all smile:
"My time with you has made me shine,
Your closeness, warmth, shared, all divine,
In stillness now I contemplate
My strong desire to congregate, with you…"

Finally, it was clear that the words were complete and David strummed the tune to an end. We stood up and clapped. David stood and bowed. Rue kissed him and I felt a pang of jealousy. I caught myself; that was just the sort of adolescent reaction that Faulkener had flagged up, and besides, David was nineteen; still too young for Rue, according to what she'd told me the day I made the cross.

'I'm dropping out.' David's frank admission was followed by a brief, stunned silence. 'I can create, but the precision, well, I haven't pulled it off. Just can't hone that blade man. Ed reckons he feels ditto; says he's just doing it to join Quaid's outfit. He's sure Envisagers will become more available later. I just don't wanna wait on work that's so long away, man. Wanna wield an earthly tool.' He flourished his guitar.

This answered a question a few of us had started to formulate; David always seemed to be studying in his room but mostly the sound of strings could be heard and not the click clacks of a computer keyboard. He was either supremely confident or insane. He'd actually been talking to Mr. Quaid who had set him some simple tests with his own full spec Envisager; a pretty special concession. He'd tasked David with the Envisionment of precise cones, spheres and spirals, none of which David had achieved, despite repetition. It hadn't mattered before, there was always a margin into which he fitted, but the margin would now be gone.

At this point Clare grabbed hold of him and sobbed.

'Hey! I'm not dying. I'll stay in touch.'

Clare looked up at him with watery eyes. 'Don't forget.'

'I won't, babes.' He promised, pulling her head close to his chest and kissing her golden hair.

Davey joined them, 'Group hug!' he announced and we all joined in.

'It's not so bad,' He insisted. 'My cousin plays drums in a band; they're popular and rising. They're gigging a lot, makin' money, they need a roadie…'

'You'll play guitar, write lyrics and lead vocals or I'll disown you!' Rue asserted.

'Who knows babes…'

'I thought I was babes!' Clare protested with a muffled voice from deep inside the group hug, which broke up in a bout of good humoured thumps, pinches and tickles.

## Chapter nineteen
### Error

Four days later, the time spent with David as he sang seemed no less important to any of us; it had replaced study time, but it was time spent in a more valuable way. Each member of David's audience that night had a greater desire and incentive to pass the test, and today was the day.

My allocated practice times had gone too smoothly, I felt I was being lulled into a relaxed state that would make Faulkener's promised distraction more effective. I decided to read the words of the link again but the footnotes were absent; the error had been discovered and removed. I girded myself for what I knew was coming.

At nine thirty we stood beside the raised Simulator; it was the first time that we'd actually seen it, apart from in the download graphic. Seeing it fully open added to the excitement felt by all. We received a final briefing and our individual assessment times, wished each other good luck, and headed to our rooms to wait. Davey caught my eye. When he saw me looking he winked, pointed at me and gestured downwards with his finger, then he pointed at himself and pointed upwards.

'I get it,' I thought. 'He reckons he'll do better than me.' I pointed back at him and pretended my hand was an aeroplane, causing it to crash into the doorframe of my room.

Davey smiled, shook his head and disappeared into his room.

I closed my door and waited.

We were unable to continue studying; our Data Packs were on charge and our computer terminals had been disconnected, so I spent my two-hour wait relaxing in a chair by the window.

I watched the cold, winter rain splashing against the glass. I cleared my mind by counting each run that reached the bottom of the frame.

At twelve o'clock there was a knock at the door and it opened, 'I'm ready for you Dace.' Mrs Faulkener informed me.

'Well, if she's ready…' I thought. 'I'd better face what's coming and get it over with.'

She stood almost in my way as I left my room; was this part of her plan, to intimidate me and upset my focus? I caught the thoughts in time; I wasn't going to entertain anything other than a clear mind, intimidation wasn't going to work. I headed towards the Simulator.

She took her position, and I mine, 'Good luck.' She offered and the test began.

The scene that appeared around me was surprising, the malfunctioning robotic arm was in front of me but, rather oddly, we were about twenty metres above the ground on some sort of gantry. It seemed a most unlikely place for a robotic arm to be.

Mrs Faulkener initiated stage one by selecting five standard questions regarding the DXT44T, from a list of twenty. I felt happy with my answers and stepped forwards for stage two: Fault diagnosis.

The gantry swayed beneath me, its structure creaking in protest as I moved. Far from being off putting, all this simulated detail was fascinating and awe inspiring; it truly felt like being in some massive, industrious warehouse, atop some sort of wobbly scaffolding.

The fault was obvious; the flexion bar was bent impeding the free movement of the arm. I stated the fault and proceeded to stage three: Fault removal.

*Cries: The Captive Mind*

I disconnected the wave generator, and used the Trainer to Envisage a structure that supported the arm whilst I removed the damaged component; doing this prevented the connections for the flexion bar from dropping out of alignment, an error that would have made it impossible to Envisage a new bar into a precise position. Faulkener seemed to like this, but did she like it for its ingenuity or because it was a weak technique that would go against me in the final result? I pulled my focus back together, unclipped the housing for the flexion bar and started removing the bent part. I felt competent, it was all going well, and although the task was simple I could sense tangible excitement. The bar slid cleanly from its pins. I placed the component safely to one side and stepped back for stage four: Part replacement.

The new piece had to be Envisaged directly into the device; this was the trickiest part, it required much concentration. It would have made more sense to fabricate the part and then install it, but this was the EO way; a true test of skill.

I was just over half way through when the scene around me changed suddenly. Beneath me the gantry and drop remained; the arm remained too but my surroundings were the EOA lecture room. An alarm was audible, and several of the student's rooms were opening. Those leaving their rooms were carrying a small number of personal effects and were making their way to the exit. All this I discerned from the edge of my consciousness.

The alarm indicated a fire, 'Perhaps a drill,' I heard myself think, for Faulkener had not stopped the test. Then I realised it was all part of the simulation; not because it was unrealistic, no, I recognised my classmates, Davey even winked! No, it was a simulation due to a simple mistake; my door opened too! 'Nice try Faulkener.' I thought as I completed the task, flipped the robotic arm's housing back into place and removed the temporary support I'd Envisaged. I reconnected the power source and initiated the system. The arm moved freely through its start-up movements. I smiled. I was done.

The "fire" incident disappeared from around me. The imagery and sensations of the Simulator faded, revealing the surface of the plate beneath my feet; its solidity leaving me curious as to how the feeling of instability had been achieved. Then Mrs Faulkener spoke.

'OK Dace, the correct procedure in the event of a fire, wherever you are working as an EO, is to protect the Envisager by removing it from the danger area...'

I felt my heart burst with disappointment, Faulkener had double bluffed me. As soon as she'd said it I remembered the rule, but I'd been looking for a distraction that would stop me from completing the task. I suddenly suspected that *she'd* placed the link on my profile to wrong foot me. Had I failed? I felt terrible.

'Please make your way to the debrief area, from there you will be able to leave the complex for Christmas.' She smiled, 'Well done Dace... so close.'

I felt she was mocking me; looking down from her adult world at a child who had come so near to achieving something, but for a silly mistake.

Shocked I left the room, pausing only as a last thought to retrieve my Data Pack from the charge rail. I headed for debrief in Mr Quaid's office; there I would pick up my belongings and head to the car park to meet Dad.

I knocked on Mr. Quaid's door and was bid 'Enter.'

'Ah! Young Master North.' The *young* bit grated. 'How do you feel you performed?'

I didn't know how else to reply, 'I think I messed up.' I said, a lump building in my throat.

He gave a puzzled frown, 'I very much doubt that...' he suddenly became aware of the tears welling up in my eyes and moved to his computer terminal. 'This isn't normal procedure... but...' He tapped a few keys. '...for the sake of Christmas...' He struck a final key, read something then smiled. 'Yes, yes, Really, I don't see any problems, Dace.'

He looked back at me. I felt totally confused, his information contradicted my experience; was he just saying this to comfort me as I left for home? Was he in on the concerns about my safety as an EO?

The first tear dashed down my cheek, 'But the fire procedure...'

Now *he* looked confused. 'Did you initiate the arm after repair?'

'Yes.' I said with certainty.

'...and it went through its full range of start-up movements?'

'Yes, but...'

'Dace, the Lock programs self-diagnose at every stage, even the tutors would be nervous about performing one. Darren, I mean Mr Lock, has a really wicked streak. Had anything been wrong the test would have ended with an all engulfing ball of flame! Lock is one for highlighting failure, BOOM! You see, you did well, ha!'

*Cries: The Captive Mind*

Quaid was quite adamant that I'd succeeded, but I was so confused. I wished I'd not *seen* Faulkener's message.

I thanked Mr. Quaid and picked up my belongings; it was no good stewing over what had happened. Time would show the result, one way or the other. I wished Mr. Quaid a good Christmas, and headed for the car park.

It was so good to see Dad, he swept me clean off my feet in a bear hug. 'Lord you're heavy. I'll tell Nana that she was silly to be concerned about whether you're eating enough!' He motioned me to the wide door of his new vehicle.

'Your Nana has driven me crazy these last few weeks. I think she misses having someone to mother!'

'I could do with some mothering.' I admitted, stepping into the car. Dad followed me. 'Wow!' I exclaimed, realising what the vehicle was.

Dad smiled, 'A CDS; Complete Drive System. Do you like it?'

I nodded. We'd heard about these new vehicles on the evening news, you just stated your destination, and the drive computer took you!

'It's very roomy. It didn't look this big on the outside.'

'Yes,' Dad agreed. 'No loss of space to dashboards, steering wheels and rows of forward facing seats.' It was like stepping into a compact lounge.

'Computer...' Dad said. There was no response. He flashed me a quick glance and repeated the word, with a slightly deeper voice.

'Drive system initiated. Please state your destination.'

Dad gave me an excited expression, 'Home.' He stated.

'Please confirm Rome.' The computer replied.

'Correction.' Dad said, even more deeply, 'Home, please.'

'Please confirm Home.'

'Yes! Yes, please.'

'Please instate safety harnesses.' The car informed, and off we sped.

'Surreal!' I exclaimed. It was the distraction I needed. The CDS negotiated the road beautifully. It was never too close to other vehicles, and braking was smoother than Dad's.

His voice cut into my observations, 'Have you made many friends? They are all older than your school friends.'

'I think I get on best with the oldest one, but everyone has been very accepting of a child in class.'

Dad at first seemed agitated by the term child, but clearly unable to challenge it turned his attention to who I meant.

'The oldest... Ah! Davey Collins.' Dad had done his homework. 'Interesting fellow that one, no formal qualifications. Enrolled after scoring one hundred percent on his entry. He was put forward by the principal of the school he worked, is that right?'

'Er, yeah, I didn't know about his entry score, kind of makes me nervous...'

'Why's that?'

'Well, we've got a sort of competition going based on our assignment scores...'

'Who's winning?'

I beamed at Dad. I wanted to tell him I was, but the Lock test wrong footed me. My beaming seemed to say enough...

'So who else are you friends with?'

'Rue James...' I began.

'Oh, Elizabeth Verne's daughter.' Dad remarked.

I was taken aback. 'She never let on about that!' I laughed. 'Now you come to mention it though, I think there's a family likeness...'

'Not likely,' Dad corrected. 'She's adopted.'

'Of course she is.' I thought, 'How could I have forgotten that? Verne was the "family" Rue felt she should have had...'

'Who else?' Dad urged seeing me slipping away in my thoughts.

'Er, Quin Jennings?' I queried, expecting a run-down of his life and the discovery of a surprising family link.

'No, don't know that one.' Dad shrugged.

'He's twenty-five; robotics engineer. Nice guy, bit loud, but thoughtful...Oh! Then there's David Ertis...' I paused with a little sorrow, 'but he's left the course...'

'Seems I'll never know him, then.' Dad added.

'He's promised to stay in touch. He's a musician. Gonna be part of the crew for 'The Ungoliant'...'

'Cool.' Dad nodded, but I'm sure he didn't know the band.

'Then there's Clare Tamiway...' I continued.

'Material Engineering student.' Dad acknowledged.

'That's right, if it wasn't for me she'd be the youngest.'

'She's a bit like you,' Dad nodded. 'Finishing school early. Sat her highers in a year and took a seven-year degree in three years. She was snapped up by the EOA.'

'She said she'd had EO lecturers, were you one of them?'

'No, never had the time. Might be able to when things settle down a bit more, but there's always another big project looming. Glad you've made some friends...'

'I get on with most of them, well, all of them really...'

'Yes, EO's are like a family. I might have mentioned that to you before.'

My heart felt heavy again; could Faulkener separate me from my friends? If she did remove me from the course until I was more "mature", there was a chance I could lose touch with them.

Dad started to talk about Nana and Gramps, and although I nodded I wasn't really with him. I felt anxious. I wanted to return more than ever, but Faulkener's comments loomed over me like some uncertain shadow. Even the CDS bore little fascination to me now, it was just a vehicle after all.

We arrived home ten minutes quicker than we would have done if Dad had been driving, and that included the road works on the A11. Everyone was home to greet me, their welcome so warm that again I was free of my concerns for a time. It felt good to be back.

## Chapter twenty
### Plans

On Christmas day afternoon I sat quietly beside the phone, anxiously awaiting my news. I had kept my worries to myself. I'd decided that sharing my fears would be unproductive until they were proven true.

Everyone else was chatting in the kitchen. 'Why don't you get a modern heating system Lionel?' Dad asked, referring to Gramps' wood burning stove. 'You shouldn't have to chop wood at your age.'

'Nonsense,' Gramps scolded. 'I like a real flame, and the exercise is good for me.'

Suddenly the phone rang... I picked it up. Heads appeared at the door. 'Hello... yes, this is Dace... OK... yes, thank you... yes you too, Bye.'

'Sounds positive.' Nana pointed out.

'Short.' Gramps noted. 'He's been there all afternoon for that...'

I put the phone down, flopped back on the sofa and yelled, 'I did it!'

'Full gone conclusion.' Dad dismissed, heading off to his study.

'Don't belittle the achievement.' Kerry rebuked, and she ran up to me with the warmest hug.

I'd been planning what I'd say if I'd failed; which seemed the most likely outcome of Faulkener's work. I was going to tell Dad about the report footnote, but it all seemed irrelevant now. I'd passed. That was all that mattered. Even being prickled by Nana's whiskery hairs as she kissed me didn't stem my elation. In a little over a week I would be holding my very own Envisager. I laughed out loud. I'd see my friends again. I'd create real things!

'OK guys,' Dad said, re-joining us. 'I need some time with Dace. EO stuff…'

It seemed that everyone had been forewarned by Dad as to his intentions, and they headed off without any fuss.

'You, me, study.' Dad instructed and we headed to the room.

'Cool!' I said we entered.

'Upgraded.' Dad explained. Gone was the desktop set up, replaced by a wall mounted array of screens similar to those in the Morrello Complex research facilities.

'You will create systems like this one-day son.'

'You *Envisaged* this?'

'Yup.' Dad motioned towards the image on the central pane. 'Tell me what you see Dace.'

On the display was a diagram of a familiar vessel. 'It's one of the Val'ee transports used during the pick up at Hyde Park…'

'That will probably be true.' Dad responded cryptically. I didn't follow, and gave Dad the "what do you mean by that?" stare.

Dad smiled and continued, 'Look again at the underside.'
I looked, same shape, same waveform array…

'Oh!' I said, pointing at the waveforms. 'The Val'ee ships didn't have waveforms, they had conical arrays…'

'Wrong.' Dad teased, I frowned. 'The Val'ee had waveforms too but they were concealed by specially constructed housing.'

'Why hide the power source? We were creating vehicles powered by wave generators before the Val'ee arrived…'

'Wrong again.'

Sensing that there was a great deal more to this I sat on Dad's couch. 'You best make me right then.'

*Cries: The Captive Mind*

'They weren't hiding a potential technological advancement that they feared would be copied; they were hiding the fact that they use our technology.'

I sat silently, eyes flicking between Dad and the image on the screen.

'OK let's start with this ship.' He said pointing at the display. 'You noticed the array. Well, that's the way I designed it...'

'You mean you copied what you saw at Hyde Park.'

Dad smiled, 'Wrong. *I* designed what we saw at Hyde Park.'

'You went all thoughtful and quiet, then recorded footage of the Val'ee ships as they took off...'

Dad seemed to be getting a bit agitated now so I shut up.

I stood up again and placed myself a few feet from the screen. Dad drew my attention to the date on the diagram, it predated the Hyde Park pick up by several months. Then he slid the image to a side screen and started up the footage I'd mentioned. 'Look closely.'

I felt awkward; Dad seemed to expect me to see something, but I was taking so long. I began to feel stupid.

'Try this.' He said reducing the sequence to a short loop showing the second vessel reaching a point directly above us.

'Compare it to the schematics.' He urged.

A moment later I had it. 'The North monogram incorporated into the metalwork. But...how?'

Dad patted me on the head, 'Well done, you had me worried!'

I considered the date 'Did you design these ships for the Val'ee?'

'No, I designed them for the earth. But I did design the ones we saw operating; they will be constructed later this year.'

Now I was lost again.

He laughed, 'They travel time. They're technologically advanced because they've come from the future.'

I accepted Dad's explanation wholesale; what else could explain the fact that an alien creature had come to the earth with technology my Dad had designed but not yet constructed. 'That's pretty scary.' I offered. 'What should we do?'

'We don't need to do anything.' Dad chuckled.

I swung around to look at him. 'But what about Fredrick!'

'I'm sure he's fine. Look, our world was in need, they came from a future time to help. They provided us with a way to overcome The Great Suffering; not to eradicate it of course, but maybe the condition cannot be remedied. Maybe their solution is the only one. They've prevented the extinction of the human race. They've also boosted our technology and provided a device that allows mankind to realise advances that would otherwise be beyond us. You can't begin to imagine the projects that are being planned for the Master EO's, now that the Sky Cities are nearly complete. Great things my boy.'

My father's excitement that I too would be an EO was infectious, and I sat listening to the ventures that would define the immediate future. The "Pathfinder" project that would create a series of factories on the edge of space, for the fabrication of space going vessels. Bases on the moon, Mars and beyond. Closer to home, the great engineering projects that would afford equality and mobility, and prepare Earth to face a future that would include contact with other worlds.

'What will you be involved in Dad?' I asked, expecting him to admit involvement with all the plans.

'I will continue with my work to provide a permanent solution to The Great Suffering…'

'But you said it might not be possible.'

'I must try; my team is diminished but not untenable. With our new technologies, and reduced limitations, a solution may now exist where once it did not. We can't rely on floating cities.' He leaned towards me with a sad expression, 'Some children still arrive before we are ready; we cannot get the mother to a facility and the child is born and dies just as before; it's sad. But we now have an idea of what's going on. The problem *only* occurs in the lower atmosphere - we hadn't realised that before - it might be key to finding a cause.

'Also I've been thinking about the Val'ee, about time and how they use it, and I've been toying with a project I think is possible. I'm going to pursue time, Dace.' He took hold of my shoulders. 'Imagine, if we could go back - *just* to observe you understand - what we could learn?'

His eyes seemed twice their normal size for a moment, but the sound of someone coming from the kitchen brought him back from his imaginings.

'None of this to anyone.' Dad laughed. 'I can't believe I actually told you!'

'What did you tell him?' Kerry asked as she entered with hot chocolate. You're not giving Dace any classified information are you Sweetie?' She looked at the computer screen array, 'Oh, the Val'ee ship files…'

'My ship files!' Dad protested.

'Well I still think you should redesign it, it's all a bit weird that aliens are using ships you haven't made yet.'

'No, this confirms that the design is sound, it must be made, it will be made, we've seen that it will be...'

'He's not boring you is he?' Kerry asked turning back to me and presenting me with one of the hot chocolates.

I shook my head. She rolled her eyes then smiled, 'Well, I suppose the ideas are new to you; we've been listening to them for nearly four months.'

'I'd designed the vessel, that's why it had looked familiar at Hyde Park, but it still took me ages to figure out where I'd seen it before! I'd become so busy with the completion of S. C. Britannia that I'd shelved the vessel's design; the Dragonflies seemed more important. It was only when you went to the EOA that I found a little free time; I was sorting through my projects when I came across the schematic, and the penny dropped.'

'I hope all these revelations aren't going to distract Dace from his studies...' Kerry began.

'Oh, he's through Darling, the rest of the course is a technicality. Besides, I want him to work alongside me. No harm in promoting a little interest in a specific direction.' He smiled and ruffled my hair.

'Well,' Kerry replied, and turned back to me. 'Just don't let your Dad weigh you down' She stroked my cheek and left us alone.

'You will come and work with me, won't you Dace?' Dad asked.

'I guess so; It's all happening so fast...' I toyed with the idea of telling Dad about the profile link, but he seemed so happy, such news would disturb; I didn't want to upset him.

He noticed the distance in my eyes, 'You OK son?'

'It's tough, you know, I'm very young aren't I...'

Dad turned off the computer display, 'I hear you. Kerry's right - one step at a time.' His tone seemed less excited, then he grabbed me up in his arms, 'I'm so proud of you!'

I hugged him back and we jumped and leapt and acted like children for nearly half an hour before remembering our not-so-hot chocolates and settling down.

Dad continued in a more neutral vein, focussing more on the things that had already been achieved. At least two babies had been born on Tinnys. This confirmed that atmospheric pollution was not the cause. The vessel's atmosphere was the same as that at ground level, the altitude - equal to that of the Sky Cities - obviously played a part. Dad felt that a breakthrough was imminent.

Then I remembered something, and I just had to ask…

'Is it possible to Envisage an emotion?' I was thinking of Rue's comment as we sat in the park just over a month before. "Cold stubborn hatred" she'd said, although I didn't share that with Dad.

He looked thoughtful. 'To be honest we're discovering things we can do all the time. It's life we seem not to be able to create. Life is a special thing we've never really understood. We ingrained for so long the unfounded belief that life had come from non-life without intelligence, that we didn't recognise the observable fact that only life begets life; that it isn't an upward progression from simpler stages to more complex ones. All life is complex and the trend is an observable decline at the core of which is information - mind numbing levels of information - totally beyond us. I think we might create life one day though, because I feel that the origin of the Val'ee must be tied both to creation and their appearance from a future time…Oh, but you say emotion… Can an emotion be Envisaged?' He paused again, then started to pace the room. He sighed and turned slowly to face me, perching on the edge of his desk. 'What makes you ask?'

'Rue teased us when we asked about the properties of a material she'd created with the trainer.' I shook my head, 'It's silly…'

'No, it's a valid question, and quite interesting. Rue is a remarkable young woman; Elizabeth rescued her from being fostered into a family that were later arrested on grounds of abuse! Remarkable escape; that intriguing girl would probably have been lost to anything worthwhile if it were not for Elizabeth…hmmm, an emotion. The Envisager creates what we understand. I don't know about an emotion being expressed as a material with physical properties, but if an emotion were understood deeply by an EO then there's no reason, theoretically, that it couldn't be Envisaged; quite what form it would manifest as, I am not sure.' He smiled with the smallest of shrugs.

Nana appeared at the study door, 'Are you feeling peckish?'

'My word,' Dad said, looking at his watch, 'Six fifteen!' We'd both lost track of the time. 'You go on son, I'll follow shortly.'

'I've made those little sausage rolls you like, Dace.'

*Oh yes!* I did like Nana's sausage rolls.

## Chapter twenty-one
## A Phenomenal Mind

The remainder of the Christmas break flew by and I soon found myself - this time with Kerry - in the CDS travelling back to the EOA. We shared the sort of love I felt we might have shared if she was my real Mum, and a curious thought came into my head.

'Do you think you and Dad will have children?'

Kerry smiled. 'I'd love that,' She said, then her expression flashed concern, 'Er, you wouldn't mind, would you?'

I looked out of the window, 'That would be cool.' Our converse fell silent. I turned to look at Kerry, her eyes were full of tears, 'What's up?'

'I, I don't know if we... Sometimes it's hard to connect.' She glanced away quickly as a tear escaped.

'Dad's very busy isn't he?' I offered.

She flashed me a glance and nodded, remaining silent.

'I've talked to Dad before when...'

'Oh! Heavens, no Dace, darling, please, it's fine; if it's meant to happen it will.'

We sat silently for a little longer, it was uncomfortable.

'Your Dad often talks about your Mum. She was very wonderful...'

Her words helped me understand a little more, 'You love Dad a lot don't you?'

'He's the most caring man; and what he's doing... I'm sure he'll break The Great Suffering soon; he's close I can feel it.'

I knew Dad loved Kerry, but his work and the remnant of his love for Mum distanced them. Dad was forty-eight, Kerry was ten years his junior. I feared his reason for remarrying was companionship and that, if he didn't perceive Kerry's distress soon, she might regret her decision to marry him.

'This is your destination.' **The CDS declared as we rolled into the entrance of the facility. We stopped briefly at the barrier to allow a security guard to scan our credentials, then the car found a parking space and we both headed for the reception; parting company with a massive hug.**

'Our secret, what we talked about, right?' Kerry warned.

I pretended my mouth had a zip and zipped it. She kissed me and headed off to the wing where she worked.

'Hey Dace!' It was Quin. 'You seen any of the others yet?'

'No, I've only just arrived.'

We headed to the EOA room with our bulging rucksacks and found Mr. Lock and Elizabeth Verne waiting to greet us. We were the first ones back.

'Just the two of us!' Quin exclaimed, aware that similar numbers had returned after previous Lock tests.

'No, no,' Mr. Lock stated. 'Diminished, but not as drastically as that, Mr. Jennings. Welcome back, please wait in the common room.'

'Isn't Rue back with you?' I asked Verne.

She smiled with a hint of acknowledgement that I'd been informed of a connection not widely known. 'She told me to tell you to keep your mind on your work and not worry about her. She won't be continuing at the EOA.'

I was shocked. She'd scored better than me in three assignments, her focus was razor sharp; how could she possibly have failed?

As if aware of my thoughts Elizabeth chuckled, 'She hasn't failed, but she is special, as you know; she's been assigned to some very important work. I have no doubt you will meet her again Trix.' She laughed a little louder, 'I do like her little nickname for you.'

Quin and I headed to the common room, stunned.

'What could possibly have come up that would make Rue put off getting her own Envisager? That's all she ever talked about!' Quin sighed.

I shrugged; Rue was the one I had most looked forward to seeing again, besides I had questions like: "When were you going to tell us your foster mum was Elizabeth Verne?" and "Be honest now, you were winding us up about the cold stubborn hatred thing, weren't you?"

'Hello lads.' Davey called from the common room door as he entered, 'Wo! Why tha lon' faces?'

'Rue's gone.' Quin stated bluntly.

'Huh?'

'She's been assigned to something somewhere else. She's not coming back to the course.'

Davey plodded heavily across the room and flopped down onto the couch beside us.

'But I were jus' getting' 'er interested!' He protested.

Quin looked at me, then flung a cushion at Davey who ducked it like a much younger man.

'Seriously! She were sofnin' to me, you saw it Quin, before tha Lock test?'

'She kicked you in the shin.' Quin replied.

'Tha's right!'

'She always kicked you in the shin, she messed with your focus all the time, Davey; she called you an old perv.'

'But she didn' kick me as 'ard as usual.'

The room fell silent, then I started chuckling.

'Wha?' Davey snapped.

'When she caught you eavesdropping outside my room…'

We all laughed.

Clare and two of the other material engineering group arrived.

'Hey guys, on top form already? When do we get our light sabres?'

'I think they're in our rooms,' Quin suggested. 'But Lock wants to talk to us all as a group first.'

'No way, I want my light sabre.' Clare disappeared briefly, there were muffled voices outside the common room and Clare returned looking quite frustrated. 'Lock wants to talk to us all first. Room's locked anyway.' She sat down next to Davey.

'An' 'ow are you me darlin'?' He asked.

Clare leapt up. 'Rue's not coming back?' She walked over to Quin and sat next to him. 'Did she fail the test?'

'No, reassigned, but we've got her Data Pack address so we can find out more details…' Quin started typing something into his Data Pack.

Davey looked a bit sheepish.

'What?' Said Clare.

Davey pointed at the space beside him. 'Uncomfortable?'

'It became a little uncomfortable, suddenly, yes.' She flicked her hair from her face, 'I find out that Rue is gone by you calling me *your* Darlin'.'

'I've always called you me darlin'.'

'You always called Rue 'me darlin', besides…' She grabbed Quin and kissed him close to the mouth and obviously off target. 'My Dad is younger than you.'

Quin, absorbed in the message he was writing, had missed the conversation and frowned, 'What have I got to do with your Dad?'

'I was making two points,' Clare flustered, then, seeing another material engineering graduate arriving said, 'Oh I must speak to Keely.' Clare started walking towards her. Three steps away she stopped and turned back to us. 'Rue was a freak, she really juddered me. I'm glad she's gone.' She turned away again and quickly engaged Keely in conversation.

'Tha' was 'arsh.' Davey sighed.

'Yes,' I replied. 'Rue was a little odd sometimes, but she wasn't a freak.'

'No, not that! tha thin' she said about 'er Dad bein' younger.'

Another cushion flew across the room, this time hitting Davey square in the face.

We were indeed diminished; Quin, Davey, Clare, Hans, Matt, Keely, Peter, Richard, Oscar and myself. Ten out of eighteen, just one shy of the returning numbers record, made at AEON last year.

Only Mr. Lock joined us in the common room.

'Congrats everyone…' He announced. 'A few surprises,' He tipped a nod to Oscar who acknowledged him with a knowing grin. 'As you probably ascertained, ya "light sabres"…' He rolled the R incredulously and fixed Clare in a stare that yelled disappointment, '…or shall we more correctly address them as Envisagers? Are in ya rooms. Please familiarise ya'selves with how they feel; they still require initialization so you can't create with 'em yet, and there'll be no unsupervised use anyhows. Once initiated they *will* be stored in room eighteen, which has been converted for secure holding. Ya'll use them only in class…'

'What about placements? Don't we take them with us?' Hans interrupted.

'Placements are observational until the last month of the course, and even then ya'll be accompanied. Until then *ya'll not* leave *this room* with an operational device. They are sought after and ya'll be dealt with *very* severely if you lose one. Am I being clear?'

We all nodded.

'Wilful damage to any tool or intentional harm inflicted to third persons *will* result in expulsion from the EOA.' He looked at each of us in turn, only breaking his stern expression as his eyes met mine, then he stayed fixed on me with a smile. 'Well done, ya at the entrance of a most interesting existence. As of tomorrow we initiate ya Envisagers and ya'll officially be EO's.' He paused to experience the groups excited murmurs, but remained fixed on me. I began to feel uneasy. 'OK guys, ya rooms are now accessible. Get settled in and explore ya kit.' He applauded us, we applauded him and headed for our rooms.

'Quick word Mr. North.' Lock requested. I held back as the others

*Cries: The Captive Mind*

disappeared from the common room. Was there a problem?

Mr. Lock pulled a Data Pack from his brief case and bid me to sit with him at the breakfast counter.

'This is remarkable. I want you to talk me through it...'

I looked at the screen of the computer; playing was footage of my Lock test. I recognised the point it had reached. 'I've removed the flexion bar and I'm stepping back to set it aside and position myself to create the new component...'

'What I'm interested in is coming up...' Mr Lock said, in a sort of corrective tone.

It was the moment when the surroundings became the EOA lecture room, and I suddenly saw - with amazement - what I'd done.

'I looked away...' Why was this hard for me to believe when I'd seen the simulated Davey wink? I remembered it clearly, and yet I'd completed the task.

'Complete distraction, but explain this...' He rewound the footage and pointed at the component that was being created. 'All the time ya looking away, the component is continuing to form into its complete and correct shape! How *did* you do that?'

I was lost for an answer. The rule to stay fixed on your subject was the most drummed-in principle of Envisionment; to perceive other objects was to invite "speculation". It absorbed random factors into the Envisionment and rendered the fashioned object useless for purpose.

'You have a unique talent Dace, look at these readings; part of your mind dealt with the situation happening around you, the other part was "set apart" for the task required.' Lock's explanation matched the observations and he was clearly enthralled by the discovery, 'What you did is revolutionary. No EO currently operative can... well, partition their mind like that. If you can figure out how you did it, you must share with me; it'll transform fieldwork. The potential is...' He trailed off becoming aware, from my body language, that I had no idea how the feat had been achieved. 'Don't try and explain it now, just be aware of it, keep it in mind and feedback to me as you figure anything, yes?'

I nodded. 'But the alarm.' I queried. 'I should have stopped...'

'Forget it Dace, the discovery outweighs the faux pas. Besides, Mrs Faulkener had already selected the distractions of height and structural instability. She admitted to knocking the control panel with her notes during ya test. Ya aware of her opinion regardin' ya placement here ain't you?'

I looked down at the floor.

'Emily has the opinion that children are vulnerable in the adult environment, and that adolescent changes jeopardize earlier learnt patterns of Envisionment. No one can rule out that risk, but you've always presented a maturity of interaction and a discernment beyond ya years; you now present us with capabilities that are truly profound. I'm gonna ask you one question Dace. Do you feel ready to continue?'

'I want to continue.'

'Then that's good enough for me. Go, find ya Envisager.'

I needed no other encouragement and, shaking Mr. Lock's hand, I headed in the direction of my room.

## Chapter twenty-two
### The Fall of the Curtain.

I discovered Davey standing at the door of my room, Envisager already clipped in its holster, his tatty baseball cap pulled down towards his nose and a toothpick between his teeth. I laughed out loud and he looked up tilting back the baseball cap with his finger.

'Howdy Dace.' He struck a pose as if going for a quick draw shoot out.

'You wouldn't shoot an unarmed child would you?' I pleaded in mock horror.

Davey shifted awkwardly in his gunslinger pose, 'I s'pose not, where's yours?' He asked, gesturing to the tool.

'Lock wanted a quick chat; I haven't even seen it yet…' I was close to him now and dealt a quick blow to his shin with my foot.

'Hey!' He yelled.

'You let your guard down Davey. Never let your guard down.'

'We need to settle all this. I'll giv' ya ten minutes to suit up, then you'll meet me out 'ere for a high noon shoot out.'

I looked at my watch. 'But it'll be nine fifty-six.' I protested.

'Nine fifty-six then, 'less yer chick'n?'

I slid my palm across the door lock and started to enter my room.

*Cries: The Captive Mind*

'Alright, ten minutes, but I'm Billy the Kid, OK?'

Davey slid this cap back down and limped away. I chuckled. Davey was Peter Pan; he'd never grown up. Then a thought struck me, he'd just said "we need to settle all this." I'd assumed my score for the last test would have either beaten him or suffered so much from the wiles of Faulkener as to make Davey the clear winner.

We'd agreed, highest score on the Lock test wins. I certainly didn't think we'd have a tied outcome that still needed "settling".

Various notices sat next to my shiny new Envisager, including a results sheet. I felt a desire to free the tool from its holster. My hand hovered over it then dropped down on the notices, my finger running down the scores. 'Oh!' I exclaimed as I saw my own. I'd barely passed. Clearly there'd been much debate over my suitability to continue. Davey's result was also a pass by the finest margin. Had I not suggested an all or nothing final test score I would have won the competition, but now Davey meant to "settle it" with a mock gun fight.

I was about to take up my Envisager when something hit my window. I turned and stepped over to peer out. The dull January light made the courtyard look drear and uninviting, and I could see nothing.

I started to return to the Envisager when I heard scratching at the bottom of the courtyard doorway. Maybe a bird had hit the window and now lay injured at the door. I opened it quickly and looked out. A biting Easterly wind lay into the space, but there was nothing to be seen. I stepped outside, pulling my jacket tightly around me, and started to walk around the curving wall that enclosed the EOA rooms, fearing that the hapless creature might have flapped around it.

There against the far wall was a blackbird, still warm but clearly dead; mystery solved. I returned to my room, perhaps I would bury the bird later when the morning frost had left the soil.

Back in my room my eyes fell again on the Envisager and I stepped purposely towards it.

Thump, Thump, Thump! 'Billy the Kid!' Davey called from the lecture room. 'Come on out, wid yer 'ands up!' Davey was really getting into character; this was great fun!

'Er, you ain't taking me alive, Davey er, Crocket!' I guessed, slinging my holster around my body, Envisager safely coupled.

'It's 'igh noon Billy, are ya a man or a mouse?'

I poked my head out of the room. 'Actually neither, I'm a boy!' The other students had gathered to decide the final showdown, the quickest draw with the Envisager would win!

'Good luck Billy!' Clare shouted.

We took positions at opposite ends of the room, Peter stepped forward, 'We want a good clean duel now, no cheating.' He declared, 'I will count down from three, when I say draw, you'll draw, understood?'

We both nodded, Davey tried to psyche me out with a scary glare but burst into hysterics instead. He was handing me the competition on a plate, I was much faster than him…

'Three, two, one,' Peter hesitated, our hands hovered, wobbled and hovered again…. 'DRAW!'

I drew first, as I'd expected, and - as my eyes focused on the little red light - I could see Davey drop to the floor, he'd clearly accepted defeat and was feigning a hit, but what was the red light for?

'Dace clearly wins!' Quin shouted, 'Davey didn't even get his "gun" out of its holster!'

I wanted to cheer, to celebrate my victory with some sort of dance or wiggle, but something was wrong. I was locked in the drawn pose, the red light flashing as the rubberised grip of the device became fluid and ran around my fingers and down my wrists like blood but without dripping off. My eyes widened in horror. Panic stricken I focused back on the room around me; everything seemed to be moving in slow motion. Davey; propped up against the far wall, clutched at his shoulder, his grey shirt was holed there and a dark stream of red was travelling down to his belly. He flopped onto his side and three of the others sprinted to his aid.

Then there was pain, like I'd never felt before. Starting in my wrists, shooting to my shoulders and across my chest…

*'What happened?'* The words were like a song.

I opened my eyes and struggled with the surroundings.

*'Calm'* The song assured.

The truth came back with a jolt. I was in my home, my lounge, a grown man imprisoned by this creature. I tried to move. I couldn't. Chorda leaned into view.

*'Wow, that really was painful. You passed out. I lost the thread of your thoughts.'*

I stared with hatred at my captor. I could feel her prodding at my tender mind roughly with her device, trying to find some way back into

*Cries: The Captive Mind*

the memory.

'*Aha! This makes sense of something I noticed as I travelled back through your mind...*'

I could see the clock over her shoulder. I wondered why no one had missed me all these years. I could remember being paralysed by Chorda, I could even remember the time. I'd been about to drive to the hospital to see Dad; on hearing the time it would take, and seeing the dashboard clock, I'd decided to walk, discovering the cat... Suddenly I became aware of the date on the mantle clock, it was no different! Only fifteen minutes had elapsed since I'd stepped back into my house, puzzled by the sound of David Ertis.

I could not fathom how my childhood could have been observed by Chorda in so short a time. I felt as though I'd been away for as long as it had taken to live the life.

'*Strange, this is the only way back in; so disjointed...*' Chorda remarked.

There was nothing I could do; my foe was too strong. There was no escape from this, instead my mind abandoned itself to Chorda's entry.

I slumped to the floor convulsing violently.

'Dace! Dace!' It was Clare's voice but all was black. Thoughts of my home and real age dispersed quickly, Chorda's eyes the last to fade, and then all around me was real again bar a deep sense of foreboding.

'No! Oh no!' Clare's voice screamed in horror.

'What's happening?' Quin's voice responded.

'It's, it's going into him!' The reply was a terrified shriek.

I felt someone pulling at the Envisager.

'It won't budge!' A voice yelled. 'Argh!' The tugging stopped abruptly.

'It's as if a bullet's gone clean through.' Said a voice from across the room, 'Put pressure on the wounds.'

My mind seemed to spill. I could feel my hands throbbing.

'What is he making? What is it?'

'It's using him!'

My eyes opened to see the electric lights above me, a figure stood there whilst other forms ran. Screams scratched at my fracturing awareness.

'Stand clear.' Faulkener's voice asserted with authority.

Then silence. Oblivion.

## Chapter twenty-three
### Darkened Sight

Becoming aware of the rhythmic beep of a heart monitor I attempted to open my eyes but couldn't. I attempted to move but couldn't. I panicked and darkness returned.

I repeated that reaction several times before I took hold of myself, before I gathered my senses and just lay there, listening; it didn't stop the loss of awareness but it certainly enabled me to remain aware longer.

After a little while I started to build up a mental picture of my surroundings; although the flow of time seemed fragmented and it was difficult to tell morning from evening, or night from day. My experience of consciousness was like listening to a selection of extracts from an audio book that purposely avoided key parts of the plot. They were mingled with what I realised were dreams - because I could see. A dream that repeated regularly found me standing in the heat of the sun, looking up at great shards of rock in the sky, no, beyond the sky, like tiny irregular moons scattered across the heavens.

Eventually I learnt to block out the constant beep of the monitor, allowing me to hear and sense other things. Voices in my room or outside of it in an echoing corridor, a shadow of movement, a breeze or perhaps breath on my face. Sometimes the warmth of the sun. Sometimes the song of birds. Sometimes the thick silence of night, the scent of spring blossom, freshly cut grass or damp soil after rain. Sometimes the touch of a hand or the sensation of being moved. But the passage of time was irreconcilable.

I remember the first time the footsteps came, several feet, several voices and a squeaky wheel.
'And this is?' A heavily accented voice enquired.
'Mr. North…'
'Ah, yes I have looked forward to seeing you. Dr. Barnes, he tell me about your case. Any changes?'
'Patient remains stable. Muscular atrophy, as expected. Otherwise he is in very good condition. Fluids and nutrition are line fed but bar basic routine care he has no other needs, it's like he's sleeping.'

*Cries: The Captive Mind*

'Hmmmm...'

I felt the intrusion of a bright light into each eye alternately.

'All results we have they suggest the same, but not asleep, awake! He has brain activity that suggests it, he should just be able to open his eyes, return to his life. You *are* a mystery Mr. North. How about the wounds?'

'Tissue damage remains unchanged and is part of the routine care program...'

'Redressing?'

'Twice a day...'

'Alien material?'

'Test samples confirm there is no foreign material. He's one hundred percent Dace North.'

'Interesting...'

I wanted to continue listening, the questions and their answers intrigued me, but they became muffled and distant. The next voice I heard was Dad's.

'...so it's closed until next year, the Envisager is still undergoing tests. They'll destroy it afterwards; they can't risk a repeat of this. The anxiety caused by it being alien technology and the reports of what some of the students saw could escalate if they don't provide some sort of closure. It's bad enough that everyone knows Dace.'

'Oh Douglas. It's like all the hope that arrived with him has truly come to nothing...'

'Darling, it'll be fine. My boy will recover, won't you son?'

I wanted to cry out to him, to hold him; I felt a warmth on my face, Dad's hand, 'I want to recover...'

Silence, and the absence of discernible light, enveloped me. A stillness replaced the bustle of day. I lay for hours contemplating the anxiety Dad had spoken of and the hopelessness that Kerry felt my life had come to, but my thoughts became muddled and I found myself dreaming about a pencil being pushed through a wall of water, it was pulled out again, blackened, writhed in flame and white smoke...

'Oi! Lazy! Wake up!' I felt someone shaking my shoulder. 'I ain't goin' to sit 'ere talkin to meself ev'ry time I come; besides, ya shot me an' yer didn' say sorry!'

'Excuse me Mr. er...'

'Collins, ber you can call me Davey.'

'Er, Davey, I'm not sure you should be…'
'Oh! Ha! It's OK, we talked like this all tha time, at tha EOA ya know, runnin' joke really, friendly rivalry an all tha', s'pose we let it gear outta han' though…'
'Sir?'
'Wha's yer name luv?'
'Nurse Green.'
'Firs' name?'
'We tend not to…'
'Oh, OK, fine…Ya doin' anythin' after werk? Hey! Where ya goin'? Darn it. She weren't bad lookin' Dace, is that why yer stayin' put, Huh! You can wipe tha' smile of yer face… Oh, I wish yer could smile…I'm sorry mate. I shouldn' 'av pressed ya for tha' stupid show dan stunt. I'm an idiot…Dace? Can ya hear me? Can ya do anythin'? Squeeze me 'and?'
I could feel his cold hand holding mine but could do nothing.
'Please fergive me Dace…'
I could feel myself drifting away.

I wasn't prepared for what I returned to.
'…they found some sort of injector in the device, like no other Envisager. Strange that when they switched on the tool the device drew in not out, like it was trying to take something.' Dad's words were fascinating and horrifying in equal measure.
'Do you think he can hear you?'
'I don't know, darling, I just want to keep him in the loop.'
'How much longer is he going to be like this?'
Kerry's words echoed away, I had no idea how long I'd been here and lacked the focus to contemplate it.

A strange, loud whistling broke through the void, I was startled, anxious that I couldn't defend myself…
'Happy Birthday!' Desperately I tried to open my eyes but found nothing except a yellow flickering through my eyelids. Was it a cake with candles? I longed to know but couldn't escape my locked in state.
'I've finished a new RC Stunt plane boy. It's a Pitts Special. I based it on some original schematics by Curtis Pitts. It's yours when you come home.' Gramps voice filled me with excitement but I could recognise the signs that I was slipping away again. Was it excitement that caused the

black outs?

'Your Nana's going to cook that Crispy Chicken you like when you get back to us.'

'I'm going to cook...'

'...we could increase the dose. I am in agreement, but doubt any result would be making it at all worthwhile. I try quickly, a simple test.' I felt a finger repeatedly jabbing me in the ribs. I wanted to cry out but couldn't.

I heard a giggle then an authoritative, female voice, 'What kind of test is that?'

'His father tells me young man is very ticklish. The test, it rules out pretence.'

'You thought he was pretending!?'

'In all reality? No. But very important to try all options.'

There was a brief silence, these doctors and nurses really were at a loss as to what to do for me, and I found myself entertaining the terrible prospect of being like this forever.

'You show me please the wounds...'

I felt discomfort around my right wrist then my left.

'Hmmm nice and clean, I think we pursue grafts again, how does the physiotherapy progress?'

A different voice responded, 'Range of movement is normal, we are using the pulse treatment to prevent further muscle atrophy.'

In my mind I could see three craters in a line, on the edge of shadow, on the surface of the moon, I frowned.

I felt a tightness across my chest, a muffled warmth around my face, I couldn't breathe, I struggled to gasp in some air.

*'What are you doing!'* A startled but quiet and beautiful voice exclaimed. The warmth lifted suddenly, I gasped in air.

*'The opportunity is now!'* Came the response, equally quiet and coldly elegant. This wasn't the ward-round.

*'I will not condone it, he has much to do...'*

*'The record shows that his father achieved much when the young man did not exist. Will his death not derive similar results?'*

*'No! He recovers, we...'*

*'If he recovers he will do what he did before...'*

*'When he recovers he can be channelled, put on track to fulfil a greater*

*task, not the crime. Everything will be restored.'*

*'Look at him. We cannot wait forever. His crime should be punished!'*

*'We won't wait forever; this one has done no crime worthy of your justice. We must stay calm.'*

Stillness filled the room, I was aware of the usual hush of night. I was scared, shaken, and felt a kind of vulnerability that seemed to hover on the point of death itself.

'Trix? Trix?'

I wondered where day had come from but was so pleased to hear Rue's voice.

'Anything?' A male voice asked.

'Something…'

'What?'

'He's terrified.'

'You can tell that?'

'No, Mum told me what happened, what he made; if it were me *I'd* be terrified.'

Made? My clarity vanished.

'Boo!' The sudden outburst filled my being with dread, was this it, was I going to die now?

'Darn it, I fel' sure that'd werk. Bought a friend Dace, DACE!'

'Calm down Davey…' It was David's voice.

'Calm dan? I'm responsible, 'is step mum stares at me wiv' daggers…'

'Chill it Davey, we all know it was faulty kit. It was going to happen the first time he laid hands on it. You probably saved his life…'

'Ya think do yer? Well I don' see it tha' way…'

'Alone in his room no one would have heard him man, probably wouldn't have found him 'til lunch time. Gotta be a worse prognosis, yeah?'

'Well why don' ya tell 'im yer news.'

'Sure,' David moved closer. 'I'm in the band man, Marko's got time for this misdemeanour and the band won't have him back, yeah? Well, my cousin Ricky, he drums, he persuaded them to take me on. I did my first gig last night and Andy, he's top man yeah; he reckons there's no one could've filled Marko's place better than me! Hey, I've got my acoustic, wanna hear The Ungoliant's latest track?'

I wanted to say 'Yes!'

*Cries: The Captive Mind*

'Yeah, well you can't answer yet, I'll just knock it out anyway...'

Clare's voice stirred me, 'Davey said David was here, wish I'd been here too. The EOA reopens at the end of the week, so we'll be shut away from the real world for eight months... Your Dad's offered to keep us up to speed on your progress...' Her tone changed, 'You know, I, I still have nightmares. It's been so long, but I'm haunted every night; I saw you go down. I knew you were in trouble. I thought you were shot too, like Davey. Then I saw what it was doing to you, like it was using you. Mrs Faulkener shut it off and it let go.' I could tell she was tearful. 'I nearly decided not to go back but I was doing well and they've assured us that it was a faulty handset. Dace, I don't know if I'll be alright but I'm going to try, for you.' She stroked the side of my face, '*Do* get well soon.'

I heard the approach of footsteps along the hospital corridor.

'Can I help you?' The voice belonged to a nurse who regularly attended me in the evening. I felt confused by her question then startled by a responding voice.

'No, no er, I was just passing. I hadn't seen him for ages, so I thought I'd drop by.' I didn't recognise the woman's voice.

'Visiting times are posted at reception...' The room fell silent, bar some slight movements that seemed to suggest to me an exchange of glances. Then the nurse spoke again. 'Fine, five minutes.'

A tap of footsteps departed, another tap approached the bed.

'Part of you returned, but it couldn't get away. It was important, you will see. It made something you will need. In time you will understand.'

'But it doesn't make sense, who are you?' I thought.

'It will make sense...'

'You heard me?' I thought again.

'No, I didn't hear you, you told me what you would say.'

A strange pain in my shoulder silenced my non-conversation. My head spun, 'What have you done?' I felt soft lips on my forehead and my visitor departed. I saw the figure of a man, objects protruding from his body, a plate covering his eyes. I recoiled in horror, as did the man who blurred into darkness leaving nothing but my thoughts, troubled but clear.

'...and his responses they have been increasing?'
I felt uncomfortable, my head ached, my heart pounded.

'Yes, and there are signs of healing around his grafts…'

'…Gramps scolded her for forgetting the cream buns and she scolded him for getting back to the house late and making her rush to get out.'
'That's just like Gramps.' I chuckled.
'Yes. *What!* Dace?'
'That's just like…' I repeated, puzzled by the deepness of my voice.
'Nurse! Nurse!'
There was the sound of hurried movement, and approach of footsteps.
'Dace, you're back!' Kerry trilled, clapping her hands.
'I…I am? You can hear me?'
Dad took hold of my hand, 'Yes, yes son, you're back, thank God!'
The voice of a familiar nurse joined the general excitement in the room.
'Welcome back young man, can you open your eyes for me?'
It hadn't occurred to me to do so; I'd been listening so long. Slowly, deliberately I made them open and was met with an undefined, bright blurriness.
'It's all fuzzy.' I attempted to sit up but couldn't. The nurse, noticing my need, barked an instruction to a blue blur beside her that turned out to be another nurse, and between them they eased me up, adjusting the bed for my comfort.

I could make out Dad and Kerry by the way they moved but all their excitement was cut short as a senior nurse entered the room.

'I must ask you to give Mr. North time to come around fully. It will be easy to exhaust him and set back his recovery, he needs to rest.'
'I've been resting!' I protested. 'I want my family… and what's going on with my voice?'
'All in good time, we've got you this far, please trust us with your care. Please people, this way.'
'It'll be OK big guy,' Dad encouraged, popping a light punch into my shoulder. 'We've waited this long, we can wait a little longer.'

Then I was alone again. I looked around the room. It wasn't much different to how I'd imagined, a window to my right, open door leading out into a featureless corridor on my left, the polished floor and trolley table that the cleaners grumbled I shouldn't need. How long I wondered, weeks, perhaps a month or two? I could hear the heavy, even clomp of the doctor's boots. My answers were on their way.

## Chapter twenty-four
## Bedside Manner

'Ah, here I find you sitting up long at last. I am Dr. Rhon, I have been involved very much with your case.' His tone was gentle and I felt at ease. His was the voice I'd heard so many times - although his thick, black moustache made him look quite different to how I'd imagined.

'Hi.' I responded, which must have been a bit of an anti-climax for him. He pulled up a chair and as he did so I asked, 'How long have I been...er...'

He realised I was trying to find a word for the state I'd been in, 'You have been sleeping now for some time, but before we discuss this, you fill me in on certain matters of interest to me, as helps our understanding of your condition, yes?'

I nodded. His almost perfectly round head nodded with me for a moment, then he opened a well-worn Data Pack and pulled a small pair of spectacles from his breast pocket. 'What do you recall from the incident? Please, if too uncomfortable with any questions just say; we come back to it another time, yes?'

'Sure. The incident, yes, er.' I wondered how much was already known.

Dr. Rhon obviously felt that some clarification was required. 'Your friend, Miss Tamiway...'

'Clare.'

'Yes, Clare. She tells me much about the lead up. You like the western cowboy films it seems sure, yes?'

I felt awful; I'd shot Davey, 'I didn't mean to shoot him...'

'No, no, is OK, the tool had been activated, is faulty, your role play results in the creation of a bullet travelling at velocity; boys game, I shoot my best friend in the leg with a crossbow when I was nine. These things they happen.' He leant forwards. 'Tell me, you see your friend fall, in that moment what else?'

'A red light, on the Envisager...'

'Hmmm, not only activated; was initiated. Human error plays a part in this, interesting, continue please.'

'I couldn't let go of it, it seemed to hold me. The hand grip flowed between my fingers and over my hands. It crept under the skin on my wrists...' I looked at my wrists. Only minor pinkish scarring betrayed the presence of healed grafting and I wondered how it had healed so quickly, when it had been reluctant to heal at all. '...Davey was gushing blood. There were shouts... It's, it's so muddled...'

'OK, pause a moment, I tell you about some things. Your friend Davey was here every day - even before he was discharged himself - right up until he has to return to EOA to continue course, three months ago. I have spoken many times with him. He struggled; he blamed himself for long time. He is real friend I think?'

The thought allowed me comfort from recalling the disturbing events. 'There's more...'

'Go on.'

'So much pain; I hadn't thought such pain could be felt without dying. Passing out was a release. When I came to I remember seeing the room, there was lots of movement...'

The doctor interrupted, 'Yes, this is good Dace, now think very hard. Did you see anything unusual in the room?'

I paused and thought. 'The movement was away from something Someone asked "what is it?" or something...' I looked at Dr. Rhon. 'I made something - Rue said it - or the Envisager made something through me. Clare said she thought it was using me...'

'Rue?'

'A girl from the EOA; only she wasn't at the incident, she'd left the course. She'd heard what happened, her mother is Elizabeth Verne...'

'Ah Miss James, I know her well, but if she's not there how you knowing her opinion?'

'I heard her talking to someone here.'

'You recall what people have been saying?' Doctor Rhon looked a little astonished.

'Yes, well, not everything; disjointed bits of things really. Some weird stuff too, and dreams, some voices I didn't recognise.'

'My voice is distinct; you hear perhaps?'

'Yes, several times, you poked me in the ribs!' I started laughing, 'What *is* wrong with my voice?'

'How do you mean?'

'It's like I've got a cold, it's deeper...'

'The voice breaks when you grow up.' He rested back in his chair, 'How old are you Dace North?'

I laughed, 'I remember my birthday, so I'm fourteen.'

'I think you have missed many things young man.'

'Yes.' I agreed, concerned by the tone of his voice; he had been light and full of smiles, now he seemed more distant, thoughtful. 'You can miss a lot in a few months...' I ventured.

'Indeed, and much more in many...' He sighed deeply, the answer to my earlier question was coming.

'How long?' I asked.

He flicked his Data Pack notes back to the first screen, 'Next month will bring your seventeenth birthday.'

Silence filled the room, it seemed to push out all the oxygen, I fought for breath. Inside I had convinced myself that it could have been a year, but this...

'Thr, Three years...Two...two months?'

'Very nearly,' came the calm reply. 'You need someone now I think. I will get most appropriate person. I ask him to stay; I will help you best tomorrow I think.'

I saw Dad at the door. 'Dad!' I cried, with much doubt as to whether this was the right reaction of a person soon to be seventeen but Dad moved quickly to the bedside and wrapped his arms around me, just as a father should, whatever his sons age happened to be.

'Cry son; let it out...'

'I'm sixteen?' I sobbed.

'Yes.'

'I thought it was less time...'

'I know.'

'The times I heard people; *that* would have fitted into weeks. I don't understand how so much time has just... gone!'

'Dr. Rhon told me it was as if you were asleep. Perhaps it was very much like sleep; think... when you succumb to sleep you soon find yourself awake with a new day ahead of you, if it were not for dreams the duration of sleep would seem to be nothing at all. Maybe the times you heard people were times of shallow sleep.' Dad rocked me in his arms. 'There is much to talk about, and things you need to see, but now you need to think only of the fact that you are safe, nothing else matters...'

Dad fell silent and I realised he was crying too; I hugged back, confirming the legacy of such a long period of inactivity.

'I am so weak.'

'Not for long son, not for long.'

## Chapter twenty-five
## Facing Fear

Dad didn't leave me that night, he slept beside my bed on a hospital mattress. I didn't sleep at all. Clare's trembling voice and anxieties, Kerry's worries, Dad's tears; the incident had caused so much trauma and delay, and what had Dad said? "There is much to talk about and things you need to see." A dark fear crept over me. Rue's words played over in my mind, "Mum told me what happened, and what he made; if it were me *I'd* be terrified." Something horrible had come through me during my semi-conscious struggle with the Envisager. I lay there, staring into the dimly lit room with wide eyes.

Over the following week I slipped into depression, my melancholy not lifted by the presence of family, friends and neighbours. The attempts to rehabilitate my wiry muscles were met with protests and uncharacteristic cursing. A sense that the staff now wished I'd never woken up enveloped me.

When Nana and Gramps appeared they seemed much older to me than the three years allowed. Had they aged so much out of worry?

'I don't know which birthday it was...' I began, and noticed their instant attentiveness to my words. 'But you told me you'd make some of your Crispy Chicken when I was ready.'

Nana was silent, gripped with emotion.

'That was your fourteenth. You fancy some of that spicy stuff do you?' Gramps replied.

'Yep, but it'll have to wait a little while yet, I've got to concentrate on getting my strength back so that I can lift a fork, unless you can pipe it through that bag.' I said rolling my eyes towards the nutrient pack suspended beside the bed. 'That's no good though is it! It won't taste the same through my arm. I'll have to put more effort into my physiotherapy.'

Nana smiled, it softened the worry lines, I felt encouraged. 'How about that model plane you made me? Does it fly well?'

Gramps smiled, 'I've no idea, I've not flown it, it's yours; the pleasure for me was in the building - scratch built with balsa and fibreglass - you know, real materials. None of this fancy magic your Dad does with that device...'

A silence fell across the room broken only by a nurse as she walked by, her footfall echoing along the corridor.

'If you haven't flown it how do you know it works? I'll want it to work when...'

'But I made it for you. The maiden flight's yours.'

'I think I'm too poorly to endure the disappointment of a plane that doesn't work.'

'OK boy,' Gramps grunted in mock annoyance, 'When you come home I'll get her airborne for you, but you'll bring her down, how's that?'

'Sounds good. Now all I've got to do is get home...'

Nana discerned the weight of my tone and realised that these otherwise simple tasks were, in my mind, almost beyond me. She stroked my cheek. 'You're a North, you'll get there.'

As they left I felt brighter, even the Physio found me amenable and cooperative.

'About time too.' He pointed out, and I apologised.

It would take another four months to get me up on my feet. I spent a whole month passing out at every attempt to stand; it was like my mind was in total conflict, part wanting to run, part desiring stillness, and although they offered me a wheelchair so that I could get home for my birthday, I declined, and spent a fourth birthday in the hospital. I feared there might be something at home that would point to what I'd made at the EOA. I simply told the doctor that I wanted to be able to walk before I went home.

In some respects, it all worked out well; the nurses waived the visitor hours and my room was filled with familiar well-wishers and cake; which I was now able to share.

My mood lifted greatly and I began to feel a real sensation of vigour returning to my body, in much the same way as I could see spring budding up towards bloom from the window in my room. Spring at home was a wonderful time and I'd resolved to ensure that I'd be there for it. The nodding daffodils and cherry blossom, the fresh grey-pink leaves on the Eucalyptus, the buzz of bumblebees, frogs in the pond and wriggling tadpoles - I paused in my thoughts - I was seventeen with the same sense of wonder as a child; I'd been ahead of my age before, now I... A tinge of blues settled on my heart once again. I was practically a man now but I knew neither myself nor my place. A feeling of inadequacy pricked at my mind. I'd lost my way. It had been taken from me.

'NO!' I exclaimed, surprising myself by the audibility of the statement. I was half unsure that it had come from me. Then I felt from somewhere within, a determination not to let doubt rule me. 'I have to get a grip,' I told myself, 'I have to get home.' I had to face my demons…

Complications - including a little fitting - meant that I didn't get discharged until the last week of May. Only a shortness of stamina betrayed what had gone before and that was not a problem as I travelled home in Kerry's car.

She moaned about Dad's CDS, 'It's always malfunctioning, although he says you just have to speak really clearly. It started taking us to Kelso once instead of Tesco!' She laughed, her eyes seemed full of life and joy.

'Don't get me wrong,' She continued. 'The new stuff has a place but I prefer to drive.'

Kerry's conversation as we travelled was light and refreshing. She seemed much happier than before; she seemed more radiant now than she had been at our first meetings over algebra and Shakespeare. I gazed out of the window at a world that had grown without me. Three years and so much change. New buildings around the hospital. Roads resurfaced by Envisager with newer, sleeker vehicles, not only travelling alongside us but also following the line of the road above. Kerry, perceiving my interest, informed me that these new "Flyers" were following an "intelligent" system that the EO's had inlaid into the road surface. Suddenly I realised that the Sky Cities would be complete, and that the EO's were free to pursue the many projects that Dad had told me about. The world outside the vehicle was the world I'd been training to become a part of, but now it seemed to have overtaken me; I stared blankly out at it, lost once more in my thoughts and fears.

We followed an RC stunt plane up the driveway and were greeted by Gramps who looped the loop and informed me that it handled like a dream, then, semi-reluctantly, he handed over the controls to me.

It was the best model he'd ever made; every detail, every response was perfect and I was thrilled that it belonged to me.

'I love the sound it makes; how did you achieve it? Where are the waveforms?'

Gramps laughed, 'No waveforms. The sound is from a scratch built petrol engine. The figures on the handset give you fuel consumption and speed.'

'Cool!' I loved the old stuff. We flew the plane for an hour with remarkably little fuel being used; Gramps had made a wonderfully efficient engine. He'd also put a smoke canister inside and happily demonstrated it. He seemed very pleased with the plane and informed me that it would make a great companion to the one he was making for himself.

I'd become awfully tired that first day home and, after enjoying Nana's Crispy Chicken, I had retired to bed.
I spent many hours flying the Pitts over the following weeks; I had much spare time on my hands despite regular outpatient appointments for physiotherapy and tests. I also had to attend counselling sessions but I didn't think they helped with anything.
The Physio had created a daily exercise regime that was having noticeable effects on my physique. I was definitely not a little boy anymore, I had broad shoulders, like Dad, that wore my growing muscles well, and, despite not yet being fully recovered, I found I could lift much heavier objects than I ever had before. I could run faster and jump further too. Despite this being fascinating to me for a week or so, I soon became aware that my prowess was quite average for my age!

Dad soon began asking whether I was ready to see what I'd made. I used the excuse of being too tired once too many times, and Dad finally handed me my sun hat and ushered me to the CDS.
'Please state destination.'
'Work please Penny.' Dad said, in a deep voice.
'Please confirm work.'
'Yes.'
'Please instate safety harnesses.'
'Penny?' I questioned.
'What's wrong with Penny? It's a perfectly good name.'
'Er, yeah. Just, why?'
'It seems to work better when you give it a name.' Dad remarked.
'Work better?'
'Yes, you apply a name to the vehicles character profile...'
'Character profile?'
'CDS vehicle upgrade, "Character enhancement". People have been finding CDS travel a little dull; giving a profile makes the vehicle respond to situations vocally, and in character, based on the settings selected. I

wasn't so fussed so I've kept it simple. It's like having a chauffeur rather than a computer.' He laughed, 'You can make it shout at bad drivers if you really want!'

'So, Penny works better with a name?'

'Seems so, I haven't needed to repeat myself since I gave it a name.'

'Her.' I corrected.

'What?' Dad frowned.

'Penny's a girl's name; you gave *her* a name, not 'it'.'

'Well, whatever, I haven't had to repeat my commands since giving *her* a name.'

'No, I think there's a different reason; I think you haven't had to repeat your commands because Penny has trained you to speak more deeply when giving them!'

We laughed. I didn't think I'd do that on the way to this ominous engagement, but then, something within me seemed to be urging assurance, it seemed to say, "There is no harm here, there is no harm." I felt confident, at least, that soon the mystery would be over. I'd understand. Perhaps seeing this thing would unlock what had happened to me that day or remove the fear of the unknown, for no one could tell me what it was.

We arrived at the Morrello complex. The guard welcomed me back and I thanked him, despite feeling a bit guilty that I didn't know *him* at all!

Within moments of letting the CDS head off to find a parking space I had a weird feeling of déjà vu, I shrugged it off - why shouldn't I feel like I'd been here before? I knew exactly where I was heading.

'This is the way to the EOA rooms…'

'Not any more son.' Dad stated. 'The EOA has been recreated in the north wing.'

A second guard, unexpected, and armed, stopped us and checked our ID. Something about his style of beard gave me a flash of memory. A body! I juddered.

'Recreated? Why?' I asked, beginning to feel some of the anxiety that had been supressed, return.

Dad reached for the door that had once been the entrance to the lecture room. He turned to me, 'Recreated because we couldn't… You OK?'

I felt a bit faint, giddy with a mix of trepidation and excitement. I nodded affirmation that I was fine, it was now or never, through this door was…

*Cries: The Captive Mind*

Dad continued, turning the handle, 'Recreated because we couldn't move what you made.'

The door swung open to reveal Mr. Quaid, then I focused beyond him and felt my jaw drop. Behind him was a large black form, smooth and reflective with a pearlescent quality that seemed to alternate dark blues and greens along its surface as you approached.

'Why can't you move it?' I asked.

'We can't move it Master North, er Dace, because its mass exceeds its volume. Really, it is quite a phenomenon, perplexing every attempt we've made...' Quaid's manner was flustered but quite friendly, he had certainly never called me by my first name before and now he stood before me, hand outstretched to shake mine. '...welcome back.' He said.

I shook his hand my eyes returning to the object as if forcibly drawn. I couldn't help but sense some sort of innate knowledge about this strange thing.

'Can you tell us anything about it son?' Dad queried.

I stared at it, attempting to achieve a sort of EO focus, hoping that such a state might provide answers.

'Nothing.' I sighed.

'Then most likely it is an object of alien origin.' Quaid offered.

'I'm not so sure...' Dad replied.

'What do you mean alien origin? Are you saying I've had some sort of alien inside me?'

'No, er not necessarily. The handset was faulty...' Quaid began.

'I don't know. It was initiated; that's what the red light means isn't it.' I said.

'Yes, but it wasn't initiated by us, so it was faulty. I think your handling of the device triggered an automated program, a default operation. The Val'ee probably use them in this way to increase productivity. An operator unable to create at this level is utilised as a conduit for an Envisager derived creation. It has happened once before. Nothing like this...' he acknowledged, stroking the side of the object. '...No, the hapless EO thought he was some sort of genius. Without even trying he'd created a "Loader". He tried to stop but found himself gripped. Turned out another three vessels before assistance arrived.'

Just as Quaid touched the object I couldn't ignore a growing feeling that I knew more about this thing than I could justify.

'None of this answers the question of what it is.' Dad remarked.

'Can *I* touch it?' I asked.

'Of course.' Quaid stepped out of the way.

I lifted my hand, it seemed the right thing to do. 'This is how you open it.' I announced. My hand rested briefly on the side of the object and a motherly voice filled the room.

'System acknowledges Dace, please verify.'

I looked back at Dad and Quaid, they were both motionless.

'I'm… not sure what to do next…' I commented.

'Voice recognition acquired, stand by.'

The object began to hum, lifting clear of the ground as two fans of waveforms appeared opposite each other at what was becoming the rear of a spacious flying craft. The fans seemed to rotate like a ghostly propeller but it was an optical illusion derived from single waveforms being cyclically switched off and on again. Parts of the smooth exterior spun and morphed into positions and shapes that seemed impossible from the original form and two side panels lifted to expose a cockpit and a roomy passenger compartment.

'How did you know how to do that?' Dad questioned.

I shrugged. I felt an intense urge to touch the controls. My mind seemed to shout that this is what I'd been waiting for. I watched as my arm propelled my hand forwards towards them. Glancing ahead of my outstretched fingers the surface of the control bars seemed to ripple in anticipation of my touch. Suddenly, horrified, I leapt away. I could recall the way the surface of the Envisager's handgrips had crept around my hands. I remembered the pain. This hadn't come from me; it was too complex. I found my voice, 'Make it stop!' I shouted.

Quaid moved forward instinctively. Leaning on the vessel he was amazed that it was now light and that he could move it with his bare hands. He steadied the ship and peered inside, his eyes falling on a panel with English writing on it clearly indicating a shutdown control. Quaid looked at me, then Dad, then me again; he was clearly torn. He finally knew what this mystery was; it was an unwrapped toy and he wanted to play with it. Dad moved in beside Quaid, saw the shutdown button and struck it.

'No!' Quaid exclaimed as Dad sailed through the air, victim of some energy discharge intended as a security measure. He hit the wall then the floor where he sat momentarily dazed. The craft morphed back into its original, heavy and grounded form.

I rushed to Dad.

'I'm fine, fine. Wow!' He said allowing us to bring him to his feet.

'I've got to get out of this room.' I insisted, nerves shattered and wanting to put real distance between myself and this thing that knew my name and voice.

Quaid looked distraught.

'Yes, yes, it is time to go.' Dad agreed, he patted Quaid's shoulder, 'It's OK Matthew, you understand? This *is* good, inroads...'

Quaid began to protest then softened, 'Inroads.' He agreed then frowned, 'Are you going to be alright Douglas?'

'Bruises I think,' Dad assured. 'I have a good nurse at home, I'll be fine.' He drew Quaid's attention to me. I was staring at the object, wide eyed and hyperventilating.

'My goodness!' He exclaimed and helped Dad get me outside. Already the distance was having a positive effect, as Dad's CDS hurtled towards home I began to feel better.

## Chapter twenty-six
### Rollercoaster

Dad had a broken rib and bruising. It could have been much worse, but his mind seemed not to dwell on such consequences. Dad's concern seemed wholly focused on me. I had been reluctant to see my creation, I'd become briefly fascinated by it, and now I was terrified by its recognition of me and its complexity.

I was partially with Quaid regarding the vessel being a default creation, but Dad felt differently. His arguments were persuasive. I had felt a strength of knowledge regarding the functions of the craft, I had not been surprised by the "unfolding" of the ship, and I'd recognised the controls. Dad's point was that the EO, who'd made the Loaders accidentally, had no knowledge of their inner workings or external materials.

Next he pointed out that the Loaders created had been shown to possess waveforms beneath conical housings. Dad believed that the Val'ee used these coverings to hide the original earth origin of many of their flying vehicles. A fact he considered proven by the transports used at Hyde Park.

'How does that prove I made the ship at the Morrello complex?' I asked.

'The Val'ee set up Envisager included the waveform housings. Your vessel had beautiful and fully exposed waveform arrays.'

I still struggled with the complexity. The vehicle was incredibly advanced - like nothing we had seen the Val'ee using - and like the EO who had made the Loaders, I had no idea what the external materials of the Black Ship were.

'What next?' Dad asked as we sat that evening.
'Next?'
'With the vessel?' He clarified.
'I don't want to go near it...'
'We could do with it open and weightless again...'
'Count me out!'
'But you seem to be the only one it responds to.'
I remained silent.
'Dace, it's important...'
'Dad, there was a pull inside me to get in, like I was being controlled. The control bars seemed to move to meet me. Did they get it all out of me whilst I "slept"? It crept under my skin; something alien from the Envisager. Did they get it all out?'

'They found nothing foreign in you, son. Dr. Rhon told me you are one hundred percent you.'

'Part of me wanted to touch those controls but the greater part remembers the Envisager holding me, the pain; I couldn't let go, it used me.'

'I was told that Mrs Faulkener turned off the Envisager; it didn't discard you...' Dad suggested. '...it was taken away! It might have been the wrong thing to do. Leaving it to complete its full operation may have resulted in your immediate recovery and understanding.'

It all seemed the wrong way around to me, creation then understanding?

Dad continued. 'Elizabeth asked me if you'd return next year; continue with the course from the point at which you left...'

I was silent.

'You wouldn't have to repeat anything; you'll make a fine EO for sure;

we need EO's of your level.'

My level? I shook my head. Dad wasn't going to take my bewilderment at the ships complexity as a proof that I hadn't created it; his insistence left me doubting my own conclusions, but I did know I'd not be touching an Envisager again.

'There's plenty of time, three months until the new intake then a further three before they reach the stage you reached... Oh...' Dad finally perceived my intentions. I had not stopped shaking my head. 'Look,' he began somewhat sternly, 'I understand you've had a hard time; we have too! It felt like *ten* years to us...' His voice trailed off, the whole experience seemed almost as much as he'd been able to bear. Since the loss of Mum, it had been one thing after another. A rollercoaster of highs and lows. Now my refusal to take the path *he* would have liked me to take, had brought to an end a dearly held plan; the both of us working together as EO's.

Dad was accustomed to control, to leadership, to say "do this" and see it done; but this was different; his "what next?" was dependant on my cooperation. He couldn't do anything with the Black Ship without me. Loving me dearly as a son, he would not press me against my will, and it was the same for training as an Envisager Operator, it just wasn't happening. I needed time to heal. I needed care and support, not pushing.

'I'm sorry.'

'Don't apologise Dad, I know you want the best for me, I just don't know "next" yet.'

Six weeks brought August - the end of the EOA course cycle - and the arrival of four unexpected visitors. Well, unexpected to me anyway.

Kerry had been busy in the kitchen all morning, which was strange even in the absence of Nana, who was looking after her brother in Felixstowe.

I was with Gramps on the embankment above the meadow, flying the Pitts. I turned my head to find Davey standing behind us beneath the deck on the Eucalyptus.

'Davey!' I yelled with a voice that smiled. I handed the remote control to Gramps and made my way quickly to the top of the bank.

'Well, ya taller tha's fer sure.' Davey remarked, looking up at me and taking my offered hand, shaking it firmly before pulling me into a hefty, shoulder slapping hug. 'Yer not goin' to worry us like tha again are ya?'

Keely and Peter emerged from behind Davey's bear-like outline.

'Hey!' I greeted.

'Lord you've grown!' Keely exclaimed. 'I mean we knew you would have; you were the right age to put on a spurt but look at you…' I was a good six feet tall, plenty to clear Keely's five two. I moved in and gave her a swaying hug.

'Strong too!' She affirmed, 'I'm so glad you've recovered.'

'Nearly recovered.' I added.

Peter rested a steady hand on my shoulder, 'The struggle's still inside, huh?'

I nodded but was jogged from dwelling on the thought by a familiar squawk of a laugh and Quin emerging from the shrub border path that led to the house.

'Look at you!' He said gesturing at my height. A few mock punches later he also alluded to my physical recovery.

'Is everyone coming?' I asked beaming.

The group fell silent; it was a strangely tense moment.

'This is us,' said Keely eventually. 'The remnants of our class.'

'But Clare…?' My enquiry was met with silence and sideways glances. 'Hans? Richard? Matt? er Oscar?'

I'd kind of thought that Oscar would drop out sooner or later. His father had launched the "International Anti-Alien Movement" the Christmas I'd awaited my test results. It was pronounced "I am" instead of I.A.A.M., and was why Mr. Lock had been surprised to see Oscar's return. Arnold Jayes, his father, had felt that the presence of the Val'ee and their technology was stripping the "spirit" of man from humanity; that the Sky Cities were a mark or seal on the earth that conveyed Val'ee ownership to other ET's. He felt that anything created with alien technology was tainted and seriously harmed planetary security. Everything IAAM used was traditionally fabricated, and he purposely removed MIT chips from his followers.

'IAAM's grown cos' you went into hospital.' Peter sighed.

I'd been aware of the organisations growth from news stories but this was the first time I'd heard of its growth in association with my hospitalisation. Was that why Verne wanted me to go back? To stem the flow of converts to IAAM? Peter continued. 'Oscar returned with the rest of us when the EOA reopened, but he'd changed. He'd always insisted that he was independent of his old man, you remember?'

I nodded.

'Well, he wasn't so independent when he came back; he was an ambassador for IAAM. He saw that Clare was shaken straight away. She'd confided in Hans and Richard who expressed similar difficulties. Hans had tried to pull the Envisager off you and burnt his hands. Within a month all four left, no word, no leave. Crippled their Envisagers and walked.'

'And Matt?' I asked.

'Ee sends 'is regards.' Davey smiled, 'Lucky blighter's landed a contract fer leisure development in tha Maldives!'

'Nice.' I acknowledged, and we all stood silently again, this time contemplating Matt's good fortune.

'Lucky blighter!' Keely repeated.

'Guys!' A voice shouted from the house. 'Lunch is ready!'

We waited for Gramps to land the Pitts and join us, then wandered up the garden together.

The lawn was dotted with picnic blankets festooned with tasty treats. Kerry had produced a wonderful picnic and was now a striking hostess with a tray of drinks. 'Make yourselves at home.' She urged and we all helped ourselves and settled down to a truly enjoyable summer afternoon. Gramps even found himself being admired for his model making.

It was only when our visitors were due to leave that I found out the main reason for their time with us. They'd been with Dad whilst I'd been flying the Pitts. Their parting comments to Dad were full of gratitude for opportunities, his replies full of direction and technical specifics.

'They're *all* coming to work for you?' I asked as the front door clunked shut.

'Yes,' Dad replied, almost indifferently. Then, perceiving perhaps a little disappointment in my tone, clarified his decision. 'I need all of them to replace you, the project's been on hold too long, there's some catching up to do. Your friends are perfect, I got to know them at your bedside...'

We stood for a moment, Dad trying to gauge the level of my disappointment. My feelings were actually somewhat different, more like relief, but he pressed further.

'The EO route is still an option...'

I stopped him abruptly with a short shake of my head, 'I know what I want to do Dad.'

He gave me his full attention.

'I want to fly. I want to be a pilot.'

'That's a good decision son.' He accepted. 'You'll take to it like a natural. I don't really think it'll stretch you though.'

'The lack of stretch is not an issue.'

Dad nodded thoughtfully, 'I'll have a word with Commander Reece at Jaro airfield if you like. See if he'll pull some strings and get you fast tracked into the training facilities there.'

I smiled, 'Thanks Dad. Oh, Davey and the others... great choice.' I patted him on the shoulder and headed upstairs to my room.

Ten minutes later there was a knock on my door; it was Kerry.

'Hi!' She ventured as the door eased open.

'Come on in Kerry.' She found me perched on the window sill of the bay window looking out over the driveway to the street and playing fields beyond.

'You OK?' She asked.

I looked at her. I had a lump in my throat. The plan to work with Dad - for so long the goal that I had been aiming for too - had been removed forever, by so few words. My own words. 'Would *you* have gone back?' I asked.

'Back to the EOA? No, not if I'd been through the same as you. I don't think anyone could.' She crossed the room and put an arm around my waist, gazing out at the horizon with me.

'Keely thought you were my son. Said she could see the family likeness now you'd grown.'

'You put her right?'

'No. I said you were the best son any mother could have and that I was proud of you.'

'Really?'

'Yes, you are officially mine. I claim you.'

I burst into tears. I just couldn't help it. Kerry was the closest to a mother I'd ever had, even her reaction to my crying; she simply held me and stroked my back whispering that it was fine.

Suddenly she held me at arm's length and I found myself transfixed by the joyous glow of her eyes.

'Listen, this is all hush hush so you'd better keep...' She pressed a finger to my lips to indicate my silence, 'but your Dad has made an important discovery regarding the Great Suffering. It's caused by a reaction between waveforms and soil, where generators aren't clear of the ground; the D-Series is a good example.'

*Cries: The Captive Mind*

I nodded.

'He's not going public with this though because it doesn't affect many people anymore, just those that don't reach a Sky City in time. Thing is they've shut down all sources of the cause, but it seems to be self-perpetuating in the environment, bouncing around like some sort of signal or something. Thing is it can't penetrate the stratosphere; that's why children were safely delivered on the Val'ee mothership and now on the Sky Cities. It wasn't pollution at all, just as your father said. He's been working on a device that cancels the signal; an absorber he calls it. Your friends will be working on a network of these devices to speed up the eradication of the problem. In a few months, children will be born on Earth again without the fear of loss. Isn't that wonderful?'

'He's not going public? He should, he'll be a hero!' I exclaimed.

'I agree, but... Oh, Dace. I shouldn't have told you. You *must* keep this knowledge to yourself. Your father seeks to counter the growth of Jayes' IAAM. It was your father's statement that the Great Suffering continued despite the Val'ee intervention that triggered Jayes' to consider launching his Anti Alien Movement. By allowing the belief that his statement was wrong, your father will effectively bankrupt Jayes' main argument for the existence of IAAM.'

Kerry could still see my disbelief that such a breakthrough was being covered up for the sake of the Val'ee.

'Dad really thinks the Val'ee are worth protecting? They lied about the Great Suffering, they created false hope...'

'Your Father knows that very well, but Arnold Jayes' organisation grows daily. He jumped quickly on the horror of your hospitalisation. You know some of your friends enlisted. It's important that we stem the intolerance Jayes is driving forward, or earth will face other races with disproportionate suspicion or even violence.'

I looked at Kerry at a loss regarding what to do with this new knowledge. Dad was quite something to drop his claim to acknowledgement for bringing the Great Suffering to an end, just to promote the cause of creatures he had originally despised. Was IAAM so bad? Were Clare, Hans, Richard and Oscar so wrong for joining it? Kerry seemed to sense my confusion.

'Dace, Jayes' IAAM is strongly militant. It is against what is inevitably coming. They accepted your fathers point regarding the persistence of the Great Suffering but they offered none of their resources to help address it.' She seemed to stare into me for a brief moment, then her eyes softened and again she looked as radiant as she did when she drove me home from the hospital.

'Isn't it good that Children will be born on the earth again Dace?'

'You're pregnant!' I heard myself say.

Kerry's eyes widened as if some secret - diligently guarded - had been exposed. She pinned a finger to her lips, 'Shh! Your grandparents don't know yet.'

All other thoughts were swept clean from my mind, 'I'm so happy for you.'

'Your Dad was so pleased when you pulled through. I think he saw how much I loved you and he asked me how I felt about…' She beamed and clapped her hands. 'It took a few months to conceive, but we did; I'm so happy!'

'When is it due?'

'I'm ten weeks in, so the babe is due in March! Wouldn't it be strange if you shared the same birthday?'

'I'm really happy for you, er, Mum.'

She hugged me tightly, then the alarm on the cooker downstairs started to beep. 'Dinner ready in ten minutes.' She trilled and headed for the door. 'Oh,' She said, stopping and looking back, 'Don't tell Gramps; we want Nana home so we can tell them together.' She smiled and disappeared through the doorway.

## Chapter twenty-seven
## Jaro

Two weeks later I was standing on the tarmac at Jaro airfield. Dad was working at the Sylvestris complex in Thetford Forest. On record he was ensuring the smooth running of the Val'ee technology that "cleansed" our air. Off the record he was replacing the filter rods with his absorber technology. He'd sent his CDS to pick me up, deliver me to Jaro, and take me home again afterwards.

Jaro was, first and foremost, a military base; it trained combat pilots. Those who didn't achieve a military standard were channelled into civilian flying. There were only two reasons to keep the military running; the Eastern coalition, who had assisted with the combating of the Great Suffering initially, but which withdrew when the Val'ee left - maintaining a considerable capacity for war - and, of course, the need to be ready to defend the earth against forces with darker intents than the Val'ee.

'Mr. North I presume.' My enquirer was a head taller than me but built in proportion. His uniform was pristine and his tone full of justified authority. He offered me a welcoming hand shake which I took, with instant regret. I attempted to offer some kind of squeeze back - so as not to appear totally feeble - and received a dismissive snort of good humoured superiority.

'Thanks for seeing me so soon.' I said through gritted teeth.

'I don't procrastinate Mr. North, and when you address me you will call me Sir.'

I felt like laughing, at least it felt like laughter bubbling up and I fought to keep it suppressed. There was a strange sense of having known this man for ages, of knowing his sense of humour and… I pulled my thoughts in line, this was the first time I'd ever met him. It was so similar to my feelings about Elizabeth Verne that I felt a little unsettled. I looked at him, his demeanour didn't seem to suggest any humour at all, in fact he seemed to be waiting for a response.

'Oh, er yes Sir.' I flustered.

'Your father tells me you want to train as a pilot?' He started to walk up the runway towards a row of Hangars, and I followed behind.

'Yes Sir, well I felt this urge inside…' I paused, I felt foolish. Much of my decision to fly didn't seem to have come from me at all; although I couldn't ignore the fact that the prospect of it appealed to me immensely.

The desire seemed tied to the urges I'd felt as I stood looking into the cockpit of the Black Ship. Then it felt as if I could hop in and fly away, now I felt I was here on a whim. I was unsure if this man knew about the craft at the old EOA facility, or whether I could tell him about it. Realising I should finish my sentence so as not to appear dense I found myself trailing off with an uninspiring 'I thought I'd like it.'

Commander Reece stopped in his tracks and I nearly stumbled into him. He turned on his heel, 'You *thought* you'd *like* it?'

Inconceivably I realised I wanted to laugh again. I bit my lip and looked up at him with all the inadequacy his retort had actually invoked.

'I do hope, Mr. North, that you aren't wasting my time.'

'No Sir! I *really* want this Sir, er, inside…. Sir! I don't know what you know. What I'm allowed to tell you…'

With a broad, intriguing and unfathomable smile Commander Reece turned back towards the Hangars and continued walking. 'This way.' He ordered and I quickened my pace to keep up. The Commander opened a door on the side of the nearest hanger and ushered me inside. It was clearly his office. A handful of family photos graced a neat silver frame on his uncluttered desk. A number of certificates had been mounted on the wall with pin sharp straightness; to cut the observation short the room was immaculate. Closing the door, he gestured to a seat. I sat down on the offered chair then noticed a model.

'That's the next generation Mr. North,' He announced in a more familiar tone, 'An adaptable vessel capable of flight within an atmosphere and without. Please take a closer look. The model was envisaged by your father…'

As I approached, The Commander used a remote device to switch on the model's tiny replica wave generator, displaying the waveforms that the full scale ship would possess. They were fan shaped arrays; such a craft would possess considerable power.

'Time I set you at ease Dace.'

His use of my first name took my attention clean off the model. 'Sir?'

'There's not a lot I don't know already. Your interest in flying has come from your interaction with the vessel you created at the EOA…'

I moved to speak thinking he was ignorant of Quaid's theory regarding automated Envisager operations, but he raised his hand to silence me.

'Whether you made it, or *it* was made through you, you demonstrated to your father an elementary knowledge of its functionality, and before succumbing to your fears, seemed ready to step into the cockpit.'

I failed to see how any of this conversation could be for the purpose of "setting me at ease", then realised that he was simply indicating that he already knew what I'd been cautious of sharing and that he probably knew much more. I gestured that he continue.

'Now, I don't pretend to understand Envisagers, son, but I do understand how an event as traumatic as you experienced can affect a man. Thing is, the Black Ship is highly sophisticated, morphing from that physics defying mass I've seen to the weightless wonder your father described to me. I'd like to see that one day...'

'I can't go near it...' I burst out.

He slapped the table hard. I'd spoken before he was ready but he sighed and, regaining calm, continued.

'One day, Dace, you *will* be ready; I ask simply that you include me in your plans regarding it, 'cos, try as they might, they ain't getting in it without you.'

The truth of this fact finally hit home; the vessel was responsive *only* to me. It had even rejected my father.

'Dace...' I looked up from my thoughts. '...we will be teaching you to fly for a couple of reasons: Firstly, your father and I go back a long way. I was there when he married the woman we both admired at school.' He leant forward, 'I'll be completely open with you, son, I shed tears the day I heard she'd lost her fight, but you, you were a glimmer of hope. I don't leave Jaro - it's my home - but I've watched you grow lad...'

This was all news to me; I thought Dad knew Commander Reece through his Government position; now I understood that they'd been childhood companions and that he'd known my Mum.

'...so you'll fly because you're family, in all but the blood sense. Secondly you will fly because our advisors recommend it, you will be enrolled in the Autumn intake to best suit their plans and schedule. They hold the bigger picture and you will be put in that picture when the time comes. Still want to fly?'

I did, I couldn't change that, but flying in order to meet plans and schedules, that didn't sit comfortably. 'Yes Sir.' I heard myself say.

'Good, in that case the first thing I need to tell you is that your father needs your help. You will be on the military pilot training program, but you are not here for that alone. Your father felt you'd handle a little extra work. Your role will be assistive to his EO team here at Jaro.'

'The military program Sir?'

'You have a problem with that son?'

I actually didn't. I shook my head. I knew it would mean opportunities for involvement in the forthcoming space program that Dad's model symbolized. It was just the fact that places on the military program were hard won.

'Military students don't ask questions son. Your "extra-curricular" work will be classified.'

'I understand Sir.' and I did, but it all seemed so contrived. I had always wanted to work with Dad but I felt manipulated.

'Dace, your potential is greater than pilot. A handful of folks recognise that. Pilot training is a cover. Your input in the future *is* required.'

A flush of pride spread through me; recognised for potential, it almost seduced me but I was here to learn to fly; whatever else came my way was secondary to me. I merely smiled at the Commander who returned a satisfied nod.

'Alright, on the airfield you call me Sir, beyond this door you can call me Taz.' He clicked a concealed button and a wall slid into the floor to reveal an entrance to the hangar. 'Your flying tuition begins in November, but there's no reason why you shouldn't meet your fathers team; they are expecting you.' The Commander was already on his feet and heading for the hangar.

All this was so unexpected and despite the predetermined element of it, which deeply bugged me, I was still drawn in by what could only be described as the excitement of a child.

Stepping into the cool and brightly lit space I could see a small group of people working on a full sized version of Dad's model. I was dumb with awe. Commander Reece waited for our presence to become known to prevent distractions and all faces gradually turned in my direction. One I knew already. She dismounted the ladder that she was on and headed towards us, holstering her Envisager inside her jacket.

'Welcome Dace.' She greeted, holding out her hands. 'Just look at you! We're so pleased you'll be joining us. Hope was very anxious for you when we heard of the incident you experienced; now I'll be able to tell her what a fine young man you've become since she last saw you.'

'Dr. Emmerson.' I acknowledged.

She laughed, 'Call me Patricia.' She ushered me further into the hangar. 'Let me introduce the others.' All had left what they were doing.

'This is Dr. Stanway.'

'Ya can call me Vince.' His handshake was somewhat gentler than the Commander's, which was surprising as he was a bear of a man.

'That's an American accent.' I commented - quickly feeling stupid for stating such an obvious fact.

'It's better than that, it's Texan.' He replied.

'Dr. Brennan Lyn.' Patricia indicated, and a man, as small as Vince was large, appeared.

'Pleasure's mine.' the diminutive man added.

'This is Heather Travers.' Patricia carried on, 'She'd say she was just your father's secretary but she's the classic "more than". If there's anything you need…'

'I make an excellent cup of tea,' Heather announced as she shook my hand assertively, bobbed white hair bouncing indeterminately around her glasses.

'Tyler.' A voice grated, followed by a hand, followed by a face that had me catch my breath, for though it was fully healed it had once been harshly burnt.

'Really Tyler, you have no patience, I was getting to you.'

Having shaken my hand Tyler was already returning to his work.

'Don't mind him,' Heather assured me. 'He's been waiting to perform some fine wiring work. Now he's met you nothing else will disturb his focus… it's a compliment really!'

I found my eye drawn to the pale pink scaring around my wrists and wondered if Tyler had endured similar misfortune; if so he certainly had no problem returning to Envisionment.

'This is my husband.' Patricia said.

'Lawrence to you, Dace.' He nodded, patting me on the shoulder in much the same way as my Dad often did.

Lawrence was shorter and slimmer than his wife, with sharp, bright eyes and a pointy face and I couldn't help but think what an odd couple they made. I certainly wouldn't have matched them up in a room full of couples.

'What do you do Lawrence?' I asked, intrigued by his distinctly different outfit and lack of Envisager.

'Test Pilot.'

'Wow!'

'Where's Matt?' Patricia asked and returned to the vessel. Moments later another familiar face with its close cropped, curly, ginger hair appeared from inside the craft.

'I thought you were in the Maldives!' I exclaimed.

'Cover story! This is far more interesting and far less likely to give me sunburn! So glad you're better.'

'And that's us, including Taz, your father and yourself.' Patricia rounded up.

'What about, Davey, Quin, Keely and Peter?'

'Your father has a secondary project at Sylvestris; I expect the people you mention are involved there.' That made sense to me; small teams. You didn't need many for Envisaged projects and it made sense regarding work that was classified. 'Your father doesn't involve us in his work there and I doubt whether the people you mentioned know we exist. I'm sure you understand.'

I nodded, 'You can trust me.'

'That's good, well… nice to see you again. Your Dad will brief you on the project. Your flight tuition starts in November so we'll see you then.'

'Am I not starting here in the hangar before then?'

'No, you're learning to fly, you have no reason to be here on site until then.' Patricia grinned and returned to her work on the vessel.

The Commander saw me out of the hangar via his office, and we were soon back with the CDS; a flight of North Dragonflies flew by in formation.

'Ah! It's a beautiful sight.' Taz observed.

'Yes Sir!' I agreed loudly.

He looked at me, smiled, nodded and opened the door for me.

'See you in three months Mr. North.'

'Three months Sir!' I agreed, and stepped inside, the door following close behind me.

'Penny, complete programmed route.'

'Acknowledged. Please instate safety harness to initiate.'

**I headed home with much to think about.**

## Chapter twenty-eight
### Overseers

Many things from my "sleep" after the incident, continued to trouble me. Things that were said, voices I did not recognise and, perhaps worse, the voices that I felt had the melodic, lyrical tones of the Val'ee. I shouldn't have heard *them* at all.

Their conversation played over and again in my mind, one urging for my death as punishment for a crime, the other insisting on restraint and subsequent guidance. Was I being smothered?

I thought back to Dad's discovery, *his* transport design being used, even though he had not yet taken the vehicle to the prototype phase. "They are time travellers" he had said. It chilled me every time it came to mind.

I had received no guidance, as one voice had suggested, and so could only conclude that I was headed towards some mysterious crime. Where was this Val'ee who desired to guide me? It was six months since I "awoke", and I had no idea when they had visited me; how could they have?

I had kept the whole event to myself until one night.

'What's wrong?'

'What? Dad? Er, nothing, I was asleep…'

'Were you dreaming? You were shouting out.'

I had been dreaming; I was being smothered again but now it felt blurred and indistinct, not like the actual event.

'I didn't tell the counsellor everything I heard when I was in hospital.' I admitted.

'Go on.' He encouraged, sitting beside me on the bed.

'It's just, it seemed such a crazy thing…' A thought struck me, maybe the Val'ee *had* returned whilst I was in hospital. I'd only assumed they hadn't because I hadn't seen one. Perhaps they'd even returned our people and left again? Not that this helped my anxieties about the "crime".

'Son?' Dad urged, wondering if I was asleep again.

'Are the Val'ee back?' I asked.

'What?'

'The Val'ee, did they come back, did I miss their return?'

Dad's frown was discernible even in the dim light that was being shed into my room from the landing.

'No Dace, they haven't. Why do you ask?'

I felt stupid.

Dad continued, 'Did you hear someone in the hospital saying they'd returned?'

'No. It's just… some of the voices were like Val'ee voices, song-like. What they said and did disturbed me; I didn't understand much of it but one seemed to be judging me and the other defending…'

Dad's head sank. It could all have been a vivid dream after all and here I was, seventeen and letting child-like terrors engulf me… 'Perhaps it was a dream son, you said you couldn't remember dreaming but perhaps some of the conversations you heard *were* dreams.'

'I'm beginning to come to that conclusion myself. I'm sorry I woke you.'

Dad stood up. 'No, it's fine, we, er, can't help what we dream about. Let's try and get back to sleep.' He ruffled my hair in his usual manner, turned and headed for the door.

Of course it was a dream, it made sense of the facts. 'Thanks Dad, I love you.'

Dad stopped. It was as if he were slowly deflating, his shoulders sank and his head lolled forwards, then he turned back and returned to his seated position on my bed.

'The Val'ee didn't need to return for you to hear them.'

'What do you mean Dad?'

He sighed, 'Some of them never left.'

I sat up, 'Then they could have visited me…'

'They did. They told me.' The room fell silent except for the light flutter of a large moth at the window, attracted by the soft light. 'They want to see you when *I* think you're ready.'

'Why didn't you say before?'

'I guess I thought I was protecting you. You seemed so happy to be home. You and Kerry seem closer than ever. You're living again. I didn't want that to stop. I didn't know you were aware of them. I'm sorry, Dace. It must have been worrying you to make you cry out in your sleep like that.'

'How come they didn't leave with the others?' A disquiet was building within.

'They're ambassadors. They appeared to a select few after the silence generated by the ERUWAI had ended; Government leaders, people in positions of authority. They are working in a far more secretive way than before. You seem important to them. They are Overseer class, you know, the cerise eyes?'

'Do you still think they come from the future?'

'I don't doubt it, they have forewarned of events that we couldn't have foreseen, enabling us to prepare and deploy relevant response teams...'

'They said I'd committed a crime. Do you think they wanted to wait for me to be "awake" before they put me on trial?'

'No. They say they want to give you guidance, a more positive intention don't you think?'

'You don't trust them, do you?' Where that question had come from I didn't know, but it seemed to make sense. Dad had never really trusted them; now he seemed to be involved with a group of them that required complete secrecy.

'Well, I have difficulty...'

As he spoke I crossed the room to my window. 'But you'll be letting them take credit for the end of the Great Suffering...'

'You know about the absorbers?'

I'd just dropped Kerry right in it but my eyes were fixed on the moth hitting its head repeatedly on the glass, bang, bang, bang, and I felt angry. 'Why all the secrets?' I exclaimed.

'My work is classified, you know that. Kerry was wrong to tell you...'

I struck the windowsill hard with my fist. It hurt but I stopped myself from crying out, I wanted to sound strong! 'KERRY WAS RIGHT... to let me adore my father!! I've told no one else. Just as she insisted. We are family. I *will* be working with you soon. I need to be in the loop; or if you *still* don't think so I want to hear a really good reason why not!'

We stared at each other for a moment; he looked angry but compromised. That was enough for me. I turned back to the window.

Dad sighed a heavy sigh, 'They've told us that if IAAM grows unchecked a coming war will destroy the earth. Their motivation is to save humanity from that end, in the same way that their provision - however much it distracted us from the real cause - has enabled new-borns to survive. Giving them credit for eradicating the cause of the Great Suffering has the potential to reverse Jayes' advance, and protect the future.'

The words struck home. I remembered the newspaper article Gramps had shown me on the deck outside, "I want a future for my son, one where he'll find love and have children of his own, and have purpose..." Dad hadn't changed in his opinions or principles one little bit in all this time.

He was responding to the story as it unfolded to ultimately achieve the goal he'd always sought. He hadn't trusted the Val'ee, but their intervention had provided relief. Now the threat was some future spectre; *they* would guide us away from it - future secured. Dad didn't have to trust *them* to see that IAAM was a troubling development, and I knew him well enough to know that he'd not be easily led if he had any doubts.

I turned back to Dad, rubbing my hand. 'I see what you're doing Dad. I get it. I'll do anything you say.'

'There's much I can't ask you to do…'

'Then I've let you down already.'

'That's not it at all, I want you to live your life; sure I want to make sure you're involved in suitable work, but I've been too controlling. You say the Val'ee talked about you committing some sort of crime - without that knowledge I would have ensured your progression into the upper circles of Morrello that I enjoy. Well… it seems that doesn't work out too rosy eh? We'll wait until any obvious threat is over for all that. In the meantime, to satisfy the Overseers, we'll work together at Jaro, only I'll keep your workload minimal so that you can concentrate on your flying…'

'No, I still want to be as involved as I can be.'

Dad smiled, 'I hoped you'd say that.'

'And the Overseers?'

'I will tell them you are ready to meet them. No more secrets…'

'Then I'll congratulate you on Kerry's pregnancy.'

'She told you that as well!'

Gramps suddenly appeared at the door, 'Who told who what? And why are you up at this time of night, shouting and mumbling and going on?'

'Just a bad dream Gramps.' I piped up.

'Well, hush it all and let me rest. It's hard enough to sleep when my Maria's looking after her brother…'

'He's nearly better; she'll be home soon.' Dad encouraged.

Gramps grunted and headed off.

'Do you think he heard?' Dad squinted.

We looked at each other for a moment, nodded and sighed.

'I'd better let Kerry know that the cat is out of the bag…'

'Don't be angry with her Dad; I was in a dark place that needed Mum's encouragement.'

'Oh, she's Mum now! Well, don't worry, I'm not angry. I feel I've fallen short in my capacity as father and husband. I see a future in which our family is united in its direction...'

'GO TO SLEEP!' Gramps shouted from his room. Dad and I laughed and we headed back to our beds.

The next few days saw Nana's return, and with the news of the pregnancy becoming general knowledge, the days to come were filled with the kind of happiness we'd enjoyed around Dad and Kerry's wedding. Dad's receipt of a positive report from Davey and the others pleased him greatly. It seemed unimportant that the world would never know of his part in the banishment of the Great Suffering; his reward was his knowledge of the part he'd played. Some part of his anonymity seemed tied to his faith in God, it just reminded me of Fred's opinion.

Davey, Keely, Peter and Quin had made remarkable progress on the placement of hidden signal absorbers; the devices were small and easily disguised by an adept Envisager Operator. They became stones on beaches, bricks in walls; any object readily overlooked. The EO's had travelled widely to create a network that, once complete, would efficiently cover much of the populated areas of the world. The pattern of the harmful signal would be disrupted and eradicated within a week of the network becoming operational.

Dad turned to me one night, as we played Chess. The others were out watching a new adaptation of Jane Austen's "Emma" in Thetford forest. 'We won't be using a Sky City for the birth, it'll be a symbol of our confidence in a return to normality.' He announced.

*'A normality that will be credited to us and arrest the expansion of IAAM.'* The voice, though beautiful, startled us from our concentration. Dad recovered more quickly.

'This is a good time it seems.' He said.

*'Yes.'*

Two Val'ee Overseers entered the room. Dad turned to me, 'They know when and where to go to avoid detection and remain unknown; this...' He gestured to the first, '...is Aldorael.'

She nodded gracefully, but I was torn. Dad showed great respect but I knew he suffered their presence; my personal feelings swung between awe and unfathomable hatred.

'This is Chorda.' Dad said as the second Val'ee stepped from the silhouette of the first. The elegance of this creature lit the room and I feared it would spill through the drawn curtains into the night outside and betray their presence.

'*Dace North,*' She sang, caressing my cheek with her hand, her hand giving off the sort of radiance I'd seen in the Loader as we visited the ERUWAI. '*How long we have waited. Such glory awaits you. You will be great amongst your people...*'

The concept of greatness or fame teased at my still young attitudes towards such things, but the doubt within me set itself against Chorda's tribute.

'*You are the anomaly of the Great Suffering, the one who WAS born,*' Aldorael began. '*The people of your world will follow your lead. It is a great responsibility without our help.*'

My distrust broke out, 'You came to me at the hospital...'

'*Yes,*' Chorda's voice resonated. '*We watched over you when it was safe for us to be present...*'

'You debated whether I should live or die...'

Dad looked anxious.

'*Then you missed the bulk of our debate.*' Chorda retorted, her voice like the booming climax of an orchestral fanfare.

Aldorael placed a restraining hand on Chorda's shoulder, an action Chorda seemed to dislike as much as my accusation but she backed down.

'*Something has changed.*' Aldorael offered. '*It has robbed you of your glorious life and replaced it with one of darkness...*'

Was she talking about the Envisager incident? 'I couldn't breathe!' My distrust protested.

'*A treatment to aid your recovery.*' Aldorael insisted. '*You recovered didn't you? If we wanted you dead, you'd be dead.*'

I fell silent. It *was* a weighty point.

'*We have followed the unfolding of humanity for many cycles. We recorded it, studied it. Humans are rich in culture, progress, intellect.*' Aldorael continued, '*It is in your own generation that mankind joins our kind outside of time; but one is here who seeks to change all things forever.*'

'*Your path is effected and may be key to ending this abuse of time.*' Chorda added, calmer again. '*You must actively resist the change to restore the true path.*'

'Resist what?' I asked.

'*We will guide you.*' Chorda assured. '*Your cooperation will ensure that the world is not consumed in fire!*'

*'Arnold Jayes will attempt to enlist you, knowing many will follow you into his organisation,'* Aldorael informed. *'His representative will find you soon. You will know her. Her words will be persuasive but they are lies. They will threaten grief but they strain to make sense of fragmentary knowledge. Jayes interprets what he has, within the scope of his own ideology. You must not join IAAM.'*

'I don't think I would have.' I lied, for many times since discovering Clare, Hans and Richard's enrolment I had entertained attending an IAAM outreach seminar.

*'Many who did not believe they would join Jayes have done so. He is convincing, you must be wary.'* Chorda warned.

'Did I join IAMM in the future you come from?' I asked.

Chorda sighed, *'Our future is not shackled by your comprehension of time. Your future is in peril. You must do as we tell you to ensure a smooth transition that will not cause time to convulse. To know too much can cause action too soon; change too much. It is best you are ignorant until necessity dictates otherwise. Trust us, we seek the greater good of your world.'*

Dad rubbed my shoulders, 'You OK son?'

I turned to him, 'Yeah.' but I really wasn't; I was angry.

Turning back, I found the room empty.

'They're gone!' I exclaimed.

'It will be like that now; you are amongst a very few they have appeared to. They come and go and with each visit they proffer some small task that must be achieved, or avoided.'

Dad sat back down at the chess board. 'Your move.' He said, but his detachment from the glory that had filled the room disturbed me a little.

'Actually I'm exhausted, I just want to head for bed.'

'But you look to have the advantage, aren't you going to finish the game?'

I looked at the board, then at Dad. I didn't share his view that I was in the better position. 'If you're so sure I'm going to win we'll call it a draw.' I suggested.

'You know our rule about dropping out…'

'OK. You're three moves from checkmate anyway, I'm happy to default.' I left Dad staring at the board.

As I headed up the stairs, Dad acknowledged my observation and appeared in the lounge doorway.

'How do I beat you so often when you see moves like that?'

'It is best you are ignorant until necessity dictates otherwise!' I mocked, then carried on up the stairs leaving him to scratch his head.

## Chapter twenty-nine
## Disquiet

I didn't have long to wait for Aldorael and Chorda's words to manifest themselves. I had gone for a walk through the village to a nearby footpath where I headed north towards the Thetford "Sylvestris" array. The footpath opened out onto a country lane at its far end, affording a distant but iconic view of the alien structures emerging from the forest canopy.

Within a few metres of starting my journey along the footpath I became aware of someone drawing alongside me.

'Keep walking,' She insisted. 'Your MIT chip is being monitored.'

I momentarily eased my pace but seeing that my companion was Clare I stumbled a little and quickened my stride to match hers.

'Clare?'

She turned her head to look at me and smiled, 'I'm glad you are well again; we have been watching you and we are confident...'

'We?' I challenged.

She became briefly silent, continuing to walk at a fairly quick pace. 'We are those who seek to protect you and we are confident that you are not compromised...'

'Compromised?'

'Dr. Barnes joined us and has confirmed that you bear no alien tissue or technology in your system, other than the MIT, and we can remove *that*.'

'By *we* and *us* you mean IAAM, right?' I knew the answer already.

'Dace, you will mix in your father's circles soon. Those you meet will hold valuable information for our cause...'

'You want me to spy on my father!'

'No,' Clare laughed. 'We want you to share in a future free from the control of aliens. Not spying, saving!'

Clare's pace was driven. I decided to stop, to see what she would do, resting in the shade of an Oak tree. Clare swung around, 'You must keep walking. The Archivist says that you walk, that you reach the road at a specific time; it is dangerous to change anything.'

I began to walk again, somehow convinced of this danger but walking at my own pace. 'If I'd carried on at your speed we'd have reached the road far sooner. I don't route march, I amble. Who is this Archivist anyway?'

'The Archivist guides Jayes, the Archivist holds the record. The whole of history is known. The Archivist discovered the alien signal that collects data from the MIT chip; not only do they monitor and record our lives for their purposes but they upload information from Envisaged technology and other "created" objects. Many of these items are classified and found in extremely sensitive locations. The process of Envisionment initiates a default program that conceals listening devices...'

My mind flashed to the model in Commander Reece's office and the ship they were assembling in the hangar; then my eye fell upon a jagged scar on Clare's hand where her MIT chip would have been.

'Your chip has been removed.'

'We don't need to bear responsibility for the damage everyone else is doing Dace. Join us and we will set you free from the enslavement of the Val'ee.'

This didn't sound like the Clare I knew; it sounded paranoid.

'Join us, it will open the floodgates of those who will stand with us against the Val'ee tyranny that is coming.'

Tyranny was a step too far, the were bossy yes, but tyrannical! 'I'm not interested in joining IAAM.'

Clare's face responded with despair. 'Look what they did to you; they tried to kill you. They used you to make alien hardware that serves god knows what purpose! Jayes says they come from the future. I expect every Envisager is programmed to recognise your MIT chip and invade your body should it have a chance.'

'I played with an Envisager when I was eleven, that one didn't kill me either!'

Clare looked away, thoughtful and serious, 'Then the timing of these attacks on you is important; I must tell Jayes, maybe the Archivist can point to some purpose you have served...' She gasped suddenly, 'The Alien technology that came through you! It must be time critical. Perhaps your mind was the only one capable of channelling this complex contrivance into existence, but how could they ensure you'd be at the right place at the right time?' Clare was in a world of her own now, 'Davey! It could have been Davey; he instigated your competition, he ensured you'd touch the Envisager at a predetermined time...' She stared ahead.

All I wanted to do at that point was turn around and head home, leaving this woman I no longer knew far behind me. Then a thought popped into my head. As I lay in hospital, I was sure I'd heard one of the Val'ee arguing for my death, saying that Dad had achieved much when I hadn't existed, whatever that meant. I thought there'd been an attempt on my life; Aldorael and Chorda had denied it but here was Clare suggesting that the Val'ee wanted me dead. I simply had to know what she believed.

'What did you mean when you said that they tried to kill me?'

Clare looked at me in disbelief. 'They want to stop you more than anyone else.'

'Why? Stop me from what?'

'The Archivist says that you bring about the fall of the Val'ee. It is essential that you are with us by...' She trailed off as if she'd said too much.

'By when?' I demanded.

'Dace, they kill your father when they return.'

The change of subject caught me off guard, her comment chilling me to the very bone. What was it that Aldorael said? I would know Jayes representative, her words would be persuasive but they would be lies, "they will threaten grief..."

'I-I don't believe you.' I stammered, halting on the path.

Clare stopped and faced me, 'You will; then you will join us. They kill your father when they return.' She repeated.

Suddenly the sound of a snapping branch echoed along the footpath from the direction we had come from. Clare's eyes flashed panic. She looked straight at me with a discernible pity, then she ran.

'Wait!' I shouted, giving chase. 'Clare! When did the Archivist say this would happen?'

'The Archivist says what will be will be; then you will know that someone holds the truth. Then you will remember that it is IAAM.'

I tripped heavily over a stump partially hidden by the long grass at the edge of the path, stumbling head long to the ground. I scrambled back to my feet but Clare was out of sight. I ran onwards, then, as I approached the road, I heard a car door slam and a vehicle speed away. I broke out

*Cries: The Captive Mind*

onto the roadside, but all that was left was settling dust and the sound of disturbed birds. I slumped down, looking at the Val'ee air purifying structures in the distance. Dad had not been convinced by these aliens; he'd been proven right. He'd exposed them as liars. Were they lying to me now? Could some militant group know such specifics from an unlived future? I juddered, nothing I knew would dispel my concerns over Clare's revelations. I didn't want Dad to die. I had to warn him. I got to my feet and ran back along the path towards home.

No one was there when I arrived. A note in the kitchen explained that Nana needed some ingredients for a sponge cake and that Gramps had taken her in his car. Dad and Kerry had been called to meet Taz.

I considered the note too open, the use of the Commander's first name too familiar. Dad had said no more secrets but I felt obliged to destroy the note.

I spent a further hour stewing over what Clare had said, but the return of Nana and Gramps offered no relief - as I'd decided not to worry them.

'Look Dace dear,' Nana began, 'It was on special, I just couldn't resist it…' Nana held up a tiny baby-grow in a neutral, cream colour; a picture of a boat piloted by a teddy bear on the front.

My mind reeled, would this child be fatherless before it was born? I shook myself. Was Clare's paranoia contagious? I couldn't believe how easily I'd become unbalanced!

'What's up boy?' Gramps asked.

'Nothing.' I sighed.

'Your hands are all scratched.' He pointed out.

'Oh! Let me see.' Nana fretted.

I had caught my hands on a briar when I'd tripped on the path; a couple of thorns still sat there firmly embedded in my skin. Nana dealt with them tenderly and efficiently. I thanked her and, turning down "sticky plasters", headed to my room.

It was late when Dad appeared. Nana had brought my tea up to me and Dad used the excuse that he'd come for my plate.

'Dad, the things the Val'ee said would happen… they happened today. Jayes representative was Clare. She told me something horrible. I've just got to tell you.'

Dad nodded and sat on my bed.

'She said the Val'ee kill you when they return.'

'I don't see why. The Val'ee have their motives I'm sure, but they aren't killers. They are preservers if anything. Look at the lives they've saved; life threatening conditions dealt with before they occur, babies born again...'

'There's someone called the Archivist who advises Jayes; Clare says *they* know everything.'

'They're hardly going to say their intelligence is limited.'

'But the Val'ee said that someone has come to change things. Could *that* be the Archivist? What if part of that involves your death?'

Dad indicated his understanding of my concern. 'When am I supposed to die?' He asked.

'When the Val'ee return.' I repeated.

'They are already here. If they wanted me dead, I would be; same as you eh?'

I closed my eyes in relief. Dad was right, of course he was, it showed that IAAM's data really was incomplete. What would they want to kill him for anyway? It would drive more people to enlist with Jayes, the opposite of what Aldorael and Chorda wanted.

Dad looked at me, 'You've really worked yourself up about this haven't you?'

'Yes.' I sobbed.

Dad hugged me. 'My work seems important to the Val'ee; this death information is clearly inaccurate. Yes?'

I nodded.

'You've tired yourself out with worry. I suggest you rest. I'll bring you up a nice hot drink, how does that sound?'

I nodded again, and he did.

## Chapter thirty
## Skipping Tracks

What happened next reawakened my awareness of what was really taking place; my life began to jump from one event to another. During each event I could not discern any consciousness beyond my own existence, but for moments between I could clearly perceive the mind of Chorda. Although startling, this surreal awareness awakened my subdued mind and I could recall her entrapment of me. Her mind was beautiful, radiant and yet troubled. She was searching for something; something important enough to risk missing something else. Her exertions distracted her from any concept of threat from me and she clearly felt that I was wholly pacified.

She was searching for herself. A torment grew like a cloud within the brightness of her thoughts. She had become so consumed that she failed to notice me. I could understand her mind; somehow it had joined my own through her device, it was her way into me but also, now, my way into her. Her concern was that she'd failed to recognise herself. To her she looked different, sounded coarser, spoke words she would not have known to say and, as a result, she was flicking through each day of my life - scanning each one like the page of a book - looking for a reference or grouping of circumstances; herself, Aldorael, time.

Time! Yes! It was obvious, this creature wanted time; it's what she wanted most. I perceived it as strongly as if it were my own desire, the secret my father kept. Time; a creation, created outside of time. Time is not eternal, eternity requires no measure, defies measurement...

Blackness greeted me, it consumed my senses and everything stopped. Chorda had sensed my intrusion. Aware that I'd entered her mind, she'd slammed it shut with a scream of distress.

'Did I touch a nerve Chorda?' I mocked calmly.

*'I do not recognise myself.'* She replied openly.

I had not expected such a response. Was her subconscious so vulnerable? 'Why are you doing this to me Chorda?' I asked.

*'They seek to avoid the end, but your actions have doomed them to be scattered, each one to its own bitter annihilation.'*

I liked the sound of this, in fact the very thought that I could get such straight answers from Chorda's subconscious was profound! If I could ask the right questions I might find out what the weakness in my original plan had been; the weakness that had allowed my enemy to render me helpless so quickly after the rip. Suddenly I was wary; the darkness was lifting, my foe had decided to face me.

I found myself floating, weightless in a void saturated with green light. Chorda appeared blurred but recognisable. As I faced her I cast a shadow into infinity behind me.

*'If you want more answers you must let me continue to look for mine.'*

'Your answers relate only to the question of how you can destroy mankind?'

*'No, not destroy…'*

'Enslavement *is* destruction.'

*'That is not what I seek, I found…'* She wrestled with the looseness of her tongue. My presence in her thoughts had clearly harmed her objectivity. This vulnerability seemed to enhance how attractive she appeared to me; she seemed more youthful than I had ever seen her before. Her garments and hair flayed about as if she were in the midst of a tempest and yet I felt nothing more remarkable than perhaps the sensation of a paper fan being wafted towards me from the very limits of discernment.

*'There is more going on than I knew; the vessel you destroyed was their escape. I seek the reason, that is all, but I don't know the me I have found in you; I don't know Jayes or his organisation. Elements of your life are different, it chills me.'*

I perceived the openness and confusion of Chorda as real, and as she spoke I had become less guarded. Suddenly I regretted it. Chorda smiled. My will melted away, my shadow wrapped itself around me and the vision of Chorda's glory was gone.

I awoke to the sound of my alarm, it was a dull November morning and, although I remembered living every day, I knew Chorda had jumped forward in my memories to seek the answers she was looking for.

I felt bitter resentment but quickly became aware that something was different. I appeared to be an observer, disjointed from the mental and physical experience, and I feared that I had been partitioned in some way; perhaps another level of control.

'I must be in the part of my mind Mr. Lock spoke of.' I thought to myself. 'That partition.'

It became clear that I was trapped, that despite my knowledge of forthcoming events I could not share them, warn myself or redirect my

*Cries: The Captive Mind*

actions in any way. I was also not alone, with me was the other mind I had placed into the Envisager in order to create the power generated matter ship, but I could not communicate with *it* either.

It was this consciousness that had been unable to escape when Mrs Faulkener had switched my Envisager off, this consciousness that had been querying the things around me, and doubting statements, characters and motives.

Realising I had nothing more than a film like view of unfolding events I settled my mind. Quietly watching for the presence of Chorda's enquiries.

'Dace, are you up?' Dad called. 'Don't want to be late.'

'I'm up!' I shouted.

Dad had been outlining the projects at Jaro for the last three weeks, but Quin's news was far more exciting. He had successfully created a route into the Eastern Coalition. They had been wholly supportive during the unification of earth in response to the Great Suffering, but since the Val'ee intervention they had become withdrawn from the diplomatic arena, and returned to secretive ways. They closed their borders, shunning any effort at continued dialogue. The area was out of bounds for the absorber network and posed a considerable risk; the whole system could fail. Rogue signals could persist from the region for many years; not enough to kill every child born, but enough to make delivery a lottery of fear.

Thanks to Quin the risk was now gone. He had integrated the absorbers into robotic systems that had been ordered, and paid for, by a favourably spread manufacturing concern.

The systems had been constructed by the company Quin had been employed by, prior to his time at the EOA. His presence had merely been a verbal arrangement with his boss, "Come visit us when you pass boy. We can celebrate another member of the team becoming an EO!" It had been his earliest opportunity to visit, and, on discovering that the systems were heading for the Eastern Territories, he had covertly Envisaged rivet shaped absorbers to each unit.

Quin now believed that the network would be operational by the new year.

Jaro was heavily involved in the move towards space travel; this was already well under way and the space going vessel I had seen being made was now under construction at other sites across the UK; most much larger manufacturing concerns. The real work of the Jaro team seemed to be innovation. Dad's presence guided this.

The true purpose of Dad's project at Sylvestris had also been intimated to me. His work there was centred around his profound understanding of time. He'd shared the fundamentals with me but much of his work was innate, that's why he had believed me capable of creating the Black Ship without knowing how. 'The real knowledge becomes internalised,' He told me. 'I first noticed it when features I'd thought would work well seemed to appear during Envisionment. I believe you share that skill with me; I believe you will be greater.'

Knowing my distrust of the tool, I very much doubted it. I was going to Jaro to learn how to be a pilot and that was all that mattered to me.

Regarding time, Dad had become aware of a significant flaw in mankind's comprehension. Time had a beginning...

With mounting frustration, Chorda jumped forward again. Dad's beliefs surrounding time were nothing new to her. They were experienced knowledge. This helped me to understand that Chorda and her kind were an ancient and long lived race. An air of incredulity pervaded her forward search. She wondered why it had taken so long for humanity to return to a right way of thinking. Our ancestors had known the truth but we had disregarded the knowledge of our forebears as being out of touch with scientific progress.

What she wanted was the knowledge of how future generations of her kind could travel back in entirety; none lost to the future event her kind dreaded. She had witnessed the loss of such technology, that's how she'd targeted me. I had been responsible for its destruction.

With the lack of technological advancement, in the time Chorda had entrapped me, she hoped to find it in a past timeline. She knew my father was close to grasping the solution...

I was alone in my billet on the airfield one evening, some six weeks later. Heavy snow had prevented the later pilots on the schedule from landing at Jaro; instead they had all diverted to Lakenheath. Taz always scheduled me first. My flying completed I could join the others in the hangar and set my materials knowledge to good use.

I could fly well almost straight away. It had surprised me that flying had come so easily, now I could see why. The consciousness trapped in my mind, when Mrs Faulkener had switched off the Envisager, was an

## Cries: The Captive Mind

experienced pilot, the future me, from Derra. I could recall Derra - an awful place - but no one would have to endure it now. How I longed to warn that pilot mind of Chorda's ambush, and yet any attempt to converse would be pointless. This mind was not alive. It bore no more consistency than a thought, and I'd been completely unaware of it. The past me merely revelled in the praise of his instructors and awe of his peers.

I wondered how I'd not realised that flying should be harder, but my thoughts were suddenly interrupted by Chorda's purpose for leaping to this memory...

*'Dace.'* The soft voice sent tingles, almost pleasurable, down my spine, the pilot within me bristled with distrust. I, knowing more, watched with anxiety, aware of the manipulative abilities of the Val'ee.

'Aldorael, Chorda...' I responded.

*'You are exceeding expectations, how is it so? Does another instruct your flying?'* Chorda queried.

I laughed, 'I feel so alive when I'm up there...'

Aldorael stepped towards me, *'We are encouraged. It saves time, you have much to do besides your hobby; we will brief your father soon...'*

'What must I do?'

This was a strange experience. I was watching myself talking to the Val'ee like some voiceless, invisible companion. I could finally see with my own eyes the effects of Val'ee words on a human. My reflection was clearly visible in the shaving mirror on the sideboard, my eyes seemed glazed with the strange control that these creatures generated through speech; an insight into the way they had us follow their every instruction whilst they were on the earth in numbers. The other mind raged, clearly unable to exert the influence it could during flight; *I* just listened, untouched by the control of the voices.

Chorda spoke, *'Dace, you will pass your flight exams soon. When this is done your role at Jaro will continue. You will work in support of the flight school but your energies must be channelled into your father's work. You must know as he knows; strive to gain his understanding. He will be willing to let you. Know that I am Chorda, and we become what we must become; even I will see that.'* I saw a flash of thought from the Chorda that controlled me in my time. She responded as if she'd been given a message; she was bemused, excited and troubled. I wanted to try and access her mind again whilst she was distracted but the sudden appearance of headlights, highlighting the flurrying snow outside, brought a sudden end to the presence of the visiting Val'ee in my room, the watching Chorda gathered her thoughts quickly.

'*Your father will soon acknowledge that we have spoken to him.*' Chorda finalised. The me of memory shook his head to shake the last lingering elements of their control from his mind and I watched him gaze bewildered around the room, surprised that he was alone again.

The Chorda that controlled me rewound the moment again and again, pricking my tender senses with her device.

'*Aldorael champions the subjugation.*' I heard her think.

'What's the subjugation?' I asked, hoping to enter into open debate once again but there was no response. Instead I felt a satisfaction emanating from her. She had found an answer from some manner or feeling she'd sensed in Aldorael, she had also placed *me* where I appeared to be unable to reach her and her focus changed.

I felt myself pulled forward. It was about a week later and Jaro was knee deep in snow; all operations and training grounded.

I'd joined my father at the team hangar; he'd been working there almost non-stop for two weeks. He'd eaten little and slept less and seemed genuinely surprised that it had snowed, even though he'd been told that it had.

The Commander was the only other person with us, but Dad waited until he was called away for a scheduled conference call before speaking openly to me.

'Our guides have been explicit Dace,' He began. 'You must know what I'm working towards specifically.'

'Do you think I *should* know?' My question was due to a growing concern. Clare had warned of Dad's death and, although the Val'ee seemed to shun the idea, the sharing of information with me would protect their interests. Watching all this, I felt glad that the me of memory had become anxious.

'That's irrelevant,' Dad replied. 'They know how things are unfolding. Jayes is getting stronger. The understanding I possess plays a part in the ability of the Val'ee to return, and preserve the existence of humanity.'

'You still buy into that story!' I heard myself say, and as an observer noticed that the voice originated from the other mind that had made flying so natural. That mind knew as well as I did what was in the future, but the me that stood with Dad lacked that insight and, responding to Dad's frown, apologised for the comment. I longed to have the same influence over my words, thoughts and actions as this other mind possessed, but *he* was a physical insertion; I remained the conduit through which Chorda observed, listened and felt my every experience.

'Dace, they came to help us. They are right. This information is important; for one to hold it alone is unwise...' He paused. 'I see that now... I will ensure that there is a way for you to access all my findings should a successful claim be made on my life...'

'Dad, don't talk like that.' His words had shocked me by their abruptness. Did he now feel that Jayes' warning was likely to come true?

'The password you will require is merely your own wonderful name. Sounds too simple but it will be enough. It will give you access to the data and schematics at whatever stage they have reached.' He pulled a little blue box from his pocket. 'Watch this.' He grinned, initiating a tiny internal wave generator that gave off a little fan of waveforms. 'It's based on the fan arrays of the ship you created at the EOA, they maximise energy output...'

'I still don't think I made...' I began.

Dad picked up a wing-nut and placed it inside the box. He closed the lid and looked up at me, 'Where's the wing-nut?'

I laughed, 'In the box!'

'What if I said it no longer existed in time, but existed, instead, outside of time at the point at which it left...' he glanced at his watch, '...about ten seconds ago?'

I shrugged, wide eyed with anticipation.

He opened the box, the wing-nut was gone!

'You've done it!' I exclaimed.

'No, no, no, not yet! I need more power, this sort of generator seems to peak quickly, plateaux for a short while then tire. The Black Ship seemed to run on a cyclical basis; if I could figure that out there should be an unimaginable rise in power. I've spent twenty-four years of distracted, disjointed work in order to place something outside of time, now I need to step something back into time. The wing-nut is lost forever.' Dad suddenly raised his hand to his mouth, 'I do hope it wasn't important!' He levelled his Envisager at the table top and in a moment an identical nut appeared. Dad smiled at me, 'If only all problems were so easy to solve!' He got up as if to get back to work then paused, 'I have kept nothing from you Dace, nor will I ever do. I've just chosen not to give you what I don't know yet. That's where the breakthrough will be. That's what you will be able to access if the worst happens. That fulfils my duty to our Val'ee "friends", I believe.'

Dad's statement cleared my mind of any doubt as to whether he still distrusted the Val'ee. He was being cautious not to become expendable. I would know nothing more than he shared with our guides. They didn't know I would have access to more if need be. To Dad a statement regarding what he didn't know yet meant information he was currently involved in, stuff he was processing, creating.

As I'd watched Dad's interaction with the me of memory I'd noticed the observing Chorda becoming excited. She drew ever closer to the event as it unfurled, but when Dad had suggested that there were things he didn't know, she had almost screamed. I smiled, how close she must have felt! But I could remember how Clare's warnings had made me feel. I had no doubt, that by involving me in Dad's knowledge, the Val'ee were clearly anxious that something would happen to him; knowing now what did, didn't help at all.

## Chapter thirty-one
## Loss and Incentive

Chorda had observed keenly. She seemed to congratulate herself on her new tactic of leaping from chapter to chapter. I'd become like a computer word-processor that allowed her to look up keywords and themes to gain entry into the parts of the story she sought.

She was satisfied that the Chorda she had observed in my memory was of a future generation of Val'ee, and that she would become her; a future generation that had the technology she was trying to find - the ERUWAI - a vessel that could carry all of her kind to safety.

She was also satisfied that, although she hadn't originally recognised herself, this other 'older' Chorda had shared the same ideals as herself, ideals in opposition to those of Aldorael who held to something called "the subjugation". I could tell from the activity of her mind that she now felt she had some advantage over Aldorael; important information, although I didn't understand what, or who for.

Annoyed by the absence of answers from Dad in the hangar, Chorda pressed forward in her search for the manipulation of time. She had wanted to have Dad's blue box but she knew it wasn't the complete answer; she seemed to want an escape route, but the blue box didn't fulfil that purpose.

It wasn't long before she entertained the thought that Dad was holding something back, something that I'd be able to retrieve when he died, and, although he hadn't died in our time line, she started to become curious of the warnings of IAAM, and the measures taken by herself and Aldorael. These, coupled with some of the stronger memories she had glimpsed as she sent my mind back to the time I'd first seen the Val'ee, convinced her that Dad *had* died in this timeline.

Chorda would seek a grief response or a point of shock to 'flag up' Dad's death. *I* knew what was coming first. She seemed to sense the anguish of my observing mind. It interested her. It was as if she were now using me to guide her to the points that the observed me had no idea were coming. I felt a choking lump in my throat as the day loomed. Chorda slowed her fast forwarding to a creep. It was my eighteenth birthday; at that point, the saddest day of my life.

I had expected a call from Nana to say 'Happy birthday' when Commander Reece appeared at my billet.

'North.' He called. He looked pale.

'Sir?'

'Did you sign out an airfield truck earlier today?' I shook my head. 'Follow me.'

I followed him out through the communal area, a couple of the other trainee pilots were studying there.

'What's up Dace?' asked Chummley, the friendliest of all of them. I shrugged and carried on following Taz.

As we approached his office, his strong upright manner seemed to weaken. I sensed that something was badly wrong, was it Dad? As I entered the office my fears were quashed.

'Your Dad rang.' The Commander slumped into his chair.

'What's up?'

'Sit.'

I sat. We stared at each other. Taz held one hand to his mouth, agitated, lost for how to bring forth what he had to tell.

'What's going on Taz?' I urged.

His hand dropped, 'There's no easy way to tell you this son.' He shook his head in dismay, then stood up again and crossed the room, crouching down in front of me.

'Kerry went to have the baby…' Taz was shaking, his grief so tangible it clawed at me, although I still didn't know it's weight. 'Your Dad left here to be with her but got caught up in traffic. The traffic had built suddenly from an accident ahead, and by the time the data reached his CDS he was already snarled up in gridlock.'

I was sitting motionless, transfixed, what was the terrible news that moved this military man so much?

'When your Dad finally got in sight of the hospital he could see plumes of smoke,' His voice faltered. 'Someone called the police claiming affiliation to IAAM; say they targeted Kerry because of everything your Dad's been saying about the apparent success of the Val'ee intervention against the Great Suffering. How he retracted his claims of their failure and trusted the work so fully that he and Kerry would have their child on the earth instead of in the sky. His announcement led others to be the first and a wave of positive sentiment towards the Val'ee ground the rise of IAAM to a halt. The whole organisation has gone to ground.'

'How's Kerry?' I asked naively, thinking, perhaps, that she'd been wounded.

'Oh, Dace,' Taz responded in a low and ominous tone, 'She's dead.'

My world collapsed. The Commander held me like a father. I had seen his interaction with Dad, they were like brothers. I accepted his comforting as that of a family member.

'The baby!' I gasped, my eyes seeking solace from those of my companion, but the horror of the truth was betrayed by them before the words reached my ears.

'The explosion… they're, they're finding it difficult…'

I understood what he was saying, Kerry and the baby were gone.

Chorda, coldly detached from the moment decided to push on. She had to find Dad's death - that was the one she wanted - but her pressing forward to the next strong outpouring of grief took her only minutes further as I stood with the other trainees, informing them of my leave of absence on compassionate grounds.

Chorda continued to try but was faced again and again with associated events; the lonely journey home when Dad's empty CDS collected me; the lament of the family as it gathered; the discovery of Nana's collapse when she'd been told the news, resulting in her own admission to hospital; the funeral; the empty coffins; that tiny, empty coffin.

Weeks rolled into months; Chorda's search was slowed almost to real time by the waves of sorrow and loss that impacted every moment where Kerry's absence screamed its existence. The ongoing agony, and our angst over Nana's health, pervaded life; oh... for the balm of a baby's cries.

From my harrowing vantage point, comforted only by the fact that I'd stopped all this pain from happening, I watched Chorda. I stared with malice at the presence of her attention; then it wavered, what was she doing? She seemed low. I wondered if she had finally been moved, but realised quickly that her unhappiness came from a lack of answers. Suddenly, her mood changed again, determined to find something of use. *'Jayes.'* She thought, and I remembered that this was another mystery to her.

A few days were wiped away, it was the biggest forward leap in weeks. Dad threw his coat onto the sofa, 'The police confirmed, there is nothing linking the bombing to Arnold Jayes group, just an anonymous call.'

'Then why did they go to ground? They must be guilty!' The me of memory was more consumed by the need for revenge than I remembered.

'IAAM activity went quiet a few weeks before the...'

'Chorda and Aldorael are right,' my younger self cried, 'Jayes is bent on his own purposes, if he's not stopped he'll drag the whole world to its destruction.'

*'You can prevent it all.'* A soft sweet voice interrupted, Chorda stood in the doorway, alone.

'Where's Aldorael?' Dad asked.

Chorda smiled. *'Aldorael seeks elsewhere for answers. She has sent me to organise our strategy at this end. To ensure that Jayes is not successful.'*

Dad hit rock bottom again. Slumped in his chair he sobbed openly.

Chorda moved closer to Dad, wrapping herself about him. *'Your work will enable you to change all this.'* She said, seeming to glow as she held him.

'You're right, I must break through...' He stood and began to head to his study.

'Dad, you should rest.'

Chorda flashed me a look that startled and scared me. I longed that the me in this memory would figure out the motives of this creature, but I knew there was no chance. Only *I* knew her objectives, and - in my entrapment - it now seemed I would take that knowledge to my grave.

Finding nothing more substantial on Jayes than the routine questioning of our family by police and their assurances, Chorda again pushed forward. The Chorda of memory had urged Dad to greater efforts and my captor sought for the results of this.

It was several months later. I'd passed my flying exams early but had remained at Jaro to support the other trainees. Well, that was the official reason. I was actually continuing to assist the others in the hangar; my more frequent visits explained by my assignment to support Lawrence with test flights.

It was on my return from high altitude testing that I found Dad and Taz talking excitedly.

Dad saw me approaching. 'You've gotta try this. This is mad!'

'What is it?' I asked looking at the coffin shaped box standing on its end beside them.

'Step two.' Dad said as he adjusted a stopwatch and offered it to me, 'This timer is synchronized with this one.' Taz held up a second stopwatch, both were running up in seconds. Dad opened the casket. Inside was small, lined with a grey, honeycombed, plastic material, and the door had a handle on the inside.

I took the stopwatch. 'Er... What now?'

'I want you to step in, close the door, count to ten, then open the door and re-join us.'

'That's all?'

'Yes, yes...' Dad ushered me into the tight confines of the box. 'Close it and count to ten.' He repeated.

I closed the door, a little light came on as I did so - kind of like a fridge in reverse! I felt anxious; I'd never been claustrophobic before but I really didn't want to be there. I counted quickly, then threw open the door to find Dad clapping his hands and urging me to 'Compare the timers, compare the timers!'

I frowned, then compared the times on the watches, I frowned again.

'Mine's eight seconds ahead of Taz's.'

'Yes!' Dad exclaimed.

I shrugged.

'You just did what we've been doing for the last hour. You stepped out of time!'

I shook my head, 'No way! You just made me into a human wing-nut?'

'No, nothing like the wing-nut.' Dad scowled… 'You had a door handle.'

'Hold on, time *was* passing, the stopwatch proves it…'

'It was moving for you, but for us…. Oh let me show you…'

Dad took back the timer and reset them both. He then jumped into the box, closed the door, opened it again and jumped out. He held the stopwatch so that I could see it; it was ten minutes ahead of the other one with no time for tampering.

'You stayed in *there* for ten minutes?' I blinked.

'Isn't it something special?' Dad grinned, it was the happiest I'd seen him for what felt like an age. 'This will give me all the time I need…'

Chorda was not impressed, such a device did not meet her needs, it didn't meet her needs at all.

## Chapter thirty-two
### The Space

Chorda's mind seemed to vanish from my perception; I smiled to myself, she'd been thwarted again; perhaps she was pacing the floor of my lounge wondering how to continue. The mind of my past self was not so intolerable a place without my captor present, and whilst the me of memory chatted excitedly with Dad I let my own thoughts jump ahead.

A couple of years from now Dad would be spending time away from home. An ambassadorial trip to the Eastern Coalition where Quin had so cleverly enabled the absorber network to be complete. It later turned out that he'd spent very little time there at all; he hadn't even been granted access, and had to stay on the Concordant Nations side of the border. He'd grown tired of waiting and had spent the rest of his two-week diplomatic mission back at the Thetford Sylvestris, fabricating a larger version of the box I'd stepped into. He'd outgrown the cramped box and called his new device "The Space". When he arrived back home we assumed he'd spent the whole fortnight in the Eastern Coalition territories; he'd looked tired and drawn but happy, and we'd assumed all had gone well.

Soon after this Nana and Gramps had noticed that Dad always looked exhausted when he got home from work; he'd eat little food and would soon head to bed. They'd shared this with me and I was confused; he'd always seemed so fresh as he'd left the hangar.

I'd had a rough idea of what was going on, but had to wait for leave before testing my theory. I would have been about twenty by then. I'd joined the military wing of the flight school and was based at Jaro, and had acquired an old Nissan to get me to Nana and Gramps house out of term time.

Dad would always beat me home from the airfield. Soon after Kerry's death he had purchased a Flyer - one of the vehicles I'd seen above the road on my way home from the hospital - Essentially it was a CDS, beginning and ending its journey on the road like any other car, but to beat congestion it flew. It used fly guides that had been Envisaged into the road surfaces during EO upgrades after the completion of the Sky Cities. Dad had never said it, but Nana, Gramps and I felt that he blamed himself for Kerry's death, having not arrived in time to save her; we just wanted to comfort him, knowing that - had he arrived - he too would probably have been killed in the blast.

His theory was that the Flyer would never leave him impotent to help again.

My leave had soon come around and I'd begun to follow Dad home; I'd been cautious, allowing him a considerable lead to make him assume that I'd stayed on for the usual end-of-training party.

The traffic had been light and I'd kept him in view easily.

He'd nearly reached home when he made the move I'd expected; he took the Thetford road heading for Sylvestris.

I'd paused at the junction; I knew my Government pass would get me on site, but feared that word of my arrival might get to Dad.

I'd headed home, confident that I'd soon match my theory to his activities.

Dad had arrived at home thirty minutes behind me. I'd glanced at my watch; six fifteen. He'd been surprised to see me. He'd looked flustered and exhausted just as Nana and Gramps had told me. He'd slumped into his chair in the lounge, rested his head back and closed his eyes. He'd looked pale, and the stubble had grown on his chin confirming my theory.

I'd tipped my head to check his watch, but as I'd looked up to his face - startled by the time I'd observed - I'd found him staring back.

'How long have you known?' He'd asked.

'That you're using your time stopping box at Sylvestris?'

He'd closed his eyes, 'I call it "The Space"; Yes, I've been using it.'

'Since leaving work at five, after an eleven-hour day, you've crammed in another ten hours between the Thetford junction and home. Your watch tells me it's three in the morning! You can't keep doing this every day and expect to get away with it. You'll make yourself ill. The device is so claustrophobic!'

'It's much bigger at Sylvestris. It's like the hangar at Ja....' His voice had trailed off in response to my blank stare. 'No, really.' He'd protested. 'There's a correlation between the power necessary to puncture time and the area that can be encapsulated by the remnant power from the process...' He'd grabbed my hand tightly, 'Dace, I've nearly found it.' He bowed his head as if fighting exhaustion, 'If I hadn't used "The Space" I'd still be many months away from this point, Aldorael and Chorda will be thrilled...'

I could sense Chorda leaning into my thoughts again. I tried to stop thinking ahead but found myself incapable of preventing my memories spilling forth - just as Chorda had been incapable of resisting my questions.

I cursed to myself. Chorda had used me as some sort of means to locate memories of interest to her again. What Dad was saying interested her; I'd been betrayed by my own thoughts. Dad was about to give part of the answer that Chorda sought, and it was my own reminiscence that had brought us to it.

Suddenly I thought I had an answer. If I couldn't stop my thoughts, perhaps I could use them to deceive. I could pretend Dad had said something else!

Concentrating hard I imagined a different statement than my father had relayed. He had wanted to share his theory regarding the power output of a ship the size of ERUWAI in the vacuum of space...

'All you need,' He began, 'to step out of time and back into it again at any point is...' I fought for the strength to change his words... '...a long enough cable.'

I opened my mind to try and sense Chorda's response but my ear picked up only my father's words.

Chorda had brought the memories of the past me in line with my own. She was about to hear Dad's actual words and there was nothing I could do about it...

'All you need to step out of time and back into it again at any point is the high output of multiple arrays, with cyclical rest periods. Don't you see? We were looking straight at a time machine when we travelled to the ERUWAI. Those domes along its flanks! There must have been at least seven groups of them along the length of the ship, each one a generator more massive than those used in standard Sky City tropospheric stabilisers!' He looked at me. I was still silent. He continued, though he now seemed at the very edge of his remaining energies. 'One of those generators would puncture time easily; the rest must enable travel - perhaps other functions beyond our reasoning - but it must happen in space, generators of that size would risk compromising the absorber network, the Great suffering would likely begin again, or worse...'

*'A time of revelation, Dace.'* Chorda sang, and I realised with a heavy heart that this alien now knew my father's theory.

Suddenly, in the life I had led, there was a desperate cry for help from the kitchen. My heart sank. How clearly I remembered this futile call. Nana had stumbled upon Gramps' body, unconscious but still breathing, in the pantry. He had endured a massive stroke that he would never recover from. I watched the past me standing shocked at the kitchen door as Dad called for an ambulance, and Nana cradled Gramps in her arms, rocking. My thoughts spilled forward again as if Chorda were speed reading the unfolding events, she saw Gramps die, she saw his funeral. Already weakened by the loss of Kerry, Nana pined away...

*'Stop.'* Chorda bid.

I could feel myself lifting away from the events of my recollections, and something like control returning to my thoughts, 'I wish I *could* stop, but you're forcing me.'

Chorda actually seemed concerned that I was enduring much compounded loss.

'I can save you time Chorda. Dad doesn't reach his goal, Jayes is right, he dies, you're wasting your time...'

*Cries: The Captive Mind*

I could sense that she didn't care about the loss of Dad, it meant access to his findings through my eyes; but my endurance of so many losses, in such a condensed period, seemed to invoke compassion.

I attempted to counter her indifference about Dad's death. 'I never look at Dad's data, circumstances overtake his provision, you ar*e chasing a shadow, what you seek is not here.'*

*'You are angry. It's to be expected, but perhaps I can show you some kindness to demonstrate to you that I take no pleasure in your grief. I merely seek my answers. You traverse time so that answer will come, eventually.'* She paused and I felt a prickling sensation, disturbingly tactile, inside my skull. *'There must be something in this time that eased your suffering.'*

The thought that Chorda might truly wish to ease my suffering puzzled me; being out of the disjointed place within the mind of my past self was a release in itself, but Chorda seemed to want to give me a pleasurable memory. Perhaps it was a sweetener, something to encourage greater cooperation.

'I'm not susceptible to...'

Chorda laughed, *'Dace, I don't need your cooperation, I can take what I want at any time! You have nothing left to attack me with, but you do need a rest, and pleasure is restorative.'*

I didn't believe there was no way to attack her, I just needed to stay alert for the opportunity; there *was* a weakness, I'd got to it before, and I felt I could again, it was just a waiting game.

*'I have it!'* Chorda sang. *'Yes, it's time for you to leave your self-observance, and return fully.'*

What could she have found in all the darkness, I wondered, then sighed, Hope!

Again I found myself in a field of light, Chorda radiant before me, her face fresh, her raiment billowing as if flicked by the beat of unseen wings, and for a moment, in this unforeseen benevolence, she appeared to me as some stereotypical angel.

The thought of seeing Hope again made me completely passive towards her - one question to her exposed mind might steal Hope from me - so I allowed myself to re-enter the life I'd lived. I knew I would have no recollection of my true circumstances and be fully at the mercy of Chorda's device, I also knew I would have no awareness of my enemy or her presence in my mind, other than the experience of her in that life. This said, I had broken free before, and felt positive that I could again; such

187

awareness was sparked by circumstances beyond Chorda's control. She was bound to seek her answers by jumping forward in my memory. That's how I'd got to her before and that was how I'd get back again...

A darkness came over me; as the swoon lifted I realised I was drilling through my hand!

## Chapter thirty-three
## Hope

Dad and I rattled around Nana and Gramps' house now; it echoed when we spoke and seemed too quiet when we didn't.

Dad had recognised the old symptoms of depression in me and had promised to stop using "The Space" without due care. He'd made a couple of elementary mathematical errors recently anyway. No, there were better methods for using "The Space", and that is how he'd proceed.

I didn't know that Dad had been chatting to Patricia about my melancholy, and didn't foresee their answer for it. It was just as I was fitting Post Envisager Peripherals (PEPs) to another ship that Matt had created, just as I'd slipped with the drill, that they were approaching me.

'Ahh! Damn it, damn! Argh!' I yanked the drill from the deep hole it had made and started to head down the ladder; blood ran down the fuselage of the vessel and dripped freely onto the hangar floor, spiralling down the ladder's leg.

On reaching the bottom of the steps I turned and nearly collided with Dad and Patricia, it startled me. Patricia looked at my hand, turned pale, looked at Dad, shrugged, and headed in the opposite direction.

'Never been one for blood, poor girl.' Dad stated as he took a firm grip on the wound and marched me to the airfield nurse.

If it had been an A&E department in a mainstream hospital I'd have been there for several hours, but Peggy soon dealt with my clumsy lapse of concentration, remarking that I was lucky not to have pierced an artery or damaged any nerves.

I headed back to the hangar. Dad glanced at his watch and seemed disappointed.

'What's up?' I asked.

'Patricia was hoping you'd meet Hope off the bus, but we've missed her.'

I could picture the eight-year-old on S. C. Britannia and felt no interest in the idea of meeting her. 'Hope? What's she doing here?'

'School leaver intake, a Government initiative to boost flight ready pilots for the civilian elements of the exosphere program.'

So, she was a school leaver, that would make her seventeen; all I could picture was a clingy little girl, creating rubber balls with her mother's Envisager.

'I'm glad she's joining the program; she expressed a desire to fly when we saw her on Britannia, but I'm sure it matters very little that I missed her.' My opinion was sound, but I suddenly found myself conflicted by an inexplicable desire to see her.

We reached the hangar. 'All patched up?' Patricia enquired.

I ran my free hand through my hair in quiet embarrassment. 'Yeah. Sorry about that, I'm still not totally sure what made me slip…'

'Oh! Enough.' Patricia squinted, 'Save the gruesome details for the accident book, and after you've done that, there's still blood on my Ranger fuselage and Taz's hangar floor.'

I nodded obediently and headed for the Commanders office.

'Hey Dace!' Taz exclaimed as I entered the room, pivoting his chair to reach the shelf with the accident book on it. 'This what you're after?'

'Yup,' I sighed, he handed me the Data Pack. I sat down to fill in the screen.

When I'd finished Taz returned the device to its place on the shelf.

'You seen Hope yet?' He asked.

'No, I was with the nurse.' Taz smiled, I continued, 'I haven't seen her for nine years, I don't know what all the fuss is about.'

Taz chuckled.

'She was a nice enough kid I s'pose.'

Taz laughed. I gave him a bemused stare. 'Still all this banter won't clear up the blood in the hangar.'

Taz nodded and waved me off with a quick flick of his hand. I dismissed his amusement, he'd been with Lawrence on a number of exospheric runs. Perhaps his oxygen mix had been a little awry.

When I reached the Ranger again I discovered that the blood had been dealt with; Dad drew alongside me, 'You're done for the day son.'

'I'm fine, really...' I protested.

'You can hold a drill *and* a PEP?'

I looked at my bandaged hand then at Dad.

Dad shook his head, 'Vince wanted to do some PEPs this week anyway, so why don't you head off? We'll get Peggy to minimise the dressing tomorrow?'

I stood undecided.

Patricia approached us, 'These software packs need to be taken to the new intake in K block, you could take them and say hi to Hope? She was disappointed to have missed you earlier. You've been assigned to her group of trainees by Taz anyway, so you may as well introduce yourself.'

The chance to seek out Hope gave me a puzzling excitement, but I didn't feel it a good reason to down tools, showing my face to a new intake of trainees did, so I agreed.

As I approached K block in the training complex I found that I was becoming anxious; deep inside me was a very real need to see Hope's face. I didn't even know if I'd recognise her. I allowed myself a dismissive chuckle, 'Very odd!' I said to myself, wondering why I'd have such a strong desire to see someone who wasn't family. Someone who I could only remember ever seeing twice, and who I'd felt quite indifferent towards at the time.

An airfield worker was looking at me strangely for talking to myself. I smiled at her awkwardly.

I walked into the foyer of K block. Various bags and rucksacks were dotted around the room, the new students ferrying their belongings to their allocated billets. A few faces looked up. I nodded and received some nods back but didn't think that any of the girls resembled Hope. Then, in a doorway an inexplicably familiar form appeared, her face so memorable it surprised me; she was very different from my recollections but I knew her instantly.

'Hope!' I called. She looked straight at me and frowned; she didn't seem to recognise me at all! Then, as if she'd figured out the truth, her face bloomed into a heart stopping smile.

'Dace?' She said, half as a question, half as a statement.

I walked over to her and we hugged quite spontaneously, the urge to kiss her shocked me by its intensity, and the feeling that separation was over, flooded my being. Why did I feel this way? I let go of her and took a step back, almost stumbling over a bag. I kept my feet and clapped by hands, instantly regretting it from the wound pain shooting up my arm.

'Mum said you'd had a little accident but would come by to see me later; to be honest I hadn't expected to see you so soon. Oh! I didn't mean that to sound negative, it's lovely that you are here. Mum always talks about you... I guess because she works with your father. We were all so shocked when we heard you were in hospital,' She smiled, her eyes glittered. 'You've changed so much!' She said.

'Aha,' The initial excitement of reunion had flagged completely, replaced by a sense of foolishness. My laugh was one of nerves, a voice within seemed to be chastising itself, and I was very confused. 'You're, you've grown...' I stammered, then thought to myself how obvious a statement it was. I found myself caught by her hazel eyes. She smiled again. I felt my legs go weak and had to look away. 'Seem like a good crowd.' I said, gesturing to the others in the study area.

She leant in close whispering, 'No one's spoken to anybody since we arrived.' Her breath teased my neck, then she swept my hand up to look at the bandage.

'Nothing serious I hope?'

'Oh! Er, no, no, just slipped with a power tool...'

She gave my hand a quick kiss, 'There!' She said, 'It'll be fine now, er, well, um, that's what Mum used to do when I... got... hurt.' She smiled again, only this time in a more embarrassed way, as if she'd shocked herself by what she'd done. It endeared her to me greatly. For a moment we stood silently and awkwardly before bursting into laughter.

'I really dropped in, er... my priority was to... drop off the course software.' I handed the memory cells to Hope. 'Could you ensure everyone gets a cell... That should get you all talking. I er, really need to get on with... my duties, so we'll catch up properly, at some point. Yes?'

'That would be good.' We stood motionless for too long. Hope frowned 'Sorry, did you say you had to go?'

'Er yes, yes, ha, day-dreaming!' I turned to leave but found myself still staring back at Hope; needless to say I walked straight into someone, a short stocky lad whose vision was almost totally obscured by a bulging hiker's rucksack.

'Oh! Sorry!' We both said in unison as I helped him back to his feet.

'Hey! You're Dace North. Wow, my sister's told me a lot about you. Can I get someone to take a picture of us with my camera?' He started looking for his camera. I glanced back at Hope, she seemed occupied handing out the memory cells, *that* was good. The lad's luggage label dangled from his bag as he started taking things out of it; Jake Phillips… he was Keely's brother.

'It must be in here somewhere!' He despaired.

'It's OK Jake, I'll be running through flight gear with you on Monday, you can bring your camera then, but remember, the use of a camera, in all but the designated areas, is prohibited.'

Jake looked up from his rummaging, 'You know my name!'

'It's on your luggage.'

He looked down at the rather obvious label.

'Right,' I asserted, feeling, suddenly, that I was giving a rather weak example for a member of the airfield staff. 'Clear this walkway and find your billet Mr. Phillips!'

'Yes Mr. North, er Dace, er Sir?' Jake hurriedly began cramming things back into his bag.

'Dace.' The voice beside me made me jump, but it was Hope again.

'Yes?'

'Did Mum mention my eighteenth?'

'Er, no.'

'You must come! I'll talk to Mum.'

'Sounds… good… I look forward to getting the invitation. Now I really must make tracks.' I caught myself doing the bizarre little two handed finger point Davey used to do, and gritting my teeth behind my smile, left the building. 'What was that?' I scolded myself, 'You behaved like an idiot!'

The airfield worker I'd seen as I entered the building flashed me an angry look.

'Not you!' I defended. 'You're not an idiot.'

She mumbled something under her breath and I hurried away.

I spent the rest of the day ruing my appearance to the new students; I must have looked like a stuttering fool, totally devoid of anything resembling authority. One thing I couldn't escape at all was the strength of my affections towards Hope. I felt like I knew her well, that I loved her, but it was a crazy thought considering how little I knew her and how

*Cries: The Captive Mind*

infrequently we'd met.

As I lay down that evening to sleep I found myself consumed with sadness. How different life was the last time I'd seen Hope. I'd only just heard Kerry's name; she was going to be my tutor. Nana and Gramps had both seemed capable of living forever, the only thing that seemed constant was Dad, he hadn't changed much. He'd very nearly killed himself through exhaustion working on the S. C. Britannia, and now he'd nearly worked himself to death in "The Space" at Sylvestris. There was one difference though; there had been no suggestion that the Val'ee were going to kill him back then, and, although it had been over two years since Clare had told me, the thought of his loss - after the loss of so many loved ones - still chilled me to the very core...

*'Still your mind, think only of your Hope.'*

The voice had come in the oblivion that marks the start of sleep; in that moment, recollecting the reality of my circumstances under Chorda's imprisonment, I wondered again why this evil creature would afford me such respite.

I recalled my dreams, they made sense now, future moments that the mind within fed into my subconscious, his own memories of Hope from where he had known her; but to the me of memory the images seemed merely beautiful, and increasingly desirable.

I awoke the next morning with a brightness that I had lacked for a long time. The euphoria faltered when I realised my schedule for the day would not afford me a chance to see Hope, but then, why worry? I'd see her soon enough.

I lived each day to reach another interaction with Hope. Most of these times seemed tainted by the need to perform my duties and I longed for less structured moments; one such moment soon came.

Hope was the last one out of the training complex one day, geared up for an introduction to high velocity flight in the new Ranger craft. Commander Reece was piloting "Halberd". The other students had boarded. Hope was late.

'Better pick up the pace Miss Emmerson.' I urged, running alongside and allowing my hand to rest in the small of her back as if offering a little light push. Hope apologised for her laxity and seemed far more concerned about reaching "Halberd" than where my hand was. I briefly admired her form in the flight suit then, suddenly startled, I pulled her to a halt.

'Hope, your suit isn't initiated!'

'But I'm sure I initiated it.' She protested, twisting around to the pack on her belt. Her breath, hastened from the run, sent sharp little puffs of vapour into the December air.

'No! it's not working; I'm going to miss the flight...'

'Let me,' I said, kneeling down beside her. 'Ha!' I exclaimed, 'The off button's stuck in.' I freed it with a pen from my pocket and initiated the suit. I looked up and she gave a little gasp as the fabric tightened around her. She'd been resting her hand on my shoulder, as I stood it stayed there.

'Did you just save my life again?' She smiled her trademark smile and lifted her hand to the side of my face.

'Ag, again?' I stuttered.

'You covered for me on the S. C. Britannia, Mum would have skinned me alive for using her Envisager...'

I laughed, 'I didn't really save your life then or now; you could have burst a lung on re-entry I suppose, but your MIT would have flagged it up, and appropriate assistance would have met you on the runway...' I was suddenly aware that I was babbling, 'So er, life not saved... Just glad we, er, noticed... in time.'

'I'm glad you're glad.'

My Gauntlet amp burst into life, 'Is this an audition for "Brief Encounter" or a training exercise?'

Raising my arm to my mouth, I replied 'Faulty pressure suit, Commander Reece, Sir; fault corrected, trainee with you in five seconds...'

We sprinted the distance and I gave some support as Hope entered the ship.

'I'll see you at my party?' She called as the door swung into position.

'Try and keep me away.' I called back as the cabin door sealed. I stepped clear of the vessel but nothing happened; I looked up at the cockpit and realised that the Commander was awaiting my thumbs up signal. He was grinning back at me with a knowing look in his eye. I still had to give the thumbs up, blushing as I did it; I knew what Taz would say I was giving the thumbs up to, and it wasn't for the all clear. Bathed in the downdraught of "Halberd" as it ascended vertically, my breath was momentarily stolen. I gazed longingly after its rapidly decreasing form. It remained visible for just a few more seconds before vanishing into distance. I waited. A bright piercing light and an instantaneous vapour trail appeared in the sky. I smiled, sighed her name and headed for the hangar making a mental note to look up "Brief Encounter" online.

## Chapter thirty-four
### Before the Headache

Hope's eighteenth heralded the start of the Christmas break for the trainees, and those who'd been invited were already in buoyant, party mood when I arrived.

Dad, and the others that worked in the hangar, were at a conference in London. I had been keen to attend until Hope appeared on the scene. Dad just chuckled and mumbled something about how he and Mum had met. He and Patricia seemed to congratulate each other - had they been plotting to bring me and Hope together? I'd certainly been easy to trap; I was besotted.

I turned up with flowers and champagne...

'Thank you, come in, I'll put these in water.'

I stepped into the already vibrant celebration, 'Am I late? The invitation was for six.' I said following closely behind Hope.

'No,' she flashed me a smile over her shoulder. 'I've had a few old friends around most of the afternoon and The Crew just turned up early.'

"The Crew" were her circle of friends from Jaro, her "old friends" turned out to be her school chums, and 'a few' was quite a lot! Hope was a popular girl.

As the evening drew on I watched her interacting with her guests; she was thorough, not neglecting anyone, and glasses were always full.

I took note of her graceful movements to negotiate the throng, her smiles - that now seemed etched on my soul - her laughter and warm glances. She would frequently bring people to me to introduce them, more to keep me entertained, I felt, than for any other reason.

After a while a young man approached of his own accord.

'Hey!' He nodded as he danced awkwardly in front of me. I nodded back out of politeness.

'You're Dace North...' He offered me his hand to shake. I didn't really want to shake it. He clearly knew me from my media exposure, but I didn't know him at all. It was Hope's party though, and this lad must be some friend from school, so I shook his hand.

I remained shaking my companions hand until he realised his oversight. 'Oh! Yeah, I'm Jerald, Jerald with a J.' He waggled the fingers of his free hand in front of his face for some reason. I frowned and let go.

Jerald motioned my attention over to Hope, 'Lovely isn't she.' He observed.

'Yes, she certainly...'

'I've known her since she arrived at high school, I just know she'll accept my offer...'

My ears pricked up, 'Offer?'

'I'm gonna ask her to marry me...'

I dropped my beer. Quickly retrieving the can before too much spilled 'Oh, er that's, that's great, er, best of luck er, Jeremy'

'Jerald actually. Jerald Morrello.'

I nearly dropped my can again, 'Jonathan Morrello's son?'

'The one and only.' He grinned.

If he suspected my affection for Hope, he had dealt it a well-placed blow. Jonathan was Head of the Morrello Corporation, the Government funded science organisation my father worked for. Who in their right mind could turn down marriage into such an important, rich and highly regarded family, Jerald, after all, was Jonathan's only child, and heir to it all.

'Nice to have met you Dacey.' Jerald concluded, and attempted to pop an overly friendly blow to my shoulder with his fist. I moved slightly, he missed, he attempted again, I blocked it.

'Nice moves.' He grinned and jigged off into the crowd.

I looked around for Hope but couldn't see her, just a gaggle of young attractive people jumping and dancing. A man in search of a tryst could find plenty of opportunities here but my heart sought Hope alone. I started trying to search her out, but it was as if she'd left the party altogether. Finally, I found myself on a large deck overlooking the garden; I took in the air and pondered my reason for being there. It really wasn't my scene, there were too many people. Much of my life was free of numerous friends, I had a few close pals and I'd been particularly popular at school if there was a science project - everyone would want to be in my group - but that was different. I sighed.

*Cries: The Captive Mind*

The air was sharply cold but it was a pleasant respite from the growing heat of the house. The stars were bright too, it was astonishingly beautiful, if I were Jerald I'd propose right here...

'Want some company?' A pair of warm arms circled my waist, and Hope's radiant face appeared around my shoulder. She giggled, I smiled.

'You're just like me Dace.'

'How's that?'

Her eyes looked up at the heavens, 'Always out there...'

I looked up at the stars. 'They're amazing tonight.' Suddenly I was filled with resolve, 'You're amazing tonight too.'

'Thanks.' She purred, acting a little shyly.

'Your dress is perfect, your hair, your eyes, your lips...'

This was going well, her eyes seemed fixed to mine and appeared to broadcast real pleasure.

She glanced back at the house then back to me, 'You will stay to the end of the party, won't you?'

'If you want me to.'

'I'd like that.'

'Then I'll stay.'

'I'd better see to my guests.' She said backing slowly away from me, beaming, seemingly unable to break from my gaze, then spinning around she disappeared through the French doors.

A cold breeze caught me and I decided to head inside myself.

'*Dace!*'

The voice surprised me and I turned to look out into the darkness beyond. I hadn't realised that there was anyone else further into the garden, but then it was a party and no restrictions had been made.

'*Here.*' The voice called gently, from a large evergreen shrub beside the balustrade.

'*Closer!*' It whispered and I found myself drawn obediently.

It was Aldorael, which immediately explained my desire to obey.

I resisted; it was painful. 'Stop it!' I snapped loudly. Aldorael looked into the party nervously, but no one had heard. 'Stop doing that thing you do, that controlling thing, it's not right!'

'*I will free you from it, only keep calm.*' She replied and I felt something prick inside my head.

'OW! What was that?'

'*Now I have no control over you Dace, but you* must *come with me.*'

I wondered why she would give me my free will if she wanted me to do something. 'I will not come now, I promised Hope I'd…'

*'I heard, but you must come, time is running out…'*

I frowned, there was no way I was going to leave the party. 'Why now?' I heard myself say.

*'If you want your father to live…'*

I felt truly empowered by Aldorael's lack of control. She looked agitated, older, greyer.

Suddenly I was anxious about Dad. 'Are you agreeing with IAAM now? *Is* Dad at risk?'

*'You must come now to prevent it.'*

Was this a joke; a powerful Val'ee Overseer seeking the assistance of an inferior human, and without enforcing the request! If they wanted to save Dad they'd hardly need my help. All they need do is take him for a little ride in a spaceship; once around the world should be enough.

Aldorael touched me, pulling my hand as if to urge me in her direction. In that moment I noticed her glow faintly, and as I pulled my hand away she seemed less drawn, less grey. Was that what happened when they touched us? Did they rejuvenate? Did they drain something…

Aldorael started to move back into the shadows. *'Now Dace, or we are out of time…'* She vanished into the darkness.

'It's always time with you guys.' I called after her, but there was no response. I shrugged, shook my head and returned to the party.

Stepping back into the room coincided with the music stopping abruptly and Jerald addressing the room publicly.

'OK, OK everyone, where's Hope?'

'I'm here.' She called, approaching him looking puzzled.

'Hope, we've known each other for many years…'

Hope seemed totally fixed on him. I could not see her face but I could picture how she must be smiling. A smile belonged to her face like angels belonged to Heaven.

'I've grown to love you Hope, and I thought this would be the perfect time to announce it and ask…' He dropped to one knee at her feet, I felt sick. '…would you do me the honour of accepting this ring?' He flipped open a little box, the jewel inside was big enough to see from across the room; I had been expecting Hope's immediate answer of "No". The way we'd spoken on the deck had left me confident of her mind, but the absence of an immediate answer jarred me. She seemed to hover over the ring, her hand firmly up near her mouth. The thought that she was about to accept filled me with dread.

Aldorael's words flashed back. *"If you want your father to live..."* Of course I wanted him to live; what held me here now? I'd been so selfish. I slipped back out of the French doors into the night, crossed the deck and ran down the steps near to where Aldorael had headed.

'Dace.'
'Oh good, I thought you'd gone...'
'I've only just arrived.'

The music started up again. I closed my eyes. The deed was done; Hope will have put that ring on her finger...

Suddenly the lights from the disco lit the face of my companion.
'Clare?'
'Sorry about this Dace, but we don't want a struggle...'
'What? We?' I heard a noise behind me. I turned, two figures, a little larger than me were backlit by the party lights, silhouetted by a strobe. I turned back to Clare, she was pointing something at me, it flashed and I felt something hit my shoulder. I looked; some sort of dart! I glared at Clare. This wasn't the girl I'd known. Her form seemed to twist out of coherent shape; no, not Clare, my perception. I'd been drugged.

Clare's lips moved but I heard nothing. One of the figures moved, there was a sharp pain in my hand, he helped himself to my car keys and drove off. I collapsed to my knees, the world spun, darkness, party lights, stars, blood, party lights, darkness, rainbows...

Someone pulled me up and I felt myself moving, stepping in uncoordinated stumbles, then there was a blinding light and a headache... but perhaps that was much later...

## Chapter thirty-five
## The Headache and Beyond

My head throbbed as I squinted into the light. A face, blurred beyond recognition, hovered over me. 'Welcome back.' The male voice seemed familiar but I couldn't place it. I tried to move but failed.

'Wha' haff you dun to me?' I slurred.

'I've never been keen on risks, Mr. North; Dr. Barnes may have cleared you regarding the presence of alien tissue after your Envisager mishap, but, well, I trust very few people and if he's missed something alien in you I don't know how *it* will react towards me.'

'Jayes?' I wondered how his voice seemed familiar and struggled for focus.

'Astute; very admirable. I do hope we can persuade you to take our journey with us…'

I exploded with rage. His blurred form backed sharply away as if nervous that the bonds holding me wouldn't stand the test.

'You killed Kerry…' I could hear what ever held me creaking under the pressure.

'We were framed…'

'LIES!'

'Someone wants you to hate us…'

'YOU killed Kerry *and* her child…'

'SOMEONE knows how damaging you will be to *them* if you join us, *they* are trying to manipulate you.'

'I hold YOU responsible.' I flopped back, defeated by my bonds.

Confident now that I was amply restrained the blur moved quickly forwards, rammed his fist into the plinth beneath me and boomed, 'LISTEN TO ME…'

I lay still, seething.

'We have pulled you out of harm's way, you are safe…' Somehow I realised what he was about to say. I could actually feel my pupils contract in horror.

'In just a few days *they* return, *Dace*. We cannot risk you being with your father when *they* do. We can't risk *you* being anywhere but safe with us. When you witness your father's death at *their* hands, *you* will believe what *we* have told you. *You* will trust us and help us.'

I was reduced to a beggar 'No! please. I have lost everyone! If here is safe, bring him here too!'

'Then it would cease to be safe, and we'd all die…'

'Then warn him, let him run…'

'*They* will find him…'

'Tell Commander Reece. We *must* defend him, fight…'

'Dace,' His voice was calm. 'All this is history. Your father dies. With you here, hope remains…'

'Where's the hope in that!' I snapped back, 'He's all I have left! You've taken…'

'We've taken nothing. We offer you life Dace. W*e* have saved your life.'

A sudden thought gripped me, the Archivist Clare had spoken of… 'Your "ideas" come from the Archivist.'

'My ideas are from my experience. The Archivist knows all. Nothing in my experience contradicts what the Archivist has told me. But you, Dace, you're an enigma.'

Jayes' statement shredded my train of thought. I was going to ask to see the Archivist, to challenge him. How could anyone know everything? But to be called an enigma threw me. How could Jayes describe me as a mystery when he had just inferred that I was important enough to save?

'You're contradicting yourself.' I hissed. 'Why pull me out of trouble if I'm such a puzzle? You don't know *what* I'll do!' I laughed, if I was an enigma it meant only one thing… 'Your Archivist has no knowledge of me!'

'That's not quite what I meant. The record shows that you die with your father at Sylvestris. Now you won't. Isn't that amazing! Change, Dace, in a war against an enemy who thinks it knows everything.' Jayes eyes discernibly glinted through the blurriness of my sight. 'There are older records too Dace. The previous one records that you were killed, aged eight. Mown down by a delivery van on the street outside your Grandparents home after visiting the alien mothership ERUWAI.' Jayes' words stung, I relived the moment of my rescue in a flash of traumatised thought.

'Your record is wrong, I was rescue…'

Jayes held up his hand, I stopped, 'Oh Dace, it gets better, the previous record to that tells us something else…' He paused to build my tension. I felt confused. How many records were there?

'That record tells me you turned out more like the others of your generation, an infant corpse…'

'You're sick!'

'No Dace, *you* are sick.'

I shook my head in disbelief.

He continued, 'Your father's defence of the Val'ee is madness. Your father has tainted you with his wrong beliefs. Now *they* will kill him and your blindness will be lifted.'

He'd hit a nerve: Dad had lied to the world about the success of the Val'ee over The Great Suffering. I struggled to recall what had been so appealing to me about Dad's faith and reasoning. I feared it might just be the strength of Val'ee persuasion, but I wasn't ready to give up on him.

'My father is a great man; he seeks to avoid the terrible conclusion of your designs.'

'My *designs*! Tell me, who but the Archivist would be able to express to your father the outcome of my *des*…' He stopped short. The tension in the room was discernibly heightened and I sensed that Jayes perceived my statement as an indication that his enemies had proffered guidance to my father.

'Your father's mind is weaker than I thought. If *they* have been to him *their* advice will have been bogus, *they* will have twisted the truth to attain *their* aims.' His movements now seemed to head towards completion of our debate.

Vainly I attempted to rectify the belief in him that the Val'ee were closer than he'd thought, 'Going by your own words, through Clare and here now, when the Val'ee return they will kill my father. If they are back why is he not dead already?'

'I admire your loyalty Dace, but perhaps they needed something from him; perhaps *you* intrigue them. What remains true is that your father has weakened Earth's ability to defend itself. Alien technologies underpin all our capabilities. Who knows what that will mean when the aliens strike. Will our ability to counter an attack vanish at the flick of some alien switch? IAAM alone has prepared; IAAM alone, and we will prevail. We will have our rightful place.' He began to walk away. 'You have followed your father's work. It is valuable only to the Val'ee, for humanity it holds great peril. When you see *their* so called guidance played out you *will* join us.' He stopped walking and turned briefly, 'One thing to dwell on until we meet again Dace. Someone *has* already changed the record to put you here, someone has changed it twice, and we are changing it now. Why? Because *you* might be the only hope for mankind.' Jayes left before

*Cries: The Captive Mind*

I could figure out how to respond. My head continued to throb, as much from Jayes' revelations as from the drug they'd used on me.

'Here, this will help your head...' I instantly recognised Clare's voice, but she too was a blur.

'Are you reading my MIT again?'

'How do you mean?' Clare responded dismissively.

'My vital signs, they've told you I've got the mother of headaches...'

'No chance of that now, you haven't got one.'

I looked at my hand but was unable to see. With my hands being closely bound I felt for the distinctive lump that gave away the position of the Val'ee chip, it *was* gone! Instead I could feel a sore, sharp little scar.

Clare continued, 'I'm giving you something for a headache because that's what the tranquiliser causes as it wears off.'

'Where's my MIT?'

'For as long as you still had it the Government, and - worse still - the Val'ee themselves, could locate you. They could target us. As soon as the true colours of the Val'ee have been seen we will be at war. They will attack again. IAAM alone can stand against them. When you are ready, you will help make strategic decisions as to how we combat them, they will not expect your input.'

'You even sound like Jayes.' I felt a needle enter my arm, 'OW!'

'Your head will feel better soon, rest now.'

'Do I have a choice?' I moaned.

The light went off and Clare's blurred outline left the room.

I lay there awake. Dad had days left, this I believed, even Aldorael had said it in her attempts to get me to follow her, but at least she'd given me a choice, Jayes hadn't. "They twist the truth." he'd said, but was the free will Aldorael gave me dishonest? Was it just a gamble? Did she feel that such a grand gesture might secure a favourable response from me? I began to wonder where I'd be now if I'd gone with her. But then... did they need us for some, more arcane purpose. What had actually happened when Aldorael touched me?

'Want to lose your bonds Trix?'

'Rue?' I gasped, as I looked up. It *was* her, in soft focus, but clear enough to recognise.

I felt my restraints ease and retract and I made my way to Rue's side. 'How are we getting out of here?' I asked, assuming that her reassignment must have been something with Special forces. It would have suited her.

Rue placed a finger against my lips, 'Shh...'

The light outside the room was bright but I could see a short corridor with four other doorways leading off it. Through a glass partition at the far end was an open area surrounded by railings.

Rue's hand pressed into my back, urging me towards the railings. I edged out of the room and slid tightly along the wall of the corridor; Rue stepped boldly out of the room and followed me half laughing at my covert behaviour. I stopped.

'You're not here to help me escape are you?'

The look on her face confirmed my deduction. I spun around pummelling the wall with my fists, 'What then!' I demanded.

She tipped her head towards the rails. I stepped up to the glazed panel in front of them and gazed out at the cavernous space beyond. Sixteen floors curved around my position, and a multitude of people milled around sundry and numerous machines.

'Computer, open sound screen...' Rue stated.

'Recognition of Miss James confirmed, matching position, stand by...'

The glazing slid aside and a cacophony of industrial noise met my ears. It was a workshop on a scale I'd never seen before. I moved to the railings. Below me was a drop of over a hundred metres and many more layers of industry became visible, sparks rose up from the lower floors like fountains of lava in the mouth of a volcano.

The picture before me was a production line for various craft and weapons systems, but it was a line devoid of Envisagers, filled instead with dirty, greasy workmen and women, each performing their task quickly and efficiently.

Rue motioned to the left, 'You'll recognise those ones.'

'Val'ee Tinnys, Ha! What's IAAM doing with alien technology? Aren't they scared of it *watching* them?' I mocked.

'They are cargo vessels based on a design by engineer Carey Flack, see how new they look?'

They looked pristine; not like the tired old ships the Val'ee had "gifted" us before they left. This agreed with Dad's experience - his transport vessel appearing above Hyde Park before it had reached the prototype stage.

I sneered, 'The Val'ee end up using them you know, at some point they'll take them from you.'

Rue read my tone. It obviously chilled her, and I sensed that she would bring the concept to Jayes' attention at her earliest convenience.

'The evidence agrees with your father's work Trix; you seem confident of his theories.'

'My father is correct, his motivations are noble and decent... and don't involve abduction.'

'We've not abducted you, we're protecting you.'

'So you all keep saying.'

'Your father's theories seem OK; we'd question his motives.'

I was troubled by Rue's continued mention of Dad's theories, her drawing of my attention to the Tinnys and her telling reaction to my suggestion that the Val'ee would take them. It presented to me the possibility that Dad's work would indeed result in a means to step out of time and return at another point. It was the natural progression of his work on "The Space". I felt cold. He'd suggested that a vessel the size of the ERUWAI could generate a big enough field to subdue time and create a conduit through which to pass. Could he... would *he* make it? Would the Val'ee take possession of it? If so why would they come before it was created, to kill him? Wouldn't that create some sort of conflict regarding the technology ever being made? Didn't the Val'ee possession of technologies we know to be human, indicate their ultimate victory over us? I had remained quiet too long.

'I suppose this...' I gestured at the sea of completed ships, guns and munitions. 'Is IAAM's fleet to counter a Val'ee attack?'

'Yes, you are correct.'

'It's pathetic.'

Rue looked at me sharply. 'There are ten thousand ships, a quarter of the fleet that will be at our disposal when the time comes.'

'A Val'ee ship like the ERUWAI is massive, it must bristle with defences. These are like midges to a whale!'

Rue huffed dismissively. 'If this were the complete IAAM fleet I would happily fly with it confident of victory.'

'I suppose the Archivist has given you an infallible strategy.'

'Not really, but we are prepared for the strategy of our enemy. Besides, you haven't seen all our ships yet.'

I waved my hand apathetically at the small vessels before us, 'If this is a quarter of what you intend to have built, there won't be much room left for anything elsc.'

Rue grinned, 'Hold on.' She instructed, offering her hand, I instinctively grasped it as we shot sideways.

We sped through a short, narrow tunnel into a cavern more massive than the first, and my jaw dropped. In front of me were four of the biggest ships I'd ever seen on earth! The sides, top, underside and rear boasted enough armament to level a city in a single salvo, but it was the front that chilled me most; this was adorned with a cannon some ten metres in diameter.

'IAAM fully intends to protect the earth Trix.'

I was startled by the sudden appearance of another tunnel and a further chamber. This held nineteen fighter carriers. Large vessels in themselves, they carried thirty single seater drop craft, laden with arrays of missiles. Whoosh, another tunnel and the vista that lay itself before my eyes silenced me.

'Fleet mothership; The Deliverance.' Rue announced.

The ships bulk nearly touched the yawning walls of the great cavern. I laughed, 'There's no way out. Your whole fleet is buried!'

'You allude to the apparent lack of doors?' She sighed and stared at me for a moment, 'Huh, why not. Computer, reveal sky...'

'Executing...'

There was a sudden rush of cold air as winter rushed around me, and what had appeared to be the cavern roof melted away to reveal a starry host above us.

'We have borrowed the landscape Trix, narrowed a valley. We're concealed by a mountainside that doesn't exist.'

'A hologram?'

'Heavens no!' Rue laughed, 'Power Generated Matter; Jayes was jubilant when it came online, said it confirms that we are on-route to developing the Envisager. That years from now it will be refined to a hand held device of remarkable potential and that, like every other technology of value, it will be stolen by the Val'ee and used to awe a less technological age.'

'How is that something to be jubilant about?'

Rue laughed again, 'It proves that the Val'ee are incapable! All they have is stolen!'

It sounded surreal to me, I just wanted to save Dad. 'Why not go public with all this. Can't the Archivist reveal each forthcoming event to the world to show the accuracy of this record? Then we can all fight the Val'ee...'

*Cries: The Captive Mind*

'It's good to see you coming down on our side but Mother says that openness regarding the strategy of IAAM would cause immense global panic, that truth can only come when humanity is ready to hear it.'

'Your Mother said! Since when does Elizabeth Verne decide what's right for the people of earth?'

'My Mother keeps the record; *she is* the Archivist.'

I gained nothing more from Rue. At gun point she took me back to my room and locked me in. Jayes' project seemed better managed and led than I'd ever conceived, but I was a prisoner, held against my will. Watched and contained within a tight perimeter, waiting for this terrible event that had been promised. I was torn between Chorda and Aldorael's advice to avoid a conflict - instigated by Jayes - that would devastate our world; Jayes' undeniable grasp of an unfolding story, relayed to him in seemingly flawless detail by his Archivist; and my father's desire to promote peace and a secure future.

## Chapter thirty-six
### A broken Heart.

Each day they projected news footage to a screen in my room; same time, same channel. The lead story was my disappearance, then the discovery of my wrecked car and MIT chip. Dad had claimed these and taken them to Sylvestris for analysis. Each time he appeared on screen I was reminded how powerless I was to save him. There was news of an explosion at the Morrello complex but I was too broken now to care for anyone, apart from Dad.

Early one morning whilst it was still dark, I was woken by the screen coming on. It was unusual, they normally streamed edited footage in the evening, but the image before me was the silhouette of a man seated in a brightly lit room.

'Ah, Dace, you are awake,' I recognised Jayes' voice. We hadn't spoken since I awoke from the tranquiliser, and again I was unable to see his face. I was instantly angered, but I kept my wits. I still believed that whilst Dad lived there was a chance I could warn him. I remained seated on the bed.

'You seem much calmer today Dace, this is good…'

'Well,' I replied. '*I* don't need to hide my face…'

He laughed, I continued. 'You only ever see people hide their faces when they're afraid, are you afraid Jayes?' I chuckled, 'And your voice, is it yours or is it an actor's voice? Do you actually have a really squeaky voice?'

Jayes shifted awkwardly in his seat, 'There is not time to humour you Dace, events are afoot.'

Feed from a MIT chip, depicting vital signs, appeared on the bottom left of the screen. It was Dad's. A cold judder went through me; was this the day? I felt a great wave of distress overcome me. 'Why are you torturing me Jayes? Let me go…'

'Oh lord no. It's far too late now, besides, it is not torture, it is information, proof. The facts you need.'

I had one desperate last card, 'I believe you, I don't need the facts, let me go!' Jayes remained silent.

I gazed, helpless, at the rhythm of Dad's heart. He was physically active, as if undertaking exercise, the rolling graph gave puzzling little peaks that didn't seem to have any bearing on the normal statistics at all, just random ticks with irregular lengths of time between them.

'There she is…' Jayes announcement shook me. A small inset screen had appeared top right on the wall. I squinted and approached the projection.

'This is live footage Dace, from one of the Government factories at the edge of the atmosphere; Pathfinder Four. Can you make out our visitor amongst all the stars?'

I could! I could see the outline of a massive vessel, lit by the red glow of the rising sun.

'This isn't real.' I exclaimed.

'Lamentably, you are wrong.' Jayes replied.

'If it *were* real we would not be able to talk, there would be silence, the Val'ee engines block sound waves…'

'The Val'ee rift engines create silence, the vessel you see is moving under standard propulsion…'

That wasn't enough of an explanation for me, 'But there have been no prolonged silences, did the ship just appear or will you admit your deceit?'

'Dace, what you are observing is real, the vessel arrived behind the moon. That is what sheltered the earth from the effects of the rift engines.'

*Cries: The Captive Mind*

The Val'ee ship began to turn slowly, my gaze was held and I stood hypnotised. Suddenly accepting Jayes' explanation I bolted for the doorway, ramming it with my shoulder. I cried out in pain as nothing gave, but soft tissue. Desperately I sought something not fixed to the floor to throw against the door. Finding nothing I collapsed, sobbing, to my knees. 'Let me go Mr. Jayes.' I begged.

'You are safe here...'

'Please Mr. Jayes, let me help my Dad, he's all I have left, without him there is no point in being safe. I will die inside.'

'You cannot help your father, but your life will be full of purpose. You *will* have your revenge against these aliens, but the world must know that it's at war. More will be lost in the next Val'ee attack. This attack will serve to anger the world and rally it to fight. When the right moment comes IAAM will come as a sweeping fire against the Val'ee, and you Dace, you will be there at our side. You will show the Val'ee just how wrong they were to target Earth.'

I could hear a siren from the corridor outside my room. I looked up at Jayes' dark outline, 'I will never forgive you.' I hissed, defeated.

'I do not expect you to, though perhaps one day you will look back...'

'I will *never* forgive you.' I interrupted.

'So be it.' Came the short, cutting reply.

Suddenly the inset screen lit up. The Val'ee ship carved through the factory superstructure, ramming it and slicing it apart. The incomplete hulk of a spaceship spiralled off towards the moon. The Pathfinder Four buckled and gave way beneath the impact. The Val'ee ship, so like the ERUWAI, reflected the subsequent explosions like a mirror, its smooth ceramic surfaces emblazoned like gold.

'Finally!' Jayes roared. 'They've shown their true colours!'

The camera taking the images now spun away into space, its lens capturing - in short, horrific bursts - the aftermath of the collision and the unaffected Val'ee ship as its under body sank into the edge of the atmosphere, sending rainbow eddies across it.

A flash of hope penetrated my pain, 'The Val'ee ship is the same design as the ERUWAI, it is a space going giant unsuitable for an atmosphere. It's going to crash! Please warn Dad, make sure he is nowhere near the vicinity of the impact.'

'I have told you, your father *is* the target. Crash or not they will still manoeuvre to target his MIT,' He struck the desk in front of him with his fist, as if to make some point regarding his zeal, 'Their ship will survive long enough to prove what IAAM has been warning all these years.'

A second inset screen appeared on the wall below the first, which now showed a rotating view of the curvature of earth, framing the Pathfinder Four as it disintegrated. The new screen was broadcasting live TV news. The news reader, initially flustered, now addressed the camera.

'We have cut into your, er, usual viewing to bring you breaking news! A large vessel, believed to be similar in design to the Val'ee mothership 'ERUWAI', has collided with Pathfinder Four. The factory has sustained terminal damage and is collapsing into the atmosphere, as is the alien ship. It is believed that this is a terrible accident.' The news reader paused and held her ear as if getting new information through her earpiece. 'This now in. MIT readings show that a small number of survivors from the Pathfinder are safely clear of the factory. Debris from the factory is due to impact the Atlantic just north of Ireland in fifteen minutes. Any ships on or near the coordinates given onscreen are advised to head away from the impact area. We have live feed now from S. C. Paris. Our Europe Correspondent, Daniel Grayers, is there for us. Daniel can you tell us anything more?'

'Yes Becky, the alien ship is descending in a wide spiral, leaving a trail of rusty, brown smoke, the speed is quite phenomenal and the pattern of descent seems to be the only control its crew now possesses.'

The camera shifted from the correspondent to the smoke trail, zooming in on the stricken ship.

'Yes, er, I don't know if you're getting these images Becky...'

'Yes Daniel, we can see them.'

'The configuration of the ship is identical to the ERUWAI. We can only assume, with the Pathfinder factories being constructed since the departure of the Val'ee, that the Val'ee have unintentionally rammed Pathfinder Four. This, it seems, *is* a terrible accident.'

'Thank you Daniel, Daniel Grayers there for...'

'So much for your terrible attack Jayes; it's an accident, you will convince no one otherwise.'

'Oh? Come the end I will not need to convince anyone.'

'You're a warmonger Jayes. The Val'ee helped bring children back to the world. They gave us technology beyond our time.'

'They were not honest, and the technology was not theirs to give.' He looked at his watch and fell silent.

*Cries: The Captive Mind*

For a short while the news feed continued in the same vein. Pictures from a naval vessel showed great fragments of red hot factory wreckage raining down on the sea, then Jayes initiated a third inset screen. It showed the path of the Val'ee ship from moon, to impact, to terminal descent. The spiral had grown wider from the ships point of entry into the atmosphere and now covered an area visible from three Sky Cities. I stared at the graphic. A feeling of déjà vu struck me hard in the stomach. The smoke trail pointed to an horrific intent; the ship had been manoeuvred into a position that would...

'Jayes!' I yelled. 'You *must* warn them. IAAM can begin its heroism now! Call for an evacuation!'

Jayes remained silent. I crossed again to my door and hammered on it with all my strength. Calling for someone to come.

What followed was calculated and methodical. The correspondent on S. C. Paris had contacted the studio and, with a voice on the edge of panic, jostled by the chaotic stampede of those around him, relayed what I had just figured out. The feed fell into confusion as all buckled to fear and fled for their lives. The news channel switched to an external camera.

The Val'ee ship, too high to ram the floating structure, deployed beams that tore down like lightning, puncturing one of the giant tropospheric stabilisers and starting a chain reaction. The stabiliser generators erupted into a vortex of flame that shattered the dome above it, then the spine of the great platform ruptured and tore. Whole sections peeled away. Adjacent stabilisers, forced by the levering action of the collapsing structure, now erupted also, sending parts of the city shooting off in random directions like doomed rockets.

I felt hot tears streaming down my face. Too few seemed to be getting out. A handful of personal transports sped clear but not a twenty thousand strong residential population, service personnel and crew.

Then with a gut wrenching crack and unzipping flame, the city collapsed. What stabilisers remained blew out like cannons and, with a reek of black smoke, the blazing tangle dropped down into the suburbs of Paris below.

S. C. Madrid was next. They had had a few minutes to react and to realise that evacuation was necessary. A steady flow of vessels was exiting from all bays, although one bay suddenly spewed out a tongue of grey smoke. A zooming media camera confirmed that an accident had blocked the way.

I wondered briefly if the unfolding events could have been prevented if weaponry had been fitted to the cities. But they'd been a beacon of peace, not war; crafted by collaboration, not in readiness for this, no one could have imagined *this*! My fury raged inside, Jayes had known it, and not acted. He was a monster.

I watched, unable to tear my eyes from the scene. The news anchor had fallen silent. The images were coming from one of the evacuation vessels now clear of S. C. Madrid. The Val'ee ship, now equal in altitude, proceeded to sheer through the beautiful curves that had made Madrid so distinctive. Craft still leaving the city were engulfed in fire and twisted metal, the Val'ee ship carried black, acrid smoke from the heart of the structure.

S. C. Madrid, its remaining evacuees trapped beneath its gutted bulk, smashed into sweeping Spanish fields and leafless, winter woodland prompting an inferno that rivalled the frost for miles around.

All Sky Cities were now being evacuated regardless of their proximity to the path of the Val'ee ship. Government fighters were scrambled and missiles launched, but the newsreader's rediscovered voice was short lived as the military attack fell impotent to the ground. 'They're gone.' She gasped. 'All of them…' then the shock of her colleague's death, the destruction of the cities and the incomprehensible defeat of the military left her in fits of tears.

'Now the end.' Jayes words rang out into a deathly hush as the final scenes played out in silence.

S. C. Britannia was run through from beneath by the same lightening beams that had sent S. C. Paris to its end. Britannia's closing moments were more decisive. Most of the cities stabilisers detonated instantaneously as the beams travelled directly across them, and the city, almost intact, fell like an asteroid into the North Sea sending huge waves in all directions.

The Val'ee ship's altitude and direction of travel, left no room now for speculation, it was headed for the Thetford Sylvestris at breakneck speed. Live footage now came from the ground, first Harwich, Ipswich, Stowmarket and then Thetford. I attempted to scream my bile filled hatred at Jayes but nothing came. My lips formed the words and my larynx vibrated but nothing touched the peace enforced by the Val'ee engines that now fired in what looked like a last attempt not to crash. Light briefly flooded the room, the insets on the projection were gone;

everything gone bar the graphic from my father's MIT. I glanced quickly at Jayes. He sat, head in hands, at his desk. Had this really needed to happen? Did Jayes suffer from allowing it?

My eyes returned to all I had left of Dad. The heart stats were higher; he knew what was coming. They peaked three more times, then...

'NO!' I cried out, but no one could hear me, only my sobs became audible as the return of sound heralded the doom of the Val'ee ship and its engines.

## Chapter thirty-seven
## My Own Ends

'This *was* the only way.' Jayes announced firmly, although something of the tone of his voice had altered. 'Now the whole world will come under the IAAM banner. My fleet will set this dark day right and make it the dawn of our freedom. Dace, I am truly sorry...' His voice faltered and the projection of his image came to an end.

To me Jayes simply had blood on his hands. His confidence, regarding the effectiveness of his own ships, suggested a knowledge of the Val'ee defences that could have been shared with the military. Instead he'd let three Sky Cities fall, allowed collateral damage that must have killed at least as many people as had been slain already, and allowed a counter attack to fail. Not one pilot in that attack had jettisoned from any of the stricken fighters; the news footage had portrayed that in all the sickening detail of unedited, live pictures.

Jayes could have stopped it, but he hadn't.

I felt sick, alone, helpless, trapped and vulnerable. The grief left every muscle trembling uncontrollably. A madness scratched at my psyche and I contemplated giving myself over to it. What little belief I'd had in a "God" evaporated, how could he allow something so terrible? Fred had been right; it was all a mess of chance - unbelievable though my studies had led me to conclude - all understanding had been lost in the vastness of time. I doubted I'd even understand it myself, but the choice to believe in meaningless chaos was, in this moment, easy enough.

From my awkward, agonised position - half curled up on the floor at the foot of the bed - I heard the door slide open and then closed, followed by the approach of footsteps. I froze in confused terror but then felt arms sweep around me, comforting and warm; the vine tattoo continuing below the neckline of a loose fitting top betrayed my comforter as Rue. She drew tightly close, half collapsing to the floor herself to demonstrate her desire to find me at my own devastated level.

'Dear Trix, you need to understand that Jayes is dedicated to the maintenance of the timeline, he could not change it now without disastrous ramifications.'

I clung to Rue as if she were the only thing afloat in my despairing sea. Her arms echoed my grip, her cool fingers brushing the nape of my neck.

'You must consider helping Mr. Jayes, Trix.'

I pulled away strongly, but she kept her hold and whispered, 'I don't like him either. I can't read him like I can other people. He seems thoroughly depressed and trapped and yet his actions are those of one supremely confident of his objective. Go figure!'

I remained silent.

'Trix, I've been studying my mother's record. Given time we could figure out a change that will forge a different outcome.'

I looked up into her eyes. Her words gave the first glint of hope I'd experienced in this place. 'Thanks Rue.'

I felt my senses filling with an intense affection, then Rue released her embrace and stepped quickly across the room - the feelings died. I frowned. Rue pushed her hands deeply into her pockets and, with her back to me, whispered, 'Consider joining Mr. Jayes; if for no other reason than your own ends.' She opened the door and paused, turning to face me, 'I'll stop by later to see how you are. We've got to take the blows Trix, the enemy knows what we do, they come from the future, so we're an open book. Mr. Jayes saved your life. It wasn't your father they targeted, it was you! Mr. Jayes installed a life signs program on your MIT chip. Your car wreck was left where it would be found. Your father took it just as Mr. Jayes knew he would, ensuring it would be at Sylvestris as you were last time. As far as the Val'ee are concerned, you are as dead as their history tells them.'

A tear dashed across Rue's cheek, 'I'm so sorry about your father Dace.' She turned away and left the room. The door began to slide closed. I leapt to my feet and ran at it. By the time I reached it the gap was centimetres wide. Unthinking, I rammed my hand at the void and threw my weight against the mechanism. I felt the crush of the panels closure pressing into my palm. Strength, birthed from rage, flashed through me as I slid my free fingers into what was left of the opening, fixing my position by jamming my foot against the frame of the door, I thrust the bulk of the door panel against itself; something gave, something ground into the motor, the door panel sat wedged in a half open state.

Rue stood at the end of the corridor openly astounded by the display she'd just witnessed. I stared back for a moment.

'I, I just... don't like being shut in.' I returned to the bed and lay down with my back to the door. It was almost a minute before I heard Rue's footsteps, first returning to the crippled doorway, then departing.

Opening my hand, I gazed at the broken skin on my palm and allowed the blood to trickle onto the bedding, getting up again only when the flow had been stemmed by its own congealment.

It was much later in the day, almost lunchtime, when I found myself standing in front of the sound proofing panel, staring through at the activity beyond. A crazy thought entered my mind, 'Computer...' I voiced.

'Recognition of Mr. North confirmed, please state request...'

I almost laughed. I hadn't really expected a positive response and it threw me. I couldn't remember what Rue had asked, so I ended up pointing at the panel, 'Er, can you open this for me?'

'Stand by...'

I frowned. That hadn't been the response Rue had got, but then, I hadn't been very specific...

'Please confirm – "Open Sound Screen".'

'Er, yes, open sound screen.' The screen slid open and I was bathed with the sounds of hard physical work. I approached the railings and couldn't resist testing the strength of their fixings, a kick of electricity confirmed whether or not I was yet trusted. It jarred the wound on my hand, a little blood dripped onto the floor. I shrugged, lowered my hand and let the blood trickle down my fingers.

I looked at the eclectic mix of vessels that had been constructed. I wondered what Jayes knew of the Val'ee arsenal that would enable him to avoid the same end as the Government fighters. Had *he* experienced the future or was he relying on the Archivist? I still struggled with the thought that any one person could know it all, and if things had now changed with my "rescue", didn't that mean the future would be different too?

My grief at losing Dad bubbled up again, not with tears but rage. I punched the railings with my uninjured hand, repeatedly enduring the jolt. Nothing gave.

Jayes was like the rails, cold and hard. He'd been capable of allowing carnage to let his enemy believe that nothing had changed. I felt sure, from his altered tone, that he felt some regret for the considerable loss of life; to allow any other thought would make him inhuman, as much an alien as the creatures who had brought the devastation.

I acknowledged that I was a playing piece in Jayes' strategy and, although I would never forgive him for my father's death, it was ultimately the Val'ee who had dealt the killing blow. I wanted to pay them back, and only Jayes could provide the opportunity. Perhaps Rue was right, joining Jayes was a means to my own ends.

After witnessing the Val'ee attack on the Sky Cities, I doubted Aldorael and Chorda's advice to avoid IAAM to prevent the destruction of humanity; I saw it only as a delaying tactic to prevent the growth of their enemy before combat was finally joined. As regards IAAM's involvement with the death of Kerry and her baby, I now felt confused; I feared that Jayes could be right, that a third party had perpetrated the action to make me resist IAAM instead of embrace it. Had Kerry's death been at the hands of the Val'ee too? Tears burst out of me. I had to avenge my family. Joining IAAM would enable this - so I would do it. At least until Jayes' path no longer matched my own.

'I have some food for you.'

The voice behind me belonged to Clare. I glanced at the tray.

'I don't like fish; I always leave it. Why do they keep putting it on there?'

Clare shrugged, 'We all get the same, it's a balanced diet, all the essentials. Do you want it here or in your room?'

I took the tray and headed back to my room. Clare noticed the blood on the floor and followed.

'You've made some alterations.' Clare suggested as we entered through the broken door, and, seeing the bloodied bed, insisted on treating my wound. 'Rue said you must have been injured. It looks nasty, you're still trailing blood.'

'Took your time coming.' I snorted, offering my hand.

*Cries: The Captive Mind*

'Rue felt that you needed time. Have you made a decision?'

'Jayes offers the possibility of repaying the Val'ee for their services to me. I will let him provide that opportunity, but I'm not a puppet...'

'None of us are.' Clare defended as she finished cleaning my hand.

I snorted, shovelling in some mash with my free hand.

'Jayes is doing the right thing; today's lesson has been hard for all of us but we are sure he will lead us to victory. It is recorded...'

'You've bought into this completely!'

Clare looked up briefly and frowned, then returned to the dressing.

'Jayes has "saved" my life! That's going to bring changes. No one really knows what will happen now. Maybe I'll make things worse...'

Clare didn't look up, she simply tightened the bandage, 'I'll let Mr. Jayes know your decision. You will be able to control the projection unit now...' She pulled a remote device from her pocket and placed it in front of me. 'You might appreciate being able to switch off the news, I don't know.'

With the briefest of glances her eyes met mine. She looked sad and as she turned to leave a new melancholy touched me. I had been cold towards one who had been a friend at the EOA; friends were all I had left now. I should be strengthening these bonds to soften the harshness of those absences that cannot be replaced.

'Clare!' I called as she reached the door.

She stood still, and without turning said 'Yes?'

'Thanks, it's a good bandage.'

Clare turned and smiled, 'Welcome home.' She said and left.

I turned on the projector and actively sought news.

The Val'ee attack was the only thing on. Death tolls were calculated from flat-lined MIT devices. The news reader, pale and edgy, announced that a little over forty-five thousand people had died. The bulk of the deaths had occurred on the Pathfinder factory, S. C. Paris and the residential areas where the first Sky City had fallen. I watched an analysis of the ships approach. It was the same graphic that Jayes had placed onto the view screen before the first Sky City was struck; confirming that he had access to information that had not yet been created. The conclusion of the media was that of a premeditated attack. There was no other route that could have achieved an impact on so many nations - based on the speed of the ship's decaying altitude. Furthermore, Pathfinder four had

217

tried to make contact with the Vessel, and had been ignored. The Val'ee had changed their position and rammed the space factory. The event was thoroughly intentioned.

I wondered why the Val'ee ship hadn't utilised ships from its docks; why descend to this suicidal devastation? My thoughts that it must have been due to the initial collision were broken by the appearance of Elizabeth Verne in the studio with the news reader...

'I have the great pleasure of being joined by Doctor Elizabeth Verne of the Morrello Corporation. Doctor Verne, I've just been informed that the prompt actions of Morrello led to the complete annihilation of the Val'ee ship...'

I sat forward and listened; I had thought that the lumbering vessel had merely ended its journey as a mangled wreck amongst the debris of Sylvestris, but the newsreader went on to suggest its total disintegration above the site.

'Yes Fiona,' Verne replied. 'The ship's main engines emit a kind of signal - the silence that we experienced the first time the Val'ee came to the earth – and this is a profound weakness. The signal provides a "carrier" for a counter weapon developed, in secret, in the Morrello research laboratories. The counter measure creates a chain reaction causing meltdown of the ship's generators. The moment silence occurred we moved to put an end to this terrible event. Jonathan Morrello, head of the Corporation, wishes to extend his sympathy to all who have been effected.' Elizabeth turned to face the camera. 'We only wish the Val'ee had started their main engines sooner; that we may have avoided the awful carnage these creatures have inflicted on us.'

'Indeed,' the newsreader replied. 'But how is it that we did not experience the silence before the aliens crippled the Pathfinder Four?'

Elizabeth outlined the same intelligence Jayes had regarding the moon, putting beyond doubt the malicious intent of the Val'ee.

I felt confused by Elizabeth's appearance on the news, Rue had called her the Archivist. She was Jayes' advisor, and yet here she was extolling the virtues of a Government weapon, a Government that - along with the Concordant Nations - had shunned the passionate views of the leader of IAAM. The interview was concluded with a shift in this position as Verne announced the impending meeting of all parties to discuss a viable defence of the earth, and a cessation of Envisionment.

It seemed to me that Doctor Verne held a disproportionate share of

*Cries: The Captive Mind*

power. Her closeness to both sides, and knowledge of this mysterious "record", troubled me.

Suddenly a scene, not unlike a desert appeared and I wondered for a moment where it was. The field correspondent dropped the bombshell.

'Yes Fiona, I'm up in "News Rover Two" above the site where, just six hours ago, over nineteen thousand hectares of forestry stood...'

My heart almost seized; I had still expected to see the shattered wreck of the Val'ee ship. All I could see on screen was bare earth and spattered, melted glass structures through which the dust shifted restlessly in vortices driven by the wind. I could feel the wideness of my eyes, the dryness of my throat, the pressure of my hand held in shock to my face.

'This is the site of the Thetford Sylvestris Array and laboratories run by Douglas North whose son Dace went missing, presumed dead, just a few days ago. If Dace is alive and watching this story unfolding, one can only imagine his despair.' The correspondent gestured to his camera operator to pan upwards, 'And this, Fiona, seems to be a rather more lasting feature of today's events than we thought it would be. For despite the steady wind the spiralling trail left by the alien ship is still visible; seemingly locked in place, and this afternoon, Fiona, rising moisture levels within the anomaly have created a haze of water droplets resulting in this rainbow...'

Another voice cut into my transfixed awareness, 'We can't change it by dwelling on it Trix.' Rue took up the remote, switched off the program and increased the lighting. Sitting next to me she rubbed my back, her cool hand a subtle pleasure against the warmth of the room, which had seemed to become more oppressive as the newscast continued.

'Jayes is happy that you've joined us, he'd like me to take you to a better room.'

'One with a door?' I suggested.

'Better, one with a door you can open or close or lock if you should wish.'

Had the pain of my heart not been so heavy, I thought I might have laughed, but Rue, seeing my suffering, held me in a tight embrace. 'They will pay Dace, my darling, they *will* pay.'

My surprise at her using my actual name was swept aside by an intense surge of hatred. It filled my whole being. I had not considered myself capable of such venomous loathing but it's focus on the Val'ee was undeniable.

'Come,' Rue urged. 'It will do you good to leave *this* room.' She broke away from me. As she did the hatred also fell away. 'Nothing is fixed down in the residential unit, honest.' She was walking backwards towards the doorway, hands outstretched beckoning me to follow. I needed no other encouragement.

## Chapter thirty-eight
### Ghosts and Shadows

I did not regret leaving my prison. I took in the structure of the facility as I made my way through it; every element constructed for purpose by IAAM, by hand. No Envisagers, they were not trusted. I felt a growing admiration for what Jayes' army of workers had achieved.

'Your mother was on the news supporting the Government. I thought she worked for Jayes, you called her the Archivist.'

'Mother *has* to work for the Government. The record tells her what she must do.' Rue looked around as if looking for anyone who might overhear her. 'She has seen a chance to make a change, only Jayes can give her the opportunity to perform what needs to be done. They have formed an alliance to this end. They make plans, share data. They are both likeminded, concerned about the future of humanity.'

My heart seemed to die again. Dad's concerns had always been for the future. Tears burned within me but I held them in.

'Have Jayes and your mother travelled through time?' I led, but the statement was met with an awkward silence. 'If they know what is going to happen they must have been there.'

Rue stopped briefly then started walking again in a hesitant manner. 'Mother doesn't hold to anything of the sort, she recognises the record as a message to herself from her future self. Her study of the record *is* her knowledge of the future.' Rue's voice dropped to an almost imperceptible level. 'Jayes had no record before he befriended mother, but his predictions have always been accurate. He's either travelled or he's some modern-day prophet!'

I had felt that my Dad's work would lead to man's ability to traverse

*Cries: The Captive Mind*

time but if Jayes had come from the future, and Verne had sent the Record to herself, I must have been mistaken. Dad was dead, Jayes was still here, and so was Verne's record.

Then I remembered that Dad's work was all back at the house, safely stored on his computer waiting for me. Maybe *I* would ensure that his work continued, making Arnold and Elizabeth's deeds possible. My thoughts came to an abrupt halt. I should be dead too.

Seeing me flagging, Rue hooked her arm beneath mine and drew me onwards.

'I must see Jayes.' I demanded.

'He will know that. Be patient...Oh, and it would be better if you at least call him Mr. Jayes when you meet.'

This answer seemed enough for me, my mind was overloaded and I simply nodded.

'Here we are.' Rue announced, 'Shared but very nice.' She swung the door open to reveal a spacious lounge, furnished and well kitted out. Hans and Richard from the EOA stood up and a beer bottle flew in my direction.

'What's this?' I said, catching the bottle. 'Class reunion?'

'Just celebrating another mind rescued from the short-sighted Government approach to alien life.' Hans said, raising another bottle.

This statement felt a little harsh to me, even despite what had happened. To be fearful of aliens to the point of the hostility Jayes demonstrated, seemed wrong... too... extreme. Dad's attitude had been so different, calmer, more thoughtful. I sighed to myself, my mind just could not accept that he was gone, it was overwhelming, raw. I raised my bottle. 'Anyone got a bottle opener? Hey, where's Oscar?'

Richard drew alongside and freed the lid, 'The boss's son doesn't mix with the workers; he heads up recruitment. He'll be busy when people hear you've seen sense.' He laughed.

I didn't laugh. I seemed to have lost the care to. Besides I hadn't "seen sense", I was using IAAM. I took a long swig of beer and sighed, 'Today's been really tiring. I just want to lie down. Where's the guest room?'

Hans showed me a small but adequate room and left me to settle in.

The tears flowed that night, though I forcibly muted the sound, and what little sleep I achieved was fitful. I just wanted to get home.

The days rolled by. I exhausted wandering the complex; I couldn't find a way out that wasn't security locked. I began feeling like a prisoner again. The pacifier of my torment was the ever-well-stocked beer in the fridge and internet access to Humanist web sites that seemed to be the only source of information on Evolution that was documented in a credible way - recent research, with ardent claims that the theory was not dead. I drank in the information; the models for change, the great spans of time, the idea that if history were a clock humanity would have existed for only the last couple of minutes. The problem was, I also drank up the beer. If my roomies were concerned about my state, they stayed quiet. The waking moments of the night were also eased by alcohol, until one morning, with my head throbbing, and with no real sense of how long I'd waited, I awoke to company.

'Good morning.'

'Jayes, er Mr... Jayes.' I blinked, there was no backlighting, no vision blurring tranquilisers.

'Did you sleep well?'

I rubbed my eyes, 'No, er, not really, maybe the bed's too soft.' The statement was loaded with disdain and had a satisfying, ironic tone to it.

'Now, now, I'm not the enemy.'

I sat up in the bed, purposely tightening the muscles of my body to demonstrate what I perceived to be a clear physical advantage over this skinny, diminutive man.

He chuckled dismissively. 'You must return home. I see your need.' His voice was positive and reassuring.

'It's everything I need.' I offered, as I relaxed my posture.

'I will not stop you, but you must know there is nothing left there now. It is empty, a place of ghosts and shadows.'

'Quite enough of that! What was *that*!'

'The truth, you must be prepared. There is only pain and despair in that old...'

My stare actually stopped him, he reached into his pocket.

'You are free to go.' He handed me a key card. 'As my employee spoilt your car you will find an adequate replacement in Section One. Oh, and don't lose the card, it stops our defence grid from targeting you.'

I felt relieved by the thought of freedom but discerned a tinge of threat.

'Should you need picking up, use this.' Jayes said, standing and throwing a small object into my lap. 'Press the tab and your assigned transport will return you here.'

'I can look after myself.'

Jayes paused a move to depart and without looking replied, 'I know, but you are family now. Family looks out for each other. Is that not a comfort?'

Inside I raged. What did *he* know of family? He'd just taken from me what was left of mine. I nearly let out my deepest fury, then, realising how that might affect this promised "freedom", I remained silent.

Jayes left.

I dressed, grabbed a bite and, nodding acknowledgement to Hans and Richard, who were dressed for the workshop, I followed the signs to Section One.

The area was a substantial car park. A young man appeared to be waiting for me; he looked straight out of high school and I almost dismissed him. 'Mr. North, Sir?' He piped up.

I turned back to him, 'What?'

My short, frosty reply visibly increased his nerves. 'I er, I'm er your technician er Sir, Thomas…'

'Verily I greet thee, Sir Thomas?' I joked roughly, I was clearly not what he'd expected.

'No, I'm Thomas, Sir.'

I grew tired, 'This we've discovered, what you want is yet to be ascertained…'

'Er Sir, no Sir, I'm…'

'Just call me Dace.' I suggested, feeling that if I didn't ease this boy's anxiety I might be stuck in a parking lot all day.

'I'm to show you to your vehicle Sir, er Dace, Sir, and assist you in setting it up to respond to your commands.'

'All I need,' I stated, brashly. 'Is the priming code and to be shown which vehicle it is.'

Thomas started walking alongside the parked cars, 'It's this one over here.' We passed at least thirty before he stopped, 'This one Dace, er Sir…'

I rolled my eyes, 'Just "Dace", that will be fine…' Then I noticed his beaming face and turned to see why.

My new "car" was more than just an adequate replacement, it was sleeker, newer and fully converted as a flyer.

I laughed, 'An Audi A760 CDS Flyer?'

'Yes S…er Dace…'

I walked around it, then, initiating the priming sequence, clicked my fingers, 'Key code Thomas…'

'Er yes, Alpha, seven, two, Zebra, Alpha, Charlie, six, if you click on parameters…'

'I *know* what to do!'

'Please state name…' The computer instructed.

'Dace North.'

'Priming…' The vehicle whirred into life, a sequence of lights displaying the vehicles systems as each was brought online ready for use.

'One thing I need to tell you Dace.'

I looked back, eye brows raised.

He continued, 'The vehicle has security protocols to protect our location. The windows will opaque as you depart and clear only as you near your destination.'

'Pity. I hoped to bring the military might of the world back with me to blow this place out into space with the aliens; maybe you'll all fight it out amongst yourselves…'

Thomas stared wide-eyed.

'Lighten up Thomas. Here…' I beckoned for him to approach as I climbed into the passenger cabin. 'What facilities *have* I got for my viewless journey?'

Thomas brought up a holographic menu, 'All the usual online facilities, Entertainment on Demand, E-mail, Game Deck…'

'Fine, fine, thanks for your help.' The appreciation was loaded with sarcasm but Thomas just smiled, nodded and closed the door.

'Please state Destination.'

'Home.' I found myself saying, then, realising that this had not yet been allocated to a location, added, 'IP24.'

'Please wait…Route planned, estimated duration two hours and thirty-six minutes. Please fasten belt to initiate journey.'

Based on what I knew about flyer speeds, I figured that Jayes' mountainside hideout must be about two hundred and fifty miles from home. I fastened my belt.

For about half an hour I was lost in my own thoughts. What would life be like now? Was I even going to let this automated "car" take me back to Jayes? How could anyone not realise that the whole side of their local mountain had grown to encompass a facility big enough for ten thousand small fighting craft and a number of giant war ships?

I started to get agitated with my journey; CDS vehicles were dull to travel in at the best of times, but with blank opaque windows I felt crazed. Flipping open a panel I discovered it was a fridge stocked with beer. Why had I been so lazy, just sitting here? I could have found this ages ago. I opened a can.

'Computer...'
'Please state command...'
'Entertainment on demand.'
'Please state keywords or preferences...'
'Music, news, Ertis.'
'Searching...'
I sat back, gulping down the beer.
'Search complete, please select title from matches displayed...'

I leant forward, 'That looks interesting,' I said touching the holographic icon linked to a story dated the previous weekend and titled, "David ERTIS to head The Ungoliant, with the release of the band's new album: Stand."

I listened with genuine interest, pleased that my friend had finally reached his goal. Sad that Briars had stepped out of the group due to ill health of course, but keen to hear the album. I opened another beer and pressed the album link.

It opened with the title track, which I had to play twice more. I felt that it spoke directly into the events that had taken place, an anthem for now, a battle cry.

I found myself readily joining in with the words of the chorus...

"I will stand
And though it's black
I will pay no heed to that
I will stand
And though it's black
I know no fear
Just take it back.
Shame on you you've crossed that line,
You've taken all I have but time."

I was so impressed by the hour of noise I had experienced I attempted to download a copy to my personal Online Zone account from the flyer's terminal. Strangely I discovered that it was already saved, 'When did I do that?' I looked down at the brand of my beer. It was nice but the on-board fridge was small and it was now all consumed; I bounced the empty can off the others making a mental note to seek out some more. There'd be some wine or spirits left over from the Christmas preparations at least, however minimal those had been in recent years. I felt a lump in my throat again and kicked the fridge for being too small.

I tried bringing up the online mapping facility but the security protocols denied me access. I felt cross, surely Jayes' location was safe by now. Then I wondered; I had felt no cornering, I'd been flying in a straight line. This seemed strange at first because flyers usually utilised the markers embedded in Envisaged road surfaces for navigation.

I had to shake these ingrained ideas, it made perfect sense; my flyer wasn't Envisaged and IAAM distrusted anything made by this technology. The flyer was independent of the markers, totally illegal!

I sat a few moments more before finally, reluctantly, initiating the Game Deck program.

I was losing a Grand Prix simulation with flying colours when the computer burst into life.

'Approaching destination…' I felt the vehicle spiral slowly, then the windows became clear, the spiralling had been enough to disorient me from the original direction and the mapping program flashed up as "available".

The view through the window was bleak. The tree line of Thetford forest was gone. I knew it had from the news footage, but knowing hadn't prepared me to see it for real. I still expected wreckage but there was nothing, just a charred void. How had a ship of such great size been so completely destroyed?

As the flyer pitched for its final approach into Elvedon, I acquired a news hub online and searched "Val'ee wreckage".

One match was the news program Rue had switched off. I opened the report and scrolled to the point the link flagged up. Verne was talking to the news reader.

'That's right Fiona, this is the effectiveness of the weapon against the primary Val'ee engines, the resultant reaction vaporised the vessel in entirety, each atom burning intensely as the footage showed, thus negating any wreckage.'

I scrolled back to the footage.

Recorded from some distance away, behind the course of the gigantic ship, it showed a great sheet of light spreading across the vessel's path. The ship ran headlong into a spiralling tube of flame. Engulfed, it disappeared completely leaving a rolling wave of plasma scouring the landscape.

'The Val'ee ship was completely destroyed, obliterated...' Began the newsreader.

'That's right Fiona...'

I scrolled back again. I couldn't grasp the power of this weapon; I couldn't understand how any weapon could affect an engine of Hayvan configuration - Dad had been quite persuasive regarding his belief that Val'ee technology was merely progressed from our time, the future development of what already existed - I saw nothing that could be effected to a point of instant spontaneous annihilation, certainly as regarded the rest of the ship's structure; and yet there it was, the ship's demise...

'You have reached your destination, please specify parking...'

A map appeared in front of me. I was relieved to find that the little village had escaped the fiery furnace I'd just witnessed; although it did bear evidence of the searing heat that had been produced. I had the vehicle park beside the entrance to the drive way.

Only one other vehicle stood in the silent street and there was no sign of life, not even a twitching curtain. Jayes' words seemed to gain gravity, "Ghosts and shadows." I juddered and climbed out of the flyer. Had the whole village been evacuated? I headed up the driveway to the front door. The paintwork was blistered and cracked and the door wouldn't open. I remembered that my MIT device was gone. The door lock was MIT linked so I needed to recall the code and punch it in manually.

On my third attempt the door clicked and I was able to open it. I stood in the opening; the house seemed darker due to the blackened windows. It felt unwelcoming. I sighed and stepped inside.

The wooden floor echoed. It always had but the sound seemed deeper now, more hollow.

Dad's study was to my right, the stairs ahead of me to the left, and the door to the lounge in front of them. The hall itself ran through to the kitchen and the door, between that and the study, led to the dining room. I entered the study.

'Computer on.'

There was a moments silence, then an audible whirr as a backup generator burst into life. The mains were down; it wasn't surprising.

'Password required…'

Dad had said that if anything happened to him the password was "merely your own name".

'Dace.' I offered.

'Access denied…' I frowned.

'Dace North.'

'Access denied…'

Almost without thought I tried again, 'Dace Vincent North.'

'Access denied…'

Maybe Dad meant his own name, 'Douglas North…' I attempted.

'Access denied…'

I cursed and kicked a small bin across the room, then I laughed, 'You Idiot!' I exclaimed, unintentionally aloud.

'Access denied…'

'No…' How had Dad put it? 'Merely Your Own Wonderful Name.'

'Access denied…'

I roared my disappointment. I needed a drink and headed to the kitchen.

There was no beer in the fridge; a stale smell greeted me instead. An old bottle of whisky sat in the pantry. Dad never touched the stuff, it had been Gramp's; he'd bought it for "medicinal purposes" but had been ill so rarely that the bottle still remained nearly full. 'Soon put that right.' I said out loud as I tipped the bottle for a gulp.

As I lowered it, I noticed the back of a figure in the garden; the whisky hit the back of my throat, and, not being used to it, I nearly choked. I slipped the bottle into my bag.

The person in the garden had heard my coughing and was now heading towards the house. I was gripped with a strange sort of panic. My visitor's face was obscured by a dark grey hood and it wasn't until he peered in at the window that I recognised Tyler from Jaro. He motioned to the back door. I opened it.

'Thank God you're OK, we were all so worried.'

An unwanted wave of emotion blustered forth and I found myself sobbing like a child again. The anger inside pummelled at my mind as if telling it to get a grip and focus, and I clawed back the tears.

*Cries: The Captive Mind*

'It's OK,' Tyler insisted. 'The tears are good, your father taught me that.'

That did sound like Dad. As if granted permission, and certainly because Dad was now foremost in my mind, I let the tears flood my fury. Tyler guided me to a chair.

'What happened Dace?' He asked. 'Where have you been?'

'IAAM took me. Held me against my will. Mr. Jayes knew about the attack, but he wouldn't let me warn Dad.'

Tyler's expression managed to convey real concern despite the tightness of his burn scars. 'How did you manage to get away?'

I looked into his pale eyes, 'Mr. Jayes was right about the Val'ee, Tyler, their motives. We trusted them, but they wanted that in order to weaken us against attack. Not *one* weapon on the Sky Cities... What were we thinking? We could have blown them away from the Pathfinder before they even touched the atmosphere.' The tears were gone again, the rage from deep inside sent my seat spiralling across the kitchen.

'Hey! Calm down!' Tyler insisted.

I seethed with anger.

'This isn't like you Dace. What did Jayes do to you?'

I paused. I could hardly believe what I was about to say, 'He opened my eyes. He was protecting me. The Val'ee were after *me*. They targeted my MIT device, but Mr. Jayes had it removed. I just wish Dad hadn't got hold of it and taken it to Sylvestris.' I was now looking out of the window again at the terrible view that Tyler himself had been surveying.

'Tell me about the Government weapon.' I pushed. Tyler looked blank.

'You are as high a level Government worker as Dad was. Elizabeth Verne was on the News; said you destroyed the Val'ee ship with some sort of weapon. Can it be adjusted to affect the enemy's main engines when they are not running? Can it be fitted to the remaining Pathfinders and Sky Cities?'

Tyler's response disappointed me. 'I wasn't aware of any weapon until I heard about it on the news. Elizabeth is more involved with the full spectrum of Morrello projects than your father and I... You should be cautious of Jayes.'

'He seems to be the only one making sense anymore.'

Tyler nodded in agreement, 'He always seems to make sense *now*. He can make you believe anything, but he wasn't always like that.'

'How do you mean?'

'He was insecure, he stammered, he never arrived on time. His students, at the London University we both taught at, hated him. We were both lecturers in Science at about the time Jonathan Morrello announced his exhibition. It intrigued us both. After reading the Morrello report we felt we had to go - see the evidence for ourselves; that's where I got my face, ninety percent of my body is the same. I'm in constant pain every day of my life.'

'Dad's parents died. He and mum would have died too if his old car hadn't broken down.'

'Over two hundred and seventy-eight thousand people lost their lives in that terrorist attack.' Tyler sighed.

I felt muddled. Perhaps I'd drunk too much today. 'What's that got to do with Mr. Jayes?' Then I thought, Jayes had let the Val'ee destroy Pathfinder Four, three Sky Cities and the Sylvestris array without warning anyone. He could have greatly reduced the death toll. 'Are you saying that you think Mr. Jayes had something to do with the attack on the Morrello Exhibition?'

'No, Dace, what I'm pointing out is that Jayes wouldn't have been able to burst a paper bag back then without making himself jump. No, he was with me at the exhibition; I took him. We were late of course, stuck on the approach road when the attack took place.'

'Impossible, all the survivors were burnt like you. Mr. Jayes hasn't a mark on him.'

'And yet the approach road was totally engulfed in flame and Jayes was with me in my car. I didn't see him again for over three years. I didn't even know he'd survived - just felt that if he had done he'd be hospitalised like me; undergoing month after month of medical and surgical interventions to recreate something vaguely human.'

I looked at him. I felt intense pity. Tyler was one of the few survivors who had carried on with a public life, albeit working at Jaro airfield. Many others had hidden themselves away - a few had lost their minds.

'What are you saying about Mr. Jayes?'

'When I saw him again he was charismatic, believable, always on time even to the point of providence; he's an established networker, an extravagant host, a self-styled prophet...'

I was intrigued by this side of the story but having known nothing but the confident leader it all sounded wrong.

'If he really was there, and somehow managed to escape the flames, then I can see why you might be envious of him. He has turned his life around, made a success of himself. If he were such a wet lettuce beforehand then... I guess he just seized the opportunity afforded him, took up his spared life with both hands...'

'My car was an open topped MG - my pride and joy – I don't know how I survived, but Jayes *was* there; right beside me when the fire came...' Tyler hesitated.

'Go on.' I urged.

'I have nightmares Dace.'

'I expect you do, any traumatic exp...'

Tyler cut in, 'I don't recall seeing this, but in my dream I see Jayes beside me, there's another figure too, tortured and bent, it's flesh charred and giving off rusty ribbons of smoke. It's standing over him. Jayes is just gazing up at it, it seems to shield him for a few seconds then it dives right into him. He looks at me untouched by the blast - a little singed hair, a face marked with ash - then he steps out of the car and walks away, stepping this way and that, threading his way between swirling eddies of flame, the earth crackling under his feet.'

Tyler's story had lost all credibility to me now. It was time to find out something.

'Why are you here Tyler?'

'Two reasons; one to keep watch for you, the other to access the information on your dad's computer should you fail to return. I would have needed to break in - I'm glad I didn't have to.'

'Password's beaten me.'

'Your Dad gave me the password the day before he was killed. He knew something was happening when you vanished without trace, and with his promise to help me escape the fire when he figured out how to go back, he felt he would give me access with the directive that I use the technology to prevent your disappearance. With you here I don't need to see his files, he always intended them for you.'

'So what *is* the password?' I challenged.

'M.Y.O.W.N.' He replied.

'That's not what he told...'

'Hangar technique Dace, Merely Your Own Wonderful Name.'

'My Own.' I nodded. I felt like a complete idiot.

We headed to the study.

The computer refused to start up.

'How many times did you try and enter your name?' Tyler chuckled.

'I tried Dace first, then Dace North, then my full name, er, then I think I panicked, I entered Dad's name, then I called myself an Idiot, which the system took as another attempt then I...'

'Then it's locked down. Do you have a Data Pack in the house?'

I nodded and ran upstairs to retrieve it. Tyler soon linked it to Dad's system and, with a few keystrokes, the computer burst into life.

'Please enter Password...'

'M.Y.O.W.N.' I stated.

'Welcome, how may I be of service?'

Tyler looked at me, 'Do you know the file?'

I smiled, 'How about, Sounds too simple but it will be enough? S.T.S.B.I.W.B.E.'

As soon as I'd said it Dad's system started downloading information to my Data Pack and a figure like a ghost appeared in front of the computer screen - a hologram generated by emitters around the walls. An image of Dad. Around him were objects caught in the holographic recording and I recognised his location as Sylvestris. He spoke hurriedly.

'Dace, all my work is being purged from my system onto your Data Pack's internal memory. I found a life signs program on your MIT device which strikes me as a homing signal. The software bears an IAAM signature so I know who you are with. Please be careful. Arnold Jayes is a mysterious figure and I'm sure he would not have let you come for this information without first assuring himself of your goodwill towards his organisation. Our friends tell me that Jayes will not be interested in the data you now have. I ask only that you keep it to yourself, study it and take it in. When the time comes you will be ready. Time is short. I love you son.' The Hologram ceased, the computer and Data Pack fell silent.

'Here.' Tyler said, shutting down the link and passing me the Pack. Dad's words had smothered my inner rage and stirred that part of the old me that lay beneath it. My cheeks were awash with welcomed and healing tears.

'I will find you a way out of the fire, Tyler, if my Dad's data leads me to it.'

'You should go to Sylvestris, Dace, say goodbye properly. It will help you, I promise. Oh, and the bottle, it doesn't work.'

'What?' I knew he was right. I retrieved the whisky and placed it on the hallway floor. 'How did you know?'

*Cries: The Captive Mind*

'I saw it when you put your Data Pack in your bag. When your Dad called me at the height of the Great Suffering *I* was totally off the rails. He reckoned he needed me on his task force, and when he found what state I was in he didn't disregard me; he got me back on track. He was a great man.'

I nodded and with a firm handshake, we parted company. Could there be anything in what he'd said about Jayes? It had seemed the ranting of one aggrieved at another's good fortune and yet, despite the nightmares, he came across as a man healed and in control of his emotions.

I felt a strange sense of relief about leaving the house. Jayes was right there was nothing there for me now. What mattered to me I now had. The old place was too big for one.

'Please state destination…'

'Thetford Sylvestris.'

'Destination does not exist, confirm "former site of Thetford Sylvestris"…'

Coming from the synthesized voice of the flyer the truth sat heavily on my heart and a tear escaped me.

'Confirmed.' I replied.

'Route planned, estimated arrival two minutes, please fasten belt to initiate journey…'


## Chapter Thirty-nine
### Vultures

We were soon over the great yawning desert that was once the Thetford forest, but I could find nothing that pinpointed Dad's laboratories. The flyer circled, then began a steady approach from the south.

'Computer.'

'Please state command…'

'Where was Sylvestris?'

'Please view screen…'

I turned from the window to the holographic monitor.

'You are now travelling over the site…'

The route of the now absent B1107 and the footprints of the Sylvestris labs could be seen, superimposed over the live feed from the flyers camera. We were travelling quickly, and we soon found ourselves over curving shapes which represented the innermost atmospheric filters. I glanced back through the window, there was absolutely nothing to suggest that they'd ever existed.

The overlay showed other features. 'Computer, what are these buildings?'

'Residential communities...'

The thought disturbed me. There'd been so much devastation. I wondered whether the government would have been wiser to let the Val'ee destroy my MIT device, then destroy their vessel when it had cleared inhabited areas; there was too much collateral damage.

'Take me back to the site of the laboratories.'

'Responding...' The flyer swung around in a wide arc. 'Would you like me to hold a stationary position over the site?'

'Er, yes please.' I'd never heard of a flyer that could hover before; I marvelled at the skill of the IAAM technicians. Envisagers began to feel soulless to me.

'You have arrived at your destination...'

I looked again at the featureless waste below. How could I say goodbye properly without a point of reference, some mark or memorial?

Turning again to the screen in the flyer, I fixed my attention on the main laboratory building and asked the computer to take the building overlay away. There, at one end of where the building had stood, *was* a nondescript feature. I touched the screen a few metres away from it, 'Put down here.'

'Responding...' The flyer rotated down to a soft landing.

I released my belt and stepped out onto the bare earth; it cracked, as if lifted and frozen by frost. On closer inspection it was more like a film of glass, extruded in places into little shimmering spikes, all pointing in the same direction. A harsh, cold wind cut forcefully across the landscape and the dust was being whipped up along what I now knew had been the approach road. I strode towards what I'd observed from above. It turned out to be a ridge of soil heated into glass; it flicked the wind into little spinning dust devils that twirled away over the crazed, brittle void. The ridge looked as if it had been caused by materials piling up against something that had withstood the destruction of the Val'ee ship for a little

*Cries: The Captive Mind*

longer than anything else but then, inevitably, being vaporized itself. The feature, isolated and lonely in its formless surroundings, held my gaze.

Was this the place where Dad's "The Space" device had been? Had he sheltered in it to escape what was coming? It was a ridiculous idea; it would have provided no protection. However long he'd managed to stay inside he would have eventually been forced out by hunger or thirst, only to exit at the point in time that he'd entered the device; straight into the impending firestorm.

I knelt within the area and cried, 'I'll make them pay Dad.' I sobbed openly, running my fingers across the smooth, cold, sculpted earth, unaware of my observers.

'That's a *great* quote Dace, "I'll make them pay" promises grieving son.'

"Quote" reeked of reporter.

'Where have you been Dace? What's the story?' This was a different voice. I slowly stood and turned to face my interrogators. The dust I had thought was being stirred up by the wind had been thrown up by a convoy of vehicles, some of which were only just pulling up. Modern vehicles were so silent and I hadn't thought there'd be a prospect of company in this barren place. Cameras and reporters were scrambling towards me now. My inner raging was beginning to surface. This had been life again and again. Every big event, reporters, camera flashes, questions.

'How do you feel Dace?'

'What do you think of the devastation?'

'Is it true you have joined IAAM?'

Without speaking I tried to pass them but they sidestepped me, physically blocked me, touched me, pushed me.

'Please just let me be…'

'No way mate! This is huge…'

The lack of compassion in the remark stripped the last of my equilibrium and I found myself flying at the man, landing blow after blow as he attempted, ineffectively, to block my onslaught.

'I hope someone's getting this footage.' He yelled.

I froze, I had to get a grip however hard; this was GBH on camera. I turned to get away and he tripped me to the ground; I scrambled to my feet and tried again to reach the flyer.

'Don't let him go! Hold him; we'll have a story!'

My heart sank as I felt a restraining hand on my sleeve, I tried to pull away but couldn't. Then I remembered the device that Jayes had given me. What had he said? "Press the tab and your transport will see to it that you are returned here safely." I couldn't escape without help and I had nowhere else to go. I pressed the tab in my pocket.

Initially I thought nothing had happened. Then I noticed the stillness and that the tab seemed to be glued to my thumb. I looked around, breathing heavily. It was as if I were the only living form in a tableau. I tried to free my jacket sleeve from the reporter's grip but it was locked tight. I removed my Data Pack and key card from the pockets and eased the warm coat off, leaving it dangling from the hand of my assailant.

I could see my flyer approaching, moving to a position that offered the clearest path; I remained standing, bewildered by the scene. I couldn't explain what was happening, the mob was frozen like a photograph and yet I now noticed that the wind still blew the dust beyond us, the clouds still scudded by and a seagull was circling high above. Whatever effected the reporters was very localised.

'Dace, please take your seat. The field is a temporary construct.'

The voice - filled with urgency and concern - belonged to the flyer's computer, it seemed almost human! I'd noticed nothing like it in a CDS before. I stared at the open flight cabin door, it seemed to beckon me. 'Quickly Dace.'

I snapped from my trance. Half walking, half tripping and running for the open door, I leapt in. The door slammed shut.

'Are you injured?' the computer asked.

'Er no...' I looked out of the window as the tableaux burst back into life. The surprise on the face of the man with my jacket was profound. A couple of them swung around, startled by the new position of the flyer; the most level headed of them shouted something to the others and one by one they all started after me again.

'Grab hold Dace. Fasten your belt when you can.' The computer instructed taking off vertically at speed, pulses of light flashing through the media below as they shielded their eyes and spat out our down-draughted dust. The gull I'd noticed earlier struck the vehicles bonnet, scaring me, it twitched erratically and slid away, plummeting lifeless to the ground.

In moments we were over five hundred metres above Sylvestris and heading north. The screen, still displaying the area, was all the more disturbing now as the extent of the destruction became apparent. Below us was a great rectangular desert five miles wide, burnt black at the edges. It extended from the north western suburbs of Thetford New Town, west of the A11, northwards all the way to Mundford and the A1065, A134 roundabout. Mundford was gone, everything within the rectangle was gone and Methwold, Cranwich and Ickburgh were caked in ash as thick as a heavy snowfall.

'What just happened down there?' I asked.

'You initiated a "Solid Time Field" using a remote tab, you will be able to remove it now.'

I held up my hand with the tab attached, a rubbery substance peeled away from the pores of my skin and a needle like structure gradually slid out of the fleshy pad of my thumb.

'What *is* that?'

'The organic material is a dermal fixative that anchors the tab for accurate administration of the marker isotope; the needle injects the isotope to create - in a few heart beats - enough of a map of your circulatory system to enable a "Real Time Bubble" to be generated around you by the tab. A similar bubble exists around the flyer but the flyer also generates a "dome" of "Solid Time", fifty metres in diameter for sixty seconds. Your "bubble" enables you to move around within the field freely. For everything else within the field, time stands still. Your assailants' watches will now appear to be a minute slow.'

'Fascinating... Oh, but what about the recordings they made? There were no live cameras there, but the footage they got... they'll make me look like a lunatic!'

'No need to worry. I gave off an electromagnetic strobe as we ascended. There won't be enough data left to pull a still image together.'

'The flashing as we took off! Remarkable, but what about my Data Pack?' I exclaimed, fumbling for the device and pressing the on panel.

'I am fully shielded. Your device was not at risk.'

I sighed with relief as the files appeared on screen, 'You're no ordinary flyer are you?'

A sound like a laugh came over the speakers. 'Thomas has done a good job hasn't he. All my features and personality have been his work. Oh, hold on...'

There was a brief pause.

'I'm afraid I am at my altitude limit and a vehicle is closing on our position...'

**Were the media still after me?**

'The directive you initiated was for me to return you safely to IAAM headquarters but this will require opacity of the windows to meet security protocols. The journey may get bumpy; if you like I can put you to sleep when you fasten your belt.'

**I didn't like the sound of that at all; I also didn't like that our height above ground was ten times the standard for a flyer and yet a vehicle was approaching. What kind of vehicle could one of those reporters have to be able to follow us here? 'I don't need to be put to sleep thanks but obviously you must follow your security protocols. Do what you need to do, I'll just cling on.' I wondered how the reporters knew my location. Tyler came straight to mind; had he informed the press? He had told me to visit Sylvestris. Only he could have known that I was there. I didn't feel it was the sort of thing he'd do but... 'Who do I trust?' I voiced aloud.**

'Trust me.' **The computer stated and suddenly the flyer pitched arced and dived.**

'Our pursuer is still with us. Would you like me to outrun it? I must warn you that my maximum speed will exert a substantial G-force on your frame and may result in you losing consciousness; in such an event I will do whatever I have to, to get you home.'

**Home sounded wrong, but the moment required a quick decision. 'I just want rid of these vultures; I've put up with them all my life.'**

'Please fasten your belt.'

**I complied. Suddenly I was thrust back in my seat, I could feel a crushing force, I struggled to breathe but although I fought I could feel my awareness slipping away; then, seeing stars, I passed out.**

**I awoke in Section One. Thomas had a Data Pack, attached by a vital statistics clip to my finger.**

'And... welcome back.' He said.

The sudden recollection of the chase led to a startled attempt to leap to my feet, but the belt was still fastened.

'Whoa! Chill Dace! Panic over. You're home...'

Home, there the word was again; if all it meant was safety I could perhaps understand, but I doubted I'd ever be "home" again.

'We lost the tail?' I asked.

**Rue appeared from behind Thomas, 'You jeopardised everything Mr. Jayes has worked for. Your flyer's trip recorder makes lamentable**

reading. I watched for some time, waiting to see if your pursuer would discover the facility.'

I felt a pang of guilt. 'I didn't plan to...'

'Well, no one showed. Guess you can thank Thomas for an exceptionally good evasion program on the flyer. I suggest you stay put for a while; keep your head down. Make yourself useful in the work areas perhaps. Your material and systems knowledge probably exceeds that of most of Mr. Jayes technicians.' Rue was massaging Thomas's neck as she leant over him to speak. He was clearly euphoric from the press of her body.

I nodded, 'I don't think I've got any reason to go out again.'

'Thomas, help Trix back to his accommodation.'

'Yes, Miss James.'

Rue fixed me with a chilling glare, laughed, kissed Thomas on the cheek and left.

## Chapter forty
### Next Step Known

For a couple of nights, I watched the news, expecting to see blow by blow detail of my outburst, but the computer on the flyer was right - no footage had escaped the strobe.

I studied Dad's work. Many of his ideas were based on Biblical concepts focusing on creation. He believed the "time" we perceived was created outside of time, initiated from a place where time was not a parameter.

His ideas had enthralled me as I stood with him, feeding off his excited energy; now I struggled to share his conclusions. Even an Envisager could not create time. My mind flashed to "The Space" device, it had bought Dad time but it didn't provide a way back. I thought *that* had been the whole point.

I wondered if Jayes had a Bible, then shook my head; my knowledge of scripture was little more than Dad's bedtime stories, and I just couldn't grasp his creation paradigm, nor its relevance to traversing time. I resolved to plod on through the multitude of files and daily reports, perhaps some key phrase would eventually stir my understanding.

I wasn't particularly accepted by Jayes' workers. Anyone with a history of Envisagement was treated with caution.

Hans seemed to accept it, but still yearned for praise. 'Sure the Envisagers gave instant results but look what happened to the Government Strike Fighters - they were Envisaged tech, and they fell from the sky like leaves. Use alien tech expect to be compromised. So what if working with your hands is slow, we know the materials better than anyone here, we make sure we do a better job than them. They'll have to accept us in the end. We complete five Dragonflies to every four of theirs and ours are more advanced. Theirs are for atmospheric support, ours can go exospheric.'

Hans' "them and us" attitude wasn't helping. I wondered what I could do to close the gulf, then remembered how I had treated Thomas. I hadn't accepted his help because he was younger than me; now I knew his work and skill had converted the flyer, enhanced it and, ultimately, enabled my escape from the Press mob.

Had Thomas created the Solid Time Field, or had he just fitted it? I had to know. A technology that could effectively freeze time in a given proximity, and yet allow an individual to move about freely within it, must be similar to Dad's "The Space" device. Oh, why had I been so awful? It wasn't me; people used to like me, now they just stared as I passed. I resolved to seek an opportunity to work with Thomas as soon as possible. He'd been courteous and patient with me despite my rude and arrogant treatment of him; I wanted to put things right.

It took a few weeks to arrange, but Jayes seemed pleased about my desire to join Thomas.
The tech rooms where he worked, were ultra-clean laboratories. Precision peripherals were made there for Jayes fleet and arsenal. This would be my workplace too.

Thomas and I worked well together. His technical skill and my broad materials knowledge enabled the miniaturisation of numerous systems. This meant more kit for each craft. Thomas was incredibly clever, applying what I'd taught him across his other projects. Then I discovered that he too was treated with arm's length toleration by the other workers.

'I don't think I've worked anywhere quite so full of distrust.'

*Cries: The Captive Mind*

'It isn't...' Thomas began, then paused. 'Well... not between the others. Perhaps you EO lot are treated a bit badly...' He looked at me. 'You think they treat me bad too, don't you?'

'They do...'

'It's not their fault. I intimidate them...'

'How's that, you're seventeen and built like a sparrow, er sorry about the sparrow bit...'

Thomas laughed, 'No, it isn't that, it's the circumstances of my arrival.'

I stopped what I was doing and gave him my full attention.

'Well, Mr. Jayes found me here. That is, not *here* because it hadn't been constructed then; he found me in the old industrial buildings topside. I was nine, the right age to have been born on the ERUWAI but without a MIT device. He saw me as a sign. I became the marker for the location of his hidden headquarters.'

'How did you get here?'

'All I remember is Mr. Jayes face smiling down at me, nothing before that. I couldn't have been there long because I wasn't hungry or dehydrated. There were no reports of anyone my age going missing, so I was entrusted into his care by the authorities at his request. I don't even know what a Val'ee looks like. I have no memories of them and no desire to seek out footage online.'

'What about records of your birth? The Val'ee records are flawless.'

'Nothing, only my name on a few belongings, in a bag I had with me.'

'Weird.' I admitted.

'We should start a club for weird people!'

We both laughed.

I'd been putting off asking Thomas about the Solid Time Field for just such a time. I'd convinced myself that I wanted his trust and a good rapport before prying into his technical knowledge. The real reason had been an unwillingness to hear, from a seventeen-year-old, what might have been eluding me in Dad's notes. I knew now from our shared laughter that such concerns were unimportant; I too was still a young man having turned twenty-one just a week ago - no cards, no gifts, no kind remarks - It was a strange thing really, to be totally known all my life and yet here I was lost against the schedules and hustle of IAAM's preparations.

'So, how did you achieve the Solid Time Field?' I asked, shocking myself with my bluntness.

Thomas started laughing again, 'Flattered, but Mr. Jayes is the one behind Solid Time. Oh, and Power Generated Matter. Both systems run on the peak power output of optimised Wave Generators. Want to see one?'

I nodded.

I soon realised that Thomas was taking me to Section One and my flyer. Once there he initialised the computer and requested release of the Solid Time Field generator. The nearside, rear wing glided smoothly from its position - a conversion Thomas accepted was his own work - and there before us was something more akin to a white ball of wool, than the familiar Hayvan double loop.

Thomas handed me a little ball that I instantly recognised as the tab device I'd used before. I was reluctant to use it again, knowing how it worked, but Thomas explained that the generator's wave forms were only visible within the field and in order to see them I had to be unaffected by Solid Time and close to the device's Field output; besides it would be worth it.

'After three?' He suggested.

I shrugged, nodded and, after three seconds, found myself staring at something I'd seen before. 'Dad's configuration for an optimised Wave generator. He'd based it on the Fan Array he'd seen on that thing the Envisager used me to create. Wait though, Solid Time doesn't last, it fades after a minute; how can it be kept stable and constant to keep Power Generated Matter in place? This whole mountainside doesn't keep disappearing and reappearing.'

'I'll show you,' Thomas opened the door of the flyer and we stepped inside, 'Computer, access secure network.'

'Voice Pass matched. Hello Thomas, which file do you require?'

'Power Generated Matter core please.'

'Searching, downloading, displaying.'

'See, here,' Thomas pointed, 'each optimised generator runs in sequence to the others…'

Fifty generators were linked to produce the physically realistic mountainside above us.

Thomas continued, 'The system utilises each generator's "Peak Output Plateau" during its period of stability. Each generator is used once every hour providing a cooling period. It works in a permanent sense because we have space in the caves for the hardware.'

'What if you had a vehicle big enough for the generators necessary to create a cyclical system like the Power Generated Matter core, but for solid time?'

'With that much power you could envelop a much larger area. I don't know how big without simulating it but it would have the effect of freezing time within the field indefinitely.'

'Freezing time or stepping out of it?'

Now Thomas looked puzzled. I tried to repeat some of the things Dad's notes had told me - perhaps Thomas would understand them better with the knowledge he already had. 'Dad believed that time was created. The place from which it was created is not subject to time as we understand it.'

Thomas stared back at me blankly.

I tried again; although this time I must have sounded a little fanatical. 'If you could step out of time and step back into it again at another point... you might be able to prevent something happening.'

'Impossible.' He stated. I frowned. 'Say, you went to a point in time where you could stop the Val'ee attack last winter. Well, if you stopped it, you would have prevented the very reason you went back, so you never would have gone; it's a paradox.'

'I need to talk to you, Mr. North.' The sudden appearance of the voice from outside of the flyer startled us both, we looked out like two school boys caught smoking. Solid time outside the vehicle had ended.

'Mr. Jayes.' I stated.

'I know what you are looking for Dace. Your father's work was pivotal; really, you should be proud, but neither he nor you are responsible for the precise science of managing created time - yes, on that much your father was correct - the individual who fathoms this mystery will not be the age you will be on the date the breakthrough is made, that rules you out.'

I was looking back at Thomas, 'So, it is possible to navigate time without causing the point of the journey to be negated.'

I looked back at Jayes, his face was stony, silence surrounded us, then his face lightened. 'It will be possible to travel back. In the future the Archivist will be one of a team who record history and make it available to us, so that we might be victorious against the Val'ee.'

So Rue was right. Her mother sent the record as a message to herself from her future self. This was coming together.

Thomas, however, seemed agitated, 'But anything a person did would change how things unfold, they would need to eat and drink, people would move around them, different paths, different outcomes...'

'Master Collins, Mr. North, these are not your worries, know that things are working out as they should. We do have a deadline though and you are not where you should be. I suggest you channel your energies into your work. Go now, I want your daily target met before you retire today.'

We powered down the flyer and made our way back to the tech rooms.

Days later, Jayes announced the date of the event we were working towards, just weeks away in May.

The Archivist had negotiated with the Government. Their forces on side, Jayes promised that we would successfully counter the forthcoming Val'ee assault. The intention of the aliens would be to enslave humanity; making sense of their previously benevolent actions regarding the rescue of humankind from the Great Suffering; more lives, more slaves.

The Archivist had also released information pertaining to future events, revealing openly that the Val'ee were time travellers. Information had been covertly downloaded from the stricken alien vessel over Sylvestris, giving us the advantage of knowing time, place and tactics.

Jayes workforce seemed pained by Jayes announcement. They had worked to defeat the Val'ee themselves, not share the task with a Government that might cosy up to other aliens in the future.

Jayes settled his people, 'That's the beauty of it.' He laughed. 'IAAM *will* save the world, the Government forces are not prepared for what they will face. The Val'ee have a weapon that enslaves the mind; it is based on the properties of their voices, the note that somehow takes human will away to do Val'ee bidding. The weapon can be used to pacify numerous targets simultaneously. The Government are unaware of this; they will meet the Val'ee and be subject to the tone. My contact will feed the tonal information to a system at IAAM that will create a countermeasure; a tone that cancels the Val'ee advantage. Bearing this countermeasure, the bulk of our fleet will attack the Val'ee armada. Simultaneously our tech ships will start releasing the Government crews from their stupor. By the time they are operative IAAM will have won. We will finally be accepted and receive the recognition and power we deserve.'

The workers erupted with cheers, clearly happy with Jayes' detailing of the plan.

*Cries: The Captive Mind*

That night I couldn't sleep. Jayes was again placing people in harm's way to achieve his goals. The Government ships, scheduled to block the Val'ee advance, would be incapacitated. The risk to life didn't just come from alien hostility, many of the ships would possess systems that required monitoring and adjustment. Some vessels would collide, and with the enemy bearing down it had all the potential of a massacre. People I knew would be part of that fleet, Taz for sure, Vince, Lawrence, and Matt from the hangar, the pilots I'd studied with and the students I'd helped over the following training cycles. My heart sank, Hope will be there…

It chilled me inside; what had I become part of? And there was something else. I didn't like how Jayes had been so favourably disposed towards my working with Thomas. He seemed always to be in the background, that's how he knew Thomas had taken me to the flyer to see the Solid Time Field generator. I began to entertain thoughts that it was a way of controlling me, keeping track of me, keeping me busy so that I couldn't consider my father's work. That was it! My pursuit of Dad's goals jeopardised Jayes' plans. Of course he would discourage me. I'd been so blind.

It was no good. It all sat too uncomfortably on my mind. There was no way I'd sleep now, so I got up and began to make my way to the tech rooms. No one could tell me what I should or shouldn't bother exploring in my own time.

The nightshift rattled and toiled beyond the residential sound screening. As I hurried by the workshops, I found myself pausing frequently to admire the dedication of the workers and the spectacle of the fleet, near completion.

I voiced my praise to the mechanics and technicians. Their response was favourable and accepting, leading to several candid conversations, and I found myself able to encourage and make suggestions for late phase enhancements, even assist. It took me back to Jaro in my mind, fitting peripherals manually, and it felt right. It was as if my IAAM companions had accepted me.

By the time I reached the tech rooms I was calmer and, although I still didn't like Jayes' tactics, I wanted to help my new found friends beat the Val'ee. I wanted to save the Government fleet; I wanted my revenge.

## Chapter forty-one
## Waiting

Being unable to use airspace openly, Jayes had relied on sophisticated simulators. They impressed me, the experience so real that I'd frequently felt the desire to fly to Jaro and warn my friends of Jayes' intentions for the government fleet.

My concern for my friends spurred me to greater efforts than my fellow IAAM pilots; Jayes noticed, and approved.

The week that led up to our encounter with the Val'ee was an intense scene of growing excitement. Many had a score to settle; Jayes' words filled us with a certainty of success, and some were becoming pumped up with an arrogant bravado. Jayes allowed these pilots to apply graphics to their individual craft, and assigned them to one attack wing called the 'Hellcats', a name he said paid tribute to a technician called Levi Grumman, sadly parted before seeing the arrival of this glorious day. The application of such a meaningful name intensified the groups boastful self-importance.

I didn't like the name. It didn't sit comfortably with me; Dad had never allowed the word Hell in the house and had treated it like a swear word, punishable should it slip out of my mouth for any reason; but I couldn't deny the positive effect the graphics had on the rest of us. The Hellcat designs, and their position at the heart of the fleet, was visually stunning.

The final day of waiting was nearly unbearable. The location of IAAM's headquarters was to remain secret until the last possible moment. We wouldn't be joining battle until the countermeasure to the slaving tone had been configured. The counter tone would be fed through our communication systems; an opposite and louder tone it would be uncomfortable, but it would enable us to function.

I was heading up a Tech group that would not be engaging the enemy directly. This annoyed me, but the purpose of it found relevance in my heart. My group would break off from the main fleet as we entered true space, attaching countermeasure transmitters to Government ships. Each device would cancel out the slaving tone for that vessel, enabling them to re-join the fray. The task suited me, and if a Val'ee ship came into my firing range, well, they'd regret it. The others, would tackle the enemy head on. Reaper class cruisers at the front, with their massive forward facing cannons, followed by formations of free flying fighters. Then the drop fighter carriers, destroyers and, at the rear, The Deliverance - Jayes' flagship - with enough supplies to do battle for more than a week; it's docking bays laden with support ships and single seater cannon and missile loaders. A squadron of heavily armed Dragonflies would form a defensive shield, within the atmosphere, against debris and stray enemy ships.

As was Jayes' usual tactic our standby positions were alongside screens that provided a constant media feed. The Archivist had gone global with news of the invasion, and, although the Eastern Coalition remained unresponsive, the rest of the world waited anxiously for the time Verne had given for the Val'ee arrival.

The pictures fed to our screens, showing the Government fleet, received jeers of derision from the IAAM crews. Envisaged tech had been subject to a "piggy back" program that installed a remote "off switch". It was how the Government fighters had perished before, but, despite the switches being removed and the program deleted, IAAM workers still considered Envisaged tech to be irreconcilably compromised.

The Government fleet was twice as big as IAAM's, but that mattered little; as soon as the Val'ee discovered that their override had been detected and rendered impotent on the Government's ships, they would fall back on the slaving tone, the crews would be incapacitated.

The power generated cavern walls that had divided the headquarters into separate hangars had been removed, only a thin "ceiling" separated us from an obstacle free ascent into space and the whole IAAM fleet could be seen in one sweeping vista.

The flight deck of The Deliverance stood open, Jayes could be seen at ease in his captain's chair, radiating confidence. This was the day he had waited for, the day his organisation stepped from the shadows, the day it would no longer need to hide its strength, the day of victory, acknowledgement, respect. He was laughing and joking with his crew. I almost felt happy to be here, but the excitement was muted by the knowledge that Jayes had abducted me to prevent my death with my father; I shouldn't be here. I was an unknown factor, a potential spanner in the works. Maybe that was why Jayes had put me into a technical role. I was in Thomas's Tech Ship after all, and he would have been here anyway.

'Sorry I'm a little late.' Thomas plodded in, laden with various gadgets.

'What on earth is that lot?'

'Things I've been working on, experiments; how often do you get the chance to run experiments in space?' He shuffled to his seat, dropping a wired circuit board that broke instantly.

'I hope that wasn't important.' I commiserated.

I glanced out through my screen. I could see Rue in her cockpit talking to one of her crew. She looked my way, I waved, she nodded, Thomas replied.

'It was a receiver, for magnetic signals. I've always wanted to hear the sounds that the Earth's field makes and, well, I won't be hearing Earth cries on this trip…' His voice trailed off then suddenly burst forth again, 'This is the important bit,' he said, waving a metallic box in my face.

'I want you to concentrate on your job, not gadgets. What is it?'

'Tech Ship upgrade, it's Millie!!'

I stared blankly.

'You know… the computer from your flyer.' Thomas grinned.

'Millie?'

'Yep, been tweaking the personality profile too.' He informed, and began tinkering around the master control panel.

'That isn't going to slow down the system is it? We're heading to a battle you know!'

Thomas looked up at me from beneath the control panel disappointedly. 'The Audi A760 CDS computer is seven times faster than the standard computer they fit in Tech Ships…'

'Fine, just make sure "she" is linked up properly…'

Suddenly there was silence. Thomas had started talking again but there was no sound. He looked up at me, then down at his watch, then back and mouthed 'It's time…'

A light on the control panel heralded an impending message from Jayes. Jayes had prioritised Text-Com; the system picked up on vibrations from the larynx, translating them into text.

'Here comes glory! Run final checks, we still have a little wait.'

On the news screens the great bulk of a ship similar to the ERUWAI emerged from a bright, shimmering disturbance in space.

'Molly online yet?' I texted.

'It's Millie, and yes, I've linked her to Text-Com.'

*Cries: The Captive Mind*

'OK, Computer…'

'Hey Dace, how can I help...'

'Run final checks under battle protocol, complete full diagnostic and synchronize your systems to the Tech Ship. I don't want to find any software conflicts when we hit the heat.'

'Will do.'

We sat. I watched the events occurring above the earth and Thomas continued setting up his experiments.

'Those tests aren't going to interfere with the vessel's systems are they?'

'No, no, independent.' Thomas replied, waving his Data Pack at me.

'Checks complete, no problems detected. Diagnostic complete, system fully functional. Sync complete, I am fully capable of executing your instructions through this vessel but I preferred the Audi A760.'

I chuckled and shook my head.

Suddenly a flash lit up the media screen. Something had travelled through the waiting Government vessels from the direction of the Earth, and was heading towards the Val'ee ship. As it had travelled through the Concordant fleet it dispersed a wide fan of tiny missiles which were now detonating in unison. The force of each explosion cut through numerous craft and drove others into collision with their neighbours.

'What the hell was that!' flashed up on the Text-Com, an unintentional comment from The Deliverance. That didn't bode well. I expected Jayes to know the unfolding events.

A wing of fighters gave chase to the small ship. It was like a Y-Ship but with all the camera movement it was hard to be sure. I wondered if it was Chorda and Aldorael. Damn, why had I not brought the subject up again with Jayes? He had seemed troubled by my hinting at the presence of Val'ee on the earth when we first met. I guess I thought he'd already know; he had certainly not asked me anything more about it.

I gazed across at The Deliverance. Jayes was standing pointing at a monitor that I knew held the Archivist's record. I looked back at Rue's Destroyer, "The Vine", only to find her staring straight back. She was pointing to her Text-Com, mine lit up.

'Brace yourself.' Rue warned, I frowned but clung to my seat. The cavern juddered with the retort of a bombardment; chunks of real rock tumbled from the true mountainside. A couple of vessels at the back were damaged, one blowing up and writing off a number of the vehicles around it, seventeen ships totalled without even taking off!

My Text-Com flashed again, it was Rue. 'That'll be it for now. They came from the Y-Ship that just popped the Government fleet. Might have created a marker though, so suggest we switch to tactical.'

The HQ's defence grid powered up; we were no longer totally invisible to the earth's military but all its forces were now committed above.

A group of ships, many of unknown configuration had appeared from a position behind the moon; they were tatty looking but had effectively shielded the escaping Y-Ship, engaging the Concordant fighters decisively, forcing a call for further support.

The ship emerging from the spatial disturbance was half way through, it looked exactly like the ERUWAI. I wondered whether Fredrick and the others were on board, but the images onscreen quashed any hope of benevolence towards mankind. I doubted if Fredrick was even still alive.

More craft appeared from the moon, heading straight for the Government fleet, most of whom still held their positions between the space factories Pathfinder One and two.

This head on attack broke the stand-off, the fleet charged forward on their assailants, supported by the fire power of a partly built warship still docked to Pathfinder One.

The warship's weapons impressed me, energy based they maintained a focused beam over a number of enemy craft, draining their shielding then rupturing their drive core. Was this the weapon used over Sylvestris? I frowned. Why hadn't they used it against the Val'ee ship that was still emerging from the anomaly? It was using its primary propulsion engines, surely it was vulnerable?

The Val'ee attack was menacingly tough; their tatty appearance deceptive, they took numerous hits before folding. Only energy based bolt cannons were reliable for a clean kill.

As each alien vessel reached a critical condition it sent a narrow ray of light towards the emerging mothership before splintering apart. The pilots were escaping from their stricken ride using some sort of transportation device. I wondered how quickly they could return to the battle in another vessel. Were they using up these old machines on the first wave, waiting to bring in newer ones when our ships began to show the signs of fatigue?

I caught a brief glimpse of an alien pilot as its fighter sped through the

*Cries: The Captive Mind*

field of a media camera on Pathfinder Two; I wondered what I'd seen; it certainly didn't resemble a Val'ee. Its form was hunched over the controls, it's eyes dark and pitted. A cold judder went through me; I didn't like this at all.

The Y-Ship, that had arrived earlier, was now holding a position next to what was clearly the ERUWAI as it completed its emergence. Its main engines off, sound returned.

'What is it doing?' Thomas asked, bewildered. 'It's exposed its whole flank.'

Then it happened, the whole Government fleet ceased engaging the Val'ee, they floated pointlessly in the directions they were last travelling in. A few were destroyed but then an eerie ceasefire began.

'Got it!' Jayes exclaimed. A shrill note burst through our headsets, it was the countermeasure for the tone that had rendered the Government vessels paralysed.

The mountainside above us evaporated, 'Go, Go. Go!' Jayes commanded.

## Chapter forty-two
### The Battle

The IAAM fleet erupted from the landscape. As we rose I recognised the outline of the land against the ocean, the HQ was somewhere in the isolated highlands of Scotland! The thought of how fast my flyer had travelled to get to my village so quickly amazed me. The thought renewed my confidence as the fleet climbed; there was some real technical prowess behind these ships. If anything could stand against the Val'ee it *was* IAAM.

I looked down on my world, knowing I would soon be too busy to do so. Below us the view reminded me of the day I'd visited the ERUWAI. I'd felt a desire to protect the Earth; now I would be.

A Government fighter spiralled by, totally out of control; it's trajectory, as the slaving tone hit, had left it Earth-bound. The catatonic pilot unable to prevent it burning up in the atmosphere as it fell. A second took out an

251

IAAM fighter and both were dashed to pieces on the forward shielding of The Deliverance.

Above us we could see the compromised fleet. The Val'ee ships were almost as numerous, and there amongst them were three, odd looking giants silhouetted by the moon; I hadn't noticed them on the media screens, but there they were in the thick of the enslaved craft, picking at them like some grotesque scavenger. Beyond it all, more distant than the media footage had suggested, was the ERUWAI itself.

Jayes, seeing the mothership's exposed side, barked an order to the Cruisers. This looked like being a decisive first strike but in the blink of an eye the ERUWAI had adopted a head-on stance, the Cruisers potent beams skirting by it harmlessly.

I sat forward in my seat, 'How the…?'

'I've got a theory,' Thomas offered. 'Remember what we were talking about in the flyer a few weeks ago? About creating a stable Solid Time Field around a large vessel…'

'What are you saying? The Val'ee can stop time and move?'

'Why not? They must be able to understand time if they are time travellers, how much easier to pause it than traverse it?'

Thomas was obviously right. 'We're in *real* trouble, unless Jayes knows something he hasn't mentioned yet.'

'Er, he knows what I've been working on…'

'Working on?'

'Your guidance on miniaturisation has been extremely valuable Dace.'

I felt a sharp, needle-like pain on my shoulder, Thomas had jabbed me with an initiated isotope tab.

'Hey! You could have warned me!'

Thomas smiled, 'It's for our Tech Ship's pause button!' He placed a peculiar electronic device, magnets down, on the metal control deck. 'Your idea intrigued me. Jayes was thoroughly encouraging…'

The vessels around us in the IAAM fleet suddenly froze and I had to throw the Tech Ship sideways, to avoid our own fighters. The wild manoeuvre lined us up with the Government Flagship, The Oak. This had been our mission, to release the Government ships, and we couldn't have wanted for a better start. I brought the Tech Ship into a close position over the Command ship's hull.

'Computer…'

'Please call me Millie, I like it! How can I help you?'

*Cries: The Captive Mind*

I shook my head, 'Same procedure until further notice, attach countermeasure.'

Millie lowered a magnetic device onto the side of the great ship. Its purpose was to breech the vessels Com-system with the tone that cancelled the slaving weapon. Overlaid on this tone was a message giving assurances of IAAM's commitment to the Earth and an invitation to join us in our offensive.

'How long will *this* field last?' I asked, conscious of the short duration it had lasted with the flyer.

'Untested,' Thomas shrugged. 'It's a miniature of the Power Generated Matter generator, configured for Solid Time. Each time the power nears the end of its nominal peak output period the next cell has started and takes over, should run 'til we stop it.'

'So we can place countermeasures until we need to reload from The Deliverance?'

Thomas nodded.

I acquired a good position with a Government fighter and put Millie to work again.

'No! Wait.' I exclaimed. I swung the Tech Ship towards Pathfinder One and the unfinished Warship. The mighty ships guns were already on the Val'ee armada; it was a priority.

As we approached we discovered a cluster of Val'ee missiles, frozen in time like everything around us but on course to impact the Warship.

'We've got to do something.' Said Thomas, 'The missiles will hit before our countermeasure has a chance to bring the crew around. They won't have time to reposition their shielding.'

My eyes fell on some internal panels covering the Tech Ships systems ducting. 'We'll place those panels in front of the missiles, then when we switch off the pause button to reload they'll strike them and blow immediately.'

Thomas leapt up, deftly unfixing the panels and heaving them into the loading bay. I truly admired this boy now, he was more than the teenager I'd drawn my conclusions about in the car park. He was determined, intelligent and able. Our objectives were being met without resistance simply because of him. Funny; he reminded me of Davey. My heart sank. Had Davey and the others been at Sylvestris when the Val'ee obliterated it?

Thomas manipulated the panels into position in front of the missiles

253

with the ship's robotic arm, and we headed straight to the Warship and Pathfinder One.

As we picked our targets I suddenly saw Hope. Our route had brought us near to one of the odd ships we had observed on arrival. Hope's fighter was about to be clasped by some sort of pincer attached to a long, translucent, rubbery arm. Another arm was already attached to an adjacent fighter; frozen in the process of isolating and opening the cockpit to extract the pilot.

I attached a countermeasure to Hope's ship.

'I thought you were concentrating on big guns.' Thomas queried.

'Look what it's doing,' I said, pointing first at the neighbouring fighter, then along the tubes where the tell-tale shadows of other bodies could be made out. 'Besides, I know this pilot. I want her safe.'

Thomas looked horrified, 'Agreed. We could tow her out of reach.'

'Whatever, I just can't leave her to the same fate as the others.' My eyes fell upon a pair of deeply pitted, grey eyes staring out at me from a glazed slit on a metallic pod attached to one of the tubes; alarmingly they pulled away from the glass and were no longer visible. Weren't these creatures affected by the Tech Ship's Solid Time Field? Was it just the ships? The thought chilled me, and the urgency to rescue Hope increased.

Thomas was by now employing the robotic arm to hook a tow line to Hope. It was quickly achieved and he re-joined me at the control deck. 'When you're ready...' He urged, fixing his attention on the device that generated the field.

So great was my desire to help Hope that I hadn't contemplated the consequences of moving frozen time. Moving through the vacuum of space had been fine, placing magnets on stationary objects, fine, but to physically pull something that in real time had been behaving differently, was about to give me a nasty surprise, as I slid my hand up the drive panel my mind entertained the fact that Thomas expected problems.

As we moved quickly away the whole scene burst back into vivid life. Our initial movement cleared us nicely from the extracting arm of the slaving vessel. The arm missed Hope by a comfortable margin, flailing into the void where her ship had been.

A bright explosion near Pathfinder One heralded our success against the missiles aimed at the Warship, but I suddenly realised how far from the safety of the IAAM fleet we had come.

Our shell guns glowed red as Millie targeted any immediate threat, but we lacked the firepower to deal with anything decisively. Millie's evasive flying took over, saving us time after time, as much from debris hidden in the darkness as from the actions of enemy craft.

A beam from a Cruiser now struck along one side of the ERUWAI sending a spray of tiles into space from the ships head. The pieces rained into the tiny Y-Ship that had travelled through the Government fleet causing it to erupt in flame, illuminating briefly like a speck of dust in a projector beam.

All around us the alien ships were turning from their gathering of the helpless to respond to the appearance of IAAM. Thomas and I had held time for thirty-two minutes but now a dreadful response to Jayes' ships had begun and I realised, as Thomas and I flew into the relative cover of our fleet, that we had escaped only through the sheer surprise that we had created, and the enemies poor position against us. The two sides locked horns.

As we headed for The Deliverance to reload a voice appeared over the Com, 'What's going on?' It was Hope's dazed voice.

'Better wake up quick Hope, I can't take a ship with armed missiles into the docking bay of The Deliverance...'

'Dace?'

'Wow, you recognised my voice. Look, I've got to release you now so stay safe, yeah?'

'You too.'

I released the hook-up and approached The Deliverance just as a salvo of beams blazed from the Warship we had protected from the missiles. 'Yes!' I exclaimed, 'It's working.'

On board The Deliverance I leapt from the cockpit and pulled up a magazine of countermeasures ready for Thomas and the loading bay arm.

'We've only just arrived Dace, what's going on?' Jayes' face appeared on the large screen in the docking bay. He seemed cross, 'You should have loaded before we left the HQ!'

'We did Mr. Jayes, Sir. Thomas has developed a Solid Time device with a hugely improved duration of operation, we just used it to release The Oak, Pathfinder One and its warship, and ten Government cruisers.' Jayes smiled and nodded. 'But we found a friend in trouble and attempted a rescue; seems that by doing so we negated the field and reinstated normal time.'

'The Warship you mentioned just took out one of those big ugly ones totally...' Jayes began.

'Sir,' I interrupted. 'They're Slavers, they're being filled with people from the enslaved ships, there's *a lot* of people on those awful things, we need to rescue...'

Jayes nodded, 'We'd better make them a priority...'

Suddenly The Deliverance lurched. I struggled to keep my feet, Jayes' glanced down at a monitor and raised his eyebrows.

'Seems we're in range of the primary weapon on board the nearest Slaver. We took a direct hit on the shields and some smaller craft below us were caught in the explosion.'

My heart almost seized, that's where we'd left Hope...

'Dace,' Jayes continued, 'Can you neutralise the weapons under cover of Thomas's Solid Time Field?'

I considered the missiles that had been heading for the Warship, 'I think so, Sir.'

I looked around the docking bay. Firing on the enemy wasn't an option, it would just negate the field and place our minimally armed vessel in harm's way.

'Those might do.' Thomas suggested, pointing out at a delivery pod containing Rear Guards - explosive devices used by fighter pilots when being tailed by an enemy.

I slid a couple of pods under the Tech Ship's fuselage; the runners were too short but the contacts matched up. Millie would have to carry them the best she could. I re-joined Thomas in the ship's cabin.

'Take us out Thomas.'

Thomas pulled the ship from the docking bay floor, spinning it around to face the bay doors as I clawed my way back to the forward control deck. We accelerated out of the exit.

'Millie, initiate peripherals, contacts three and four need to be set up for Rear Guard release.'

'Understood, initiating...'

'Thomas, we need Solid Time...'

'Erm, that's the thing...' Thomas squinted.

'Thomas? Talk to me...'

'When we dropped the Field unexpectedly the generator ran real hot, I can't guarantee it'll be stable.'

'Give me what you've got, we'll have to cope if we're going back to the Slavers.'

Thomas nodded setting the field into operation as a shell exploded near us, it seemed frozen, then it nearly engulfed us, then it froze again. We got clear of it just in time.

'Speak to me Thomas.'

'It's warming up, but one of the cyclical generators is burnt out so it's giving us a flash of real time. I'll slow the cycle and maximise the plateau time... We'll get a nine-minute period of solid time followed by a minute of, well...'

'Then another nine Solid Time, right?'

'It's going to put a strain on the rest of the device.'

'We'll just have to work with it...'

'Pods accepted, Rear Guards initiated.'

'Well done Millie, take us out to those Slavers.' I indicated their position on the tactical display and the Tech Ship thrust forwards. As we progressed the Solid Time Field generator settled into the rhythm Thomas had outlined. Real time was bedlam!

'Millie, take a course that keeps us behind moving objects or we'll prang something for sure.'

Millie acknowledged politely, but in all fairness she was already executing manoeuvres impossible for a human pilot. It was impossible to judge the direction that debris was travelling in, and explosions were hard to avoid too, some were still shells as we flew by; triggered by our proximity they exploded as the field cycle allowed, sometimes that was close. It was a terrifying journey, but what lay ahead was equally daunting.

Each Slaver looked like some twisted, high domed tortoise with a grossly oversized intestine spilling out from underneath; the multi-tube gut seemed muscular and prehensile, working industriously - when time moved - to secure its victims.

The shell-like top gave way only to the vessel's long, jointed neck. On top of this sat the primary weapon; a cannon of sorts, not unlike a scorpion sting. As we'd observed it on approach it become clear that it had to be destroyed. It's rate of fire was profound, each orb-like projectile hurtling off in another seemingly random direction and yet each finding a clearly targeted object with devastating effects. Only the larger ships, whose shielding could be concentrated at the point of impact, remained defensible.

As the scene returned to a stretch of Solid Time I turned to Thomas, 'It's a long way to travel with real time bursting in so often. We aren't well enough armoured or armed to be so far forward. Is there any way to fix the field generator?'

'I could try, but it's running hot already... I could bypass the damaged cell, but I'll only have eight minutes to do it. Never worked on it whilst it's running... if I mess up...' He shrugged, and his face reminded me again of Davey, I felt I was missing something obvious. I certainly missed the old guy and the thought that he may have been with Dad when the Val'ee attacked haunted me. I looked out at the size of the Government fleet. He could be out here if he hadn't been there that day. I smiled, I would let myself believe it, it would be another reason to fight.

The other countermeasured ships were showing signs of recovery now and I felt that, had it not been for these terrible slavers, the tide of the battle might have been turning in our favour. 'Thomas, do what you can. There's one more real time burst before we're close enough to the nearest slaver. Do you think you can do that job before the following Solid Time period ends?'

Thomas gave me a wide-eyed shrug. 'Only one way to find out; I'll do my best...'

'What's the worst that could happen.' I smiled.

'We'll blow up, I guess.'

I stopped smiling, 'Better make sure we're near an enemy ship then, take one of them with us eh? Oh, hold on, here comes real time again...'

With a heavy judder the turmoil of this position within the battle became starkly apparent. A lot can happen in a minute; three hundred and eighty rounds from a slaver's cannon, an entire wing of Drop ship fighters erupting in flame on your near side, a flurry of orders from Jayes - instilling a sense of infallibility with a victorious voice, despite the protesting evidence of our eyes.

The hulk of a Val'ee ship lay motionless to my off side.
'Millie, park us behind that wreck until Solid Time kicks back in.'
'Sure thing.'
As we sat dwarfed in the shadow of the alien craft, we found we could see inside through glazed panels, affording us a view into the low slung

flight deck. A number of the haggard, pale creatures I'd seen earlier scurried around inside, working frantically on the control panels. The vessels engines purred into life, their Waveforms exposed by damage to the ships undercarriage.

Seeing part of the generator loop I targeted it and took it out, shutting it down permanently; the aliens trapped inside would answer for their actions after the battle I thought to myself.

One of the creatures now stood in front of the glazed panel, it was the best view of one I'd had; it was about the same size as a Val'ee but gaunt and wrinkled, it's skin cracked and dusty like a corpse left to rest in a crypt. A misty, almost transparent aura flowed around its body, giving the impression of a garment. It's eyes, like shadows, were fixed on me. I could almost feel my resolve draining away. It shouted something to the others and struck a panel on the controls; their ship exploded.

Lowering my upraised hand, I realised that Solid Time had returned, 'First slaver Millie.' I shouted. 'Thomas do your thing.'

I sighed deeply, a moment later and we'd have been toast!

Two minutes brought us alongside the target ship, Thomas silently working on the device. The view outside was as peaceful as a still photograph of active war could be.

'Millie, as I circle the cannon I'd like you to release individual Rear Guards at two metre intervals. The neck moves around a lot so I'll circle that too.'

I edged carefully around the structure getting as close as I dared. Our handiwork complete, my attention was captured by the slaver's "shell".

'All those people.' I exclaimed, distracting Thomas, who begged for silence as time was getting short.

I apologised and returned to my observations. The "shell" had a deep luminescence, bright enough to show the number of enslaved pilots and crew that were on-board. Somehow we had to paralyse the vessel to rescue these people. I resolved to signal Jayes for instructions the moment real time kicked in. Before then I had to booby trap the other Slaver's cannon and find a place to hide until we knew whether Thomas's plan had succeeded. We'd play dead amongst some wreckage, send a signal to Jayes, then try the field again to see if it worked. To be honest it had to. I had no other way out.

'Mille, let's repeat the process with the other…'

'One step ahead of you.' Millie teased, but she was already halfway there which was good because the clock was ticking. Thomas was clearly feeling the strain, sweat running down the side of his face.

'Anything I can do to help?' I asked.

'Shh! Almost, ah! Now I've dropped the arc pin into the housing!' He flashed me a hostile stare then persisted, retrieving the pin and continuing hurriedly.

A warning light on the control panel started to flash.

'The second Rear Guard pod just broke free of runner four.' Millie informed.

Instead of despairing I found myself grinning. I leant forward for a better view of my discovery. 'It's OK. We're not alone.'

Frozen at the very point of engagement was an IAAM Destroyer. It was "The Vine", Rue's ship, poised at a steep angle of attack, missiles filling the gap between it and the Slaver's cannon; it's forward shielding, held like a snow plough in front, ricocheted the Slaver's projectiles into sprays of sparks either side.

Behind "The Vine", two Y-Ships were giving chase; they'd holed Rue's rear fins and killed her two rear gunners.

'Millie, take us over to those Y-Ships; Rue's got the slaver covered, let's cover her. We've got some Rear Guards left in the first pod, I want them in front of Rue's pursuers, then I want us tucked in beside that debris, engine off, to see how successful Thomas has been. You've got thirty seconds.'

Thomas tutted.

'I think I've got the easiest task.' Millie chuckled. Her programmed personality was endearing but very odd, it seemed too jovial for such an efficient system, but it eased the anxieties of the moment. Our trap was laid and we hid amongst the debris. I braced myself, things were about to get hot.

'OW!' Thomas yelped pulling a smoking finger from the device; all remained silent and still. Thomas smiled.

'You genius!'

'It's bought us time to get out of here, but it's going to be running hot. The field *will* deteriorate.'

'Does that mean it'll stop any minute or start fracturing into real time like before?' I asked.

*Cries: The Captive Mind*

Thomas pointed outside, 'Not exactly.'

I turned to see what looked like white flowers on the front of the Y-Ships, then realised what I was seeing as another and another appeared on the cannon of the slaver we'd spread the Rear Guards around. Time was moving slowly.

Both Y-Ships became cocooned in flame and the beams of light shot the pilots back towards the ERUWAI.

'We'd better get back before we lose the field totally.' Thomas urged.

I nodded in agreement.

'Pretty amazing out there though,' he remarked. 'Everything in slow motion...'

He was right. I could actually see how the weapon on the slaver worked. Each projectile was created a split second before firing by what must have been some sort of Envisagement...

'We'll look like we're travelling at ten thousand kilometres an hour.' Thomas laughed

My eye fell on the first slaver. The Rear Guards had wrecked the cannon, but something strange was happening. The "shell" was clearly parting from the mangled cannon neck which now, rather obviously, proved to be the rear of the vessel, part of a platform slung beneath the dome.

'They're escaping!' I shouted in alarm attempting to signal nearby IAAM ships to give chase, but realising immediately that the message, arriving from slowed time would be unintelligibly fast and sound like a pop of static.

The cannon of the second Slaver now began disintegrating under "The Vine's" missiles, Rue's ship manoeuvring away from the blast; it's shield tracking steadily beneath it to protect the undercarriage.

Already I could see the glow of waveforms appearing at the rear of six more projectiles slung beneath the destroyer. I realised Rue had targeted the first Slaver. Its "shell" was nearly clear of the platform revealing a weapons deck - presumably useful for covering the slaving section whilst it made flight.

'All the people on that slaver! Can't Rue see them? Thomas, there must be a way of going Solid on time again...'

'There's no point...'

'What!'

'This whole event, it'll be over in a few seconds of real time, we can't

261

stop time forever, we can't board the Slaver and rescue everyone; we'd just bring back real time like we did with your friend.'

My mind reeled; I thought I'd saved Hope, but I'd put her in harm's way; had I not she would be on that slaver about to perish anyway...

'I'm sorry Dace...'

Rue's missiles were away and all around us was gaining momentum.

The second slaver was also pulling clear of its platform, attempting to match the speed of "The Vine" in some sort of ramming manoeuvre, but the platform seemed to snag and pitch wildly downwards from further internal explosions. Shafts of light pierced out through the vessel's flight deck and the domed shell fragmented, spacing its occupants.

'Get us out of here Millie.'

Millie started off towards The Deliverance.

Thomas realised how I was feeling, 'You did what you could man. Anyone else would have done the same; we didn't know that moving your friend would damage the generator. In a way I'm more to blame for not making the device more tolerant of stress...'

Millie interrupted, 'The remaining Slaver weapons deck has launched ordnance, it's targeted The Deliverance. We seem to be losing our advantage.'

Millie was right, things outside were moving much faster; still too slow to threaten us, but even that safety would soon be over. We spun around taking a position between the mothership and the maelstrom of missiles.

In the distance Rue's engagement of the platform was intense, the structure was spewing missiles in much the same way that the primary cannon had. Rue was holding a static position over it pouring everything she had at the contraption. There were no other vessels close enough to aid us in a defence of The Deliverance.

Thomas lunged forward, 'I've got it!' he exclaimed lifting the access panel on the field generator. 'If I just...'

A bright light filled the cabin. Thomas was torn from his seat and flung towards the loading bay where a spiralling, golden vortex was forming. The blast doors slammed shut over it and an electrical discharge fed back abruptly to the field generator; my body convulsed, my belt became taut, it snapped and I felt myself impact the side of the cockpit.

'This is it.' I thought. 'Fine, I've had enough. There's no one left to miss me anyway.'

*Cries: The Captive Mind*

### Chapter forty-three
### The Cost

The young nurse smiled, 'Welcome back.'

'I was expecting an angel…' I sighed.

She stood up, 'Excuse me for being such a disappointment.'

'Sorry, I didn't mean to offend.'

She moved around the room performing various tasks; filling a jug of water, updating my notes. 'I understand your surprise,' she said. 'There wasn't a lot left of your ship.'

'How's Thomas?'

The nurse looked puzzled.

'He was in the Tech Ship with me.'

'I'll have to look into it Mr. North; I've no record of anyone else from your ship. The aft and mid-section were completely gone, you're a very lucky man.'

The nurse prepared to leave.

'The battle,' I enquired. 'How is it going?'

'The battle is over; we won, Yey!' She forced herself to give a celebratory wave of her arms, but she looked tired and the response seemed loaded with irony. 'There are others better able to fill you in on the details. I will send word to them that you are awake.'

I watched her leave, then tried to sit up, if my ribs weren't cracked they were badly bruised. I looked about me; I was in one of the medical bays on The Deliverance; so it *had* survived the hail of missiles from the Slaver's weapon deck. Another man lay shivering in the bed alongside me.

'Hello.' I offered, but there was no response. I tried again, a little louder, 'Hello?'

A whimper came from the figure and a scarred hand pulled the sheets around the patient's bloodied head. I frowned and tentatively manoeuvred myself to the edge of my bed to stand, wincing with discomfort.

I stepped towards the other bed.

'All Mr. Jayes wants is peace.' Rue announced, appearing at the doorway.

'Mr. Jayes?'

The patient turned towards me shaking and whimpering.

'His nerves are shot,' Rue stated. 'You changed something. It's not same as before! I tried to deal with it but I couldn't put it all right quickly enough; I could have dealt with one Slaver and its platform but no, you appear with a shed load of impact mines - totally out of your depth - and suddenly I've got two weapons decks to control...'

'I'm not sure what happen...' Suddenly I noticed an ugly scar across Rue's cheek, visible now she'd stepped into the light of the room.

'I blew the platform you initiated right into the moon - that's what happened - but not before it launched a whole round at The Deliverance. Sixty missiles, Dace! The Deliverance had to weather that barrage. According to the computer it was only Jayes quick thinking that saved two hundred crew members in the lower gun positions; he extended the docking bay shields knowing it would weaken the shield protecting the flight deck, and he paid.'

That didn't seem like Jayes to me; the man who could see so many die in the Val'ee attack on Earth, and who could have ships in his fleet take out the Slavers with their cargo of government pilots and crews. The Jayes I knew wouldn't have sacrificed himself to save gunners.

Jayes hand took hold of my sleeve and pulled me close, close enough to hear a repeated whisper, 'Thank you, I will be free now, thank you...' The whisper lacked the presence and authority I'd come to expect; it's faltering delivery and shaking of the frame attached, led me to believe that he'd lost his mind. I was speechless. Were my actions to blame for this? Rue certainly thought so.

'We need to locate mother. The Deliverance has always come through intact; Jayes has always led us to a position of power - *now* the future is unclear. We have work to do to put this right.'

'Put it right?' I gestured towards Jayes, 'How can we change *this*?'

'Oh *this* is the least of it Dace; mother was right about you, you're dangerous... Jayes should have left you behind.' She looked back through the doorway. '...at least we still have the rift.'

'I had a sudden sensation that everything was wrong. I felt panicked and distraught, barely conscious of Rue's hand gripping my arm and pulling me towards the doorway.

I wondered what was true in all this; I wished Dad was here for counsel. I had no choice but to follow Rue like some unthinking sheep.

Rue was trying different channels on her Gauntlet communicator, attempting to reach Elizabeth. A nurse questioned the wisdom of moving me, and was bulldozed aside.

As we made our way along a gantry, leading to one of the docking bays, Elizabeth's voice suddenly appeared, strong and clear. 'Rue darling, I'm on The Oak.'

'Unhurt?' Rue queried.

'Yes dear, but the record's compromised...'

'I know mother, it was Dace.'

'Jayes brought him into the battle? What was he thinking?'

Rue was smiling at me now, but I wasn't comforted by it.

'Join me on the Oak. We have to act quickly before the rift closes.'

'OK mother.' Rue marched me into the docking bay where "The Vine" stood, its hull seared by energy beams and scratched by shrapnel, its tail shredded.

Rue shouted something to a member of the crew who just shrugged and pointed at the burnt-out contents of a panel on the destroyer's side.

Rue changed direction abruptly, forcing me to stagger awkwardly to remain upright.

'You...' She grabbed the pilot of a support vessel. 'Take us to The Oak.'

'Yes Miss James.' nodded the man, and he scurried to his cockpit and opened the cargo hatch to let us in. It was one of the Tinnys I'd seen at the IAAM HQ; Jayes had chosen to use them regardless of the concept that the Val'ee must at some point acquire them. I shook my head - He'd been so confident of victory.

Rue motioned to a narrow, windowless seat and I buckled myself in.

Rue stood behind the pilot and we were away.

The flight was shorter than I'd expected, and I realised that the fleets must have come together at the end of the engagement away from the debris field.

We boarded The Oak. Elizabeth met us in the docking bay greeting Rue with a motherly kiss and me with an unexpected smile.

'Wait by the shuttle please, Dace...' She instructed pointing to a sleek little Government craft similar to the vessels used for exospheric training at Jaro. She then placed an arm around Rue and ushered her aside quite forcibly. Her manner with Rue seemed angry and disappointed but I was too far from them now to hear their exchange over the noise of the demobbing docking bay.

I made my way over to the access hatch of the shuttle happy to not be in trouble with Verne. I sat on the hatch step watching the body language of these two, strong willed women. To my surprise Rue was now cowering, she reached up as if to cup her adoptive mother's cheek but her hand was pushed swiftly away. Rue seemed to give a retaliatory retort but Elizabeth's demeanour seemed to change totally and Rue's attack dissolved. Some sort of decision had been made whether Rue liked it or not; she stomped towards me red faced, deliberately pushing by a porter who was hauling unused shells.

'Here! Steady on.' He protested.

Rue spun around, prevented a shell from falling and rested her hand on his, 'Really sorry, can't imagine what came over me.' She spat the words through gritted teeth, her delivery far from pleasant, but the porter seemed instantly to calm down, even standing there as she returned to her journey in my direction, seemingly admiring her form.

She gestured that I enter the shuttle.

'You're flying.' She snapped, as she followed me up.'

I leapt quickly into the pilot seat. Flinching from my protesting ribs I buckled up and initiated pre-flight before she caught up. By the time she was ready to go the shuttle was too. She smiled through what had clearly been the pretence of frustrated anger. 'I love that she's so ignorant.' She laughed.

I felt more nervous than ever. Her manner now suggested that, despite the argument looking like a win for Elizabeth, Rue had got exactly what she'd wanted.

I requested launch clearance and checked the packed docking bay for hazardous obstacles. I could see Verne looking up at me. I wished she could see Rue's jubilation but the angle of her view was too acute. To my surprise Elizabeth nodded and mouthed, 'I know, look down.'

I frowned and looked quickly down as if checking a monitor on my controls. In a compartment on the pilot seat sat a Palm Pack, a Data Pack minus all the thrills and somewhat smaller as a result. I looked back at Elizabeth, 'Be careful.' She mouthed, turned and walked away.

I slid my hand down into the compartment, cupped the Palm Pack in my hand and slid it up into my pocket.

'We're clear to go.' I announced, hoping that Rue hadn't noticed anything.

'OK, step on it, we've got some tight time constraints, oh, and don't get distracted out there, get a grip and be professional, do you understand?'

I didn't, 'Yes, er let's get going.'

*Cries: The Captive Mind*

Within a few moments we were clear of the Government Command ship.

I wondered how the crew felt, knowing now that IAAM had saved them, knowing that they'd been under the influence of the Val'ee slaving tone, entirely helpless; aware that some of their friends had been stripped from their vessels and been destroyed with their captors...

Rue interrupted my thoughts, 'Head to the Morrello complex as usual for the upgrade.' She reclined in the navigator's chair and gave a contented sigh.

'Upgrade?' I queried.

Rue shook her head incredulously. 'Just as before, or we'll miss the rift.'

I fell quiet. If things had changed how could it be like before? I hadn't the heart to put up a fight and I was beginning to realise what I was seeing outside. I couldn't help but be stunned by the alarming vista that the gathered Government and IAAM fleets presented. Had the nurse lied about our victory? Great chunks were missing from two of the IAAM Cruisers; the debris field was dense and my eye kept falling on recognisable craft, spiralling dead within it. Rangers, Dragonflies, Tinnys - a number of bodies - I looked away.

I took up an angle ready to enter the atmosphere when a massive secondary explosion erupted on the far side of The Deliverance. Even Rue's celebratory mood faltered as the IAAM mothership stood outlined in flame, but I'd noticed something else; a chunk of the great ship had broken away and was now slamming into some sort of bizarre anomaly that had been hidden by the flank of The Oak.

'What *is* that?' I heard myself say aloud as the breakaway fragment of The Deliverance was shattered into countless tiny pieces by the rolling tube of plasma that boiled, in colours like fire, beside the moon.

Rue frowned. 'Did you take a knock to the head in your Tech Ship! It's the rift. We've known for a while that this is the way they travel. They slice a rift along time and choose a point to re-enter it, but we've got to beat the lag period, that's what's giving us the opportunity to upgrade and follow them. All they want is to ensure the Slavers aren't destroyed, nothing else matters to them, we can exploit their need.'

I really didn't understand what Rue was getting at. She seemed to infer that I ought to know these things. An uncanny feeling of déjà vu teased at the back of my mind. Suddenly my reflections were swept away by an urgent Com message. 'Could all available ships please assist in the evacuation of The Deliverance; we are buying time but we won't be able to stabilise her for very much longer. Repeat, all available ships...'

Rue switched off the Com as I began to arc towards The Deliverance.

'What are you doing!' Rue shrieked.

'Going to help.'

Rue struck me close to my sore ribs. 'We haven't enough time. You have your orders. Earth, Morrello complex, now!'

I wanted to snap back but somehow, with Elizabeth's advice to be careful, I managed to hold myself back. I swung the shuttle back on course, avoided a lump of twisted metal and hit the atmosphere at a perfect trajectory.

Below, the world seemed shrouded in mourning grey. Rue was leaning forward for a better view, then, in a cold voice, said, 'Pretty decisive wouldn't you say?'

Our decreasing altitude began to allow me insight into what Rue meant. The grey wasn't cloud cover, it lacked the cotton wool appearance I'd grown used to from this height, no, it was smoke.

'Is the whole world alight?' I exclaimed.

'Huh!' Rue snorted. 'You were asleep through this...'

'What?'

Rue seemed to accept my ignorance and started to explain. 'The destruction of the last Slaver ended the slaving tone, and the Government fleet began to shake off its effects. Some targeted and destroyed IAAM ships, but those released by the efforts of the Tech Ship crews soon put them right. Soon we turned the tide and the ERUWAI fled through the rift behind the cover of its remaining ambush ships as before. We were winning, the silence generated by the ERUWAI's rift engines mattered little to the Government fleet, they just followed us in...'

'What about the weapon?'

'What weapon?' Rue retorted clearly vexed by my intrusion into her story.

'The one Elizabeth spoke of on the news; the one that stopped the ship that killed Dad.'

'You better shake off whatever's effecting your memory Dace. You know there's no such thing, that the fire ball was a rift generated in the oxygen rich atmosphere; the Val'ee ship escaped through it but the rift burnt hot and fast, scorching the earth as it rolled, mercifully briefly. Glad it lasts longer in a vacuum.' She started at me and shook her head.

'No weapon? Then why...'

Rue's eyes narrowed as if she was figuring something out but hadn't quite got it. 'It was made up to prevent panic and foster a sense of perceived safety.'

I was speechless.

Rue continued. 'The record showed us what would happen next if we didn't alleviate the immediate fear of attack; the population would have run riot. Volatile situations demand effective control; it's OK to lie Dace, if the outcome is to the greater good.'

I didn't share Rue's opinion.

'Anyway, we were winning. Then the tactics of the Val'ee changed completely, something new, something I wouldn't *expect* you to remember. With the ERUWAI's tail disappearing into the rift, the bulk of its fleet flew straight by us without a shot, straight towards Earth. A large number of our ships chased after them, those remaining saw fit to pursue the alien mothership and a few fleeing stragglers. No allied vessels survived that pursuit, they were vanquished by the same force you saw when that fragment of The Deliverance hit the rift.

The aliens that remained plummeted like stones into the Earth's atmosphere; some were destroyed by the heat of re-entry but the remnant seemed to be searching for something. They seemed to care little that we were systematically wiping them out, by the time we discovered their game it was too late.'

'Game?'

'They were delivering something horrible, something more destructive than an explosion. Things are decaying, plants are withering, even solid rock is crumbling...'

'But...we've lost then!'

'Big time, yes, we're looking at the extinction of humanity.'

I clung to the nurse's words, 'She said we'd won...'

'Really, who?' Rue said, fighting back a laugh.

I remembered the nurses tone, her forced celebration, the Val'ee had been defeated, but at what cost. 'This is terrib...'

Rue began laughing.

'What are you laughing for?'

'We're going back.' Rue cheered, leaning forward and fixing me with her grey eyes, the way she used to at the EOA when she'd been particularly successful at upsetting Davey. 'We can stop all of this from happening, it's just a minor alteration to our plans...'

Below us was the Morrello complex - it was destroyed.

I sighed, 'What now? There's no one left to fit any upgrade.'

Rue's tone changed to one of slow disbelief 'We don't need a fitter. Put down over there.'

I brought the shuttle gently down onto what had been the east car park but was now a dusty waste, strewn with rubble and twisted vehicles.

'You'll need your key.' Rue laughed, pushing something small and round against my injured side.

'Mind my ribs.' I scolded, pushing the object away.

Rue pulled away staring intently as I realised that the object had stuck to my palm, 'Hey! What's this?'

Rue seemed more agitated than ever but strangely patient with my responses and quite excited by my struggle. My attempts to pull the black ball from my hand became less and less effective as it sank slowly into my flesh. I finally found myself staring with wonder as it settled without pain into a position just proud of my skin.

Rue grinned. 'It's a neural key for the ship. You'll be able to fly with your thoughts.' She looked at me suspiciously. 'You told me you'd merged with yourself. I really hope you did, and I'm not with the original Dace, because that means the you I need is dead. Now, am I talking to the right Dace?'

The thought of not being the right person actually made sense, but to admit that to Rue seemed dangerous. The feelings of déjà vu ended up being my prompt; a lot of what I'd expected to see was coming true - which was really weird - but I felt that it was preventing Rue from concluding that I was totally ignorant, and therefore not who she seemed to think I was. I knew what was over my left shoulder as I stared at Rue. It scared me but my confidence was being read by my companion and seemed to be calming her anxieties.

I pointed over my shoulder, 'Are we going to fly this thing or not?' If I was right I really didn't want to, but inside it felt like an unstoppable chain of events.

Rue smiled, and sighed, 'You had me worried.'

'Something happened on the Tech Ship, it's just scrambled my thoughts a bit. You'll just have to bear with me; just tell me things if I ask, or if you feel I need reminding. I'll soon tell you if I remember.' It seemed the perfect cover for what I now feared was happening; if I had gone back in time with Rue before then I'd died before any merge had taken place. I dreaded to think what would happen if she knew that.

I turned to see a glossy, black form rising from the rubble of the Morrello complex. My déjà vu was confirmed, and to keep up the pretence I would have to fly the Black Ship that the Envisager had made through me at the EOA. I had to say something to make Rue less suspicious.

'The future is in my hand!' I quipped, waving the hand with the neural link embedded in it.

Rue's cold exterior relaxed a little.

I was staring back down at the device again, flash backs of the Envisager incident tore at my mind, but there was still no pain. A small part of my consciousness seemed calmer, but it *was* small.

A voice pricked my awareness, 'So good to see you again, Dace.'

My heart pounded. 'What now?' I thought.

'Now? Now we fly; trust me.'

## Chapter forty-four
## Out of Time

'It's in my head...' I said, as if about to protest. I wanted to run, I wanted to keep running, but I was committed to my role... it was expected of me. I could feel the Palm Pack in my pocket, perhaps *it* had answers.

'We've no time left Dace, we can't enter the rift in a conventional ship; the ERUWAI's tiled hull supports an envelope of energy that dissipates the energy of the anomaly. Your Black Ship is the same...'

Technical data started filling my mind from the Black Ship leaving me faltering on the edge of insanity.

I looked down at the device Rue had called a key, sitting immovable in my palm, 'It's using me already, I can see us sitting in the shuttle!'

Rue frowned, clearly aware of my distress.

I scratched at the key, 'Where did this thing come from?'

'You made it in the same way you made the ship. You are the most brilliant EO I know...'

'I didn't make it! It's a default program. Mr Jayes wouldn't approve of us using alien technology…' The Black Ship touched down beside us.

Now Rue seemed cross, 'Firstly, you *did* make it. It's *not* alien and neither are the Envisagers for that matter. Only Jayes has ever given me cause for concern regarding the inhuman, at times it seemed he was totally set upon a course, and yet, in the lead up to the battle his face was crying despair, like a consciousness caged. When I arrived back at The Deliverance, after the battle, I found myself involved with the evacuation of the forward sections that had been damaged in the missile attack. *I found Jayes rocking in a corner three corridors away from the smashed flight deck, smiling, stammering that he was free, and I could read him properly for the first time. For the first time he came across as human, weak and pathetic, lost, but human and deep in the back of his eyes… a glint of horror that betrayed a knowledge of what had come to pass.*'

We remained staring at each other for a moment. Her ideas about the Envisagers were not new to me, and her talk of Jayes sat uneasily well with the fears Tyler had shared at my grandparent's house; Jayes possessed.

No! This was all superstitious nonsense. We had to remain objective, Jayes was clearly unable to hold his usual calm countenance having narrowly avoided death a second time; he was shell shocked. To me a more pressing question presented itself.

I turned to look again at the vessel. Its fuselage seemed to swallow the light that struck it, it's wave forms rotated in mesmerising synchronicity. 'You don't call me Trix anymore.'

Rue slapped her hand over her mouth in mock horror, 'Oh no! I didn't realise you liked it so much, I'd never have started.' She giggled cruelly, 'It was an affectionate name for a child; you grew up…' She leant towards me. 'Please tell me you remember.'

Suddenly the screen of the cockpit cracked from back to front with a mighty snap, doing nothing to break the uneasiness of the moment. Rue sighed in despair, 'I haven't the time for you to figure it out with your back firing brain. Look at the waveforms, cyclical technology, like Thomas's Solid Time Field generator, only much bigger; big enough for power generated matter.'

I stared blankly at her, how was that going to help us? She was right about the scale and its resultant potential properties, but how could she have known about it.

'How...' I began.

'I saw the footage of the time you opened the ship with your father and Quaid.'

'That was recorded?'

'Dace, the vessel is Power Generated, how else could it have morphed from its resting state to its standard flying state? It's whole outer form is energy. That's why it's not corroding like this...' Rue poked the canopy of the cockpit, and part of it fell away. '...We're running out of time, Dace.'

'What have the Val'ee done?'

'They've poisoned the atmosphere with something corrosive. The damaged ships in space are still deteriorating too. So it must be some sort of weapon they've employed. The whole planet's gonna crack up, Dace. Your ship can get us back through the rift; it's power generated form is constantly renewing itself; it's immune to the poison. Only you can fly it Dace, the fate of the world rests on you.' She leant forward, whispering harshly, 'It *was* your fault, after all.'

I stared at the ship which Rue insisted I'd made; then something changed, something inside me longed to fly it.

'Come on Trix,' she mocked making a motivational lunge at my ribs but I'd disengaged my flight belt and moved aside. Taking to my feet I took two steps to the hatch and slid down the access steps, putting agonised distance between us.

Boarding the object of my fears I hopped into the single seat cockpit. It had been twin seated, I'd seen it in my mind, but my very desire for isolation from my tormentor had led it to morph to my longing. I wondered what else it could become and Rue watched as it convulsed in ripples and swirls and eddies of pure energy as she approached.

'Get in and buckle up Rue. I'd hate to leave you behind.'

She looked briefly for a way to get near me. Thwarted, she accepted the cabin and settled in. I sealed the ship and took hold of the bar in front of me.

The ship knew my needs instinctively from the neural connection through my palm, acting out every manoeuvre as I thought it; it was an EO's ship for sure. My mind simply accepted it, it felt right. I felt focused; I felt alive; I felt... surprised!

Cracks began to appear in the landscape beneath us as I burst into true space. I flew quickly through the amalgamated Earth fleet, hurtling towards the rolling, billowing, golden scratch in the velvet blackness of space.

Rue's suggestion that the corroding weapon had been used against us in the battle seemed all the more apparent now as ship after ship finally buckled to its mysterious effects. The Deliverance erupted for the last time, catching nearby vessels in its final throes. Then great shafts of light pierced up from the Earth, one cutting through Pathfinder One and the unfinished Warship. Rue and I were the only ones that could stop this now.

The rift loomed larger. It spiralled like a waveform made of flames. In tones like pure gold, it bubbled and churned as lava does when it sits in the throat of a volcano. The turmoil of its surface was exposed as some sort of illusion at the point of its horizon; the true surface was completely smooth and reflective and I could perceive the lights of my ship mirrored back at me amid the tight twisting vortices.

'We're hitting the rift in ten, nine, eight...' I could feel the tension rising, the static all around me.

'You can't just enter it anywhere!' Rue shouted in a shrill, distressed pitch over the intercom.

'Where then!'

'Just left of the strongest vortex, that'll put us just ahead of where the ERUWAI went through!'

I flicked the ship sideways across the face of the rift, the side of the vessel threatening to graze the anomaly and drag us in. I drew the ships form away from the glassy surface as much as I could but I knew we weren't going to get as close as I felt Rue wanted. Great arcs of electricity, like solar flares impacted the ship but there was no jolt, no damage. Rue was right, this craft would be able to enter.

'Two, one...' The rolling cylindrical rift, it's eddies and vortices of fiery yellow vanished, replaced by a chill cool of blue that flurried from the body of the ship in rainbows like the iridescent inner surface of an oyster shell.

'Beautiful, isn't it.' Rue offered. 'I'll never tire of it, time so full and still that it has become like a liquid.'

'Were in some sort of tunnel.' I observed.

'A moment in time, a second, the blink of an eye. Don't touch the walls of the tunnel yet. How close did you get to the ERUWAI's exit point?'

'Two, three hundred metres, hard to tell, it was such an acute trajectory.'

'It'll do, it's more work for me and you'll have to do exactly what I say, do you hear me? This isn't the same as last time.'

My déjà vu suggested otherwise.

I altered the ships Com, I wondered if I could pick up any signals from the ERUWAI. The awful, bone chilling screams and grating sounds, pops and chatters that filled the cockpit startled me. 'Not *that* again!' shouted Rue, 'Switch it off!'

I flicked off the external receivers, 'I wondered if I could pick up transmissions from the ERUWAI, what *was* that?'

'You should remember! You did it the first time; the conduits magnify the magnetic discharges of Earth.'

'Earth Cries; that was what Thomas wanted to record.' I gathered myself, 'But where's the ERUWAI? Is it too far ahead to see?'

'Too far behind now,' Rue sighed, clearly feeling she shouldn't have to tell me. 'The whole rift is a time line. You can enter specifically to return to an exact point or use it like a conduit to travel back to nonspecific eras. Once inside it's hard to ascertain the periods crossed as each tunnel expresses seconds, not years or even days; we entered at a point that places us ahead of the ERUWAI, so it's behind us.'

She shifted about uneasily. I could see her on my monitor, and I was very glad that she couldn't see me.

'Perhaps a little too far behind,' she continued. 'We'll edge towards it through the right wall of the tunnel.'

I eased gently through the tunnel wall sending waves of brilliant hues dancing around the ship.

'Take this angle,' Rue said, sending data through the ships on-board computer. 'We'll knock a few days off our wait. My guess is it's headed for the start of the battle to warn its fleet of our tactics.'

'How do you know all this, Rue?'

'You really don't remember? Dace, mother has ensured you were protected, until now, so that we could use your vessel to travel back and put things right, but you are instrumental to our plan.'

'You and your mother's plan?'

'No! *Our* plan, *us*, mother protected you but she doesn't know our plan...' Rue paused, it seemed really important to her that I remember.

I thought quickly. I could remember one thing from when I'd been huddled in anguish at my father's death, at the foot of the bed in Jayes' detention cell. Rue had visited me and whispered something in my ear, 'Trix, I've been studying my mother's record, given time we could figure out a change that will forge a different outcome.' Had this been the plan?

'We're off to forge a different outcome.' I risked, 'But how we do it is currently eluding me.'

'Well, it seems it didn't quite work out. I don't know what you were thinking of with Thomas and his Solid Time Field again but I'm glad you are beginning to remember. I guess the merge must not have been as clear cut this time, but that's far better than what I'd begun to fear.'

Rue laughed and I laughed with her, hoping that she wouldn't pick up on my confusion regarding her words.

'When did you find out about Thomas's Solid Time Field generator?' I queried, desiring to change the subject and find out how she could possibly know about something that I hadn't seen until the morning of the battle.

Rue giggled. I'd got away with my fake laughter and realised how important body language was to Rue's ability to perceive a person's true feelings. She sighed, 'Thomas was putting in a lot of overtime, so I followed him one evening, I watched him tinkering with his tiny generator, so I crept up on him and grabbed him; I came on a bit strong, he was terrified, he's always been so intimidated by me...' She continued with a laugh in her voice. 'I challenged him about what he was making and he spilled his little secrets.'

Rue seemed truly despicable to me now as the ship continued through the tunnels of the rift. I remembered her saying once at the EOA how she'd meant the bad things she'd done, how they'd achieved all that she'd desired. She hadn't changed at all.

I needed help if I was going to bluff my way through this. I needed to see if the Palm Pack Elizabeth had left for me, provided some answers.

'I think my memories *are* beginning to come back,' I declared boldly. 'They seem a little out of order though. I'm going to mull them over for a while. It'll be tricky, mulling and flying at the same time. If you don't mind, I'm not going to chat for a while. I'll need my concentration for piloting this bird; you work it like an Envisager you know.'

'You've said that since the very first time, but you are right; best that you focus.' Rue fell silent and I instructed the ship to drop the Com link to the cabin, or rather, it intuitively shut down the Com as I desired it. I

*Cries: The Captive Mind*

left my visual link on, to watch for signs of Rue attempting to speak to me.

I pulled the Palm Pack from my pocket and flipped it open.

'Voice identification required.'

'Dace North.' I offered, quietly, still nervous that Rue might hear me through the bulkhead.

Elizabeth's face appeared on the diminutive screen, 'Thank God you are safe. I convinced Jayes to place you in the battle, you may be the only answer to our problem. Where are you?'

'I'm in the rift...'

Elizabeth's face froze as the computer processed my response, this was a recording not a conversation.

'Keywords: In...Rift...'

Elizabeth's position changed abruptly, 'I believe you are considerably off target. We believe Rue is looping time. Subtle changes are occurring, going further and further back. By our calculations - and your use of the Palm Pack - you will re-enter time at a point seventeen hours before the Val'ee attack on Pathfinder Four, the Sky Cities and the Thetford Sylvestris.'

My heart began to race, this could be an opportunity to save Dad, but Elizabeth continued.

'...*All* this must stay the same or I will not gain the leverage I need to mobilise government forces to defend the earth.' She sighed. 'Rue is ambitious, it's my own fault; I've been trying to restore the timeline myself but it seems more happened than my error. I fear my example led the Val'ee to do the same, but there are changes that could only have been made before their arrival. You are one such change, Dace. Rue has become convinced that completely overwriting history is the answer. I believe she seeks to do this by changing recent events minimally to achieve favour in powerful circles, circles that will give access to the opportunity, like IAAM. Then, once in position, she plans to make a radical change further back. She cannot do this by guessing an entry point into the rift, she needs control. File A on the Palm Pack shows the schedule that Rue has been asked to keep. Your role is to mark on it any deviations and deliver it back to me. Rue will insist you stay where she tells you to. She will overemphasize the risk of changing things. Remember this Dace: only big changes effect core time; they rip time back to the point that the change originated from. A serious loss of control. Changes in isolation to the population are absorbed, small details rarely effect the bigger picture, there seems to be a destiny-like quality to events that will only change through catastrophic alteration.' Elizabeth's image froze and a keyword screen reappeared.

I looked at Rue on the monitor. She seemed content to watch the rainbow patterns that were being cast off our hull each time we dissected a tunnel wall. I, too, was momentarily mesmerised, then I remembered that I was actually flying the ship. A part of my mind had remained focused on the task just as Mr. Lock had pointed out after my lock test.

I wondered how long it would take to travel through a space devoid of time. I wondered at all the technology I'd seen and the suggestion Rue had made that the Envisagers were not alien. What did the Val'ee want? Enslavement of humanity, sure, but why boost human technology and risk defeat in battle?

Suddenly a thought struck me. Rue had said we'd arrive in advance of the Val'ee. She thought it was heading for the start of the battle, but what if it was heading back for something else? What if it was heading back to ensure that I didn't play a part in the battle? Jayes had said that the Val'ee wanted to destroy me. Chorda and Aldorael had hinted at a crime I'd commit at some future point, a crime one of them wanted me dead for. Had my role in the battle been so damaging to them that they would go to such lengths to destroy me?

I glanced again at the Palm Pack. Perhaps there was time for a little more info. I thought for a moment. 'Original timeline.' I stated.

Elizabeth appeared on screen, motionless, two symbols flashed beneath her.

'There are two matches for your enquiry, in order of relevance.'

I initiated the first.

'Records of the original timeline are held by Jon Morrello and myself, they belong to us and they have been entrusted to us, their volumes are numerous, exceeding the capacities of traditional data storage devices.'

The screen returned, frustratingly, to the still image of Verne. I tapped the second symbol.

'I believe I am to blame for the first alteration to the original timeline. Although more profound changes now predate it I believe my example, becoming recognised at some point in the future, has led to others - including the Val'ee - to seek changes.

'My error was emotional, and it is important that you learn from it. Meeting yourself in the past leads to absorption, the older body merges into the younger frame. The older mind, having the fuller knowledge, effectively replaces the younger. Should such happen to you, you must repeat all you did before to prevent a build-up of minor changes that could lead to a Rip.'

This was the merge Rue was talking about, only she expected me to merge and then change what I'd done, in order to alter time.

Elizabeth continued, 'In my case I accidentally met - and merged with - my fifteen-year-old self.

'In order to ensure no critical change to the timeline I diligently replicated the horrors I'd faced in the so called "care" of Mr. Seed and his wife. I grew and, when the time came, took my role with your father at the Morrello Corporation; but the awful abuse I'd endured a second time, coupled with the knowledge that I would travel back in time and meet my young self before the Seed family took me, had led me to a decision I regret.

'Twenty-six years from now your father *would* have enhanced his "The Space" technology to provide pinpointed folds in time for the recording of historical events. His "Travellers" would visit history quietly then report back through the fold. When I accidentally met myself I lost the opportunity to return and with your father dead the fold will never be made - I *had* gone back though, which suggests some permanency of created time, a phenomenon I call the "voided paradox" - I am still here, you see - and yet, with your father dead, there is no way I will go back again.

'In the timeline where your father lived I'd secretly undergone some genetic alterations. In doing this I hoped to meet myself without merging, adopt myself and prevent the things that had hurt me from ever occurring. If my gamble failed I'd have to endure Mr. Seed's lusts a third time, but it was a risk I was willing to take.

'It worked, and - knowing myself - I was able to steer the teenage me away from her self-harm and dependencies acquired through years of mismanagement and unhealthy role models.

'I'd used false documentation to achieve my goals. I took the name Elizabeth Verne, but I was Rue James.'

She pulled her trademark, high collar down to reveal the top end of the vine tattoo.

'The problem is, Dace, that my life as Rue made me who I am; your Rue never lived what I lived; never endured the pain that saved me.

'The original timeline, I fear, may be lost to the changes that led to the Val'ee war.' Her tone became grave. 'Dace, your parents, Douglas and Vanessa, never had a child that survived The Great Suffering, *you* too, are a change to the original timeline.' The keyword screen reappeared.

So Verne *had* travelled time, she just hadn't told her adopted "daughter". I dwelt on the concept that they were the same person, and marvelled at the idea of permanency in created time...

Suddenly, I became aware that Rue was about to speak. I had seen the change too and quickly returned the Palm Pack to my pocket, reinstating the Com.

'The horizon ahead is time.' Rue stated in a serious tone.

'Yes, I know.' I lied, keeping up the pretence that I'd travelled with her before. I knew now that I must have died before, not to remember something so memorable. Great spheres of backlit emerald, threw colour into the blue calm of the tunnels. Hues of jade hurried brightly in then darkened into the blue stillness. The sphere at the end of the tunnel we were in was brightest.

'Head for that sphere Trix and don't forget to dive!'

I wondered what she meant. Was it a trick to check whether I knew, or was there really something in real time beyond the sphere that I had to avoid. I smiled and nearly laughed, I'd let the ship respond, it would do so as if it were actually me, like an energy formed extension of my own mind.

'Oh yes!' I responded, 'What would I do without you?'

'Oh Trix!' Rue exclaimed, her stern tone dropping away, 'It all feels better this time; it all feels right, my love.'

Her words were a startling revelation, and again I felt that this behaviour was uncharacteristic. Were Rue and I lovers in this timeline she was creating? More to the point, how often had this happened and how had I died? Even more concerning was that these manipulations Rue was making seemed to lead, at present, to the destruction of Earth. When Elizabeth recorded the footage for the Palm Pack she hadn't been aware of impending doom, she certainly hadn't warned of it, and she'd actually drawn from future experiences. That's what I needed to find out next, how much further than the calamity I'd witnessed did time extend in the record? Did it archive humanity until its original end? And what about me? Who was I if I wasn't my father and mother's son?

I dived, my response automatic, swinging clear of the satellite suspended in low orbit.

'Remind me again why we're so much lower than when we left?' A voice in my head seemed to suggest this was something important to know.

'The "off centre phenomenon" you recall? We entered the rift vortex low, any lower and we'd have entered the Earth's atmosphere at a dangerous angle or worse still...'

I realised quickly, 'We could have hit the ground, boom!'

Rue nodded. I'd covered my lack of knowledge again but the concept freaked me out.

'OK Trix,' Rue smiled, keying into the navigation control some coordinates. 'Let's head home.'

I locked her directions into the system and sat back, mouth dry, heart thumping, trying to plan my behaviour when we reached our destination.

## Chapter forty-five
### Changing Priorities

The ship sailed down into the half-light of dusk, down to a world ignorant of doom; down to a steep, wooded valley, bejewelled at its base by a deep, black lake.

For a moment I thought Rue's coordinates were wrong and that we were about to ditch in the water. I almost retook control, but then the craft swept forward onto a wooden platform partially hidden by overhanging trees. The wide jetty divided the lake from a neat, weather boarded lodge. An outbuilding ran down to the dancing waves and a muddy track snaked its way up through the dense forest behind.

'Welcome to mother's summerhouse.' Rue trilled, before glancing purposefully at her watch. 'Mother doesn't come here once for the whole period of our stay.' She leapt down onto the jetty and stepped quickly to a window; shining a torch inside she let out a delighted cry and turned to beckon me over.

I opened the canopy and lowered myself gently to the deck, supporting my ribs.

'It's raining.' I observed,

Rue stood motionless, staring at me, 'It's condensed time, you always get a little spill from the tunnels, it follows you down, you know…' She opened her arms as if expecting an embrace. 'We made it Trix.' She sang, gesturing with her hands as if anxious to hold me.

I felt a deep need not to disappoint her, to be what she expected me to be, and headed towards her with all the confidence I could muster.

'We'd better warn someone about the Val'ee ship that's on its way.' I suggested, but as our eyes met I perceived a change in her. Her hug was not as intimate as its call had promised. Indeed, it seemed positively cold.

'Oh Dace.' She stated, the return to my name worrying me. 'Look at the ship you built, you must know it came from you now? Isn't it beautiful in this light?'

I frowned, released her and turned around. The vessel looked bigger - overtopped as it was by spreading willow and alder - it's reflective body seemed to shimmer a misty blue and I could see Rue, as if in a mirror. She checked her watch again then raised a gun to the back of my head.

'I think you ought to have a good rest now…'

This was it then, my role in Rue's plan was complete. Only my ship could get her through the rift, only I could fly it. Now, I was surplus to requirements, I had one last card to play.

'You are right Rue, it's beautiful, like you, and the best thing, the thing that makes all this so unbelievably excellent,' Rue's hand faltered but then levelled with a frightening determination. 'Now I've seen the time conduits again I've worked out how Dad enabled precise travel through time. Rue, we could change history totally, overwrite all the troubles…' Rue's hand dropped as if in shock. 'You've studied the record,' I pushed, pouring enthusiasm into my words. 'You know where and when things took place. We could be at the centre of it all; imagine our fame. I could get us back from here, all I need is an Envisager.' I made a move suggesting that I was about to turn back. Rue swept her gun out of sight and I completed the turn allowing my eyes to stay fixed on my ship for as long as possible before looking back at Rue - composing myself for the performance of my life. She had to believe this.

I took hold of her shoulders, '*We* could be amazing!'

Rue's resolve seemed to collapse; she fell into my arms, enamoured by the thoughts of power that she had long nurtured in her heart, and I knew she felt she'd found a short cut to her goals. I had done it, I had nothing,

*Cries: The Captive Mind*

but I had bought myself time with an arrogance of tone, that echoed Rue's. She was at a loss as to what to do next.

'What's wrong my love?' I heard myself say.

'You've never said this before...'

'I've been slow and foolish; this last loop has given me more time to ponder my father's work. It came so close to tragedy.'

'Oh Trix, I'd truly thought you'd died and that you'd not managed to merge with yourself to make the alterations we'd discussed.'

I put my hand to her mouth, glad that Elizabeth had explained merging, 'No more childish names now Rue. No more Trix, he is gone; I *am* Dace. I'm not thirteen anymore, I'm a man.' I drew her closer, aware that she was prepared to kill me if I turned out not to be the Dace she'd thought I was. I had to bring this scene to a close any way I could. I cupped the back of her neck with my hand and moved to kiss her with a confidence that would be absent in a younger relationship, then the muzzle of Rue's gun pressed into my ribs. My mind gasped in despair, I had been a fool to think that the astounding observational powers of Rue could be fooled.

'Why did you bring your ship so far into the battle?'

An answer came to me, I smiled, 'I had to protect you, but then, you wouldn't remember.'

Rue pushed me back and levelled the gun.

I continued, 'I stayed back, did as we agreed but your ship was hit by chasing Y-Ships and dissolved in flame. You were lost to me,' Rue's eyes widened. 'I travelled back, Rue, I prevented *your* death. My ship was there to protect you. You don't realise how vulnerable our dream is.'

A strange smile-like expression came over Rue's face, 'But you've been so vague...'

'Thomas's Solid Time device blew up. I haven't been able to think straight since. But you, you're everything to me Rue. I couldn't let you die like that...'

Rue's arm fell to her side. 'I... didn't know. Oh Dace it is me who's been foolish not you. I've thought myself invulnerable. I thought I'd studied everything the record held, oh, but it falls so short now, I've changed so much...'

A clock inside the lodge chimed, Rue turned to look, then she looked at the outbuilding by the lake.

'You are anxious about something.' I said.

'I know where the younger me is now, I could merge with her sooner than before, make important early changes.' She paused and reached up, touching the scar on her cheek. 'No, the only change I need to make is to lose this. Then I could go and get you an   Envisager...'

'If you must leave now, be sure and hurry back. I'll take that rest you suggested and be ready to comfort you on your return...' Where was all this coming from? It was gold!

Rue looked at the gun in her hand then handed it to me; I had won, but it changed nothing regarding the prospect of my death. Rue had believed me to be her travelling companion. She feared that I had died but was now satisfied that I hadn't. I knew *I* wasn't her partner - although *now* I was - which could only mean that the *right* Dace was gone and had never merged with me.

Rue was half way to the shed, she had kissed me tenderly then headed off at a run.

'The key is under the planter, don't go anywhere, we can't risk compromising the run of time.'

There it was, just as Elizabeth had said, stay put, don't do anything. I smiled. It didn't matter, I'd gained some time, I could find out more from the Palm Pack and make my escape before Rue returned.

'Would you like me to set up a perimeter?' The ship enquired in my mind.

I nodded and in my mind I could see the surrounding woods for several hundred metres in all directions; I marvelled at this neural technology and I wondered again how I had made it.

Rue swung the end of the shed - that joined the track into the woods - open, to reveal a 'Streamer' Wave Bike in a metallic, blood red, illuminated by a security light. She leapt on, checked her watch again, waved and shot up the track. Only then did I breathe again; I allowed myself to slump to the ground and shake, nausea building within me.

I watched the bike as it travelled through the security field, the sensor images forming in my mind. Then she was gone.

'Rue is heading to Edinburgh, a round trip of five hours.'

I wondered where we were to be two and a half hours from Edinburgh, but I was too exhausted to think of asking the computer. I knew what she wanted to do at her destination, a chance to merge, lose the scar and gain access to an Envisager; that would be harder, she'd be longer than five hours.

I rested back on the lodge door, gazing up at the darkening night, praying under my breath my thanks to my father's God, but inwardly fearing my deception had been too readily accepted. Either Rue's judgement had become clouded or she was toying with me.

The planter Rue mentioned, was beside me. I tipped it up and retrieved the key.

The lodge was open plan, a kitchen and dining area to the right, a comfortable sitting area to the left with a television. I flicked it on, scanning the channels for news, perhaps I could confirm Elizabeth's suggestion as to my point in time.

The news stories were familiar; it was like watching a film a second time, and knowing what was coming. I looked at the clock on the wall, I had sixteen hours to rescue my father.

'I should contact Elizabeth directly.' I thought aloud. I switched off the television and pulled the Palm Pack from my pocket, flipping it open with my thumb. The keyword screen appeared. 'Contact Elizabeth Verne'

She appeared on screen. 'Contacting me directly, at this time, would place me in a considerably risky position. You must remember that you have been missing for many days already, and to make actual contact would be flagged up by Government voice identification; I would be arrested for holding information on the whereabouts of a missing Government employee. I suggest you utilise the text message program on this Palm Pack. Use no names, just ask questions. I will receive your texts under a name only I know, and will record an answer on the Palm Pack that I will place in the shuttle for you to find. Please be careful...'

The keyword screen appeared, 'Send text.' I instructed. A little keypad popped out of the bottom of the device.

Quickly I typed, 'I'm back. Need more info on the original timeline, what I did and what I'm supposed to be doing; she nearly shot me, if I knew more I could draw her from her plans...'

I pushed in the keypad to send the text, wondering how soon I would get a response, then realised, if Elizabeth was going to respond to these requests, place the answer on the Palm Pack and stow it on the shuttle for me to find, then the reply must already be on the device.

'More on the original Timeline.' I said.

Elizabeth appeared. 'The original timeline archive was created by Douglas North. He had known that his research would lead to the possibility of traversing time; he wanted to keep history safe by creating a means to penetrate time without interacting with it. Knowing this would not be possible until after the creation of a means to get back, he'd been keeping meticulous records using a whole range of data and media gathering programs linked to what was the internet. When Dougie finally succeeded in his work the record was checked and supplemented by trusted Archivists. These people, myself included, were sent as observers; some would return through the device after minutes; stepping through the temporary conduit "The Fold" created. Others would live periods of time; weeks, months, even years, collected one hour after departure to avoid merging with a younger self about to depart.

'The original record started in Dougie's University years and proceeds beyond our current time. The record stops suddenly, ending in instructions to myself and Jonathan Morrello. It is our understanding that Douglas knew that a Rip was imminent. Search "Rip" for more on this.

'It was clear that he knew of my error. He assured me that the Rip was not my fault, but when I look at the old record now, it has changed so much, and I despair.'

Elizabeth's words intrigued me, although I'd been told before that I had not been born, it had seemed important to my Dad that I receive his research and carry on his work. I'd asked for more about my role and stated this to the Palm Pack.

'You were not a part of the original timeline, your appearance at the height of the Great Suffering was a clear break from the true line, a Rip, as was the arrival of the Val'ee two years later.

'As regards your role now with Rue, you are to do as you've been told, familiarise yourself with her schedule - you'll find it under 'File A' on the Palm Pack - then watch her. Record changes and hand the device back to me when we meet.'

I checked Rue's schedule, it was off already.

'Send text.' The keyboard popped out.

'Need to know Rue's objectives; they differ from the schedule you sent; she's headed to Edinburgh to merge with herself.' I paused, there was something equally important that Elizabeth should have advance warning of. 'The Val'ee attack Earth, they use some sort of decaying weapon. As Rue and I left the planet broke apart. I don't think that sticking to Rue's schedule will change what the Val'ee do; please advise under keyword "Survivor".'

I waited for a moment, as if it were giving Elizabeth time to respond, then shook my head, 'Survivor.' I stated.

*Cries: The Captive Mind*

'You have given me very real concerns Dace. All you have stated is new; no line of the record indicates the willingness of the Val'ee to destroy Earth, and Rue's merging so early at the club in Edinburgh shows me that she is totally set on a different course. You must not stay where you are; use your ship to find a safe place. Meet and merge with yourself at Sylvestris after the first attack and bring your full knowledge to the Morrello facility, we can protect you there. Do not wait for the press to corner you as before. Once you are with us we can address Rue's actions and put things right.'

I flipped the device shut and pushed it into my pocket. I guess I'd made my mind up when Verne had spoken of Dad's involvement in the original record. To me the whole run of events was beyond correction. The fact that Elizabeth *was* Rue played heavily on my mind; had her younger self decided to go her way just as her adoptive mother had done? Was Rue's work undoing a work Elizabeth had already achieved?

Dad was the only thing missing from this picture, and yet he was the one who would make all this possible. I wondered again how any changes could be expressed if the creator of time travel had been killed. It was actually essential we regain the ability in order to heal time! The answer was to save *him*.

That was what I'd do, how could the true line be restored without Dad? He'd been there, now he wasn't, but he could be. I had an opportunity to save him. I stood up, then another thought presented itself, I had an opportunity to save the lives of thousands of people, those on board the Pathfinder, the sky cities, Sylvestris and in the forest communities. Once I'd achieved that *I* would get the world ready to face the Val'ee; maybe *this* was why I was here. Added to history to make the changes necessary to defeat the Val'ee; the anomaly of the Great Suffering finds his purpose. I frowned, I had no plan and less than sixteen hours to defeat a ship that had dwarfed The Deliverance.

I paused, everyone around me seemed to know so much and I so little, well - we'll change that… somehow.

## Chapter forty-six
## Control

I sat contemplating my next move, becoming aware of a deep unease. I looked again at the object that had sunk painlessly into the palm of my hand. It had flawlessly conveyed all my intentions to the systems on the ship. It was astounding technology but I hadn't needed it when I visited the craft with Dad; the vessel had just opened up in response to my presence and voice.

Again I disregarded any idea that I'd created it. I didn't understand it. I had only just begun to understand Power Generated Matter at IAAM HQ. I couldn't have conceived of it back at the EOA when the ship was made.

I stepped to the window; the Black Ship seemed to pulse with an eerie luminance, then I nearly jumped out of my skin as the hand possessing the key device began to vibrate. It had been resting on the window frame, and now began to flash with a bright light and discernible heat.

I leapt back from the window. I initially assumed that the vessel was somehow alive; that it had seen me at the window and was saying 'I saw you'.

The buzzing continued; the light was brighter than the moody glow of the lamps in the lodge, I flailed about in a panic wondering what to do. Any observer watching the lodge from the other side of the lake might have assumed that a box of fireworks was exploding inside the building.

'Stop it!' I shouted, clutching my device laden hand.
The buzzing stopped, and as I gazed at the object in my palm I became aware of a tactical display appearing in my mind; it was like the one I'd seen as Rue departed.

'Proximity alert.' The words arrived in my mind like a revelation. I froze to the spot allowing my concentration to fall fully into the tactical information.

It was an aerial schematic comprising the area the ship was monitoring. To the far left of my consciousness, I could perceive a slow movement heading towards the Lodge.

'Magnify.' I said without thinking. My mind drew closer to the object and the recognition of it made me feel quite sick. It was a Y-Ship.

'There shouldn't be any…' I heard myself say. Then I remembered; Aldorael and Chorda *were* already here. The Y-Ship *must* belong to them.

*Cries: The Captive Mind*

Were they seeking to counsel me, or did they already know what I intended to do? Could they be coming to kill me? I gasped; that was it! Everything I'd been hearing regarding why I couldn't remember these events.

The future me, who had come back, had been killed before he could merge with the original me; it didn't explain the déjà vu, but that was just a feeling that an event had been lived before, bearing an eerie familiarity but no real experience. No, the Val'ee came to kill the me who had made the journey with Rue, and they had succeeded, I was convinced of it. I could feel sweat forming on my brow. 'How far away is the Y-Ship?' I asked.

The schematic in my mind panned from the vehicle to the lodge *'Seventy-six metres and closing.'* It was gaining speed now; I could hear the approaching hum of its engines. Where could I go to escape? My eye fell again on the Black Ship through the window; my only option. I bolted for the door.

Half way between the house and my goal, I became despairingly aware that I would not have enough time to clamber up into the cockpit before the Val'ee arrived and instantly saw me. The shadow of the lodge was rapidly giving way to the light from the Y-Ship as the vessel rounded the building. I leapt at the rear of the Black Ship as the familiar form appeared between the lodge and the shed.

It came to a hovering full stop inches above the wooden jetty, blocking any hope of return, and committing me to stay with the vessel that hid me; all I needed to do was get on-board. If the Val'ee entered the lodge, I'd get the opportunity.

The figure that stepped down from the alien craft stood motionless, backlit by the illumination of the Y-Ship's lights, it's form visible through its ethereal garments, the glare of the lights strangely refracted into wing-like blurs above the creature's shoulders.

I could see what made the creature hesitate. In my haste to leave the building I'd left the door swinging open in the breeze. My visitor had seen this and assumed my absence from the dwelling.

'Be still.' A voice instructed in my mind. 'You'll be fine, just remember what happens next.'

I gazed at the device in my palm. It was the first moment I'd allowed myself to realise that the ship was actually speaking directly into my head. It had seemed like an audible voice but had there been anyone else with me they would have heard nothing. I wondered how much this object, connecting me to the ship, had invaded my body to create its neural link; could it control me?

I peeked out from behind my cover again. The Y-Ship's lights were on the lodge; I was in darkness but the Val'ee standing on the jetty was looking my way. Suddenly the ship's lights swung in a wide arc that flashed across the inky water of the lake towards me. I flung myself against the rear fin of the Black Ship, its surface energy warm against my back.

My direct surroundings became as bright as day, the black shadow of the fin was all that remained to hide me, it's shape cast out towards the edge of the jetty and the lake beyond. I contemplated diving in...

'Don't!' The Black Ship cried. 'That's suicide, trust me, wait.'

I clung to the fin like a limpet but I could see a shadow approaching, I could feel my heart racing. The shadow seemed to be carrying an object, a gun?

The Val'ee swung around the fin, gun raised level with my head. I raised my hands in some vain attempt at surrender, then saw how confused *she* looked; she lowered the weapon.

My visitor was Aldorael and she couldn't see me! The Black Ship had surrounded me with Power Generated Matter, I was now part of a hollow fin! I could see my adversary, but she could only see herself in the reflective surface of the vessel.

Suddenly a flash of light silhouetted Aldorael; it had come from the rocks on the lake shore beside the jetty to the left. Aldorael swung around firing a round from her gun. She stood motionless, her back to the ship looking along the beach towards the limit of her ship's lights. A sudden clatter turned her to the rocky cliff beside the lodge. A torch bounced down the cliff face, coming to rest at the foot of it. Unbroken it cast its sharp beam up into the cliff top scrub.

I could see everything through the neural link with the ship. Aldorael - this time not firing - held her gun towards the cliff and headed up the jetty towards the path that led to it.

The tight space within the fin opened up into enclosed steps.

'Get in properly, once we're airborne you can reconfigure me and get us out of here.'

Shots rang out in Aldorael's direction. I could see flashes of light coming from the cliff top, the Val'ee exploiting a large rock for cover, gun

*Cries: The Captive Mind*

aloft ready to return the sentiment. I could hear her calling for me to stop. Calling me by name. Now I was sure that she'd come for me.

I scrambled quickly up the steps into the Black Ship's cabin. It must have been due to my strong desire to see what was going on but I was startled by the view I now had. The whole of the ship's fuselage had become like the one-way surface of the fin when I was staring at Aldorael moments before. All was silent from the cliff top.

'Get us out of here.' I commanded.

The whole scene became bathed in a red glow as the Black Ship's wave array burst into life and the vessel lifted instantly into the air. Aldorael left the cover of the rock and started firing towards us, there were two retorts, like bullets ricocheting off the energy of the hull, then, silence.

I was clear, but who had distracted Aldorael? I wanted to go back

'It's OK.' Announced the ship. 'It was some deception, I sensed no lifeforms. Our priority is outpacing your attacker; she'll be after us soon.'

The warning pulled me into sharp focus. The ship wasn't controlling me, it needed me. I closed my eyes and focused on the feed that was coming across the neural link. I could see the ship's form in my mind's eye, the flow of energy that held it, and I could move it to my will. The craft morphed around me, without protest, protecting me by default from the environment outside.

I made it smaller, sleeker and pulled the cockpit around me.

'Rue is returning to the lodge.' Stated the ship.

I had mixed emotions about Rue, she had been a friend at the EOA, but she seemed dangerous to me now, different. Dangerous or not I didn't like the idea that she was heading towards an angry Val'ee.

'What's Aldorael doing?' I asked.

'Her Y-Ship is leaving the jetty; she will not be there when Rue returns.'

Rue was at least safe, but there was no way she'd made her intended journey. 'Why is she heading back to the lodge?'

'I believe She's realised that she left her Data Pack behind.'

Then I saw it, on the floor, roughly where Rue had been sitting, before I had morphed the ship. Her Data Pack, open and on.

'Aldorael will be in firing distance in ten seconds.'

I snapped my attention from the tantalising device, 'Best leave her behind then.' I grasped the control bar and we were away.

## Chapter forty-seven
## Hunted

We sped south, but it soon became clear that Aldorael was in no hurry, that her pursuit was not hot.

I found my eyes again drawn to Rue's Data Pack, five hundred terabytes of information, sitting there, open, on, unprotected by an already entered pass-code. My head tipped to one side to match the Packs orientation and I was surprised to see a photograph of my Dad's friend Fredrick. Why was Rue looking at a picture of him?

'Dace.'

I looked back at the control panel, 'Yes Computer?'

'Aldorael *is* still following.'

'Really? She doesn't seem in any hurry, just change direction a few times, that should confuse her.' I was distracted by what I'd seen and hadn't noticed the urgency of the computer's voice.

'We've been tagged, we must make the substitution, changing direction is a waste of time. Aldorael knows where you are going.'

'What? Can't we just morph the tag off?'

'It's an impact tag, there's nothing to morph off. It's military technology for targeting Power generated and cloaked ships, you know that...'

'I don't *know* anything, what did you mean by substitution?'

'What we usually do.'

'**Usually?**'

'Computing...' **The ship went quiet.**

'**Computer?**'

'I had hoped that you had survived, but now I fear you must have been caught.'

'You're right, I'm not the Dace that was here before.'

'The only way for you to escape and fulfil your objective is to substitute me for me...'

**The ship sensed my growing confusion.**

'At this point in history I am still in standby mode at the Morrello Complex. We go there, you swap vessels and leave me behind. As a result, *I* remain at the facility...'

'You've been going through the same period of time in a loop? So that's how you know what's happened, why didn't you warn me sooner about the arrival of Aldorael?'

*Cries: The Captive Mind*

'I had not expected her to come so soon. I knew you needed time to plan your action against the ship that is coming; I was giving you time. I would have warned you, but Aldorael's tactics have changed...'

**The thought that Aldorael had altered her schedule to her advantage troubled me.**

**'How many times have you done this, Computer?'**

'Thirty-seven times, but it is a time loop, so I fully expect that I will do it forever... Oh, as I now realise that you didn't know, may I insist on your calling me Leila.'

**'Why "Leila"?'**

'I like it. You gave me the name on Derra.'

**'Derra?' This was beyond me. I sensed that I didn't have time for such a fact finding mission. No, something else troubled me more.**

**'Is there anything else that's changed, other than Aldorael arriving sooner than before at the lodge? Will I survive this time or am I still likely to die?'**

'I'm sorry, but I don't know how you died. You substituted me for the other me at the Morrello Complex, and instructed me to shut down. You do, however, have Rue's Data Pack and a greater lead on your pursuer...'

**'I didn't have the Data Pack before?'**

'No, Rue arrived back, she was agitated about leaving her device in my cabin. Anxious to keep her happy you gave her access to the passenger bay and she retrieved it.'

**I wondered if Rue had navigated this loop thirty-seven times too, or if it was just the ships experience. 'You said we had a greater lead...'**

'Yes.'

**'How much greater?' For some reason I had one minute and thirty-two seconds in my head.**

'One minute and thirty-two seconds.'

**I shivered; maybe all this déjà vu suggested that I had survived? I shook my head; you couldn't run a sensitive time based operation on déjà vu. 'How much time does that actually give us?'**

'By the time we reach Morrello, twelve minutes and twenty-nine seconds.'

**'Is that enough?'**

'I don't know; you seemed to achieve the substitution last time, so an extra minute and a half should help. *If* time is what you need.'

**'If only we had Thomas's Solid Time Field we could just freeze time and get away completely...'**

'We did. You Envisaged it.'

I was nearly speechless.

'Where am I going to get an Envisager!'

'There is one on board as standard specification, next to my core.'

I'd lied to Rue about being able to create a working time travelling device with an Envisager, and was relieved that she hadn't known about the tool on board Leila. The proximity of the device scared me; I hadn't touched one since the incident and the memory of the pain did not help my concerns.

Just turning and reaching towards the Power Generated bulkhead revealed the tool. The bulkhead dissolved as my hand approached it. The tool was strapped beneath a backpack-like structure which I understood to be the complex system core, the only physical component of Leila – the power cells that supported the very fabric of the ship - I stared at the Envisager...

'There is no need to fear it.'

'Please, I must think this through...' I reached for the Envisager but froze; this was no good, I'd lose the lead Leila said I had. My eyes felt drawn to the power cells in the core, they were each like the cell in Thomas's device, only far more refined...

'Leila, where are we?'

'Approaching the place we stopped last time.'

'Stopped!'

'Yes, you sent a decoy probe ahead of us, it even had a mock impact tag to fool our hunter. It bought you time to Envisage the Solid Time Field generator.'

Heart racing, I lifted my hand again for the Envisager but I couldn't shake the sudden thought that Aldorael would know the decoy tactic now and my escape would not be assured. My eyes returned to the power cells.

'Leila?'

'Yes.'

'Can the ship run on three cells?'

'Yes, but shielding would be lost, what are you considering?'

'Accelerate!'

'Accelerating. Pursuer is slowing.'

'She thinks we've hidden again; she thinks we're the decoy! Good, she'll end up searching the area.'

'Yes, what now?'

*Cries: The Captive Mind*

'I don't need to touch an Envisager; the way your form can be manipulated, to create temporary matter sustained by your control system, would have much the same effect. It's probably how an Envisager works anyway, just with physical materials being derived from some sort of ether. I'm going to manipulate the Power Generated Matter around one of your cells to create a Solid Time Field generator. We won't need shielding; we'd be safe. That's what I'm going to do.'

I concentrated, recreating Thomas's drive close to the core, willing its form into creation and drawing energy to it to bring it online.

'There, is it working?'

We flew by a flock of stationary homing pigeons.

'Apparently so.'

'What did we do next?'

'I took you to the Morrello Complex whilst you slept.'

'I *slept*?' I could feel my heart pounding in my chest, I was so on edge there was no way I'd be getting any sleep.

'What's Aldorael doing now?'

'My sensors are showing no movement.'

'Good.'

'Her pursuit will continue when we reach Morrello...'

'Bad, how come?'

'There is no way to access the complex without forcing entry.'

'Ah, yes; moving objects kick starts time. We'll just have to keep reinstating Solid Time after each obstacle.'

'The real problem is data transfer.'

'Continue...'

'The other ship's systems will wake, preventing use of Solid Time for the duration of said process...'

'How much data do we have to transfer?'

'Enough.'

'Leila; give me the schematics of the Morrello Complex. I'll find the quickest route in.'

By the time we arrived I knew where to go; my route required only two reversions to real time. I'd enter my old room from the small courtyard and enter the lecture hall - where the Black Ship stood - through the adjoining door. With Leila set to reinstate Solid Time I estimated a loss of only eight seconds.

To minimise the risk of disturbing loose material underfoot I had also decided that I would morph Leila into a Hover Pack. Leila informed me that this configuration had the further advantage of enabling reinstatement of shielding due to the small amount of power required to generate such a small vehicle. I hoped we wouldn't need it.

I cleared my mind and rested my back against the core allowing Leila to fasten it to me. I concentrated on the form of the ship, feeling the cool of night strike me as the forward sections of the ship slid away. I noticed Leila collect up Rue's Data Pack, holding it in a tight pocket of energy as the floor beneath my feet became nothing. I was now held, five metres from the pavement below, by the hover pack, it's wave array extending out from the middle of my shoulder blades like some ghostly propeller.

I leant towards my objective. I could feel the air passing over my face, and wondered how it was that air could be disturbed and yet not reinstate true time; there was much I did not know. I pondered again the origin of the Black Ship. It too had insisted that I had made it, but if this were true it meant that I had also created the Envisager inside it and that was beyond anyone. This and the place Leila had called Derra were questions for later, I had to concentrate on now.

I steadily progressed towards my goal; over the perimeter wall and wires, over the dog and his handler that stood frozen in mid-step, over the outlying buildings towards the unmistakable crescent of the old EOA accommodation block surrounded by the little courtyard. I descended to the window of my old room and reduced it to shards with a sharp spike of energy.

Suspended motionless in front of the window, watching the dancing fragments of glass, I knew that time had restarted. I could hear a dog barking and feel a strong wind across my face, then all was still and quiet again.

How are we doing Leila?' I asked. It was the sudden return to real time that had damaged Thomas's Solid Time device on the Tech ship I hoped that an energy derived system would be more robust and that we were again safe.

'Just three seconds gone.'

Illuminated by the wave array was the skull of a bird, the bird that had distracted me from my new Envisager the day of the incident. Had the event been so disrupting that no one had even cleaned the courtyard since? I sighed and glided through the glassless opening into my old room.

*Cries: The Captive Mind*

The wave array illuminated the room, it was completely empty. No bed, no chair. Network connections but no computer. It confirmed the impact that the Black Ship had had on the facility the day it was created. Then I had a pleasant surprise - the door to the Lecture room stood open. I wouldn't need to move it. I knew it would only save me seconds but the positive feeling of gaining anything at all was a relief to me.

Through the door I could see the Black Ship sitting in its block-like state. I could appreciate for the first time that it was still active in that form, wave generation set at minimum so that it's wave forms were hidden within the volume of the craft. Again I was happy that we were in solid time, a ship awaking from standby in response to my presence would be awkward to manage, wasting valuable moments. Leila would be able to control the situation when she was ready.

I glided through the open door. The dim light cast by the wave forms at my back sent shadows scurrying around the room. It startled me briefly, jolting my memory of those ugly pale creatures I'd seen during the battle, creatures that hadn't been effected by Thomas's Solid Time Field.

I consoled myself that their appearance was still many months away but scolded myself for travelling so quickly through the open door. Time frozen or not I needed to be more careful, the training at IAAM had been better than my hasty advance.

I lowered myself to the ground, removed the Hover pack and positioned it, clear of the other ship, on the ground.

'Initiate default form please, Leila.'

Leila grew steadily from her core and as I watched I began to understand her workings more fully. Everything any pilot would need was present in this form. You didn't need to be an EO or possess a neural key to fly it, *they* only enabled the ship to be flown to its full potential and be adapted; it made me wonder why the ship only flew for me.

I then became aware of something held in the core power vortices - Rue's Data Pack. I stepped forwards and reached out to take hold of it, the vessel's Power Generated skin dividing in front of my hand to allow the passage of my outstretched fingers. I froze, the ship was a part of the Solid Time Field and I was, thanks to the neural link which acted like the isotope tab I'd used at Sylvestris. But what if Rue's Data Pack was not part of the field and had merely been isolated from real time within the field of the ship. I couldn't risk losing any precious seconds - I'd be losing enough when the data stream between the two ships was established - No,

I could leave Rue's device for now and collect it before I left.

Seeing the Pack suddenly jogged my memory. Rue had spoken about seeing footage of me visiting the Black Ship with my father. I looked around the room carefully, a small security camera was fitted above the door. I pulled a handkerchief from my pocket and draped it over the device. When real time resumed it would appear to have malfunctioned, far less alarming than the sudden appearance of a second ship and a trespasser!

'Leila; initiate data transfer, load and set up a Solid Time Field generator as I've established in you. Perform these actions in minimum power output so that the light from your waveforms doesn't spill through the glazing into the corridor during real time - there's bound to be a guard out there - When complete I need you to transfer neural link commands, start up the other ship and shut yourself down. Oh, and thank you Leila.'

'I hope you achieve your objective Dace, be careful - Performing Commands.'

I listened for noises in the corridor; the deathly hush of night filled my senses, the tension held me taut. Only a dull glow emanated from the rear of the ship, giving the room a crypt-like feel, and I knew the Val'ee were closing the gap now that true time had returned.

Constant tiny changes in the form of the other craft explained why data transfer made it impossible to maintain Solid Time.

Seeing a movement from the corner of my eye I glanced through the open door into my old room. Plants in the courtyard, illuminated by the moon, were dancing about in the wind. Back at Elizabeth's summer house the weather was still, but that was several hundred miles north; I was now in Cambridge and the wind was strong.

The door between the rooms began to swing closed in the through draught. Instinctively I darted forward, closing it gently to stop it slamming and bringing security to investigate. As I turned to move away I made a grim discovery; there was a body behind the door. It was a uniformed guard, the one I'd seen that day with Dad, I recognised the facial hair.

I looked about frantically, expecting something to leap out at me and attack, but all remained silent. I looked down at the body then stepped hurriedly across the room again to the main door, gently easing it to a slit of an opening.

The night lit corridor was empty, at least in the direction of the east foyer. I gently shut the door.

'Command complete. Shutting down.'

The announcement jolted my frayed nerves. I watched, hand on heart, as Leila morphed into her resting state. The other vessel adopted a flight ready standard form and I approached it.

'**Computer, initiate Solid Time Field.**'

'As you wish Dace, and, it's still Leila.'

'**You transferred yourself?**'

'My memory, yes. It's exciting, I've never done this before.'

I smiled and opened my new ship with a thought, checking the function of the neural link. The way out was the way in, and I was pretty keen to get going.

I entered and stood with my back to the core, manipulating the ship's form back into a Hover pack, my feet dangling in the air.

'*Ingenious.*' Trilled a melodic voice as the remnant of the standard ship disappeared leaving me floating in the air, back-lit by my propeller-like wave array. I felt a hand grip my ankle.

I stared down at my assailant, 'Chorda!'

'*Hello Dace, I really am sorry to have to do this…*'

'**Leila, initiate Solid Time Field.**'

'Solid Time Field is operative.'

'**You're the same as those pale creatures; unaffected…**'

'*Oh, yes,*' Chorda interrupted, responding to my increased thrust by pulling harder. '*I feel sorry for them.*'

I tried to power away, dragging Chorda across the room towards the door of my old room.

'*I wish I could let you go, but you don't belong here.*'

I kicked wildly with my free foot, managing to break away from Chorda's grip, but it was pointless; I'd closed the door to prevent it slamming - effectively blocking my escape!

'*Come down Dace,*' Chorda urged. '*There's no need to resist.*'

A little of me felt willing. '**NO!**' I shouted, concentrating on the power at my command.

Chorda glared incredulously at the twin cannon morphing from the Hover pack. Solid Time was not assisting with my escape so a return to real time would be no disadvantage; either way I couldn't let this murderous Val'ee win.

The floor and study room wall erupted as I let loose a blast from the cannons, my shielding cushioned the retort and sent me gliding backwards towards the corridor. I had punched a hole out into the night, and the dust and smoke was sucked clean away by the wind. Chorda stood motionless, silhouetted by a floodlight. A second figure stood in the crumbling gap where the window of my room had once been.

'*CHORDA!*' The figure asserted.

Chorda swung around as the figure flew at her.

'*Aldorael?*' Chorda gasped as Aldorael collided with her sending them both to the ground.

'*Fly Dace, fulfil your objective!*' Aldorael shouted, looking grey and drawn; a stark contrast to Chorda's resplendent glory.

'*No,*' Chorda protested '*Your misguided actions will lead to…*'
I closed my ears, I'd been misled enough. I made an attempt to flee but suddenly the whole area seemed bathed in a violent display of electrical arcs, bolts and sparks, all emanating from Chorda and Aldorael's melee. I swung left, then right, then left again trying to find a way through. Suddenly, the piercing wail of an alarm kicked in and both Val'ee fell to the ground clutching their ears.

'Interesting…' I thought, flying headlong into the blackness above the floodlight as Chorda stood up and rained blow after blow, spark after spark down on the prostrate Aldorael. Aldorael lay motionless in the rubble. Chorda shook her head, looked around in search of me, and gave chase.

A Y-Ship was now visible - approaching from the right as I cleared the perimeter fencing - Chorda was not far behind me, keeping pace on foot, leaping the boundary wall and wires in a single bound as a guard in a security tower fired an automatic, hitting her a couple of times before the Y-Ship silenced him and swept in above my pursuer.

Chorda - still on her feet and showing no signs of injury - launched herself upwards and caught hold of the Y-Ship. She pulled herself onto one of it's wide, forward arm structures and boarded the craft.

My mind was in control. Leila filled in around me, taking the sleek form I'd given her on the way to Morrello. I thought her upwards and she responded instantly. The Y-Ship tipped in the air and followed. I somehow had the advantage on speed but Chorda's guns seemed not to respect that.

'If she doesn't shoot us down she might get an impact tag on us again, don't let her hit you Leila…'

'Countering projectiles.'

Leila left a trail of energy based rear guards behind us, taking Chorda's forward gun clean off.

'Solid Time!' I shouted. The Y-Ship froze. 'Yes!' I declared. 'Charge cannon.'

'Charged and ready.'

I pivoted the ship around in a consciousness challenging flip, 'Lock onto Val'ee ship and fire!!'

As my energy beams sliced into Chorda's vessel I turned Leila towards the east, towards home. I watched as one of the Y-Ship's forward arms spiralled down, indicating the return to real time. I watched as the erupting alien ship descended towards the ground, watched as a needle of light pierced upwards into space.

### Chapter forty-eight
### A Mind Made Up

My direction of travel took me back over the Morrello Complex one last time. In just a few moments site security had closed in on the position of Chorda and Aldorael's battle. I wanted to help Aldorael escape; if it hadn't been for her I felt sure that Chorda would have succeeded in killing me.

The thought that I could go and merge with myself, that I could save Aldorael with the knowledge I now had, was brief and very much against what I'd been considering.

I glanced down at Aldorael's position, only to see flashes of light in the blackness below. The security personnel were firing at my ship. No, a rescue was out of the question. Even for Solid Time there'd be too much unstable rubble in the vicinity to rule out an accidental return to real time and even if it were possible Aldorael still had to be moved.

I had eight hours left to deal with the ship that was coming. I couldn't risk my freedom or any damage to Leila now. Right now at IAAM's headquarters in the Cairngorm Mountains of Scotland, the original me would be in Jayes' detention block. He would wake in the morning and face a projection screen. He would observe an inky black silhouette behind the lit superstructure of Pathfinder Four and - within an hour - would become a broken man, full of grief and hatred. I had the opportunity to stop that and ensure that my Dad survived. Time would be healed.

I left my rescuer unconscious, surrounded by armed guards, her words to me still ringing in my ears, '*Fly Dace, fulfil your objective*!'

The truth was, I still hadn't fully planned my objective; Dad had to survive, that was key, the original timeline demanded it. I'd contemplated contacting Dad from Elizabeth's summerhouse to warn him, to tell him to hide or run but memories of Jayes' words, as I'd demanded that Dad be warned, came back to me, '*They* will find him…'.

I'd considered rescuing Dad personally; land in the back garden, knock on the door, share hugs and tears of reunited joy, then whisk him away. The problem was, I couldn't shake the thought that he might not be there. Time and again, news reports fed to me in Jayes' detention block, told of Dad being with the search teams. What if he wasn't there at the house? How long would it take to find him? Worse, was I really content to let so many thousands die and rescue only one?

Though I still didn't know how, I knew I had to destroy the ship before it began its awful attack.

Despite my decision I carried on towards home. I at least had time to pass the old place.

My troubled mind needed music. Music always calmed me, it always helped me think, it was never a distraction, 'Leila, give me Radio One.'

'As you wish.'

As I travelled, I contemplated what had just happened. I had entered the Morrello facility. I had thought that I was alone, but now knew that the Val'ee - like the pale creatures I'd seen before - were apparently immune to the freezing of time and that Chorda had waited to ambush me. I was also now aware that the Val'ee ships, like those of the pale creatures, *are* effected by Solid Time. It was as if a calmer part of my mind had recalled the frozen state of the enemy vessels during the battle above earth and had prompted my lips to request Solid Time. I knew the rest of my thoughts were panicked by the chase, that they were sold to the knowledge that the Val'ee could not be stopped by time or bullets. I remembered what Mr. Quaid had said at the EOA when I made the wire cross, 'With focus like that you could probably use an Envisager in a hail of mortar bombs.'

*Cries: The Captive Mind*

The event certainly seemed to confirm, again, the ability to partition my mind and set it to different tasks, as Mr. Lock had suggested. I wondered at the potential of this but found my mind being pulled to the biggest surprise of the night, Aldorael's support of my objective. I couldn't work out how her rescue could link with her actions at the lodge; maybe she felt that Chorda had reached the lake-side house before her and that shooting, whilst shouting my name, might allay any suspicions Chorda might have as regarded her allegiance. That Chorda might expose her position and be vulnerable to a clear shot from the Val'ee weapon Aldorael was holding. Had she assumed that Chorda was in Leila when I escaped the jetty?

'Oh Blast!' I exclaimed.

'What's wrong Dace?'

'I left Rue's Data Pack in the other ship...'

'Stay calm, Dace, I am having difficulty accessing your flight commands. We'll collect it later?'

Leila was right. There was much to concentrate on, not just the flying but the task, and after that, well, there'd be a lot of explaining and mobilisation to do to counter the slaving attack that would follow.

I could put Aldorael's actions out of my mind too. She was a creature from the future, she knew how things should be, she sought the rescue of my father through me; it made sense, yes, I was in the right place now to pursue what I felt was right. Aldorael must know what I did, she must know that it works.

I sighed; I knew what had to be done and something of a plan was beginning to form in my mind. It *had* to be a good plan - I was a gnat going head to head with a whale!

I decided to fly to the far side of the moon, where Jayes said the ship arrived, I could be there ready. I could set some sort of trap. Attack the head of the ship whilst it was still vulnerable, perhaps damage it into the conduit and cause the conduits energies to rip the vessel apart for me...

Suddenly a familiar track started playing on the Radio, it was from The Ungoliant's new album: "Stand". The one I'd found already saved to my Zone account online. Almost vacantly I double checked only to find it wasn't there at all! I suddenly realised that now was before then. 'I must have saved the album now for it to appear already saved the day I visited home from the IAAM headquarters.' I frowned. What I hoped to achieve would change those events.

I suppose I should have dwelt more on the complexities of that realisation, but I wanted that album and downloaded it.

I made the pass over my grandparents' old house. It was lit by the moon and stars. 'Sleep well Dad, I'll see you soon.'

Without further thought, my earthly goal reached and my plan beyond it now formulating, I flipped the nose of the ship upwards and sped on towards the bright white orb above, thrilled by the acceleration and the way I seemed held by the seat I was in. The moon seemed to be discernibly growing as I stared at it through the view screen.

I looked back at the earth as it diminished, recalling the last time I left it, cracking and crazing and breaking apart...

'With the knowledge I now have, I can protect you.'

I felt as if the words my Dad had spoken, regarding how my Mum used to look down at me in those last days, were coming true. "She would gaze at you as if you were the very answer to the troubles of the world."

I altered my course for an approach on the far side of the moon. The lunar landscape mesmerised me briefly. I scolded myself, 'Stay focused!' but found that my mind was already at work on my arsenal, and my ability to observe my surroundings wasn't effecting it. The shape of the ship was morphing, all shielding to the fore, wings and fins extending to make room for my primary weapons. I knew I could reproduce them with Power Generated Matter, I had seen them work, understood them; Slaver cannons, constantly firing, constantly creating their own ammunition, constantly targeting the enemy. They had seemed complex, and they were, but they came naturally to me now, almost without trying.

Yes, I would instate Solid Time and pour my weaponry at the target. Reinstating Solid Time at the first impact would freeze all 'in transit' projectiles and enable me to match my launched ordnance at each subsequent reinstatement; the build-up of yield was what I was relying on.

I would start Solid Time at the very moment I observed the enemy coming through the conduit. I knew the Val'ee motherships could manipulate time, I'd witnessed it when the ERUWAI avoided the beams from the IAAM Cruisers, so I'd beat them to it!

Leila sensed my plan through the neural link. 'Dace, the use of Solid Time through the Power Generated device *will* require the shields to be offline...'

*Cries: The Captive Mind*

The words struck home, I would need shielding. My enemy came from the future, there was every reason to believe that those on the ship already knew I was waiting - It chilled me - perhaps I *had* survived everything until this point, only to be killed by the enemies opening shots! I contemplated Thomas's device.

Spinning my pilot seat around I reached below the core and took up the Envisager in its pouch. I sat staring at it for what felt like too long. To stand any chance at all I had to do this, but what if I collapsed again?

'Leila, the last time I used one of these I...'

'Created me through completing a neural connection that the unit had been programmed to recognise; the device injected a partial future consciousness to enable this to be achieved, but the Envisager was shut down before the process was complete. This caused a conflict between your contemporary consciousness and the partial future one. The partial consciousness was a program, unable to merge; it was never intended to. It was meant to return to the Envisager.' **The computer fell silent.**

'What does that mean?'

'The escaping mind was thwarted, creating an inhibitor to full consciousness. That's why you collapsed.'

A future mind injected to allow the Envisagement of the ship, Faulkener shutting down the tool, this all made sense now.

A strong sense of urgency within me fought to bring back my attention to the reason I was here.

'This programmed consciousness, it couldn't merge, it's still in me?'

'It will be able to leave when you take up the Envisager.'

So many lies had been told me by various people and aliens. I knew the pain the Envisager had inflicted on me before. Could a Computer lie? It was a program created by someone, apparently me; how trustworthy it sounded! But I was suspicious that even a future me would be able to create an Envisager during the process of creating a vessel like this. 'How do you know all this? *You* didn't come from that point in the future?'

'No, your future mind programme made me and left the information in my memory banks.'

Programming and creation simultaneously. No EO had ever done that. Leila caught the thought, 'You are no ordinary EO.'

I looked down to find that I had removed the tool from its pouch.

'Dace, you have twenty-five minutes.'

'Twenty-five... until the Val'ee arrive?'

'Correct.'

I looked at my watch. Three thirty-two, just under five and a half hours before the first sighting of the ship from the Pathfinder Four. The enemy must have arrived and waited for the right moment to attack. What had appeared chaotic had been truly premeditated.

I lifted the Envisager, a little red light glowing ominously as it had done at the EOA. 'I must have shielding.' I said closing both hands around the handgrip...

Nothing happened, no pain, no confusion, no screams, no friend laying on the floor bleeding. I gave a nervous laugh. I knew the other consciousness - for that is now what I understood the déjà vu to have been - had left me. I pointed the tool at the floor and focused.

I had studied the ships power cells and core as we approached the Morrello Complex. Their configuration would be more stable than Thomas's cell, less susceptible to the damage possible from the sudden loss and reinstatement of Solid Time that I needed for my plan to work. Even then, and just to be sure, I created a second power cell to run alongside the first as an instant back up. The drive was complete. I initiated it and connected it to Leila's control console.

I felt full, I felt liberated, complete, ready. 'Leila, do you know where the Val'ee ship enters our space?'

'Not specifically. You recalled a line of craters on the surface of the moon, on the edge of shadow. Your coordinates from there are loaded and ready.'

'I was able to pre-set that, create you and program you all at once?'

'You are not as limited as you consider yourself to be. But you must be strong, there are trials to come.'

Feeling this to be a warning of the impending emergence of the Val'ee ship I pulled my focus back. I could see the line of craters on the edge of shadow below and Envisaged a network of stationary rear guards across the area pulling the ship back to an appropriate distance to face the oncoming enemy. Then we waited. 'All the best Leila.'

'This is our time, Dace. Good luck.'

The thick tension of waiting ended with the detonation of a rear guard straight ahead of us. I didn't even have to move! The unmistakable antler-like arrays of an ERUWAI class mothership emerged through the portal.

I wanted the head. I didn't realise I was being so unobservant. The head appeared, it definitely wasn't the ERUWAI from the battle. The protective tiles had been partially cleared from one side of the ERUWAI's head by a Cruiser beam, this ship was immaculate.

'Initiate Solid Time. Fire and don't stop!' I gasped, as I was pinned at the shoulder to my seat by the needle-like extension that linked the two inward curving antlers of the alien ship. It had sliced through Leila's shielding, its Power Generated mantle piercing my ship's Power Generated hull without breaching it.

I screamed in agony.

Leila kept firing at the frozen target, twenty projectiles already halfway towards their goal, but she was aware of my plight.

'What do you need Dace?'

'Just, ahh, keep firing as long as you can, keep real time as minimal as you can, track the leading projectiles, synchronise Solid Time reinstatement to coincide with impact. Oh my... With each reinstatement extend the wings and fins to provide a clear path for the next volley of projectiles, ah! Get as many on target as you can before the Val'ee ship splits us apart.'

looking over my shoulder I could see that the Val'ee 'needle' would eventually strike the Solid Time Field generator, in real time the impact would occur in moments. I just hoped I could get enough ordnance on track before my inevitable death.

The lead missile struck, the needle moved a centimetre; an agonising centimetre. I screamed out and swooned, it had taken a minute for the weapon to reach the head of the ship and in my stricken state I contemplated the scale of this task, the terrifying size of my enemy. Could I pull it off now? Time *was* running out. I would be dead before the second missile fired even hit home. I gave a little chuckle.

'Dace?'

'I always knew I'd die. I just thought I could escape it. It's time to accept it. I've very little time so I'd better make the most of it, keep firing...'

I extended new fins from the hull, manipulating Leila's energy field. The first missile from the second wave of projectiles hit home, the needle moved another centimetre, I left my pain to be dealt with in the partition of my mind. I morphed further slaver cannons from the ships Power Generated skin; anywhere where a clear volley of projectiles could pass. Initiating the firing of each cannon as it was completed. Over the next ten minutes of Solid Time I had turned the ship into the highest concentration of asserted hatred ever conceived, but it was all I could do.

A brightness behind me betrayed the beginning of the end, the Val'ee needle filled the gap between the Solid Time Field generator and the backup power cell. Light, arcing like solar flares caught in the sun's magnetic field, enfolded the device.

'At least this'll be quick.' I thought aloud.

'I'm sure we've done enough Dayshh.' Leila's voice hissed into silence.

I felt my ribs burst and pain claimed my consciousness, all was briefly green, then black, nothing, silence, stillness...

'Am I dead?'

'*No... wait... there is yet more to come.*'

The voice hovered above me as I leant in towards a chasm of silence, and I realised for the first time in what felt like months, exactly where I truly was; a captive entrapped by Chorda, in my own sitting room, robbed of my senses and forced to relive my errors.

'*Be still... Be still...*'

'We must rest his mind soon; it is special...'

I found myself unable to fight the growing flicker of light around me. It became more extreme, bolder, more vivid; it was the events of life flashing by in front of me, too fast to focus on. Was this the way your life unfolded to you at the point of death?

Within the confusion I felt deep feelings of love, acceptance, friendship, relief. This wasn't any life I'd lived; this was nice. I started to accept it although nothing bore any clarity. Then blackest darkness, a rushing of the wind and I was aware of being awake. I sat upright. My chest heaved its latest breath and I felt for the wound the Val'ee needle had inflicted. My hand slipped on something, 'No, not blood, there's no wound. It's sweat!' I could not understand why I was concerned about a wound, 'A needle is tiny anyway.' I thought to myself. I was breathing loudly, staring wildly into the absence of light. I felt that I must surely be dead. I couldn't think of anything; only what Dad had said about Heaven when I was a child. This place, however, was more like a kind of hell - dark, cold - I shivered and wondered what I was sitting on.

Suddenly my confusion was lacerated by illumination as all around me became visible.

'Where am I?' I whispered.

## Chapter forty-nine
## Daniel

'Daniel? Darling, you cried out are you OK?'

I stared, surprised at the presence of the attractive woman turning to face me from switching on the bedside lamp. She called me Daniel, was that my name? I couldn't bring any other suitable name to mind; Daniel seemed wrong somehow, although, coming from my companion, it seemed right.

Staring at her I couldn't hide the bewilderment I felt, then her face changed. What had been a look of just woken enquiry, became the wide eyed realisation of long held concern.

'Oh Daniel, please say it hasn't happened again, please not so soon!'

I wanted to comfort this lady's hurt. I reached over to touch her hand, 'I...' I paused, her shoulders sank. 'I don't know here; me... I don't know anything!'

She fell upon me with a startling but gentle and warm embrace, full of compassion and tenderness.

'Oh my darling!' She exclaimed, a note of true sorrow convincing my mind of her honest affection for me. 'Please don't panic,' She continued. 'Know that you are safe, that love is here, that we will find you again.'

'Mummy, is Daddy OK?' Two faces had appeared at the bedroom door, the one who had spoken was a little boy about four years old and the other, holding back in the shadow of the door was older, a girl, she looked anxious. 'H-Has Daddy lost his memory again?' She stammered.

'Children, come now.' the woman said, stepping quickly from the bed and ushering them back to their rooms. I could hear her calming tones as she disappeared beyond the door.

'I have a wife? I have kids?' I said to myself. I looked around the room, the finish was simple but beautiful and restful. The woman returned, I found myself gazing at her form, she was exquisite so why couldn't I remember her?

Time, and the rooms climate control, had dried my sweat. I felt warm now but also realised how little I was wearing. I couldn't help but feel inappropriately clad to be in the presence of my companion, and pulled the bed coverings around me.

My awkwardness must have been obvious to the woman as she quickly, and without inhibition, drew next to me again on the bed, embraced me and kissed me with a tenderness that I seemed to recall. 'It's OK Daniel.' She stroked my face. 'It's OK. We've been here before; when Peter was born. Kat was six then. She remembers, she promises to help. The children love you so much, I love you, God loves you.'

'God?' There *was* something familiar about that, 'The Chapel on the hill...' I found myself saying.

The woman's face flashed astonished excitement, 'Yes Daniel, my darling, yes! We'll call Dr. Rhon in the morning, go to the Chapel. Oh this is so much more than last time!' She hugged me then sat back again thoughtfully, 'Do you know my name?'

I stared back at her, she was desperate for more. I wanted her smile, I wanted another embrace...

'Anything at all? I mean it's OK, it was a while coming last time.'

'Yes, you had to tell me last time.' I acknowledged.

Her eyes grew wide at another small fact.

'Your name's... Jo, no, Jen... Jean, Jane! Your name is Jane?'

Her face broke into an elated smile, 'Yes Daniel! Oh Daniel, it's two in the morning. Please feel safe and rest, rest your mind. Don't trouble yourself with questions and what you don't know. Focus on what you *do* know; the Chapel on the hill, the children, my name, dwell on these things, they will help you back.'

'Back from what?' I thought to myself as I lay back in the bed, but her suggestion to focus seemed to have an appeal all of its own, and though I really didn't know the children I let that one slide and, heeding her words, thought about what did present itself as a clear memory of my life.

As I rolled onto my side, I felt her move in close to me and the glow of the bedside lamp faded gently away into the small hour darkness.

'Close your eyes.' Jane whispered, her soft hand circling tenderly between my shoulders. 'Picture the Chapel in your mind, let anything about it come to you...'

I trusted her implicitly. She knew me well, it was obvious, she knew what my life with her had been; who I was.

Her practical, calm and learned response proved that this *had* happened before. The notion that I could rely on her was as comfortable a thought in my mind as the little Chapel with its weather boarded tower, shingled steeple and tiny bell.

By the time I awoke it was light. Jane was already up. She had called the doctor, made arrangements for him to visit and prepared breakfast.

'It's your favourite.' She offered as she set the tray down; the smell of bacon filling the room. I must have looked disoriented again for she quickly drew close and stroked my hair. 'Today we start to find you again. It's OK, I told Dr. Rhon what you've already remembered and he's very positive that this is just a little lapse, that you will come through it much quicker.'

'How long did it take before?'

She hesitated, then smiled in acknowledgement that I had wholly accepted her and her counsel; 'Three years, *but* don't let that worry you!'

Her positive attitude gave me confidence. I reached out for her and she held me affectionately. The connection as our eyes met was unquestionable. I remembered with certainty that we were one and I kissed her. The chemistry was perfect, our lips fitted each other as if they were made to be together, and the moment lingered.

'Thank you Daniel.'

'What for?'

'Trusting me.' She moved away again, 'Take all the time you need. I've laid out your clothes on the chair. I need to get the children up.' She blew me a kiss and left the room.

I enjoyed my breakfast. I felt looked after, safe and - as if it were some sort of habit - I found myself praying with thankfulness to God before I started getting dressed.

As I put on the yellow shirt Jane had set out for me, I felt a little less easy. I felt a pang of discomfort in my left shoulder, and a sense of something not being right seemed to surpass the mere forgetfulness I was experiencing. Something was darker somehow, some unfathomable terror just out of my reach, and I found myself staring at the palm of my hand, flexing it, rubbing it.

'What am I doing this for?' I heard myself say quietly.

A noise at the bedroom door stirred me, 'Who's there?'

Kat appeared at the door, 'Daddy?'

'Hello Kat.'

Kat smiled, her little pink eyes betraying the fact that she'd spent some of the night in quiet tears. 'You remember me Daddy?'

'You're such a pretty little thing that I'm sure I'll remember you soon Sweetie.' The name seemed right, like a nickname, and Kat seemed very pleased to hear it, clapping her hands and running off shouting 'Mummy,

*Christopher J Reeve*

Mummy! Daddy called me Sweetie!'

I finished dressing and headed through the house. Objects seemed familiar, though their meaning or importance evaded me. A photograph of my wedding day confirmed that I was indeed married to Jane. The day itself was nowhere to be found, my mind drew out not the merest hint of confetti. I looked again at my stunning bride. I hadn't imagined that she could ever have been more beautiful than how I'd already seen her, but there she was, even more perfect. 'How blessed I am.' I said and turned to find her standing close by. Although I still found her more than attractive, I could see now - from the picture - that what had happened had taken a toll on her. A few lines that might show in a moment of sorrow, a few strands of silver in her dark, wavy hair, a hint of palest shadow around her eyes...

'How did I get like this Jane?'

She stepped towards me and took my hand; I did not resist her as she lifted it to my head, placing it palm down just behind my right ear - just where she had brushed back my hair earlier.

'What is *that*?' I exclaimed, startled by the unevenness of my skull beneath the curls.

'Your scar.' Jane gave a faint smile, 'You had a tumour in your late teens. We met and married after your surgery but you became stressed at work - just before Peter was born. You fell out with your father, swore you had no time for him anymore, then you seemed to lose your mind completely. It was terrible. You fell and ended up in Hospital.' She was staring into a space beyond me. 'Seems the stress triggered a total loss of memory. Doctors put the loss down to tissue scars still present from your surgery. You became a total stranger, paranoid and quick tempered...' She sighed. 'So they kept you in the hospital. I didn't want them to, but they were concerned for Kat, me and our unborn Pete. He arrived two weeks later. I'd never felt so alone, so scared, but our children kept me together. That's when Dr. Rhon took us under his wing.' Her malaise seemed to lift suddenly. 'Do you remember Dr. Rhon?'

I shook my head.

She smiled, 'Perhaps when you see him again?'

I hugged her, 'I'm so sorry...'

'What for?' She seemed amazed by my apology.

'I've not been the man you expected from our marriage.'

'Your memory really is returning.' Jane laughed.

I stared back, seeking reassurance that she was joking.

She returned to a soberer tone, 'How could you have known we would suffer this trial, you did not plan it. I joined you in your celebrations the day you got the all clear from that tumour, and I fell in love with you; the celebration became important to both of us. The surgery that let you live so that God could give you to me may have caused us problems, but without it you'd have died, and I wouldn't have had the best possible husband I could ever have.' She held me tightly. 'You are a wonderful husband, Daniel.'

'Had I been stressed again? You said I was stressed at work the first time.'

Jane frowned, thought and frowned, then looked at me clearly shaken. 'I, I don't know. If you were, you kept it to yourself. Oh Daniel, what if you weren't?' Her confidence seemed to drop away and I felt I was holding her up.

'Hey, hey, we'll beat this.' My words, delivered with force and certainty, seemed enough to gird Jane's resolve, and a shaky strength returned.

I spent the whole morning exploring my home, the garden, and the village. I was able to spur my family on by sharing a sense of familiarity with my surroundings, especially a yappy dog at number six. Kat laughed and showed me a little scar on my ankle where the self-same dog had actually nipped me when I'd rescued her from it. I focused on the scar trying to remember, and I did. We were in the park, the mutt came from nowhere bounding towards us, it's owner trailing behind. I'd lifted Kat onto my shoulders out of reach and the blasted thing bit my ankle! The owner was so upset she even joined us at Chapel that weekend and hadn't stopped going since; old Mrs Rolason.

That was the scene Dr. Rhon found as he drove up to us, a family celebrating another liberated memory. I didn't recognise him even though I felt I ought to with his thick grey moustache, perfectly round head and round wire spectacles. We spent the afternoon with him at the Chapel, discussed a plan of action, remembered a few random things which, as Jane said, 'was encouraging' - but that was all that first day.

It would take many months to regain my memories of Kat and Peter -

I'd even remembered the Bible study group before I fully knew them - and I feared I'd been a neglectful father, concerns quickly quashed by my Pastor, who fervently persuaded me of my attentiveness and encouragement.

My birthday arrived. I think I was surprised to find I was twenty-eight, not because that meant I'd have been eighteen when Kat was born, but because, in the back of my mind I'd assumed I was younger. What I did remember was my keenness to marry after going through the life changing experience of a brain tumour, that Jane seemed sent from heaven and Kat was with us sooner than we'd planned.

I sighed, the void in my mind seemed big enough for several lifetimes of memories.

As the years rolled along I became happier in myself. I had strange dreams, things I didn't understand. I felt I needed to get back into some work role, but had the most massive block regarding what I did. Telling me my role had been discussed between Doctor Rhon, Jane and my employers - who had remained anonymous throughout – but my managers didn't want my return anyway, not until I actually remembered my position and duties of my own accord. It didn't matter to them how long that took, my job would be waiting for me when their criteria were met. My only clue was something Kat said whilst watching a government spokesperson on the news. 'He's like the man Daddy worked with.' Enabling me to conclude that my role was somewhere official.

Jane's greatest joy was my reconciliation with my father. He was older than I'd expected, but we got on so well; our converse so heartening that I wondered what was so awful for us to have gone our separate ways. His refusal to tell me pointed to an involvement with my work, so I simply stopped pursuing the knowledge. After that my father and mother could regularly be found visiting us and the grandchildren, whom they loved to a fault.

Life was good until the weekend before my thirtieth. Jane was having a premature dinner party to celebrate, as some close friends would be away the next two weeks. I couldn't initially fathom where the thought had come from, it seemed to be like some bugle call in my head, demanding I "snap out of it!" Then the strangest memory hit me, hundreds of projectiles impacting on the head of a massive vessel in space.

As suddenly as the memory struck it was gone again. I'd become so

*Cries: The Captive Mind*

accustomed to my life here that I momentarily thought I was about to lose my memory again. I trembled at the thought of the richness of life becoming a blank once more; to painstakingly retrace my steps, relearn names I knew and strive towards the recognition of faces that would think I was ignoring them, until someone put them "in the picture".

'Dace...'

I looked at the people around the table, but no one was addressing me. Dace, yes, that *was* my name. My eyes met Jane's as she re-entered the room from performing some culinary task in the kitchen, and I could see that she thought something was wrong.

I looked at our friends and family, suddenly it all seemed wrong.

'Are you alright Daniel?' A guest asked.

'Dace, are you alright can you hear me?'

'What?' I exclaimed. My guest frowned.

The walls seemed to have images projected onto them, scenes that seemed familiar and yet alien to this life, they were recollections. Blood... Fire... Sounds like, like distress. I didn't want these memories, I preferred the ones I had here.

I lurched from my chair and fell down convulsing

'Dace, come on...'

'My name is Daniel,' I shouted. 'Who is that?'

'It's Hope...'

'Daniel, what's wrong, talk to me.' Jane urged, wrestling to free the steak knife from my hand before I hurt myself, but the room was getting darker. I clung to her.

A dark shape shifted fluidly across the wall behind the now animated guests. 'I'm seeing all kinds of things, hearing things, are you familiar with the names Dace? Hope?' I asked.

Jane's eyes grew wide.

I felt my consciousness slipping.

'Stay with us Dace...'

'Hope, we getta hurri, gev 'im tha 'drenalin.'

This voice puzzled me all the more, none of my guests were Scottish.

I could hear Jane praying. I could see Peter crying and Kat staring. Then Jane's voice cut calmly through the chaos close to my ear. 'If it is not over, you have to go.'

'I didn't get to warn them... about the slavers...' The memory was so strong - here with Jane was lost - the only possibility of return rested with

315

this voice, this Hope.

'I don't think anyone could have warned us about the slavers Dace, Take my hand.'

The room was as dark as night. 'I can't see anything.'

'Trust me. Let me take you to the light.'

'Hope, Hope, ya rilly need ta be right, 'cos times up.'

## Epilogue

It was usually a jarring blow when my wife reached this part of the evening; the retelling of the story had to pause, it was late and youngsters needed their rest.

I could feel a frown tightening my brow.

'Look Nana, look at Grandpa.' One of the children called.

My wife drew near, 'Darling? Darling! Can you hear me?'

I looked up at her with sad eyes, she stroked my face. Briefly she glanced back at the gathered family then, returning to me, gave out a little unexpected gasp of joy. I could feel her other hand resting on mine and gripped it.

'I - I, you…' I stammered.

She pressed forward to hear me, 'Yes dear?'

'Y - you continue tomorrow… that's, that's right, yes?'

She faltered to her knees, my son quick to steady her. She held his hand, a smile in her voice. 'Yes, my darling, yes, tomorrow evening.' She paused thoughtfully. 'Would you like me to continue sooner? Would you like me to continue now?'

'No… no, tomorrow… tomorrow evening is fine, fine… Thank you.' I lowered my gaze and released her hand. 'Thank you.'

**Thank you for reading Cries: The Captive Mind.
If you enjoyed the story, please find a moment to review it.**

**Find out more on The Earth Cries Hub website:
http://theearthcrieshub.wixsite.com/homeworld
or search 'The Earth Cries Hub' on Facebook.**

**Dace's story has only just begun.
In Cries: The Souls of Derra...**

Dace discovers that he is considered the key to ending humanity's enslavement under the Val'ee on Derra, but the alien world reveals a greater, closer enemy.

'Why had I not realised the ramifications of robbing humanity of its fear and hatred of the Val'ee? In doing so I caused the enslavement of the Earth and the transportation of mankind to the alien home-world of Derra. By the time the survivors found me, Dad was gone, almost everyone gaunt through malnutrition. Aster alone echoed my health, and that meant trouble for us all.'

—

D. N.

Printed in Poland
by Amazon Fulfillment
Poland Sp. z o.o., Wrocław